The BERYLFORD *Scandals*

LUST & LIBERTY

or
The Scandalous Tale of the Countess of
Vyrrington

DALE HURST

<u>Dedications</u>

my critics
Mum, Nan
Auntie Jackie
Jon Appleby

my friends
Will Ackrill, Shahan Ahmed, Fahim Ali, James Boxall,
Dean Connor, Craig Coogan, Tom Crocker,
Dan Gibson, Mantas Gliaudelis, Alex Hardwick,
Kelly Kingham, Ashlie Kitching, Matt Lawson,
Conor Macleish, Kyle Munn, Rianna Oak,
Alex Sampson, Emily Taylor, Jack Tunney

and my illustrator **Dan Lipski**

Contents

List of Characters

PART 3 – THE RETURN

PART 4 – THE LETTERS

PART 5 – THE TRIAL

Dear Lauren,

All the very best
and hope you enjoy
the book.
From Dale

LIST *of* CHARACTERS
in order of appearance

Lady OLIVIERA VYRRINGTON, Countess of Vyrrington – reigning social matriarch of Berylford

Lady VENETIA VYRRINGTON – Lady Vyrrington's eldest daughter

Lady MINERVA VYRRINGTON – the second-remaining Vyrrington child

The Hon. SPENCER VYRRINGTON – the year-old heir apparent to the Vyrrington estate

The Hon. EDWARD VYRRINGTON – the baby Vyrrington child

GEORGE WHITLOCKE – the Vyrrington family butler

Lord WILSON VYRRINGTON, Earl of Vyrrington & Viscount Beryl – the Lord presiding over his seat at Berylford

REVEREND HELTON – Berylford's clergyman

Mrs TRUDGEDAWES – the Vyrrington family cook

AMETHYST CHESHILL – Lady Vyrrington's lady's maid

JESSE BLAMEFORD – the Vyrrington household footman

JOSHUA – the Vyrrington household boots boy

ELSPETH URMSTONE – chief gossip in Berylford and one of Lady Vyrrington's best friends

JUDITH-ANN HAFFISIDGE – calming influence over Mrs Urmstone and one of Lady Vyrrington's best friends

ALICIA WARWICK – Mrs Haffisidge's niece, whom she adopted as a daughter

LUKE WARWICK – Mrs Warwick's obtuse husband, whom Mrs Haffisidge mutually despises

ABEL STIRKWHISTLE – Lady Vyrrington's politically-ambitious cousin

Lord GRIGGSDEN – an eccentric old friend of Mrs Haffisidge

Lady HILDA ALBION – a socialite

Lady LEDDINDSHAM – a socialite

Lady OXBORROW – a socialite

Major NEWMAN ROYALL – a widely-talked-about military man

Mrs ROYALL – Major Royall's wife

Lady JACQUELINE RHÉSEL-D'IVRE – a French noblewoman

CHRISTOPHER TRATSLY – a former cart driver and acquaintance of Mrs Haffisidge

Doctor JONATHAN STREET – Berylford's physician

Mrs EARLY – Berylford's nurse and midwife

JULIA OSBORNE – one of the town's two haberdashers, a cousin of Miss Gwynne

AGNES GWYNNE – one of the town's two haberdashers, a cousin of Miss Gwynne

CLARA RUDGERLEIGH – Berylford's schoolmistress

ZEPHANIAH GUSSAGE – Berylford's schoolkeeper

Lady LAVINIA ISSACS – Lady Vyrrington's eldest sister

Lady CLEMENTINA ISAACS – Lady Vyrrington's second-eldest sister

Lady DIANA ISAACS – Lady Vyrrington's favourite sister

Lady GEORGIANA ISAACS – Lady Vyrrington's fourth-eldest sister

The Hon. JUVELIA ULLSWELL – Mrs Urmstone's sister

The Hon. BLATCHFORD ULLSWELL – Mrs Ullswell's husband

Mr JACKDAWE – the Vyrrington family lawyer

REBECCA STIRKWHISTLE – Abel's younger sister

LIZA STIRKWHISTLE – Abel's wife

Mrs KNYVETON – a military wife

Constable MARRIS – a lawman

Sir JOSEPH EZRINGTON – one of the judges presiding over West Hampshire

Mr ICKRELL – a prosecutor

Captain A. H. KNYVETON – a well-decorated officer

PART 1
THE <u>DISAPPEARANCE</u>

Book One
A CONFLICTED HOUSEHOLD

Chapter I
At the Mausoleum

THE SEAT OF THE VYRRINGTON earldom, a family that had existed for four generations, was *Beryl Court*: a grand and stately mass of brick and stone – the only decoration on an otherwise featureless hill, that stood watch over its tenants in the market town of Berylford St. Barbara – Berylford for short – like a gigantic vulture awaiting carrion. The home of the Earl and Countess of Vyrrington – Lord Wilson and Lady Oliviera – a pair who fit the bill of every society romance – a well-decorated former officer who had retired early to take up his noble duties, and a great aristocratic beauty. However, the years had not been kind to either party; while both still in their thirties, both the Lord and Lady Vyrrington had souls that would welcome the grave, were it not for the stubbornness of their bodies. Their hearts had endured many blows over the years, and with a total issue of seven children, only four remained. A recent epidemic of Scarlet Fever had claimed young lives throughout the county, and in *Beryl Court*, two of the Vyrrington children – Felix, the heir apparent, and his brother Augustus – had also fallen victim.

Away from public view, behind the attractive veneer of *Beryl Court*'s outer walls, in the house's somewhat neglected gardens, stood the family mausoleum; a massive domed stone heap wherein the bones of every obscure Vyrrington relative found their final resting places. There, on this dismal grey October morning in 1793, the remaining household, with their servants and retainers – few as they were – gathered to pay respect and remembrance to the late Vyrrington children. The Countess, rendered icy and hollow in her grief, clad to the throat in black, her dark locks worn loosely bound and draped over one shoulder, topped with a hat that reflected the latest fashion, cascaded slowly down the line of servants, none of whom dared look at her directly, towards the entryway to the mausoleum, a rose locked between her well-bejewelled fingers. She had not noticed that some of the thorns had pierced her skin, such was her heartache that she was numb to all other superfluous forms of pain. Following her was her barely-adolescent eldest child Lady Venetia Vyrrington and her younger sister by one year, Lady Minerva. In both daughters' arms, they carried a boy child each – the newest additions to the Earl and Countess' brood – Spencer, the new elder son and heir, and the baby, Edward.

Lady Vyrrington stood waiting by the mausoleum door, calmly yet cautiously awaiting her husband, who was yet to appear. There was not a sound but for the occasional hiss of wind as it attacked the nearby trees, or the babbling of the infant Edward. But as the minutes continued to pass, the Countess became more and more unsettled by the absence of her husband. Having had enough of waiting, she swiftly started walking back along the line of servants – the maids all shuddering as she passed as though she froze the very air that followed her – until she reached a tall and somewhat stoutly built man with narrow eyes, lank blonde hair and a seemingly-permanent scowl. This was George Whitlocke, *Beryl Court*'s butler.

"Was His Lordship ready when you left him?" Lady Vyrrington asked him quietly.

"His manservant had finished dressing him, yes," was Whitlocke's stern reply. The feelings between the Countess and her butler were not amicable to say the least.

"Then go and find him!" she commanded, through gritted teeth, "It's his sons' burials, for Heaven's sake!"

Not speaking, merely nodding, Whitlocke turned and went back into the house. The Countess waited where he had been stood; she resolved to stay there until Lord Wilson arrived.

The grand house was a labyrinth of staircases, corridors, nooks and passageways, seemingly endless and without determinate direction. Indeed, it would only take a sharp mind and memory, such as those of George Whitlocke, to know them encyclopaedically. Such as it was, assuming that the butler found Lord Wilson quickly and that they would be along presently, Lady Vyrrington had contemplated starting their sons' burials without her husband for all the time she had spent waiting. She pursed her lips angrily, eyes white with frustration when, a good ten minutes later, she finally beheld the figure of Lord Vyrrington walking toward her and the line of servants, Whitlocke following shortly behind.

Though her ire at his being late for one of very few events that warranted his absolute punctuality blinded her to it at the time, Lord Wilson was still of attractive frame for his age. He was not a tall man, standing at no higher than five-foot-six or seven, but what there was of him was all but pure muscle. He had a fair complexion, short dark locks, broad shoulders, a flat stomach and well-shaped legs. Were the occasion different, Lady Vyrrington would have a mind to recall him in uniform, becoming attire for one of such a build. Black became him just as well; more suitable for the event of the day. Her thoughts could not own any of this good opinion; she was far too annoyed at his tardiness.

"At last you deign to turn up to your sons' burials!" she hissed at him, "On this of all days, Lord Wilson, I expected you to have some compassion – if not for me, then at least for your remaining children."

"I have nothing to say on the matter, Oliviera. If you don't mind, I think we have delayed this deplorable affair long enough."

"*We*-?" Lady Vyrrington expostulated, but her husband interrupted her.

"Take my arm, My Lady; let us see our boys to rest."

She was shocked to see his face was already wet with shed tears. Her mouth still ajar, she hooked her slender arm around his, only then noticing she had shed blood from the thorns of the rose she had been carrying. Caring little about it, she gripped the fabric of her husband's frock coat and walked at his pace back to the entryway of the Vyrrington mausoleum, wherein would lie the mortal remains of their late sons.

At nine and seven years of age respectively, the young Lordships' coffins were small, dark, brass-handled boxes. It had barely entered the Countess' mind that it was her own flesh and blood within them. The mausoleum was otherwise filled with the bones of Vyrringtons that even her husband had never known or met. This time it was two of her sons, borne from her body and suckled at her breast. Such was the risk of betraying her emotions that Lady Vyrrington clutched her husband's arm tightly, and bowed her head, so her eyes met only the ground on which they stood. She dared not look up as the pallbearers brought forth the caskets and stopped by the Earl and Countess. Lady Oliviera kept her head averted downward, until her husband whispered,

"My Lady? My dear – the rose."

She sighed heavily. It was her only duty for the entire ceremony. Still clasped betwixt her now blood-stained fingers, she slowly and almost reluctantly placed the flower atop the coffin of one of her sons – it had not occurred to her to read the inscriptions on the caskets. The Countess took a step back and could not bear to watch as the pallbearers proceeded into the great stone tomb: their eternal resting place.

The Reverend Helton, a sombre and, even on more joyful occasions, somewhat severe-faced man of intimidating height and visage appeared before the Lord and Lady. He bowed, before reciting in Latin the Requiem Mass.

Though she was loath to admit it, the Countess normally found the words to the Requiem pretty in their own way. In all the funerals she had attended prior to this, her attendance had been more a formality and she had shed few, if any, tears at most of them, giving her ample time to appreciate the words spoken. On this day, the Mass was a long, monotonous and torturous effusion she wished they had never asked for. And following the reading of the *Pie Jesu Domine* lines, her "amen" was said as soft and weak as the feeble chirp of a dying chick.

She felt ill.

After the reverend and the pallbearers had left, the servants returned inside, even her husband had had to finally repair back to the house lest the rain should descend, Lady Vyrrington remained stanced in silent, ineffable grief before the great sepulchre.

"This vessel of despair, sorrow and anguish…" she spoke to herself, about the mausoleum, "…This excrescence on the face of my beautiful home. It's nothing more than a delusion of grandeur. For the sake of keeping old bones…"
The Countess approached it, placing her hands on its outer walls.

"…And young ones," to herself she continued, before slowly leaning into the wall and sliding down to her knees. She would have probably wept more, were her tears not all spent. Instead she could only gasp, wheeze and sniffle; the expressions of a mother's pain for the loss of not just one but two of her children she could still muster.

And thus she remained for a few minutes, though to her it seemed as though ages passed. She heard a distant chiming from the church, the hour had struck, and sooner or later it would be time for her to dine. It mattered not whether she wanted to eat or not; it mattered only that she attended dinner at all. Pulling herself together, as much as she could anyway, she rose to her feet, sculpted her facial expression to extinguish all sign of mourning, and returned to the house.

Chapter II
Whitlocke Has Objections

THE LORD AND LADY VYRRINGTON dined without their children, all of whom had been confined to their own rooms. Not as a punishment or because they showed them all little affection – the Earl and Countess adored children and were firmly resolved to care for theirs themselves, rather than employ a governess. The grief-stricken parents merely could not bear for their remaining issue to behold them in such utter anguish.

After serving his employers upstairs, the butler George Whitlocke returned downstairs for his own dinner, which was partaken with the other servants. Or, at least, what remained of them. It had not occurred to him when they were lined up outside by the mausoleum earlier that day, but when Whitlocke entered the servants' hall, he realised the startling lack of people sat around the table. As he sat at the head of it, he did not even notice the food before him; instead much preoccupied by where half of the servants had gone.

"Mr Whitlocke?" Mrs Trudgedawes, the household cook, addressed him, "Is something amiss with your dinner?"

Whitlocke had only partly paid attention, only then realising he was being spoken to.

"Hmmm? What?" he said.

"I shan't be offended if you aren't happy with the food, Mr Whitlocke," Mrs Trudgedawes returned, "But I would like to know what's wrong, so I don't make the same mistake again!"

"No, no, nothing's wrong with dinner, Mrs Trudgedawes, thank you. Where are half of the servants?"

"Gone, Mr Whitlocke. Dismissed last night. I'd have thought you of all people would have known about that!"

"I did *not* know about that! I would not have sanctioned any such thing without good cause."
Still ultimately ignoring his food, to Mrs Trudgedawes' chagrin, Whitlocke swiftly went back upstairs. The Lord and Lady Vyrrington were still eating, silently, in the dining room. Sensing his temper might flare, Whitlocke thought about how he would address the issue; this day would not be the best to start an argument with either of his employers. He turned the corner, so he was in sight of both of them. They stopped eating when he appeared.

"Yes, Whitlocke?" Lady Vyrrington said.

"Forgive the intrusion, My Lord, My Lady; I have just been informed as to the dismissal of around half the household staff last night."

Lady Vyrrington looked across at her husband, whose eyes were currently directed downward towards the table. Whitlocke went on:

"Of course, you are at liberty to hire and fire as you see fit-"

"I thank you for that acknowledgement, Whitlocke," Lord Wilson interrupted.

"-But you must understand it is an administrative difficulty for me to rearrange duties around the running of the house with only a fraction of the pairs of hands on deck, so to speak."

"What are you saying, Whitlocke?" Lady Vyrrington asked sharply, "That you would like to be *consulted* before Lord Wilson decides to make changes around here? What right do you reserve that you should be informed of such dealings, if only that to avoid 'administrative difficulty', as you put it?"

Whitlocke was seething behind the calm and submissive exterior he was trying so hard to maintain. He knew it in mind, heart and body that the Countess was the cause of this; that the loss of servants was a deliberate attempt to make his job more difficult.

"Very good, My Lady," he finally said, after a momentary pause to consider how to continue diplomatically, "I will take this under advisement and… will not pursue the subject further. Please ring when you await your second course."

"That would be now, Whitlocke, quick as you like," she returned, looking up at him shrewishly and placing her hands in her lap, waiting for him to lean over her to clear her crockery away. Unable to do or say anything, Whitlocke conceded defeat – this time – doing his duty with the efficiency for which he was known; biting his lip while he did so.

Upon returning downstairs, which he had done slowly and with his temper a little short of frayed by this point, he placed the plates down firmly on the servants' dining table, they clattered so loudly that they startled one or two of the housemaids and perturbed Mrs Trudgedawes as to Whitlocke's current state of irritation.

"Second courses, please, Mrs T." he muttered.

"Right you are, Mr Whitlocke," she returned, still keeping her distance, "Jesse, Amethyst – if you wouldn't mind. Quick as you like – these quenelles are not going to stay hot forever."

One of the senior footmen, a twenty-something young man of medium height but attractive build, took one of the trays from Mrs Trudgedawes, but nearly dropped it in turning to go through the doorway, for the young boots boy of no older than seven or eight – known only as Joshua – came hurtling through it at the same time – he was late for dinner, a punishable offence downstairs at *Beryl Court.*

"Will someone tell the little idiot to watch where he's going?" the footman – Jesse – shouted at him.

"Yes, *yes,* just get that tray upstairs!" Mrs Trudgedawes shrieked back, before taking off one of her kitchen sleeves and giving Joshua a sharp slap across the back of the head with it.

"Amethyst – vegetables, now!" she then addressed the young housemaid, "Or do I have to hit you with this too?"

"Yes, Mrs Trudgedawes. No, Mrs Trudgedawes," Amethyst squeaked fearfully as she scuttled after Jesse with a steaming silver tureen. Clutching her chest and breathing very deeply in and out, Mrs Trudgedawes collapsed into her chair and fanned herself with her hand, looking at Whitlocke exhaustedly.

"Dinner for two of them should not be this difficult, should it?" she wheezed.

"When you only have a fraction of the workers on hand, *yes!*" Whitlocke replied, "Lord Wilson dismissed all those maids and footmen without consulting me and I know that bitch had something to do with it. If it wasn't all her idea in the first place, that is!"

"Oh, let it go, Mr Whitlocke. They're gone, it's done. We're managing – *just* – and you never know, there may have been a good reason."

"*Nothing* Lady Oliviera has ever done has been for a good reason."

"I would like to argue with you, but I'm fagged out already and there's still the sweet course to do yet!"

They both relaxed for a mere moment before bustling came from out in the hallway. Jesse came storming down the corridor, incensed.

"That little bastard needs to go. Tonight!" he roared, pointing directly at Joshua, who, scared out of his wits, hid under the table.

"What's all this about?" asked Whitlocke.

"I have a gravy stain down my livery from the quenelles – caused by that idiot's carelessness. And as such I have just had to serve the Lord and Lady in a dirty uniform!"

"Do you not think you're overreacting a bit, Jesse?" asked Mrs Trudgedawes.

"I would not normally make such a fuss, Mrs T., but Lord and Lady Vyrrington *noticed* and *commented* on it," returned Jesse, now much calmer, "*I* don't want

to be accused of letting standards fall in this house –
especially when another is at fault."

Mrs Trudgedawes and Whitlocke looked at one
another, realising that Jesse had a point.

"I will see to it that Joshua is disciplined, Jesse,"
said Whitlocke, "He can go to his room without
supper."

Joshua came out from under the table, looking almost
as if he wanted to protest, but Mrs Trudgedawes took
him firmly by the shoulder and led him out. Jesse
looked at Whitlocke incredulously.

"Seriously? Bed without supper? That's your
idea of discipline?"

"As butler here, Jesse, I shall not be questioned
with regard to my decisions by the likes of you."

"You're too merciful, Mr Whitlocke," returned
Jesse, "Be wary or people may think you've gone soft."

"Joshua is an orphan, Jesse – no family, no other
place to go. Were it not for my mercy, he would have
died in a *workhouse* somewhere…"

He stood up and went to go upstairs, before turning
again in the doorway and continuing.

"…And also, need I remind you, he is not the
only one whose life has been saved by mercy." Then he
disappeared down the corridor, leaving Jesse alone in
the kitchen.

It was a thought that gave Whitlocke restored belief in his own goodness and hope in times of doubt. He was an arbiter of fates; he could mete out a person's future if they were in his employment. He could save lives should the occasion arise and could likewise destroy them. But only with good reason. He would have loved nothing more than to turn Jesse Blameford out of *Beryl Court* forever. This impudent and argumentative senior footman, whose cocksure strutting around the corridors of the house played merry Hell with Whitlocke's temper. But for all his swaggering like a cockerel, Blameford was too effectual at his job to be dismissed without the risk of question or protest. With the little orphan boots boy Joshua, the opposite was true. Being childless despite pushing forty with not such a long stick, Whitlocke felt as close to a paternal feeling toward the lad as he knew to recognise, but with Joshua's lack of years and experience, under any other authoritarian butler, the boy would have been dispelled from the house immediately. To die? To go to the workhouse, that is also, to die? What other human being, too preoccupied with the feathering of his own nest, would care? It did not seem right in the mind of George Whitlocke.

As he cascaded the narrow corridor that led to his pantry, he caressed those thoughts. 'How do I mete out the fate of this child here?' his words from his mind were, 'Now with so few hands on deck, we will have to compromise. More training – that is the answer! Train him for a new position and watch his every move.'

Chapter III
Confidences at the Looking Glass

LADY VYRRINGTON, WITH HER EMOTIONS spent, her mind exhausted and her soul besieged, could barely walk to ascend the stairs to retire for the night. Such had been her anguish, she felt like a centuries-old crone imprisoned in her thirty-six-year-old body, her strength barely existent. As she was making it to the first landing, Whitlocke appeared at the foot of the stairs. He did not look pleased, but that was his usual expression, as the Countess well knew. Her exhaustion notwithstanding, she closed her eyes before turning to face downstairs, where her butler was stood. She needed to speak with him.

"Retiring for the night, My Lady?" Whitlocke asked her.

"I must speak with you first, if you please."

"As I you."

"How did you find His Lordship earlier?" she asked, totally unintrigued by what the butler wanted to talk to *her* about at this hour. Whitlocke did not look comfortable in answering.

"Well, I found him in his study, where I expected to find him," he returned, somewhat defensively.

"I meant in the sense of his demeanour. His *precise* disposition!" the Countess pressed. Whitlocke's expression once again resumed a scowl. Lady Vyrrington did not look amused.

"What?" she asked.

"He was burying his *sons*, for goodness' sake!" Whitlocke gasped exasperatedly.

"As was I."

"Surely his demeanour when I found him in his study would go without saying, My Lady?"

"You found him grieving."

"Smoking a cigar, but yes, very grief-stricken by the look of things, as if one could expect anything else."

"And nothing else?"

"Nothing else, My Lady!" Whitlocke now turned uptight and officious. Had the Countess the energy to pursue the conversation any further and to think any more on the subject, she would have suspected her butler of secreting something from her.

"Then very good, Whitlocke. I shall see you in the morning."

"Pardon me, My Lady. There was one other small matter."

"That cannot wait until morning?"

"Just a quick 'yes' or 'no' would suffice."

"Go on."

"Permission to train up the junior staff into undertaking further positions downstairs. We will not have to increase wages."

Exhaling deeply through her nose, eyes firmly closed, the Countess sighed:

"Permission granted, Mr Whitlocke. If I may take to bed any sooner, permission granted to whatever you please. Good night."

Leaving Whitlocke almost astonished that she had made a decision in his favour, and once again at her old woman's pace, Lady Vyrrington took herself off to her bedchamber. There, as she had expected, the Countess found Amethyst within, waiting on Her Ladyship's instruction.

Alongside her duties as a serving maid, Amethyst Cheshill also served as Lady Vyrrington's lady's maid, a position she had held since she was fourteen. She had entered Her Ladyship's service by no happy or fortunate circumstance. Fatherless from before birth, and her mother Judith Cheshill was dismissed from her employment as a charwoman when the child born out-of-wedlock was discovered. As such, Amethyst was thrown upon the workhouse's mercy from her earliest years. There, both she and her mother faced vicious torment in that abhorrent institution. Eventually poor Amethyst was left parentless when her mother had been beaten so savagely and starved so mercilessly that God would no longer permit her body to endure.

The only good fortune in Amethyst's tale occurred when an old man, rich, knowing, kindly and charitable, visited the workhouse and selected from among the youngest inmates to add to his household. Amethyst was among the first the old man chose. He belonged to the name of Lord Ensbury Isaacs, the master of a house in Dover called *Vellhampton Park*, and the father to Lady Oliviera and her four sisters. Immediately installed as a lady's maid-in-training to the then-fifteen-year-old Lady Oliviera Isaacs under a stern but nonetheless fair mentor, Amethyst and Her Ladyship had developed a close, sisterly bond, and the Countess was one of the very few people around whom Amethyst did not feel frightened. Though the years since the workhouse had been far kinder to her, Amethyst still bore many a scar from her experiences in her youth. She was timid and easily-startled, like a rabbit escaping the hawk, but also with an ineffable sense of inferiority.

The nightly ritual began, whereupon Amethyst would brush Her Ladyship's hair before retiring, and one would usually confide in the other.

"A pleasant service today, My Lady, did you not think?" Amethyst addressed her mistress.

"As pleasant as one could expect, I suppose, yes."

"Though I wish you could wear it in better circumstances, forgive me for saying so, milady, black does become you."

Lady Vyrrington chuckled.

"Thank you. I wish I agreed – I fear it makes me look like a corpse."

"No, not at all, milady. It becomes Lord Wilson as well. And even Mr Whitlocke."

The Countess' expression suddenly turned cold.

"Well Mr Whitlocke is to be dressed in a black uniform until the end of his days, much as I tire of it."

Amethyst looked disheartened by her mistress' reaction.

"My Lady does not care for Mr Whitlocke?"

"No, I do not. An insolent, indignant and irksome man. But he is efficient, and that pleases Lord Wilson. For all the heartache we have endured in these last months, it pleases *me* to see Lord *Wilson* pleased. Even if that means putting up with Mr Whitlocke indefinitely."

She looked up at Amethyst in the mirror, noticing her maid had gone silent and become completely preoccupied with her hair brushing.

"I care for *you*, though, Amethyst," she said, taking one of her maid's hands and holding it, "Which is why, though it pains me to own it, I could never let you give yourself to such a man."

"Give myself? To Mr Whitlocke, milady? Please know it, milady, I mean to do no such thing. *Especially* if it would displease you."

"I would hope that you would never part with me, Amethyst. Not even for a husband."

"Never, milady, never."

"Good," Lady Vyrrington whispered, kissing Amethyst's hand and smiling.

Book Two
MRS HAFFISIDGE HOLDS A DINNER

Chapter IV
A Vagrant Approaches

WHILE LADY VYRRINGTON HAD LONG since reconciled herself with the fact that the majority of Berylford's society was made up of labourers, farmers and traders – none of whom someone of her status would sanely be seen with socially – she did have a close circle of female friends. The two lynchpins of that circle were a pair of ladies who may as well have been joined at the hip – they were so seldom not in one another's company.

One was Mrs Elspeth Urmstone, a small and shrewish woman of Scottish descent, whose father and grandfather had had close professional connections to the English royal family. Particularly George I, his wife Queen Sophia Dorothea, whom he imprisoned, and her mother Éléonore d'Ésmier d'Olbreuse, of whom tales of increasing embellishment and exaggeration would frequently be regaled from Mrs Urmstone's lips.

The other was Mrs Judith-Ann Haffisidge, who was mousy in the face but possessed a prominent beak of a nose, of similar build to Mrs Urmstone but of a great deal milder temperament and in possession of better-informed, more liberal, views.

Both devout women, albeit not zealously so, they attended church together every Sunday. However, this was only in part for worship, but also as a means to gossip about the other townspeople. Mrs Urmstone, in particular, having been widowed only very recently and with no children, had no affairs of her own important enough to eclipse her interest in those of everyone around her. And where there were no instances of talking behind hands or shifty body language, this only paved the way for her highly speculative and cynical mind to conjure some often-half-credible story of her own. Unknown to no one but herself, her stories were taken with the pinch of salt they merited by everyone who heard them, for it was a well-credited fact that she intended no malice. Mrs Haffisidge was usually on-hand to rein Mrs Urmstone in if her zealous rumourmongering began to go beyond control.

However, on her way out of church that Sunday, it was Mrs Haffisidge who found herself the subject of undue attention. After thanking the rector for his sermon, she and Mrs Urmstone walked arm-in-arm back down the hill toward town, where it was their Sunday custom to have a modest repast at one or the other's home. Amid discussions of whether or not their close friend and fellow townswoman – the schoolmistress Clara Rudgerleigh – and her lodger Zephaniah Gussage were guilty of immoral relations, Mrs Haffisidge spied a figure out of the corner of her eye. Not thinking at the time, she stopped dead in her tracks while the figure approached, despite Mrs Urmstone's frantic questioning as to why they had stopped. She too looked up and saw the figure, which belonged to a middle-aged, dishevelled and pot-bellied man – a vagrant, he must have been, by all accounts.

"Fortune told for a penny ma'am?" he murmured directly at Mrs Haffisidge between well-whiskered lips – his beard and moustache were in a most unkempt condition; in truth, it was any wonder he could be understood at all. Mrs Urmstone shrieked at the vagrant:

"Go on! *Shoo*! There's no money for you here! This is sacred ground! Go on!"
He backed away from them, turned and walked on. Mrs Haffisidge remained frozen on the gravel path on which she stood, her mouth ajar and eyes white with an inexplicable fear.

"Mrs Haffisidge?" Mrs Urmstone asked her quietly, "*Mrs Haffisidge!*"
Her friend awoke from her trance.

"*Hmmmm? What?*" she said, shaking her head and blinking vigorously.

"Did you know that vagabond?"

She turned to face Mrs Urmstone; her expression had not changed in the slightest – still worry-stricken and mouth open.

"Of course not," she finally said, "I have enough vagabonds in my life as it is with my niece's husband living with us at present."

While she closed her mouth, her eyes were still fixed on where the vagrant had approached her. Eventually, Mrs Urmstone had to drag her friend along.

"Tea, Mrs Haffisidge. *Tea* and luncheon at my house. You appear traumatised, so I might well afford you a piece of Dundee Cake as well."

Mrs Haffisidge finally re-engaged with the world and laughed at Mrs Urmstone's facetiousness.

"Actually, Elspeth – might we turn luncheon into dinner and invite Lady Vyrrington to my house tonight? We have not seen her much in her mourning. It might do her good. And I would like to see her."

"If it will take your mind off the abominable creature that trespassed on Our Lord's holy ground, anything, Mrs Haffisidge. On the condition that I bring my Dundee Cake for afters."

In going their separate ways, and upon returning to her house, Mrs Haffisidge quickly composed a lengthy correspondence to the Countess, to serve as a formal dinner invitation. After writing and sealing it, she gave it to a little urchin boy with a ha'penny with express instructions to away straight to *Beryl Court*, and hand the letter to the butler at the door without question or comment.

When delivered, it read:
My dear Lady Vyrrington,

Please forgive the negligence with which I have conducted our friendship these recent weeks. Friends can be of the most healing of comforts when one is in mourning. The most melancholy chapter your house has suffered, I fear, would not have been in any way alleviated by mine and Mrs Urmstone's presence; rather much to the contrary, and we both believed you and your husband should just be left well enough alone.
Mrs Urmstone's own grief has kept her out of society of late, but we both feel a little merriment is warranted, to drive out the sorrow. Thus I am cordially inviting you to join us for a little supper this very evening. I apologise for the lack of notice – but then you have always known me to be a creature of spontaneity. Mrs Urmstone, my niece Mrs Warwick and her husband will also be in attendance, and will be all enthused to see you.

I hope you will accept, and to see you around five this evening, before it becomes too dark to traverse into town.

My everlasting affectionate regards,
Judith-Ann Haffisidge

Chapter V
Remember: Juliette Harrowsleigh

N O MORE THAN AN HOUR after sending her invitation was Mrs Haffisidge in receipt of a reply. Elegantly written, in a cursive hand in crimson-coloured ink, Mrs Haffisidge almost felt guilty breaking the seal on the Countess' response; she almost regarded the handwriting as she would a work of art.

Dear Judith-Ann,

Allow me to begin by attempting to dispel any anxieties you may have – I know my family and I were in your thoughts in the heart of our emotional turmoil.

I myself wish that I could have been a pillar for our dear Elspeth to lean on, bearing in mind her own recent loss. I too have exiled myself from society since the death of my sons – for too long, though it shames me to own the words.
Therefore, I will be delighted to attend dinner this evening; you may expect me on time.

Affection as always,
Oliviera

Not that she expected Her Ladyship to decline her invitation, Mrs Haffisidge flew into a frenzied flutter of anxiety at the notion of the Countess' attendance. Was the silver polished enough? Were there plenty of cushions to ensure every possible comfort for Lady Vyrrington? Was the wine of a rarity and decent-enough vintage to present to a lady of such status? Just a thimbleful of the questions that darted through Mrs Haffisidge's head all at the same time. After composing herself, she knew she had everything in hand – the Countess was a gracious enough guest, and had been frequently enough in Mrs Haffisidge's house, to appreciate whatever hospitality was afforded her.

Berylford was not a large town, and *Beryl Court* itself was not situated too far away from it – it looked further away than it was when perched so solitarily atop its hill. The town consisted of only four main streets – conjoined by a square at the centre – down which were situated the numerous houses of varying size and character, and businesses. Down Kellford Road sat Mrs Haffisidge's house – a moderately-sized property – not on so grand a scale as *Beryl Court* but big enough for a woman of her status – quaintly decorated externally with a small garden of berry bushes. She did not herself employ servants, since there were but two others who resided with her – her niece Mrs Alicia Warwick, and her husband Luke, who worked as a farm labourer on the edge of town. Mrs Warwick's mother – Mrs Haffisidge's sister – had died very young and, as her godmother, Mrs Haffisidge adopted her as her own daughter. As such, she exhibited great protectiveness over Mrs Warwick, and despised her nephew-in-law.

Lady Vyrrington was punctual as ever – she relied on arriving a good quarter-hour – at least – before the scheduled time, for her maxim was that to be just on-time was to be late all the same. And lateness was discourteous. Mrs Haffisidge's eyes glistened at the sight of the Countess' elegance as she glided through her little front garden, garbed in purples and mauves, with accents of black to indicate her mourning had not yet completely ended. She was a stupendous woman, so beauteous and intelligent, and yet, beloved friend to both her and Mrs Urmstone.
After a warm welcome and a short apéritif in the parlour, Lady Vyrrington and Mrs Urmstone were led by their hostess to the dining room, wherein sat the Warwicks.

Throughout the dinner, despite her best efforts, Mrs Haffisidge, who was sat at the head of the table, stared daggers down at Mr Warwick, sat at the foot. He was an indolent, uncouth, feckless and impudent man in his early thirties, but was nonetheless an attractive sight to behold with bright eyes shining icy blue from a square-jawed, freckled face. It was a pity that even the most basic codes of courtesy were lost on him, especially in front of a guest as esteemed as the Countess of Vyrrington. He slurped his soup loudly, chewed his meat as a cow would a mouthful of grass, and ate peas off his knife. Each transgression irked Mrs Haffisidge more and more, to a point where she was certain Mr Warwick was trying her patience on purpose. Eventually, her temper, which she rarely lost, could not hold out any longer.

She slammed her spoon down before standing up and storming down the other end of the table.

"Out. *Out! Off with you, Mr Warwick!*" she shrieked as she approached him with a vehement pace, "*If you're going to behave like a pig you can go and eat* with *the pigs up at the farm but not here in* my *house!*"

Rather than look incredulous as some men would, or apologetic as others, Mr Warwick smirked out of one corner of his mouth, intent on causing his aunt-in-law further distress. He stood up from his chair, letting it fall over behind him, and sized Mrs Haffisidge up.

"Are you worried I'm embarrassing you in front of your friends?" he sneered.

"You embarrass yourself, this house and this *family!*" Mrs Haffisidge returned, "Lord knows why I gave my consent to your marrying Alicia when I did!"

"Well, too late to do anything about it now, isn't it?"

"I think I told you to leave."

"I will away to my room. You cannot eject me without good enough reason."

He left the fallen chair where it was and exited, not bowing or even nodding courteously to the other ladies -- even his wife.

Upon his closing the dining room door, Mrs Haffisidge sighed deeply, leaning on the dining table as though the entire experience had exhausted her completely.

"Are you all right, Auntie?" asked Mrs Warwick.

"I shall be, my dear. Elspeth; My Lady – I must apologise for my outburst just then. May I offer you a small digestif? Port, or a sherry?"

"I think that sounds a wonderful idea," Mrs Urmstone replied, "We'll help ourselves? In the parlour?"

"That's it. I'll be with you presently."

She stood firmly where she was; Mrs Urmstone and Lady Vyrrington making their way out into the adjacent parlour. Mrs Warwick then stood by her aunt and placed a hand on her shoulder.

"You know he does it because he enjoys your reaction," she said, "If you didn't concede to it-"

"How can I sit by and let him run rings around me and get away with it?" Mrs Haffisidge hissed in reply, "I cannot, Alicia. I *will* not! He's a coarse, chauvinistic, ungentlemanly creature. The very epitome of the sort of man you should have avoided. *All* women should avoid, failing that!"

"You gave your consent, Auntie."

"I did, though the Devil won't let me forget it. The one thing in my life I singularly regret."

"He must have had qualities you did like, or you never would have done it."

Mrs Haffisidge exhaled deeply through her beak-like nose, her nostrils flaring to such a size that she was in danger of inhaling something quite large with her next breath. She could not retort to her niece's last remark – Mrs Warwick was right.

"Go upstairs to him, my dear. I am quite tired. We'll see to the plates in the morning."

Making her way into her parlour, Mrs Haffisidge found Mrs Urmstone and Lady Vyrrington both sitting in armchairs by the picture window, conveniently placed to look out onto the goings-on on Kellford Road. An opportune spying ground for the scandalmongering eyes of Mrs Urmstone. Pouring herself a glass of port,

Mrs Haffisidge walked over and stood between the two armchairs, placing her free hand on the Countess' shoulder.

"As the guest of honour tonight, My Lady, I must apologise to you once again for that abominable display in there," she said.

"I will hear no more of it, Judith-Ann," returned Lady Vyrrington, "I was myself offended by Mr Warwick's behaviour – such disrespect should not have gone unaddressed."

"Agreed," Mrs Urmstone piped up, her attention still half-occupied on any potential happenings outside.

Mrs Haffisidge pulled up a well-cushioned chair and sat between them, sipping her port pensively and watching, and waiting.

*

Before they knew it, they had fallen asleep – all three – but it was not the mantle clock and its chiming nine at night that woke Mrs Haffisidge with a start. It was the silhouette of a male figure stood in the berry bushes outside her house – a faceless shadow nevertheless staring in at her. She cried in horror, which in turn woke Lady Vyrrington and Mrs Urmstone.

While both of her friends tried to get an answer out of her as to what the matter was, Mrs Haffisidge's face was quite as it had been earlier at church: mouth agape and eyes white with fright, only this time her fear was justified; the silhouette had vanished. Her finger pointed at the window, unendingly as though *rigor mortis* had set in while she still lived.

"There was… a man… in my garden," she stammered, her voice quavering and tremoring.

"Should we wake Mr Warwick?" Mrs Urmstone whispered.

"Do not speak to me of Mr Warwick!" Mrs Haffisidge expostulated, "For all I know, he may have hired one of his friends to scare me for sport."

"Judith-Ann, I hardly think that *that's* possible – even for one like Mr Warwick," Lady Vyrrington said, trying to calm her, "Perhaps it was a nightmare?"

"I was fully conscious and saw a male figure, a face cloaked in black and shadow standing 'twixt my berry bushes. And if he lingers there, he'll be on the receiving end of the *poker.*"

She took up arms – a long and well-used cast iron poker – and slowly approached the front door, the Countess and Mrs Urmstone following her closely. She made way for Mrs Urmstone, who unlatched the door cautiously and opened it. Mrs Haffisidge held the poker outstretched, at the ready to brandish at any would-be assailant. There was no one out there, but she was not relieved in the slightest, for it answered no questions. Lady Vyrrington wrapped her purple and black shawl tight around her shoulders and exited the doorway.

"It has been a most *exhilarating* evening, my dear Judith-Ann," she said, kissing her friend on both cheeks, "But if you'll forgive me, fantastical episodes may still be a bridge too far for me at this stage of my grief."

"I assure you, My Lady, that next time you are invited here, it will be much less eventful," replied Mrs Haffisidge.

"The excitement is what I enjoy, my dear friend. I shall see you at some point this week. Both of you must come to the house for cards."
She turned on her heel and began to leave, until her shawl became caught on something in the berry bushes.

"Be careful, My Lady Vyrrington or you will tear your shawl!" Mrs Urmstone cried out.

"What on earth has-?" the Countess muttered, trying to free herself from whatever she was caught on, but found it not to be a bush thorn, but a long metal pin, threaded through the leaves and something else. A piece of paper, to be precise.

She took the paper and held it to Mrs Haffisidge's lamplight to read it. It was an awkward scrawl – a spider dipped in ink could probably have made more legible hand – but in the right light, three words were distinguishable.

Remember: Juliette Harrowsleigh

Lady Vyrrington looked up at Mrs Haffisidge and Mrs Urmstone, who looked at each other with the same mixture of confusion and fear.

"Maybe there *was* someone in your bushes, Judith-Ann," said Mrs Urmstone, "And they know this Juliette Harrowsleigh?"

"Who is she? Or who *was* she?" asked Lady Vyrrington.

"I haven't the slightest idea," Mrs Haffisidge scoffed dismissively, taking the paper from Lady Vyrrington, "Look at this hand – it is that of a child or some such. This is a practical joke of extremely *low* calibre, designed to scare a lady on a dark night. Nothing more."

"You said you saw a man!" said Mrs Urmstone.

"I thought I saw the *shadow* of a man. Upon waking up the shadow of a boy could easily be manipulated by the mind and the eyes as that of a man or worse. You and I both, Elspeth, have lived in

Berylford our whole lives and never known a Juliette Harrowsleigh. Or any Harrowsleighs anywhere!"

"That is true."

"Then I think there's an end to it. My Lady, Elspeth: I bid you both good night."

Book Three
TWO UNUSUAL EVENINGS

Chapter VI
Vanished in the Night

THOUGH SHE WAS NOT A creature of fragile nerve, Lady Vyrrington would have been lying had she claimed not to have been greatly perturbed by the events in the latter part of her visit to Mrs Haffisidge's house. She kept a quick and frantic pace on her way back to *Beryl Court*, with every flicker of shadow provoking her every caution and suspicion. She was relieved to see there were still candles alight in the house as she neared it, but did not think so highly of Whitlocke not being at the door to receive her. Such was her frame of mind that she let herself in anyway, with not a single servant to be found upstairs, to her dismay. Deciding that, in light of what had happened that night, the need to feel safe in her own house, away from men cloaked in shadow lurking in bushes, was paramount. However, upon descending the stairs to the servants' quarters, she found mayhem had already begun to unfold.

Every servant that still worked at the house appeared to be awake, alert and looking for something. Or someone. Some were so preoccupied with their present task that they did not even acknowledge their mistress the Countess stood there in the stairwell. Eventually Mrs Trudgedawes bustled past, and had to look twice before noticing Lady Vyrrington, giving a short curtsey in response.

"My Lady? Is everything all right?" she asked

"I should ask the same of you, Mrs Trudgedawes!" the Countess returned, "What on *Earth* is going on down here?"

Mrs Trudgedawes hindered in her answer.

"I fear Mr Whitlocke is the best one to explain, milady, if you please. He's in the kitchen at present."

Silently and suspiciously, Lady Vyrrington turned the corner and found Whitlocke sat at the head of the kitchen table, his fingers steepled in deep contemplation – quite unlike his fellow servants, who were frantically bustling around.

"Mr Whitlocke?" Lady Vyrrington asked hoarsely, "Tell me the meaning of this agitation."

"The boots boy Joshua. He has gone missing," Whitlocke did not turn to face his mistress as he spoke, "Vanished in the night."

The Countess remained silent, and it was only her lack of reaction that caused Whitlocke to finally look at her. Her lips were pursed and her expression severe.

"What?" he asked.

"Get yourself and the other servants to bed this instant," she returned, an air of disgust about her voice, "You all have work in the morning. With or without the *boots boy*."

"A child has gone missing, My Lady," Whitlocke stated, "Be he a boots boy or a baron's son, he is a child all the same."

"What point are you exactly trying to make here, Whitlocke?"

"A missing child usually leads to a dead child, My Lady. In this town, at any rate. Have you so little compassion that the life of this one particular boy means nothing?"

Lady Vyrrington approached Whitlocke, leaning in as close to his face as she could without touching him.

"Do not speak to *me* of dead children, Whitlocke," she whispered sinisterly, "I have suffered the sight of them more times than I ever intended. Or have you forgotten the two we buried only *days* ago? You will excuse me if I don't allow a *third* child to trespass on my conscience." She moved away and turned to go back out the door. Whitlocke tried to speak:

"My Lady, I-"

"If you do not order your servants to cease the chaos going on out there in the hall before I do, your job will be forfeit," she returned coldly, "Is that clear, Whitlocke?"

Glaring at her behind her back, Whitlocke remained silent, defiantly.

"I said 'is that *clear*, Whitlocke?'"

"*Quite* clear, Lady Vyrrington."

Satisfied with herself, the Countess made her way back upstairs and ascended higher to the upstairs rooms. She did not share a bed with her husband these days, since their own respective grief was too much for the other to bear. Nonetheless she moved past Lord Wilson's door and caressed it softly, wanting with all her might to go in and see him, but knew too well she would be rejected. Instead, she made her way round the corridor to her own bedchamber and sat on a cushioned settee beneath one of the hallway windows outside, putting her head in her hands.

To her surprise, she found she was weeping, however silently, knowing that what Whitlocke had said was correct. Though this was long before she came to Berylford, she knew the tale of a series of five child abductions and murders that had occurred across two months in the town. No child that went missing ever came back alive. The situation had become so bad that the presiding judge had ordered constables from

London across to investigate. Though motives established at that time were bereft of any foundation, many suspected the mayor, while others thought an old Jewish émigré responsible. Others still believed the murderer to be a travelling schoolteacher, since the disappearances and deaths had started occurring only upon his arrival. The tale itself was almost twenty years-old; one of the three was arrested, tried and hanged, though which man changed with every retelling. The Countess certainly had no idea who was truly responsible.

She was loath to admit it to Whitlocke, but she was strongly contemplating that the same had happened to Joshua, a boy she barely knew or even saw. But for a child, as Whitlocke had correctly pointed out, to meet such a grisly end, was more awful a thought than Lady Vyrrington could endure.

As she began to dab beneath her eyes with her handkerchief, she heard footsteps coming down the hallway.

"Lord Wilson?" she said, hoarsely.

It was not her husband, but rather the footman, Jesse Blameford. The Countess sighed deeply.

"My Lady is troubled?" he said, "Dry those eyes."

"And *you*, footman, are too familiar," she replied, "I was not crying, not that it's anyone's business."

"You made it my business, the first time you did this."

He sat down beside her and kissed her lips gently, stroking her cheek with one hand. Trembling at first, Lady Vyrrington then reciprocated, taking his face with both hands and holding it in place as they continued to kiss. Jesse began to make his way along her face and down her neck, whereupon her hands ran their way through his thick, luscious hair.

She then remembered where they were, and jolted upright. Jesse stopped and looked at her.

"What's wrong?" he asked.

"Where were you just now when I was downstairs?"

"With all the other servants, looking for the damn boots boy."

Lady Vyrrington looked back and forwards thinking for a moment, her mouth slightly ajar and her eyes wide.

"I can't Jesse. I can't help thinking–"

"What?"

"All these terrible things that are happening in my life, and to the ones I love. It's all because of this – what we're doing now."

"You're talking nonsense; it's just a boy who decided to run away. Nothing more."

"Oh, it's more than just the wretched boots boy!"

"Then what? *Tell* me!"

He stroked her arm, trying to rekindle her attention, but she looked away.

"I think you should go back downstairs now before someone catches you up here," she said coldly. Realising there would be no profit for him to argue with her in the corridor in the middle of the night, Jesse stood up and walked back down from whence he came. As soon as he fell out of eyeshot, Lady Vyrrington tossed her head back and exhaled deeply. She then rose and walked in the same direction Jesse had gone, as if to follow him downstairs. But instead, without even knocking, she entered her husband's room.

Lord Wilson was sat up in bed still, though his expression and reaction to his wife entering his chambers implied he was not expecting her.

"What's the meaning of this?" he asked.

She remained silent and approached him slowly, undressing herself as she did so. Before he had time to react, she straddled him on the bed and kissed his lips passionately, stroking his face roughly. She reached down and found his prick, hard and throbbing – he hissed as she handled it and gradually allowed him to enter her. It was their first intimate encounter in many months; as such it did not take either of them long to reach their climax. After finishing, the Countess rolled to the other side of the bed, panting harder than she ever had before. Completely exhausted, she fell asleep without a word.

Chapter VII
With the Countess' Connivance

LADY VYRRINGTON AWOKE SLOWLY; SHE thought she could hear the distant sound of knocking. It was not coming from the door to Lord Wilson's bedchamber – it was a room further away.

"It's probably Amethyst," came a voice. The Countess wheeled around to see her husband watching her. He was smiling.

"Why, of course!" returned Lady Vyrrington, "How foolish of me. She will not know where I am. She'll probably think *I* was stolen away too!"

"What do you mean?"

"Oh, just some nonsense with the servants last night – one of them allegedly went missing; it'll all be resolved today I'm sure of it."

"As you say."

"Thank you very much, I will see you at breakfast I suppose?" she continued as she quickly dressed again.

"Thank *me*?" Lord Wilson said incredulously, "Thank *you*, My Lady! For being so… obliging!"

"Doing merely my wifely duty, sir," she returned somewhat curtly, before exiting the room.

The knocking continued and became louder as she neared her own bedroom door. To her surprise, she saw it was Whitlocke outside it, rather than Amethyst as she had expected.

"Can I help you, Whitlocke?" she asked. The butler was somewhat startled to find her in the corridor.

"Thank God, My Lady; I began to grow concerned!" he said.

"If that were true, you would have stopped knocking ten minutes ago and come to Lord Wilson. Where you would have *found* me," she replied sardonically.

Whitlocke did not answer – his mistress had beaten him very easily on that one.

"Well you may as well come out with it," she continued, letting herself into her bedchamber and allowing him to follow her, "To what do I owe the early disturbance this morning? Have you found that boots boy yet?"

"Not yet, milady, no."

"Have you at least recommenced your search?"

"No, milady, we have not."

"May I ask why?"

"Because, with all due respect, milady, as I put to you last night, I don't expect we'll *find* Joshua. Not alive, at any rate."

"Are those the same lips that accused *me* of a lack of compassion last night, Mr Whitlocke?"

"It is a display not so much of a lack of compassion, rather a lack of hope. Especially as I think one of our own may be involved."
Lady Vyrrington's eyes widened.

"Whom do you suspect?"

"Jesse Blameford, of course."
The Countess' expression remained as it was.

"Why so?"

"I know very few are aware of his background and his reputation, but I am one, and *you* are another. I needn't bother answering the question any further."

"Your hate clouds your judgment, Whitlocke. What *possible* motive could a footman have for abducting a boots boy? Hardly worth a ransom, do you agree?"

"Still My Lady, such as it is, I do not consider the household safe while Mr Blameford works and resides within it."

"Innocent until proven guilty, Whitlocke!" Lady Vyrrington said sharply, "I will cast not one single servant out of this house because of an ill-informed hunch you have."

"You need not do anything My Lady. If Lord Wilson is convinced, I will have his leave to do as I please…"

Now *she* knew she had lost; the Countess remained silent.

"...I'll send Amethyst to you directly," Whitlocke finished, turning his back on his mistress and exiting the bedchamber.

Infuriated she had conceded defeat so easily, Lady Vyrrington sat down on the edge of her bed, and exhaled slowly through her nose in dormant anger.

'I'll be damned if that's the last I say on the matter!' she thought to herself, 'I have power enough and influence enough. Why don't I just get rid of Whitlocke?'

As she thought that last thought, Amethyst came through the bedchamber door, and the Countess smiled at her.

'Ah, that's why,' she reminded herself, 'If I sacked Whitlocke, I would lose Amethyst forever. She would never forgive me.'

After being dressed in among her finer blacks and purple shades, the Countess joined her husband in breakfasting quietly with the children; they did not speak very much in the mornings, even when their marriage had been very young and love-filled; preferring to peruse over their respective correspondences. Lord Wilson, while retired from the army himself, was still responsible for the local militia in not only Berylford but also the neighbouring towns of Hinxstone and Wraxhill-on-the-Test; most of his letters were longwinded effusions of no entertainment value at all.

The Lady Vyrrington was in close contact with her numerous cousins and four sisters – all of them perpetually-unmarried middle-aged creatures with no love of society whatsoever – but was often in receipt of an invitation to a party, soirée or salon somewhere. While attempting to take the numerous social summonses she had received somewhat seriously that morning, her thoughts were preoccupied by Whitlocke's threats, and how she would attempt to thwart her enemy. She gritted her teeth hatefully as she watched him observe the service from the side of the room, breaking the seal on the next letter with vehement force. However, it was a correspondence that would gain her undivided attention – a letter from her cousin Abel Stirkwhistle, a gentleman with some involvement in politics, who lived in London.

My dearest cousin Oliviera,

I pray that this letter finds you well, regardless of how well I am in the writing of it. I am in much distress

to have heard in your last letter of the passing of your
young sons, and how very sorry I was to not be of any
service to you during that time. However, to own the
truth, my distress is twofold, for I regret to inform you
that my father – your mother's cousin-by-law – is gravely
ill, currently in convalescence in Italy, but it is feared his
health will not endure much longer.

This letter is written to inform you that I am to
set sail for Naples within the fortnight, but as soon as I
return, with good news or bad, I will endeavour to make
myself more available to you in whatever form or fashion
you deem merited.

> *Regards to you and the family,*
> *Abel Stirkwhistle, Esq.*

The opportunity could not have been more perfect,
Lady Oliviera thought. Her cousin was a man of rich
and expensive tastes, and so did not keep servants so as
to afford to indulge himself and his wide and varied
social circles in magnanimous forms of entertainment
all the more. A voyage abroad, however, would be quite
different, the Countess knew, for while Abel was
notoriously independent, he would not be seen to be
carrying his own luggage around. A more-than-
adequate reason to send one of her own servants – Jesse

Blameford, namely – to serve as the manservant her cousin Abel would require. She smiled as she folded the letter back up. Lord Wilson noticed.

"Something droll, my dear?" he asked.

"Quite the opposite, my love," she replied, "'Tis from Abel. His father – my great-uncle Adam Stirkwhistle – is ill; he is to make for Italy soon. I wondered, given it is such an arduous journey for one man to undertake with baggage, if we might loan one of the footman out to serve as manservant?" Whitlocke's attention piqued, and only then upon hearing her did he attend at the table.

"I can't imagine that would be a problem – we have no pressing engagements here," said Lord Wilson, "Whom did you have in mind?"

"The young one – Jesse, I think his name is?"

"With all due respect, Your Ladyship, do you not think someone with more *experience* would be of benefit on a trip such as this?" Whitlocke asked, a note of anxiety present in his voice. He knew his hold on his mistress was weakening with every word.

"Jesse will not *gain* the experience if he is not given these responsibilities," the Countess returned, "Besides Abel is not a patient man; Jesse is young and fast from what I have seen – he will be able to keep up with Mr Stirkwhistle's pace and attend to his whims efficiently."

"You'd know all about how young and fast he is," Whitlocke muttered under his breath.

"What was that, Whitlocke?" asked Lord Wilson.

"I was merely confirming to myself that Her Ladyship makes an excellent point, Your Lordship. I shall inform Jesse immediately."

Whitlocke took the plates away, exchanging glances with Lady Vyrrington, who had been stunned to silence. She had heard the butler's 'young and fast' remark. Until now she thought her liaison with the footman Jesse Blameford was a secret. She decided she would have to confront him on the issue, but later; once the other servants and members of her family had retired for the night.

Chapter VIII
A Shove in the Dark

THE COUNTESS KEPT HER DISTANCE from the remainder of the household practically all day; she had only watched from her sitting room window the carriage taking Jesse to London to meet with Abel Stirkwhistle. He had been affixed with a letter from Lady Vyrrington reading:

My very dear Abel,

With each passing day, I am sure you can imagine, I miss my sons more than I dare express. Your wisdom and goodness were both much needed and, indeed, much missed at the time.

But how can I rightfully talk of my own suffering when fully aware of your own plight? I am utterly overwrought to hear such sad tidings of your father, of whom I possess such a fond remembrance. I would not wish for this period to be any more difficult or incommodious than it already is, and while I would also not dare overstep my bounds, as family I feel duty-bound to help wherever I can.

As such, I am delivering the individual with whom this letter arrives into your service. His name is Jesse Blameford; he has been in my service since he was nineteen, as a footman under both my father's household in town, and in my own household in Berylford. He has demonstrated exemplary skill, efficiency and discretion. May he attend the same in your employ.

Likewise unto you, if there is any comfort I can bring should the worst arise, I will gladly be at your service.

As ever, your affectionate and devoted cousin,
Oliviera

'At least that's *one* problem out of the way', she thought to herself, 'Now to deal with Whitlocke.'
She rang for tea once it had become dark – she knew when Amethyst ate, so she was assured it would be the butler who would attend her call.
He knocked briskly and let himself in, not even allowing his mistress to instruct him to enter. He was perturbed to find her facing him, only sat a short distance from the doorway.
  "You know, then?" she said coldly.
  "Of course I know," he scoffed in reply, "It isn't exactly discreet the way you carry on."

"I thought it was *very* discreet! Dear God! – does anyone else know?"

"If they do, they haven't said as much to me. And nor will they. As butler, I run downstairs with an iron fist as necessary."

"Yes, yes, all right, very well."

"Whether he *is* behind Joshua's disappearance, or in any way involved, sending him away for his own protection will do no good, My Lady, let me make that very clear now."

"I am sure I don't know what you're talking about."

"If anything, you have made my job easier. I can reveal all. About his past, and his *present*, and take you down in the process."

"Don't be so naïve, Mr Whitlocke – I credited you with more intelligence than you rightfully merited, 'twould appear! You think that *this* will ruin *me*?"

"A great lady having a sordid affair with a servant – I think it would cause a stir, definitely."

"No one who moves in the same circles as I would believe anything of the sort."

"And what about his past?"

"My influence is greater than you think. Whatever people hear in society, I will merely say that I too was deceived about Mr Blameford's life before he

came here, and sent him away upon learning the truth –
his whereabouts now *unknown* to me..."
There was a light knocking and someone else entered –
this time it was the Countess' maid Amethyst.
However, Lady Vyrrington did not altogether notice
her maid had come in and carried on talking to
Whitlocke.

"...Let me assure you now Whitlocke that if you
threaten me again you can not only say goodbye to your
position here but all hope of a marriage with... *her*..."
She smirked nastily and held the door open for him to
leave.

"...Thank you for the tea, Whitlocke. Amethyst,
if you'd be so kind as to pour me a cup?"
Whitlocke, now almost purple in the face with fury,
stormed out, slamming the Countess' door behind him.

*

Hours passed, almost without Lady Vyrrington even
noticing. The clock on her bedchamber mantlepiece
read close-to-midnight. Her Ladyship had fallen asleep
in her armchair. However, something woke her – a
disturbance or just a sudden subconscious anxiety – she
could not be sure.

She rubbed her neck as she rose, for it had stiffened in her sleep; compelled to examine the corridor. En route back, depending on how she felt, she thought she might or might not visit Lord Wilson again. She turned the corner from her own bedchamber to the main corridor and the top of the stairs. She glared in the darkness, such was her wariness – she was certain a noise had woken her.

However, before she had time to contemplate any further, she felt a shove of almighty force in the dark, and cried out as she went down the stairs headfirst, tumbling down to the very foot. The commotion stirred Lord Wilson, who exited his room, candle in hand, to investigate further.

"My dear!" he shouted as he observed his wife at the bottom of the stairs, running down swiftly to attend to her. He felt her wrist and detected she was, thankfully, still alive. Displaying great strength despite his waning youth, he swung the Countess over his shoulder and carried her back up the stairs, passing Whitlocke, Amethyst and Mrs Trudgedawes, who had lined in the corridor having come down from their own sleeping quarters one floor above to see what was going on.

"Ensure the house is searched, Whitlocke," the Lord Vyrrington commanded, "And see to it that all doors and windows are checked and locked before anyone else sleeps this night. If whoever attacked Lady Vyrrington is still in the house, it is imperative that we catch them!"

"Yes, My Lord," returned the butler, through however gritted teeth.

PART 2
THE <u>SICKNESS</u>

Book Four
A SOCIETY PARTY

Chapter IX
Mrs Urmstone is Coaxed

NEWS QUICKLY SPREAD OF THE attack on Lady Vyrrington in her own home, despite the efforts of Lord Wilson to keep the event a secret. By way of Mrs Trudgedawes, who had occasion to mention it to the schoolmistress Mrs Rudgerleigh in town, tidings of the violent happenings at *Beryl Court* were eventually iterated all the way across town, and by midday Berylford was rife with mindless speculation, but also fear. Fear that the same assailant may still be at large. After hearing the story via the town's haberdashers Miss Osborne and Miss Gwynne, Mrs Urmstone made her way home quickly, yet cautiously. She examined the garden around her own sizeable house, to ensure that no potential assailant was concealed anywhere awaiting her return home, and eventually went inside. She entered her parlour to find Mrs Haffisidge there. She had a pair of envelopes in her hand.

"My dear Mrs Haffisidge?" she said with an air of confusion, "How-? Who-?"

"Your door was unlocked, Elspeth," returned Mrs Haffisidge, "To own the truth, you left it *ajar* when you left for Osborne and Gwynne's."
Mrs Urmstone's mouth hung open at the response. Such must have been her excitement and animation to venture to the haberdashery that her mind must have neglected all thought to her own security.

"I cannot believe I did that!" she gasped.

"Mr Gussage from the schoolhouse was fortunately walking by when he heard it creaking. Realising the situation, he came to find me, and I have been waiting here for your return ever since."

Mrs Urmstone blinked several times trying to contain her perplexedness. In truth, she was used to the late Mr Urmstone being at home, to warrant such measures unnecessary. It had been not yet eight weeks since his burial; in the main, she had grieved. For she had watched his descent into the fever that rendered him bedridden, had many a grave conversation with Doctor Street and the nurse Mrs Early, sat in quiet prayer and watchful contemplation for a whole fortnight, before the inevitable occurred; she was at once the widow of the Lord Mayor of the town.

These things she knew and carried with her each day. And yet, for all of that, Mrs Urmstone was still unused to the fact her husband was gone in the small matters. While he served in his office, he preferred to operate as much as possible from the house, consulting privately the views and opinions of his wife when composing speeches, motions and manifestos – though never admitting as much publicly lest respect should be lost for him and his authority – a fact that Mrs Urmstone could not help but appreciate. When he was not at home, she was usually by his side attending a variety of events that merited both their presences. As such, a trivial thing like locking the door – Mrs Urmstone had difficulty recalling the last time she had to remember such a thing. She came and sat on one of her settees, facing Mrs Haffisidge in one of the armchairs. Placing her hands in her lap, she closed her eyes and exhaled deeply and slowly.

"My mind is besieged, Judith-Ann," she sighed, "I am quite overwrought, I fear."

"'Tis of little surprise; we have seen such losses these last few weeks, my dear," Mrs Haffisidge stood and placed a reassuring hand on her friend's shoulder, "We are closer to Lady Oliviera than any in Berylford; to see those beautiful children taken so suddenly. Not to mention your own grief, of course. And now the Countess *herself* attacked."

Mrs Urmstone rubbed her eyes with one hand, pulling it down her face in exhaustion.

"I am unsure how to proceed from this," she said, "I never expected to be *married*, let alone widowed. Now I have a house that's too big for me. In truth I have never felt more alone in my life. My Lady Oliviera was very lucky she still has a husband and servants to attend her. If a man should throw *me* down the stairs, I can hardly rely on Zephaniah Gussage to be walking by *then*! Or for *you* to be in the parlour!"

"Then we should return to what gives us pleasure, Madam," Mrs Haffisidge said straightforwardly, "We should go into society."

Again, Mrs Urmstone's mind turned to her grief and her husband. 'Two months – that's all it's been, two months!' she thought, 'Besides, I am not even out of black yet.'

"What do you think, Elspeth?"

"I barely had enough energy to attend dinner with you just a couple of weeks ago, Judith-Ann! And that was a *private* engagement. Society will involve many other people; so recently grieved, Mrs Haffisidge, would I not be thought... *brisk*?"

"Better to be brisk than not to be *brave*, my dear Elspeth," returned Mrs Haffisidge, "I have here in my hand two invitations to a party at Griggsden Manor – the Lord Griggsden was a comrade of my late husband's and we've always kept in touch..."
Mrs Urmstone still did not look certain.

"...Listen to me Elspeth, Mr Urmstone would not want you to hide away indoors forever, and neither will Lady Vyrrington! Griggsden is not all that far either; we could be there in a carriage in quarter-of-an-hour. If you go and cannot endure it, then we'll come home again. Give yourself a chance. You were at your happiest *in* society, Madam."

Mrs Haffisidge had made a very valid argument. Extravagant soirées and parties were perfect stamping grounds for Mrs Urmstone. 'Drawing room talk' was one of her favourite pastimes, especially if it was about people she neither knew, nor expected to see again any time soon. She sighed again, long, haggard and fatigued.

"Very well, Mrs Haffisidge," she said, "If I am to be thrown down my stairs in the dead of night, I may as well enjoy a night of revels and frivolity before I run afoul of that fate!"

Mrs Haffisidge smiled and chuckled.

"That's the spirit!" she returned, "I will arrange for the fly to pick you up tomorrow at seven."

"You could come by here first for an apéritif?"

"Only if that will be agreeable to you."

"Of course – just let yourself in."

"Whether you're in or not?"

Mrs Urmstone laughed harder at that response than she had in weeks, so much that she also wept a little. Mrs Haffisidge placed a well-ringed hand on her friend's shoulder.

"This is the Elspeth Urmstone I knew and loved. Beginning to dispel the darkness from her life. As rightly she should…" then her smile turned neutral and her eyes sad,

"…Do not be governed by your grief, Madam, for it leads only to ruin and despair."

Mrs Urmstone was unsure now how to respond. Mrs Haffisidge came to herself and blinked a few times, before her face transformed once again to bear its mousy grin.

"Forgive me, Elspeth."

"Freely granted, Mrs Haffisidge."

"See you tomorrow, then," she returned, before turning and exiting the house, giving her friend no chance to pursue further conversation.

Chapter X
The Griggsden Party

KEEPING TO HER WORD, MRS Haffisidge had arranged a carriage to pick her and Mrs Urmstone from Portchester Road at seven the following evening. The apéritif idea was actually a ploy of Mrs Haffisidge's, to ensure her friend did not disinvite them both at the last minute. She feared, in spite of her unquenchable optimism and desire to see her happy, Mrs Urmstone would have shut herself away in her house, perhaps never to emerge again.

The roads to the house of Mrs Haffisidge's old friend Lord Griggsden were unusually smooth; a small blessing for the springs of a hired carriage seldom made for a comfortable journey – even if it were only a quarter-hour ride outside Berylford itself. Had the weather been finer, and if it were a private engagement, Mrs Haffisidge may have been prone to suggest walking there – but there were always rumours of thieves, bandits, brigands and vagabonds squatting along the road – wild and violent creatures with whom the ladies would not dare acquaint themselves if they could avoid as much.

Mrs Haffisidge, knowing her friend was attending half-reluctantly, attempted very little conversation; though did recite a few names whom she thought might stimulate Mrs Urmstone's scandalmongering appetite. Major Royall, who had espoused a much younger woman, for example; or the French noblewoman Lady Jacqueline Rhésel-d'Ivre, who had, so rumour told, fled the revolution, the Guillotine – by extension and encompassment, *The Terror* – by way of being smuggled in a fishing boat, fish being one of the few things to which Madame Rhésel-d'Ivre was not allergic. The objective of "the game of gossip", as Mrs Urmstone was prone to calling it, was not to mock, lie or offend the subject or subjects (though it was ultimately of little consequence if any such thing was caused), but to see the lengths of exaggeration and embellishment that could be given to a merely-overheard or eavesdropped misinterpretation. It was not uncommon that, especially in Berylford, these embroideries and superfluities to the truth, their arrant wildness and ridiculousness notwithstanding, became the believed version of the tale, and by extension, part of public record and history. Tonight, looked to be one of the first and only times Mrs Haffisidge beheld Mrs Urmstone's utter disinterest in playing the game tonight. Instead her eyes were unwaveringly fixed out of the carriage window.

Griggsden Manor was a grand building, in the same league as *Beryl Court*. After exiting their carriage, Mrs Haffisidge saw her friend appeared to have rallied a little at the sight of the magnanimous house. A liveried majordomo escorted the ladies up thirty-or-so large marble steps – woe betide any who should slip down them ("It would not have ended well for Cinderella if the ball had been held here! Imagine losing a shoe on *these* stairs!" Mrs Urmstone quipped *sotto voce* to Mrs Haffisidge once they had survived to the top of them) – and through a series of winding corridors, lined on both sides with gilded portraits of many a Griggsden family member, whose relationship to the house had no doubt increasing dubiousness and obscurity.

Music, light and loud frivolity emanated from a large drawing room, filled with at least two-hundred people, all, by the looks of them, of varied class and character. Gossiping or being gossiped about.

The most colourful and exuberant presence was in the centre, a short and skinny, yet well-tanned and handsome gentleman who appeared to be wearing Persian costume. He was smiling as he spoke between three ladies, but this smile broadened into a beaming grin when he beheld Mrs Haffisidge before him. He excused himself from the ladies and approached her.

"Mrs Haffisidge, it is a joy and an honour to see you again," he said, leaning in to embrace her and kiss her cheek. The bristles of his dark beard tickled her face and she giggled girlishly. Mrs Urmstone looked unsure what to think.

"Oh Lord Griggsden, you remain a disgrace to the last," she jovially quipped in response, "And you attire yourself so eccentrically. Typical of you."

"My travels in Persia have been most fruitful, Madam, not least for discovery of their taste in clothes," he replied, "When one is a bachelor, one can afford such luxuries."

"Are there no plans for a *Lady* Griggsden any time soon?" Mrs Haffisidge asked.

"One adventure at a time, I think," returned Lord Griggsden, maintaining his broad grin, "The world has many other unseen wonders. I won't be satisfied with marriage before I have seen them all, and it would be unjust to neglect the wife I choose for favour of them."

"An admirable sentiment, My Lord," Mrs Urmstone finally piped up.

"Ah Lord Griggsden, may I introduce one of my closest friends and neighbours, Mrs Elspeth Urmstone. Daughter of The Honourable Marcus Hawthcourt."

"Honoured and charmed that you could attend my little salon, Mrs Urmstone," Lord Griggsden displayed surprising gentleness when taking and kissing Mrs Urmstone's gloved hand, "Word did reach us of your husband's recent passing. I am very sorry. I did back him when he was running for mayor, you know?"

"Your Lordship is very kind."

As Mrs Urmstone's attention was occupied by their host, Mrs Haffisidge had time to survey the other invitees. The three ladies to whom Lord Griggsden had been speaking prior to their arrival, Mrs Haffisidge only knew by sight – they were a trio of higher-class society ornaments who, given their spindly, statuesque figures and choice of clothes and headdress, could just as easily have been mistaken for coatracks and lampshades. By name, the Lady Hilda Albion, the Lady Leddindsham and the Lady Oxborrow. Mrs Haffisidge reciprocated their condescending stare-downs of her, and turned her gaze across the drawing room.

She spied the Major Royall, in a uniform of red and gold, a couple of medals catching the light and gleaming, stood with a tall, blonde-haired lady in an ice blue gown – she could not have yet been five-and-twenty despite his being relatively similar in age to Mrs Haffisidge herself. The young lady – presumably until proven otherwise to be Mrs Royall – looked awkward and uncomfortable, so she was obviously the topic of some talk somewhere about the room.

Mrs Haffisidge's gaze then found a small woman wearing a highly-becoiffed powdered wig stood by the buffet table, looking very indecisive at the selection. There was a large bowl of a punch made with brandy and port, of which the lady was holding a glass, sipping almost reluctantly from it as she surveyed the food on offer. A spread hardly bereft of colour or extravagance, quite like their host. A great jelly in the shape of a pyramid flushed a pinkish orange as it was jewelled with tiny crayfish within. Oranges, pineapples and grapes adorned the corners of the table, at which were countless bowls of trifles and syllabubs. On the more savoury side, a massive tureen of a soup of mutton and veal, platters of cold roast beef and stuffed quails.

For all her hesitating and dilly-dallying, the lady was observed by Mrs Haffisidge to turn from the table altogether, shaking her head, holding her punch glass closely and protectively in both hands as though it were some precious heirloom. This could be none other than

Lady Jacqueline Rhésel-d'Ivre. She thought Mrs Urmstone would at least be intrigued by details of a conversation with Lady Jacqueline, so Mrs Haffisidge started towards her.

She had to stop dead though, for suddenly her eyes met those of a man, pot-bellied yet in all other articles thin and not especially tall, with dark shadows under his eyes. The frock coat he was wearing, unevenly embroidered and even patched on one elbow, looked rented. Upon seeing her, he smirked somewhat, and made his way out onto the terrace through the open doors.
She felt as though she had been revisited by an evil spirit, but Mrs Haffisidge nevertheless felt compelled to follow him. She turned around, and found that Mrs Urmstone was now being introduced to people by Lord Griggsden, and thus felt well in leaving her while she pursued the man she had seen.

The terrace was empty save for Mrs Haffisidge and the mysterious gentleman. He had his back to her when she arrived.

"Do I know you, sir?" she asked, "I *do*, don't I?"
The man turned to face her. He bore an unsettling grin.

"Wouldn't expect you to remember a lowly cart driver, Mrs Upholland."

Mrs Haffisidge pointed her chin at him, her lips uncharacteristically pursed with displeasure.

"I no longer answer to that name. My name is Haffisidge as it was before my marriage."

The man chuckled.

"I had a feeling you may have changed your name," he continued, "Indeed, it surprises me you can bear to be seen in public at all."

"Pray convey to me the point of this, sir. Who are you?"

"My name is Christopher Tratsly, not that you would recall; we were not formally introduced before and it was not important. Just as it is not now."

"It would seem so. I have no recollection of ever meeting a *cart* driver, nor ever needing one," Mrs Haffisidge condescended to him, "speaking of which: how did you acquire an invitation here?"

"Driving people from place to place does not pay awfully well. Posing as others can, depending on where and whom."

"You conned your way in. Then forgive me, sir, but I must take leave of your presence." She turned on her heel and went to go back into the drawing room.

"You really have denied it all these years; even maybe convinced yourself the lies you tell your friends is the truth. Only you know the truth of your disgrace. And *hers...*"

Mrs Haffisidge stopped dead in her path. She turned to face Mr Tratsly again.

"...Only you. And me," he continued, his tone had become sinister.

She had been reduced almost to silence.

"I don't know what you're talking about," she said, barely stomaching the words.

"I think you do, Mrs Haffisidge. And unless I am paid two thousand pounds, so will the entire of Lord Griggsden's party."

Mrs Haffisidge shook her head and ran back into the drawing room. He followed her, intent on drawing attention to them both. Fortunately for her, she found the majordomo.

"That man over by the terrace doors has not formally been invited, and has just insulted me gravely," she explained, "Please have him removed at once."

The majordomo did not question her at all, and walked straight over to Tratsly and took him by the arm. Aggressively, he shook himself free and began to call out to Mrs Haffisidge as he was restrained:

"I'll ruin you, Madam. The people you know! The people you *love*! They will all know your disgrace. *Remember: Juliette Harrowsleigh!*"

His cries were cut off as he was successfully removed from the room.

Those three last words were haunting her again. She knew now whose silhouette she had seen in her garden those nights ago. She wanted to think further on it, but, realising all eyes were on her, Mrs Haffisidge knew she had few options, and so to spare her dignity, she chose to laugh loudly.

"What theatrics, My Lord Griggsden. Oh my, you do entertain us!" she exclaimed.

Chapter XI
The Society Spindles Speak

THE REST OF THE ROOM all started to laugh at Mrs Haffisidge's response. Thankfully, they believed the entire event to be a spectacle on the part of their host, who played along despite being confused in his head. He was merely happy to see frivolity and amusement restored. In all, except for the society spindles themselves Ladies Leddindsham, Albion and Oxborrow.

"Who is she, again?" Lady Oxborrow asked *sotto voce* regarding Mrs Haffisidge.

"Some old friend of Griggsden's. No one really," to the question Lady Leddindsham returned.

"Turned up with that one over there," said Lady Oxborrow, inclining her head to Mrs Urmstone, "Not that I know of her either."

"Oh, *that's* Elspeth Urmstone," Lady Albion whispered, "Elspeth *Hawthcourt* as was. Berylford society woman, but with high connections in Scotland."

"Any title?"

"No, she has no title; she's the younger daughter after all. Just a plain old Missus, to the last. The only reason she can move in the same circles as we, is down to her joined-at-the-hip association with Lady Oliviera Vyrrington, *whom* – I might add – rumour has it, has been a guest head on more than one pillow, if you get my drift."

Unbeknownst to the ladies, Mrs Urmstone had been listening to them speak about her, and while she was more than happy to endure their ignorance and arrogance regarding her, to pay Her Lady Oliviera Vyrrington insult was a bridge too far. Her lip curling angrily, she turned sharply, lips pursed so tight they were white, and quickly approached Lady Albion. The three were unsettled by her vehement expression.

"You may insult *me*, Lady Albion -- oh yes you may do that to whatever end you will, and I will stand back and hear whatever poison you decide to spout despite my being so recently *grieved*. But I would be *drawn, quartered and devoured by mongrels before I heed words against My Lady Oliviera Vyrrington*! If ever there were another lady in existence of such kindness, wisdom or beauty then she would still walk thence as a nun, creeping in my Countess' shadow."

She had almost become entranced by her own ire and had almost forgotten they were in society. Lord Griggsden and Mrs Haffisidge were both stood behind her, bearing concerned expressions.

"Is everything quite well, Mrs Urmstone?" Lord Griggsden asked.

"I think not, My Lord. Judith-Ann, my dear, I knew it was a mistake to come here. I think my mourning should continue formally a little longer. Please can we leave?"

"Of course, Elspeth," returned Mrs Haffisidge, "I must apologise, Lord Griggsden, could you have the majordomo arrange for our carriage?"

"By all means, madam. I am sorry to see you leave so soon."

Thankfully for them, it was not long before Mrs Urmstone and Mrs Haffisidge, both perturbed by their respective experiences, were able to depart. Lord Griggsden, mortified that they had both been treated thus expressed his dismay most regrettably by not only arranging their transport home himself, but by seeing them to the foot of the deadly-steep front steps, and was furtherly gracious enough a host to invite them both to dine with him privately as his guests. Both ladies accepted, but also said they would write to confirm officially.

In the carriage, the two ladies sat side-by-side in silence. Mrs Urmstone eventually broke it.

"That man, Mrs Haffisidge," she asked her friend, "Who was he?"

"A stranger," Mrs Haffisidge replied, "A creature with little better to do than profit from a fictional scandal. 'Remember: Juliette Harrowsleigh', indeed! I have never known any Harrowsleighs to remember one in the first place!"

"It could mean something else, Judith-Ann!"

"Well if it's supposed to imply towards something, it's beyond *me*! At any rate, I refuse to afford the subject any further attention. I would advise you to do the same, Elspeth. Just as you should give the remarks of those three witches no credence."

"'Twas what they said about Lady Vyrrington that vexed me," returned Mrs Urmstone, "'a guest head on more than one pillow'? If it's adultery they're implying, could you blame the Countess? For all the attention Lord Wilson pays her?"

"The lack thereof, you mean."

"Exactly! As long as it was with one of equal breeding and status. In all seriousness, though, My Lady Oliviera is a woman of the most superior moral character. I would not think her capable of anything unbecoming of her standing!"

"And *I* would agree with you."

Book Five

WHITLOCKE AND AMETHYST

Chapter XII
Lady Vyrrington Makes Accusations

THE COUNTESS WAS FIVE DAYS in bed. She had barely woken since her attack, and even when she did, it was a reluctant attempt. One-eyed at first, heavy and indecisive. The room around her was dimly lit, and her vision blurred. She tried to pivot herself to see more around her, blinking as she did so, and suddenly she screwed her eyes shut and hissed in pain as she felt an agonising shot come from her back. She clutched the area in question with a sharply-clawed hand, bit her lip as it continued to afflict her.

'What in God's name happened to me?' she exclaimed in her head.
She wanted to move again, but the position she was in, skewed and awkward as it was, was the least painful way to sit at present for her.
"My Lady, you're awake!" came a woman's voice.
Lady Vyrrington opened her eyes again, not moving from the now-awkward position in which she was lying. She recognised the voice as that belonging to Amethyst.

"What on Earth happened, Amethyst?" she asked slowly and painedly, "And why is it so dark in here?"

"The doctor recommended the curtains be kept closed, milady, in case the light would hurt your eyes."

"I think the light would be welcome compared to the pain in my back."

"You broke a rib, I believe the doctor said." The Countess' vision was now clear enough to see where Amethyst was in the room, now that she had drawn the curtains a little and allowed some light in.

"*What*?" she returned hoarsely.

"Do you really not remember, milady?" Lady Oliviera blinked a few times more; this time it was more out of confusion than an attempt to see clearer.

"Doctor Street did warn us you might have hit your head on the way down. That you may have trouble remembering things," Amethyst continued to explain. The Countess remained just as perplexed as before.

"I remember seeing Mr Whitlocke before retiring for the night, as is my habit. What do you mean 'on my way down'? When did I do such a thing as hit my head, or break a *rib*?" All the mystery was exasperating her, and she kept forgetting the pains, and, in attempting to move out of bed, reminded herself the hard way.

"Oh, this is ridiculous!" she exclaimed to herself, aloud, "How did this happen to *me* of all people?"

"You fell down the stairs in the night, my love," then answered a male voice. Her husband Lord Wilson was stood in the doorway. The Countess scoffed.

"If the last thing I remember was a conversation with Whitlocke, I wouldn't put it past him to push me down the stairs and leave me for dead."

"Don't be absurd. You just missed a step on your way down for a glass of water."

"I have a jug on the nightstand for such a purpose, Lord Wilson!" returned Lady Vyrrington, "I can think of no reason for wanting to go down the stairs on my own accord. Apparently Whitlocke wanted me to in however forceful a way he thought appropriate."
She looked him in the eyes, lips pursed.

At first her husband looked to be considering her accusation seriously, but then he smiled at her.

"This is hysteria, My Lady," he said, "You did not even remember the fall until just now; you can't just go around blaming the last person you spoke to as an easy explanation."
He sat and leant across the bed to kiss his wife's cheek.

"Get rest," he continued, "We will have some breakfast sent up. Come, Amethyst – let us leave Her Ladyship in peace."

"Yes milord;" returned Amethyst, "I will be back in due course with your breakfast tray, milady."

"Mind my words, My Lord Wilson!" Lady Vyrrington called after her husband, before he exited the room – he allowed Amethyst to go before him, "Mind them seriously. Whatever you do – believe me or otherwise – do *not* allow George Whitlocke into this bedchamber alone."

"If you're serious about this, I will question him myself on the matter," returned Lord Wilson, "But I bid you, My Lady, to give this accusation a moment's consideration. It is no secret your management style *clashes* with that of Whitlocke in this house-"

"That he should question it *at all* is rank insubordination!" the Countess interrupted.

"-But you cannot give credence to the idea he would feel compelled to attack you."

"I am usually of such robust self-awareness, sir. I cannot think I could have just 'missed a step' as you put it! Have you at least considered that I was attacked – if not by Whitlocke, then by someone? The same someone who took that young boots boy?"

"We searched the house, Oliviera," to his Lady Lord Wilson replied, "Not a servant slept until we ensured every brick and stone of *Beryl Court* was checked. We found nothing; we found no one. I know not what else I can tell."

"Assure me you will protect me. You must promise to do this."
Lord Wilson approached his wife and sat beside her on the bed, kissing her on the temple.

"I am duty-bound to do nothing else, My Lady," he whispered, before getting up again and leaving.

Chapter XIII
Amethyst Wounds Whitlocke

WHITLOCKE WAS SAT PENSIVELY AT the head of the kitchen table, with Mrs Trudgedawes bustling around in the background to make preparations for dinner. He drummed his fingers in aimless and fruitless thought.

His senses returned when Amethyst entered, and he stood up as soon as she did so. Even though when she first came to *Beryl Court* she had been little more than the wretched creature Lady Vyrrington's father Lord Isaacs had saved from the workhouse, George Whitlocke's otherwise stone-cold officiousness and stern aspect were all but rent to shreds upon first beholding Amethyst. She was not pretty, but then, half-starved human beings rarely are. Even so, Whitlocke had seen past it to the innocence and sweetness within. Behind the sorrow and behind the fear.

He in turn had been admired by her. Amethyst always maintained he looked well in livery, though his build had become more corpulent with age. She cared not, for she too had possessed the sight to distinguish the kindness that was masked by the authoritarian visage he carried with his occupation. Nevertheless, as

Whitlocke was somewhat taken aback to see when she entered the kitchen that morning, Amethyst looked nervously at him. He could not fathom to himself the reason, and continued to watch her, though sat back down.

"Her Ladyship has woken, Mrs Trudgedawes," Amethyst told the cook *sotto voce*, "Is there any of the mackerel left for her breakfast?"

"There's only the one fillet so I'll do her some eggs as well," Mrs Trudgedawes returned.
She left for the pantry, whereupon Amethyst was left alone with Whitlocke. It was a harrowingly awkward silence, both of them wanting to scream words at the other but neither of them in possession of the right ones.

Instead they just stared at each other. Whitlocke could not help himself in the end. He had to say something.

"What's the matter, Amethyst?" he asked.

"Where were you the night Lady Vyrrington fell?" she replied straightforwardly.
He was utterly gobsmacked by the response. It had been the last thing he had anticipated her to say.

"I beg your pardon?" he managed to utter, still hindered in his speech somewhat in surprise, "Where was I when-?"

"My Lady said you were the last person she saw before she took the fall," Amethyst explained, "and that you pushed her."

There was very little that rendered Whitlocke bereft of words. He had all manner of razor-sharp quips and quarrels up his sleeve for the likes of Lady Vyrrington, sometimes His Lordship, and even once or twice, Mrs Trudgedawes, but for Amethyst he had nothing. His mouth just hung there, open in unadulterated disbelief.

"Tell me it isn't true, Mr Whitlocke," Amethyst continued.

"It is *not* true, Amethyst," Whitlocke returned almost instantly, regaining the full use of his mouth and mind, and sounding insulted, "And I am hurt that not only you would think me capable of such a thing, but also that you would doubt my integrity."

Angrily, he stood up. Amethyst's eyes widened for fear of him.

"My Lady is no foolish judge of character, Mr Whitlocke, nor prone to hysterics. She wouldn't say these things if she didn't think them true!"

Now it was time to confront the Countess; thus he left Amethyst, fearful and alone at the kitchen table. He ascended those stairs so quickly the carpet might have caught fire, navigating the corridors to Lady Vyrrington's bedchamber. He knocked – force of habit, rather than genuine courtesy – and let himself in without waiting for a response from the bedbound Ladyship. His face suggested fury, nostrils flaring, skin red and eyes wide. However, he was taken aback when the first thing he saw was a poker pointing just a breath away from his head, being held by Lady Vyrrington herself from her bed.

"I dare you to approach me one more inch, George Whitlocke," she hissed, "Just you dare. I will skewer you with this poker – mind my words."
His vehemence had replaced itself with confusion.

"So it *is* true!" he said quietly, "You actually believe I tried to kill you?"

"I don't just believe it – I *know* it! I am unashamed to own the fact, Whitlocke. Who else in this house would see me dead?"

"The one who pushed you, perhaps?"

"Don't take that clever tone with *me*, or so help me-"

"Regardless of what you believe, My Lady, turning Amethyst against me is hardly what I would call a fair fight."

"Have you not threatened to do the same by me to Lord Wilson?" Lady Vyrrington returned, "Of all the things I thought you were, Whitlocke, a hypocrite was never on the list until now."

Whitlocke remained quiet. He could not argue with her on that point.

"Amethyst comes to her *own* conclusions," the Countess continued, "She does not have them dictated to by me. I afford her *that* much respect, I can assure you. Apparently, *you* do not."

They stared at each other as though they had pistols ready for duel at ten paces, interrupted by a loud and frantic knocking on the front door downstairs. Whitlocke did not immediately move.

"I would consider answering the door if I were you, Whitlocke. Or we may have to find a replacement butler, after all," the Countess sneered. Whitlocke eyed her narrowly, as she did him as he exited the room, both giving the message of 'this isn't over yet.'

The knocking at the door was becoming harder and more frequent until Whitlocke finally made it. The culprit was Mrs Urmstone, who bustled into the front hallway without so much as a "hello" to Whitlocke.

"I am come, rather, I am *sent* to fetch Amethyst," Mrs Urmstone gasped, trying to catch her breath – she had probably run from town to *Beryl Court* directly.

"What is it regarding?"

"Oh the *baby*! Mrs Warwick is in labour!" she returned, her exasperation flaring, "Mrs Early the midwife is ironically bedbound in her *own* confinement to assist. Amethyst is the next most-qualified."

"She has duties downstairs, Madam. I'll fetch her post-haste."

"No need, Mr Whitlocke – I'm here," Amethyst appeared from the stairs leading to the kitchen and servants' quarters, "I heard Mrs Urmstone from afar."

"Come, child – *make haste!*" Mrs Urmstone shouted at her, becoming more enflamed by the minute. Whitlocke wanted to speak to Amethyst before she left, but could not stop her as she was almost frogmarched out of the house by Mrs Urmstone down the front grounds of *Beryl Court*. He needed to apologise to her.

Chapter XIV
A Lustful Quake

M R WARWICK WAS STOOD OUTSIDE Mrs Haffisidge's house, having been ordered there by his aunt-in-law.

"Men, apart from the good doctor, are just in the way during childbirth. They have no business trying to be on-hand. So off with you, Mr Warwick!" she had said, to his disgruntlement.

He had been abandoned to anxious thought, and was wringing his hands while leant up against the front wall. Not out of fear for the welfare of his wife, but out of impatience to see his son, as it *was* to be a son or nothing else. Nevertheless, he could not help but have a little concern for the sounds coming from within the house, for they could be heard from outside. A turbulent period mixed with loud, heavy agonised breathing and panting, and harrowing screams. The kind that would make those of frailer heart and mind screw their eyes shut in the hope it was merely a warped and depraved nightmare. A cruel trick of the subconscious mind. Especially in that the otherwise blessed thing of childbirth killed so many in Hampshire. Mr Warwick was of shallow mind, though, as was the case with many men like him, and it had never occurred to him to imagine the pain his wife was enduring for the benefit of his family line. He merely paced up and down across the garden, the dirt, wet from the recent rainfall, grating beneath his boots. There were more screams from inside the house; Mr Warwick gasped with exasperation.

'Why is this taking so long?' he thought to himself.

Until it came to pass. The screams had ended, then an awful silence, at which at once a mere glimmer of worry happened upon his thoughts. But once the squeaks of the newborn baby were heard, he gasped in relief. Rather than wait for permission to enter the house again, Mr Warwick let himself in, treading mud into the carpet as he did so, and ascended the stairs to Mrs Haffisidge's bedroom, where Mrs Warwick was laid up. Doctor Street appeared at the door as he was about to let himself in yet again.

"Ah, Luke – you may enter now," said the Doctor, "And you should be very proud."

"How are they?" was Mr Warwick's abrupt reply.

"All is well with both of them."

"Have I a son?" Mr Warwick now sounded very brusque and impatient, "Doctor Street, is my child a *boy*?"

Unsure as to what sort of tone was best to respond to such intolerance, Doctor Street spoke slowly:

"You are the father of a healthy boy, Mr Warwick."

He smiled, and went in to see his wife. He sat beside her on the bed, looking at his son as he was cradled about his mother's breast, warmly wrapped in swaddling cloth.

"I thought Paul for a name," said Mrs Warwick, weakly, her energy all but spent, "After your father. Do you like it?"

"I love it," returned Mr Warwick, "I love him, and I love *you*."

He kissed her forehead, getting carefully back up.

"I owe you all thanks: Doctor…"

He then stopped and surveyed Amethyst up and down.

"…And erm… Miss Cheshill. *Yes*, I thank you all!"

Mrs Haffisidge cleared her throat loudly, and Mr Warwick turned back.

"I did not catch that Mr Warwick!" she said.

Mrs Warwick smiled in amusement as she observed her aunt's expression toward him.

"And *thank you* Miss *Cheshill*!" he reiterated spitefully, once again looking at Amethyst. Upon looking at her again, he was suddenly charged with a passion that he had not felt in a long time. Hitherto his wife's condition, he was bereft of means to quench his sexual thirst. And while not pretty, Amethyst cut a figure that was nevertheless attractive to a man, especially one suffering such a lustful quake.

He walked out immediately with these thoughts at the brim of his mind, leaving Mrs Haffisidge (amidst expressing how little she was surprised by Mr Warwick's actions) and Mrs Warwick to convey their own thanks to Amethyst and Doctor Street.

Mr Warwick skulked in an alley beside Mrs Haffisidge's house, watching Doctor Street leave. He was waiting for Amethyst; his desire stewing. Mrs Warwick was still in no position to acquiesce to his passions, and there were no brothels for miles; the majority of the women in Berylford were otherwise married, too superior to speak to him, or in the course of middle-age and beyond. Amethyst was in her mid-thirties (only a year or two older than Mr Warwick himself) engaged to no one and a servant. She fit the bill perfectly. She was last to exit, and as she passed the alley, Mr Warwick grabbed her and pulled her towards him, his hand clasped over her mouth, so she could not cry out.

"You must not make a sound, do you hear me?" he whispered to her, sinisterly, releasing her mouth.

"Please sir, what are you about?" Amethyst asked, very frightened.

"I am about to show you what it feels like to have a man inside you."
He grabbed her blouse. She writhed in order to resist him and protested quietly. Eventually, Mr Warwick pinned her against the wall of the alley, and started to kiss at her neck. Again, Amethyst did the best she could to stop him, but it was not good enough.

It only took a swipe of a wooden cane by Whitlocke, who had come running from *Beryl Court* to find Amethyst, to end the depraved display.

"*Get off of her!*" Whitlocke shouted. Mr Warwick fell to the ground when struck with the cane.

"Do you defend her?" said Mr Warwick, clutching at the back of his head where Whitlock had struck him.

"I certainly don't defend *you!*" returned Whitlocke, "Get out of here before I send for a constable."
Mr Warwick got up and slowly moved away from the alley.

"And if I ever hear you've laid a finger on this woman again, I will have you thrown from Berylford quicker than you can blink!"

"Really? If a butler has so much power, then why is he still a butler?"

"I never said that it would be *I* who *personally* threw you from here. But I *do* have friends who may." They stared each other down; Whitlocke's hand still clutched around the cane at the ready. But Mr Warwick said no more, quickly retreating back inside his aunt-in-law's house.

Chapter XV
Whitlocke's Declaration

THEIR CANTER BACK TO *BERYL Court* was slow and silent. The butler and the maidservant. Theirs was a story insignificant to many, a fact for which they were very thankful. Both being servants, their employers notwithstanding, they were not prey to the rapacious speculations of Berylford's gossips.

Whitlocke was certain that he had frightened Amethyst earlier that morning, and was deliberately remaining silent, though he still wanted to look at her when she was not looking at him.

"I admire your courage, Mr Whitlocke," she said while still looking ahead; he felt his face flush red in embarrassment. She had obviously been conscious he had been watching her. "And I owe you thanks," she continued.

"Not at all, Amethyst," he returned humbly, after having first to stifle any visible displays of awkwardness, "Think nothing of it."
They carried on walking, again the silence recommenced, and again it was Amethyst who broke it.

"What made you come into town after me?" she asked.

"I felt I owed you an apology for the way I spoke to you earlier. If I offended you, or frightened you, I pray you'll forgive me."

"I didn't expect you to react the way you did. But I suppose I owe you an apology too, for ever thinking you capable of such a thing."

"Freely granted, I assure you."

"I feel so dirty; his hands all over me," Amethyst had to stop walking and almost winced at the notion she was describing, "The man had just had his son delivered. What sort of man would want to have his way with the midwife straight afterwards?"

"A man with little about his brain," said Whitlocke, "And don't you worry; he'll get what's coming to him once Lady Vyrrington is told about it. Mrs Haffisidge will have him out before the town for a *very* public shaming. I think she would have him in the stockade, or *worse*."

"Oh no, *please*! Please, Mr Whitlocke, I beg you – don't tell Lady Vyrrington about this. Or anyone else for that matter. I don't need any sort of fuss, thank you."

"Even from a man who loves you?"

"Indeed, even from the man who – *what*?" Her eyes had returned to the wide-set position they had been in that morning, but this time the expression stemmed from shock, not terror and fear. Whitlocke was smiling warmly at her.

"We have worked beside each other all these long years and you haven't once realised I love you?" he said.

"Well I-"

"And I know you feel something as well."

"Doesn't matter what I feel."

"It's the only thing that matters, as far as I'm concerned."

"'Tisn't as simple as that, Mr Whitlocke," returned Amethyst, "I am pledged to serve My Lady Vyrrington. I am bound never to leave her side."

"We would still live and work at Beryl Court."

"She would never sanction the match, though. *Especially* knowing what she suspects you of!" Whitlocke dropped to his knees, one hand about his chest, the other behind his back. Amethyst did not look like she knew what to think or say.

"I told you before and swear to you now, Amethyst, with my life as forfeit, I did not attack Lady Vyrrington," he said slowly and clearly, "And in the same vein, I swear to you that I love you."
Amethyst chuckled, looking around her to see if any passersby were watching.

"I think you should get up now, Mr Whitlocke," she said, still laughing, "I'm quite overcome – you do look a little ridiculous. What will people think?"

"That I wish for us to marry."

"Well *really*, Mr Whitlocke!"

"*George!*"

"George, I know full well that *marriage* isn't even possible. I would require Lady Vyrrington's permission and-"

"Do you love me?"

"What?"

"Do you *love* me?"

Amethyst's mouth hung ajar in contemplation of how best to answer.

"Why yes, of course! Of course I love you, *George* Whitlocke."

She approached him, and they embraced tightly.

"And of course I agree to marry you," she continued, "If the Lord and Lady give their consent to it."

"We are not children, Amethyst," returned Whitlocke, "If we wish to marry, we will do so with or without their blessing."

Chapter XVI
Mr Warwick's Cogs Begin to Turn

ALL THE MEANWHILE, MR WARWICK, who had lingered in Mrs Haffisidge's downstairs hallway since re-entering the house, had been considering the potential consequences of his actions. It was not an extensive list, but none of the outcomes were good by him – for why should they be? He was well aware of what he had done and that it was neither moral, decent nor gentlemanly – though he never professed to being any of those things.

The assaulted party was a member of the Vyrrington household, and a close confidante of the Countess herself, a great friend of Mrs Haffisidge. Lady Vyrrington, if she were to become aware, could in turn tell Mrs Haffisidge, who would relish the opportunity to oust him from the house and end his marriage to Mrs Warwick once and for all. Or worse, Whitlocke – the witness Mr Warwick had not planned – he could tell the Lord Vyrrington. Mrs Haffisidge's wrath, while uncharacteristic of such an otherwise mild-tempered and sweet-natured lady, endowed her with a great formidability; God only knew of what Lord Wilson would be capable if he knew about what had happened.

In the best case, he would exercise his power to eject Warwick from Berylford altogether.

It would more likely end in the courts, whereupon Whitlocke would testify he saw the attempt in action. Death was still the penalty for rape (while not a learned man, Mr Warwick knew this much), though he had failed in his attempt; it would be likely that Whitlocke and, by extension Lord and Lady Vyrrington, would not care too much about the finer details, and there would be no reliable character witness to vouch for him in any way that might redeem him.
With so much to blockade his thoughts, and being the self-absorbed and shallow-minded man he was, these considerations were only pondered on for a short while. He did not have much of a choice, for Mrs Haffisidge had descended from upstairs.

She noticed him stood there, loitering in the entry hall, and glared at him, relishing the opportunity to administer another tirade to him:

"It's no skin off *my* nose, Mr Warwick, if you only want to see your son for a few seconds, but it may do your wife some good," she quipped.
Mr Warwick did not answer.

"This is utterly typical of you Mr Warwick," his aunt-in-law continued, "You are completely engrossed in nothing but yourself! What my niece was thinking in giving you the added responsibility of a child is *beyond* me! If I had my way now, I'd have the union dissolved and you out of my sights forever."

Mr Warwick then smiled maliciously, intent on annoying his aunt-in-law further. He had pretended very well all the years he had been married to Mrs Warwick to not listen to anything his aunt-in-law said: her ponderances and anecdotes, and tangents and flights of fancy. What he had come to understand, again not that he was a man of any great intelligence or common sense, as was quite common in an individual of his character, was what truly could drive Mrs Haffisidge to distraction and fury.

"Her mother would have approved!" he said, and immediately and inevitably, Mrs Haffisidge's eyes whitened with rage.

"You dare, Mr Warwick – just you *dare* test my nerves! By what *right* do you presume to tell *me* what my sister would have done! You never met her! If she'd been alive she would *never* have consented."

"Then why did *you*? As Alicia's surrogate mother?"

"To this day it remains a mystery – I cannot speak for what *madness* drove me to it! I must have been bereft of every shred of good sense, and mistook you for an honourable man at the time. Whatever decent creature you masqueraded as, that which veiled every ugliness about your character has since been rent to nought. For I see the good-for-nothing scoundrel, the chauvinistic audacious wastrel, as clearly as I behold my own reflection in the mirror."

"I'm just a typical Berylford farmhand Mrs Haffisidge."

"Typical is *right*! A typical *man*! *Self-obsessed; self-serving;* overtly and deliberately *vulgar*! No desire to assist a woman and *every* desire to assert your superiority over one!"

"Those are strong words, madam."

"I told you to test my nerves and you did. Strong words where strong words are *due*, Mr Warwick and due they *are* when a person tests my nerves!"

Mr Warwick huffed and pushed past her to away upstairs to his room, shutting the door behind him. While he could not deny any of what Mrs Haffisidge had told him was true, he was certain that, for all that, and the events of the day notwithstanding, he did truly love his wife. Trying to have his way with Amethyst as he had done was a release of inner, previously-dormant

- 109 -

lust, which he would have visited unto Mrs Warwick had she been in the condition to receive him. Not because he had forsaken his feelings for her.

He began to feel a little sentimental, not that it was common for him to feel thus, and reminisced briefly about how happy he and his wife had been on their wedding day, when even Mrs Haffisidge had compliments to give to him. Adding to his reminiscence, he looked through the top drawer of his bedside cabinet and something caught his eye. He took it out and surveyed it, and while he did not fully understand what he had before him, it bore words he knew how to read. He decided, the questions he had would be answered by a more intelligent power. Not only to quench his curiosity, but also to get a final, lasting revenge on his aunt-in-law, and set her reputation in Berylford ablaze once and for all.

Chapter XVII
Berylford En Fête

THE MAJORITY OF THE TENANTS to the Vyrrington estate, in other words, most of Berylford's citizenry, were independent labouring businesspeople – the joinery owned by a Mr Dyer, the rag-and-bone warehouse whose proprietor was a Mr Devonshire, plus *The St. Barbara's Arms* tavern and the haberdashery and millinery shop owned by the Misses Osborne and Gwynne – Lady Vyrrington, Mrs Urmstone and Mrs Haffisidge's close friends – among them.

However, the main source of income to the estate, and to the town, was Cox Farm – a large plot of land to the north of Berylford – a business rich in commerce with exports of game, poultry, dairy and grain going out to nearby towns such as Hinxstone, Wraxhill-on-the-Test and Andover. A business worth taking care of, especially now that winter was setting in. When December was imminent, it was necessary that any last crops that had not been ready during the harvest time were to be reaped before the winter cold arrived. These crops, by the connivance between Reverend Helton and Mrs Early, one of his more devout parishioners and mistress of Cox Farm (married to its owner, Mr Early) were to be taken to an area that stood not far from Berylford known as the Farthing-'Twixt-'Em Cottages, a slummy parade of hovels named thus because the inhabitants – treacherously poor and wretched creatures – otherwise only had about a quarter-penny between them to live on. As such they would either benefit from the charity of the Berylford citizenry and bear it graciously, or starve and freeze to eventually die.

A machine – newly imported from overseas – which reportedly would speed the reaping process harnessing the power of steam – was being put through its paces; if the hands at Cox Farm, who counted Mr Warwick among their ranks, did not make haste, their efforts for the brick-makers would be ill-spent.

The Yuletide was a well-relished celebration in town. Thus, it was nothing extraordinary for Berylford's people to be going about their business preparing for parties and banquets in honour of the Christmas season – one in particular was given every year by Mrs Urmstone and her late husband. The fastidious and feisty lady was as usual in the company of Mrs Haffisidge, readying for a day at the market, and in turn for eyeing out a potential scandal or rumour worth embellishing. Or rather, Mrs Urmstone was faffing and fussing before the looking glass in the parlour, while Mrs Haffisidge waited patiently – or tried her utmost to – for her to finally be prepared. Mrs Urmstone was once again distracted, looking about her parlour, a dissatisfied look on her face – the kind that suggested weariness with just making do with one's lot.

"I am not so sure I shall bother giving a party this year," she soliloquised, "I never *did* like hosting in this room; it's not at all the correct size for entertaining larger numbers of people."
Mrs Haffisidge chuckled, but at the same time rolled her eyes.

"You don't fool me, Elspeth Urmstone – I know what your game is!" she quipped, "There's no shame in admitting you still miss Mr Urmstone. No one would lay blame to you for *that*! Your grief is still very near. It has not been yet three months since his passing. Lord knows *I* can speak to the difficulty of the first Yuletide a widow!"

"Mr Urmstone used to handle all the administrative duties: arranging the servants, sending the invitations. I hate all that."
Mrs Haffisidge had been avoiding her next sentence as much as possible, but it was becoming clearer and

clearer that she would be bereft of peace if she did not utter it.

"I will happily bear half of the hostessing, if it would please you?" said she, endowed to the last with that careful *savoir-faire* to mask her reluctance to make such an offer – even though it was made in genuine kindness – and that which rendered her being one of the few in Berylford who could pacify Mrs Urmstone.

"Oh Judith-Ann! I am quite overcome," to her Mrs Urmstone replied, "In which case we'll do it at *your* house."

"At my-?"

"Your house is bigger, and in a better part of town. And more to the point, it is better-practised, not to mention *better-suited* for entertaining!"

"With a baby upstairs. And a Mr Warwick," responded Mrs Haffisidge, "Much as I hate to own it, I cannot oust the latter; I must account for his convenience."

"Send him up the tavern with a five-pound note; he'll find ways to occupy himself."

"He deserves tuppence, but I'll honour him two guineas if he agrees to vacate the house."

"There we are, you see! Compromise! Well struck!"

"To be sure," murmured Mrs Haffisidge out of the corner of her mouth; regretting as she knew she would raising the entire suggestion in the first place.

"Let us go and invite everyone!" said her friend, excitedly.

Mrs Urmstone made for her front door, but Mrs Haffisidge delayed.

"Are we not sending cards?" she asked, with an air of uncertainty adrift her tone of voice.

"Oh, why bother when we can invite them all in person?" Mrs Urmstone replied. Then she gasped with magnificent pleasure and cried, "I do so *love* Berylford en fête!" Then she exited her house before Mrs Haffisidge could hinder her further, and so she went after her. 'What use is there in opposing her?' she thought to herself.

Chapter XVIII
The Well-Connected Lady

WHILE HIS COUNTESS MADE A sure but gradual recovery in an otherwise-bedridden state, duty fell to Lord Vyrrington to visit their tenants in Berylford. As the keepers of the estate, they tried to maintain friendly relationships with the townsfolk, so as to keep them living happily and comfortably, and as such rents, fees and surcharges made their way to *Beryl Court* without any fuss or complaint. In short, neither of them felt wary or apprehensive about going about town.

While it was true that they ranked high above most of the residents, the majority of whom were working-class, the likes of Mrs Urmstone, whose family had kept company and been entertained in circles with the royal family, and Mrs Haffisidge, the widow of a commander in the army, were of status that could be seen by otherwise judgemental eyes to be acceptable. His visit, as luck would have it for him, on this day coincided just as Mrs Urmstone was exiting her house, Mrs Haffisidge following behind her somewhat reluctantly.

"Come *along*, Mrs Haffisidge!" she badgered her friend excitedly, "Look – there's Lord Wilson, of all people, I *do* declare!"

Mrs Haffisidge looked as though she wished to protest, but had no time, for all of a sudden Mrs Urmstone was in Lord Wilson's face at a hair's breadth away.

"I do hope we can expect you and My Lady Oliviera to attend this year My Lord?" Mrs Urmstone cried loudly, after exchanging the usual pleasantries, "Mrs Haffisidge and I have agreed it shall be hosted at her house."

"That's a thing to call it," Mrs Haffisidge muttered, "I fear we would need strong men about the place that night, sir!" She raised her voice somewhat, "Strange things have occurred on my street of late, and in *your* house too, we understand. It's no wonder I barely sleep well these days!"

Her voice had turned sardonic on the latter sentence, as if to incline to Mrs Urmstone she was not altogether sure about the idea of hosting the party after all. But Mrs Urmstone was too concerned with the guest list matter in hand to notice, but did add to her friend's comment regarding the attack on Lady Vyrrington:

"Why yes! Such a terrible business that should be visited onto such a noble and knowledgeable creature as our Countess. It beggars belief what kind of wretch is capable of such violence!"

Lord Wilson wanted to answer and opened his mouth to do so, but before he knew it, Mrs Haffisidge had interjected again:

"It makes even Mr *Warwick* look noble in comparison. And those are words I never thought I'd own!"

"Yes, *speaking* of your nephew-in-law, Mrs Haffisidge I was just on my way to Cox Farm now," the Earl finally found his window to speak, and a bye to slip away, "I'll send your compliments, shall I?"

He began to walk away as Mrs Urmstone squawked:

"My Lord Wilson? May we expect you Christmas Eve?"

"I thought it would have gone without saying Mrs Urmstone. Of *course,* My Lady and I will attend! Good day now!"

She meant to pursue him – any chance of a conversation with any member of the Vyrrington family was a very public reminder for all passersby that Mrs Urmstone was a well-connected lady in the town. Her experience at *Griggsden Manor*, and the snobbish slights of the society spindles Ladies Albion, Leddindsham and Oxborrow, had left her with a lingering anxiety about her true social standing. She then turned to Mrs Haffisidge, who seemed off in another world, and looked quite anxious herself.

"Whatever is the matter with you, Judith-Ann?" she asked, sounding genuinely concerned.

"I have not really wanted to host in that house since..." and Mrs Haffisidge lowered her voice and leant in close so her friend could still hear, "...*that* night! The night of the shape at the window."
Mrs Urmstone gasped, mouth agape in shock of her own insensitivity, but before she was able to contemplate speaking another syllable, she found they had been joined by the Misses Osborne and Gwynne, who had both run quickly out of their haberdashery shop to approach Mrs Haffisidge.

"I have forgotten what it was you told me for your new winter gloves, Mrs Haffisidge," said Miss Osborne, "Was it to be red with gold trim or gold with red trim?"

"The former, Miss Osborne, if you don't mind," replied Mrs Haffisidge after a brief hesitation to collect her thoughts, "And please do not hasten to complete them. Just give surety to their being finished in time for when the cold *does* set in."

"If it is yet to," piped up another voice – the ladies all wheeled around to find Mrs Warwick, her baby son well-wrapped in her arms, "We actually had to excuse our candles last night!"

"And light the fire instead;" Mrs Haffisidge interjected, "I had been hoping the cold would remain averse to our house until December. It has not listened to me, unfortunately."

"And where were you headed, Mrs Warwick? With the young prince?" asked Mrs Urmstone.

"Up to Cox Farm – my husband rarely sees his son these days, he spends so long at work," said Mrs Warwick.

"Agreeable as I find that arrangement, we *ourselves* were headed that way, to deliver their invitations to the Christmas Eve party," returned Mrs Haffisidge, "We may venture there together in that case. I think Elspeth wanted to chat to the Lord Vyrrington a little more."

"Then so we shall!" returned Mrs Warwick There was then a moment of silence, sliced apart by a loud explosion of sound that had occurred up Elxham Road, right by Cox Farm.

"What on Earth was that?" asked Mrs Urmstone, "*Oh Judith-Ann*! I see *smoke* emitting from Cox Farm! Oh, *Alicia*! *Miss Osborne*! *Miss Gwynne*! *Someone* fetch Mr Zephaniah Gussage from the schoolhouse. Tell him 'tis of the utmost *urgency*!"

As someone – for all the commotion it was impossible to tell whom exactly – did as Mrs Urmstone had instructed, the other ladies rushed with the rest of the marketplace to Cox Farm to investigate further.

Chapter XIX
Disaster at Cox Farm

A T *BERYL COURT*, SAT IN the garden was Lady Vyrrington, betraying doctor's orders and sitting with her feet elevated on a well-cushioned hassock, attended by both Amethyst and Whitlocke, had also observed what had happened at Cox Farm, for the smoke was visible, as had been the explosion from inside the barn. Without words, the Countess attempted to stand, with her two servants having to assist her.

"We must go to them," she murmured, weakly and in pain.

"My Lady, I don't advise it," returned Whitlocke, "Not in your condition."

"I will keep my own counsel about my condition, Whitlocke. Lord Wilson is down there – no doubt attempting something very brave but nonetheless foolish. Old habits – military or otherwise – die hard. Now fetch my fur shawl, Amethyst. We *must* go to them. You too, Whitlocke."

The carriage was summoned in haste, and the horses were whipped sharply and strikingly to provoke speed into town. As they were nearing Elxham Road, their vehicle was halted a fair distance from the scene, not by any authority or official, but by the crowd the disaster had attracted.

Whitlocke alerted them to Lady Vyrrington's presence by commanding the people to make way for her, especially difficult bearing in mind her condition. Very soon, all three of them found themselves at the forefront of the farmhouse with its barn adjoined – completely wreathed in flame and blanketed with smoke. She eventually found Mrs Urmstone, Mrs Haffisidge, Mrs Warwick and the Misses Osborne and Gwynne, who were all stood frozen with fright as to what the incident could lead to, and who, if anyone, had died.

The Countess placed hands on a shoulder each of Mrs Urmstone and Mrs Haffisidge, who took her hands in their own, all looks of despair and intense worry expressed from their faces.

"Elspeth? Judith-Ann? Where is my husband?" she asked them loudly, unable to otherwise hear herself speak through the noise and commotion.

"Oh, my Lady," Mrs Haffisidge placed her hands about Lady Vyrrington's shoulders, "He went into the barn. With Zephaniah Gussage. There are men still in there."

The Countess shut her eyes in growing anguish.

"I knew as much," she said, tightly grasping her two close friends' hands in her own, waiting for something or someone to emerge from the ablaze building.

After what seemed like a lifetime, the silhouette of a man, short and hunchbacked appeared – that of Mr Gussage, the schoolkeeper, who displayed strength that belied his years – for he could not have been far off fifty – in carrying another man on his back. He staggered from the smoke and the heat, then dropped the one he had rescued – a young farmhand, who was completely unconscious yet, having been blackened by the smoke, it was unclear how badly he was burned, if at all. Lady Vyrrington and her friends were anxiously hoping Mr Gussage would not be the last to exit the inferno. Again, an overwhelming length of time passed, and then it happened. Another figure became visible from the doorway in a similar fashion to that of Mr Gussage.

To the Countess' sheer relief, joy and a number of other emotions even she could not describe or explain, Lord Vyrrington appeared; he had forsaken his jacket and waistcoat, his cravat wrapped around his mouth to filter the smoke. To the gladness of Mrs Warwick, he had saved her husband, who he had placed down next to Mr Gussage's rescuee. Unlike the other farmhand, Mr Warwick was conscious, but groaning in agony from the burns that had afflicted his arms.

Mrs Warwick knelt by her husband.

"What happened, Luke?" she said, "Can you tell us?"

"The machine," he cried from the ground, "Cinders from the machine caught the hay. Up in flames in seconds."

To Lady Vyrrington's shock, both her husband and Mr Gussage turned to go back inside, but the inevitable happened first. Another explosion occurred from within the barn, shaking it to its foundations, to such an extent that they could no longer sustain it. The building groaned, cracked and snapped before panel-by-panel and beam-by-beam, it collapsed.

"What was that? How did that-?" Mrs Warwick began.

"There was gunpowder in there. For the game shooting," her husband groaned, before falling unconscious.

The commotion had waned, and was followed by a harrowing silence – not even the slightest tremor from a member of the crown until, at last, Doctor Street arrived, only to see the two men that had been saved, and those who had saved them.

Lord Wilson politely declined the good doctor's attentions, and approached Whitlocke, who helped his master put his jacket back on, having removed it when entering the immolated building. He then faced Lady Vyrrington.

"You should be in bed, my dear Lady," he said, calmly.

"*You* should allow Doctor Street to examine you," returned his wife, sharply, "The smoke may have afflicted your heart or God-knows-what else."

"No, I am sure I am quite as I was when I arrived," answered Lord Wilson.

"Lord Wilson knows his own health and his own heart," said Whitlocke.

"I know they say a soldier's habits never really leave him," continued Her Ladyship, seemingly ignoring Whitlocke, "but *really*, what were you thinking of?"

"Men needed saving, My Lady," he said, "I couldn't just stand there."

"It would give *me* peace of mind though..." the Countess continued pushing, "...if you were to permit Doctor Street to examine you."

"I told you, Lord Wilson *knows* his own health," Whitlocke sternly replied.

"*Thank you*, Whitlocke," Lord Wilson addressed the butler sternly, "You will do well to remember who speaks to *you* and who speaks to *me*."

"Yes, My Lord. So sorry, My Lord."

"No, I shall excuse myself of an examination. Although I *shall* oversee the welfare of the two patients..."

He trailed off, observing Zephaniah Gussage, who, also having refused to allow Doctor Street to examine him for any unseen injury, was beginning to remove some of the planks to see if he could find any bodies.

Lord Wilson continued:

"...And I shall oversee the funerals of those we *know* to be deceased."

Chapter XX
The Torment of Costs

WHILE IT WAS WITH NOBLE intent that Lord Wilson offered to pay for the funerals of the dead from the Cox Farm disaster, he had thought nothing of how ruinous it would be to the contents of his purse.

The day before Christmas Eve, the accountant had been in to review income and expenditure in time for the Yuletide, and left Lord Wilson's study twice as stressed as he had been when he entered. To afford Christmas for his own household, he was told he would have to lay off at least one other servant – even when accounting for the wages no longer paid to the missing-presumed-dead Joshua, and Jesse Blameford, whose wages were now paid by the Stirkwhistle family. 'How will I then pay for four funerals after that?' he thought to himself, anguished by the idea of failing those poor families.

Lord Wilson slouched in his chair, surveying around his study, thinking how on Earth he could resolve his predicament and not turn out a member of his staff to the workhouse in the heart of winter.
The clock struck the hour, a little sooner than he expected, and so he pulled out his pocket watch to

inspect. It was a number of minutes slow, but as he went to correct it, he suddenly beheld how superfluous a possession it was. It was no heirloom of his family's, nor a gift of any great affection. In actuality, a trinket of enough gold to pay for four decent coffins.

'As for paying for Christmas, we'll just have to manage,' he thought to himself as he stood to go out. As he did so, he felt a sudden painful lurch from within and he coughed loudly, so hard and often he had to clasp his handkerchief to his lips. What he thought was phlegm he had ejected from his mouth had actually stained the cloth with spots of red. He dabbed at his tongue with a couple of fingers and found blood at their tips. He merely swallowed and thought it was not worth worrying about, and even more particularly, not worth worrying his wife about.

The motivation to do good endowed him with enough energy to ride to the neighbouring town of Wraxhill-on-the-Test (or Wraxhill, for short), where was established the only pawnbrokers for around twenty leagues. The watch, which he sold outright, gave him twenty-five pounds (though even the pawnbroker was aware it was worth at least twice that amount), which did his finances a good turn, but not so much to his health. It was only a ten-minute journey in clear weather by horse, but when he returned home, he was exhausted.

He retired without supper without so much as a word to Lady Vyrrington, who was much-preoccupied with choosing between dresses for Mrs Urmstone and Mrs Haffisidge's Christmas Eve party the following day to notice. Despite his exhaustion, Lord Wilson was still adamant to himself that he would attend the party – if only to ensure himself a peaceful following year from the no-doubt endless tirade from Mrs Urmstone should he not.

Chapter XXI
The First Tale

WHEN THE CLOCK IN MRS Haffisidge's parlour
chimed its seventh chime Christmas Eve,
the hostesses presented themselves with
great festive decoration – Mrs Haffisidge wearing a new
silk gown of a deep red colour, that of a ruby shade
which endowed also the richest wines of Portugal, with
her best gold earrings and necklace encrusted with
garnets and opals. The embroidery in the gown had
been done in a golden thread. Below her neck was a
brooch, the design of which bore the likeness of a holly
leaf and berries. She was anxiously examining and re-
examining her appearance before the looking-glass –
not because she was afraid there was anything wrong
about her, but because she wanted every distraction
possible to occupy her mind, lest it should turn to less
savoury notions, that would disturb and frighten her,
and incommode her pleasure only further. The idea
that Christopher Tratsly – if, indeed, that was his real
name – knew who she was – prior to her widowhood
and now following it – and, even worse, possibly, where
she lived, was almost too much for her mind to endure.

Before it could take over her thoughts, however, Mrs
Urmstone arrived next to her in the mirror, dressed in

green and silver, emeralds and diamonds set within her silver jewellery, and a brooch that bore the design of three mistletoe berries – represented in pearls. Mrs Haffisidge looked her friend up-and-down.

"You are looking very regal this night, Elspeth," she said.

"As are you, Judith-Ann," replied Mrs Urmstone, "Though I'm not in the position to eclipse My Lady Vyrrington, am I?"

After a slight pause at whether the true answer would give offence, Mrs Haffisidge returned:

"I don't think there's any hazard for that, madam: Lady Vyrrington always impresses with her fashion sense."

There was a long pause, as they both beheld their reflections in the mirror.

"Elspeth," said Mrs Haffisidge, a tone of fear lingering in her voice, "You will never think unkindly of me, will you? Regardless of what you may hear?"

"Well really, Judith-Ann, I'm sure I don't know what you're talking about."

"Oh, pay me no heed, my dear!" Mrs Haffisidge opted against that line of conversation, "This madness with the whole Juliette Harrowsleigh nonsense has my mind on the edge of a knife."

Mrs Urmstone took her friend's hands in hers.

"Tonight, we make merriment in all who enter our company," she said sweetly, "In food, in drink and in music, we will make it. That is your duty tonight, my dear Judith-Ann."

They smiled at one another, and before the conversation could continue, a knock came at the door.

A woman of unfailing punctuality, Lady Vyrrington arrived first, embracing the latest hairstyle – her dark hair built upward at a backward-diagonal angle. She had presented herself in a cream-coloured silk gown, with a bejewelled crimson bodice patterned with brocade and elaborate crimson and gold stitching ascending from the hems. She had brought with her a thick crimson and gold shawl, for the plan was later that night, they would depart the house to light the candles up at the Church, as was the tradition in Berylford. She did not like to pull rank around her friends, so the Countess let herself into the house.

"Lady Oliviera, my dear," said Mrs Urmstone, descending the stairs with Mrs Haffisidge following, "You come alone, I see?"

"Oh, so I do!" the Countess replied with an air of sarcasm as though she had not noticed her husband's absence, "Lord Wilson said he would arrive after me – a matter of urgent business. Estate management and so forth."

"Urgent business? At *Christmas*?" Mrs Urmstone expostulated, turning to Mrs Haffisidge and muttering, "He knew when the party was."

"You both look elegant this evening, ladies," Lady Vyrrington quickly changed the subject.

"Why thank you, My Lady. As do you," returned Mrs Haffisidge, having to push past Mrs Urmstone on the stairs and inclining into the parlour to invite the Countess in that direction, "That is a most beautiful decoration you wear, by the way."
She referred to the brooch pinned on the right-hand side of the Countess' dress at the level of her breast. It came in the form of four large spherical jewels: representing winter berries, two of which looked to have been frosted. They were bound into a brooch with four intertwining pieces of wire, and a purple ribbon.

"Thank you, Mrs Haffisidge;" returned Lady Oliviera, "It was a gift from my late mother."

"It most certainly is an *unusual* bauble," and she then inclined at her own brooch, "My mother had *this* heirloom handed down from generations away. Though the less said about them, the better, I fear."

"For what reason, pray?" said the Countess, "Is there something of a scandalous nature about it?"

"Of the *most unspeakably* scandalous nature...!" Mrs Urmstone cried, returning to the parlour holding a platter of small wine glasses, "...so do not pursue your account any further, Judith-Ann, or you may very well have reason to rue *this* Christmas Eve party!"

"Oh, keep your tongue held, Elspeth. For goodness' sake, what harm can *possibly* be caused? She is not here among us to incommode our pleasure! If you allow my account's resumption, I shall see it permissible for you to recount that story that you say your Grandfather Farquhar told you all the time." Mrs Urmstone gasped in a brief breath of laughter.

"*That* account is *scarcely* appropriate for a gathering such as this. It is better suited for All Hallows *Eve*!"

"Does it involve some sort of mystic creature, or a wicked spirit?" Lady Oliviera quizzed.

"Not necessarily, but it is disconcerting for an occasion on which we are *merrymaking*! This is no séance, after all," Mrs Urmstone diverted the subject abruptly, at the moment when a knocking came from the door.

"*Elspeth*!" Mrs Haffisidge hissed, "Would you *mind* forsaking your duties in the parlour, temporarily, and seeing to those awaiting the pleasure of our company at the *door*?"

"Yes *madam*," returned Mrs Urmstone acidly, curtseying sharply in a gesture of indignance, before strutting off to answer the door. Mrs Haffisidge stood by the parlour window, very anxious. Their guest list was not long, given the recent events, but as her experience at *Griggsden Manor* had taught her, the man who called himself Christopher Tratsly paid little heed to trivialities such as invitations. She could not see who was at her door from her parlour window.

"Judith-Ann?" came a voice. Mrs Haffisidge started, placing a hand at her chest and shutting her eyes in shock. "My dear lady, I do believe I scared you!" The Countess stood before her, her hands now clasped around her friend's wrist. Mrs Haffisidge opened her eyes slowly, and smiled with an expression that spoke relief from every corner.

"My Lady! Forgive me; I was in a world of my own for the moment."

"I fear 'tis thee who should forgive *me*, madam!" returned Lady Vyrrington, "Whatever could be the matter?"

Mrs Haffisidge hesitated. She did want desperately to pour her every fear out to the Countess, but she could not. Such was her paranoia, like a rabbit scrambling to evade an omnipresent hawk, she could not risk one of such wisdom, elegance and unquestionable reputation as Lady Oliviera, being drawn into this situation of hers, and worse, being approached by he who called himself Christopher Tratsly.

"Merely everything is going so well thus far, My Lady," Mrs Haffisidge had to improvise quickly – whenever in doubt, she would blame her nephew-in-law – "I sent Mr Warwick away with two pounds and half a crown, and strict instructions to stay out until after midnight!"

"And you're worried he'll return early?"

"That, and he has probably some no-doubt merry prank prepared at my expense."

At that event another voice joined the conversation:

"Auntie Judith, I made Luke swear to me he would do no such thing."

To her relief, it was only her niece Mrs Warwick, followed by Mrs Urmstone, who offered her some of the cold hors d'œuvres – consisting of a variety of savoury biscuits, each topped with a slice of one of a variety of cheeses, and either a red or a green grape.

"Mrs Warwick!" cried Lady Vyrrington, "Where is the young Master Warwick?"

"I left him upstairs asleep with my aunt's attention on-hand," returned Mrs Warwick, "No troubles, I trust, Auntie?"

"None. Mr Warwick has remained true to his word and instruction thus far, though I scarcely believe I can own that." She then had a thought, and her expression, which had hitherto held signs of distress and anxiety, turned to a mischievous smile. She half-turned her face in the direction of Mrs Urmstone, and raised her voice somewhat.

"Though still I cared not for you being abroad alone at this dark hour, my dear Alicia. It is all too redolent a scene from *another Christmas Eve* in this town."

She then leered at Mrs Urmstone, who turned around; causing Lady Vyrrington and a slightly-confused Mrs Warwick to chuckle.

"I'm not telling that story, Mrs Haffisidge – glower at me all you like!" she quipped.

"Your aunt was just in the process of telling us about a distant ancestor of hers," the Countess said to Mrs Warwick.

"Indeed. Her name was Rachael Yeatminster!" Mrs Haffisidge explained, "...Her supposedly '*scandalous*' deed was done after the Battle of Sedgemoor. She collaborated closely with the Lady Alice Lisle; a woman who had obtained her title after her husband – Sir John – had been a member of Cromwell's House of Lords. He was a judge at the trial of Charles the First. Anyway – these two ladies, both very old women – gave shelter to a man named John Hickes, who was a Nonconformist minister. They were both living in Ringwood in Dorsetshire – the Lady

Lisle's residence was known as Moyles Court. With him was a man named Richard Nelthorpe; a man under sentence for outlawry! The morning after the ladies gave them shelter, the men were found–"

"As were their *hostesses*!" Mrs Urmstone joined in on her friend's recount, "Who *both* had claimed their alleged guests were not at Moyles Court! A servant had alerted the authorities!"

"Yes, thank you Elspeth. And so the two ladies: The Lady Lisle and my so-many-times-great-grandmother Rachel Yeatminster were arrested for having harboured fugitives. They were sentenced in Winchester once *The Bloody Assizes* had begun."

"There were *five* judges presiding over The Bloody Assizes," said Mrs Urmstone, "They were–"

"*Six* judges, Elspeth!" Mrs Haffisidge recommenced, "Led under the Lord Chief Justice Jeffreys and his like-minded compatriots–"

Again, Mrs Urmstone interrupted:

"They saw fit to charge both ladies. And they were executed *forthwith*!"

"That was the Judge Jeffreys' *initial* decision, yet the King allowed a few days respite–".

"Before they were *burned*! At the *stake*!"

"*Decapitated*, actually Elspeth. I was told His Majesty substituted the usual means of execution to

something less painful. Bearing in mind the Lady Lisle
was nearing her seventieth year of life!"
Their guests all applauded.

Chapter XXII
The Second Tale

A T THAT MOMENT, MISS GWYNNE and Miss Osborne entered the room. Mrs Urmstone and Mrs Haffisidge both looked at each other. There were no servants employed in the house so there was no conceivable way of their coming in unannounced, Mrs Haffisidge began to fear.

"Who let you in?" Mrs Haffisidge asked brusquely.

The two haberdashers were somewhat taken aback.

"And Merry Christmas to you *too*, I'm sure!" Miss Osborne returned acerbically, "The door was left *ajar*, actually."

"We *assumed*, on *purpose!*" added Miss Gwynne. Mrs Haffisidge turned with an acid expression to Mrs Urmstone, whose face was quite the opposite of its usual fiery and quarrelsome aspect, rather one of submission and fear – more becoming of the likes of Amethyst.

"Was it, indeed? Left ajar?" Mrs Haffisidge said, sardonically.

"I think you have a faulty latch, Judith-Ann," Mrs Urmstone replied very nervously.

"I'll give you 'faulty latch', Elspeth Urmstone; you *know* I'm at my wits' end!" she growled at her friend in an uncharacteristic display of dormant temper.

"'Tis no matter, we're here now!" declared Miss Osborne, intent on defusing the obvious tension and quickly taking a seat, "Have we missed much?"

"Oh Miss Osborne; Miss Gwynne..." remarked Lady Oliviera, "...you have just missed the story of Lady Alice Lisle and Rachael Yeatminster."

"Well told! *Well told*!" Mrs Warwick commented.

"And as a punishment, Elspeth, for your blunder just now, you can tell us the tale of what Mrs Trimwitt saw!" Mrs Haffisidge instructed her friend.

"Please do, Elspeth," said Lady Oliviera, "I am *most* interested."

"I can tell you, Lady Oliviera..." sighed Mrs Urmstone after a few moments of pained contemplation, "...*since* you have shown such an extraordinary interest in this tale, I am resolved. Just as I remember my grandfather, *The Honourable* Farquhar Hawthcourt, telling it to me:

Mrs Trimwitt, whose Christian name – forgive me – I am unable to recollect, was a lonely old widow who lived here in Berylford– in a house that she named *Kellford End*. She was a resident here at around the same time as the aforementioned Rachael Yeatminster. The story – I suppose – *is* appropriate for its first chapter takes place on this night – Christmas Eve. It was described as a night like the one under which we sit now – cloaked in the dark of the early-coming night, the snow was imminent, and the cold was bitter. Mrs Trimwitt sat by her sitting room window – two candles atop the windowsill. The snowfall had commenced when the clock struck to end its first quarter of the eleventh hour of the night. The chimes had fallen and Mrs Trimwitt was stunned to see, amidst the snowflakes, the figure of a local boy-child – whom she identified as Little Tommy Oates – of no older than seven or eight years.

Mrs Trimwitt distinguished immediately from her view at her candlelit windowsill that he was lost in the snow, separated from his mother. Of course, Mrs Trimwitt rose to bring him in from the cold – yet at the very minute that she stood from her seat did she hear the neighing of a nearby horse. Immediately to her horror did it come swiftly galloping across the square – the figure astride it merely a silhouette to Mrs Trimwitt; shrouded in both the darkness of the night and the blizzard of snowflakes. He was riding too quickly to even see."

Lady Vyrrington and Mrs Warwick both gasped. Miss Gwynne's hands were clasped over her mouth –

her eyes whitened in a mixture of horror and excitement.

Mrs Urmstone continued – her intonation unfamiliarly darkened throughout her recount:

"The boy was *struck* by the dark steed's front hooves. And most likely its hind ones too. And in front of Mrs Trimwitt, Little Tommy Oates *disappeared*!"
Again, there were gasps throughout the parlour.

"It ends not there, for the second chapter begins in the early morning of Christmas Day.
Mrs Trimwitt – Grandfather Farquhar told me – was a woman of *superstitious* manner. So she would not refuse an offer of apparent *good luck* from even one so much as a *gypsy*!
Grandfather Farquhar told me that the woman who came that day was grotesquely deformed: one *eye*; no front *teeth*; and of *dwarfed stature*! Her hands seemed to have been affected by causes of leprosy; some of her fingers apparently *amputated* to an amateur standard. She offered to Mrs Trimwitt what was held in, what it had remained to be, her *claw* of a hand. A *rounded* object wrapped in cloth. The gypsy claimed this object would offer to Mrs Trimwitt good luck and thusly she received it willingly. The dwarfed grotesque of a gypsy was observed from the sitting room window to walk

back from whence she came, and then Mrs Trimwitt removed the cloth, only to drop the object in the utter and extraordinary proportion of fear and revulsion of what it concealed. *She* had expected something such as a crystal ball, yet instead the object the gypsy had given to her was nothing other than the *head* of Little Tommy Oates! The neck had not been kept; the remains of its attachment to the skull were naught but *sinew*!"

The parlour was silent – consumed in both shock at this revelation and anticipation for Mrs Urmstone's concluding chapter.

"The day after Saint Stephen's Day, Mrs Trimwitt, who in those recent events seemed to have been driven to all but madness, took a walk in the snow-covered woodland near the grounds of where Beryl Court stands now. She was silent and staring, and her destination seemed nonexistent. Nearing the lake, she sat herself down upon a log – her gaze still blank and gaunt. She looked downwards, and screamed in her growing insanity, as the torso of a boy-child lay before her – its head severed from its neck. Only she knew too well that that was the body of Little Tommy Oates."

Mrs Urmstone stopped.

"What happened to Mrs Trimwitt?" Miss Osborne asked.

"Grandfather Farquhar did not know, and thusly, *I* do not know. Some say she drowned herself in her madness – either by merely walking into the lake or weighing her corset and petticoat down with stones. Others say she just froze to death. Others still, claimed her terrified screams were heard and she was incarcerated in an asylum for the rest of her life. Who knows?"

"It is a mystery," said Miss Gwynne, "And a compelling one at that."
The parlour all applauded.

"I fear it may be time for *whist*, My Lady Oliviera," sighed Mrs Urmstone, seemingly worn weary from the telling of her tale, "Have you the cards, Miss Osborne?"

"I brought *two* decks..." piped up Miss Osborne, "...for I was not enlightened as to how many would be playing, nor was I certain as to how many people would indeed attend tonight."

"Our little party is only just *begun*, Miss Osborne," said Mrs Urmstone, sounding slightly offended, "I am sure we will be delighted by the presences of Lord Wilson Vyrrington, Mrs Rudgerleigh and Mr Gussage before too long."

Had this been a soirée of one such as Lord Griggsden, the revels may have taken the shape of a magnanimous Bacchanalian feast, with wine spouting purple from silver fountains at every corner and edge of the room and the table practically invisible beneath a spread laden as every fashion and culture would permit with sugary and savoury delights. Mrs Urmstone had lesser ambitions for frivolity, but hers and Mrs Haffisidge's table was not immodestly stocked. There was a ham, darned with cloves and spices (a gift sent from *Griggsden Manor* with the compliments of His Lordship himself), a salmon adorned with oranges and red wine. There were cheeses bought from the traders; canapés of pastry with all sorts of rich flavours – anchovies, mackerel and garlic. There were also trifles, the alcoholic potency of which prohibited any close proximity to flame lest they should be set ablaze, and finally a great Dundee Cake – from the hands of Mrs Urmstone herself, from a recipe laid down by her grandmother Murdina McLaer. All this was partaken of before, during and after the numerous rounds of whist played around Mrs Haffisidge's table – even though there were only few of them – with Lord Wilson yet to arrive, and the presumption that Mrs Rudgerleigh, whose brother had been amongst those killed in the barn fire at Cox Farm, would not attend – it was difficult not to enjoy. In fact, it was one of the first times in what felt like an age that Mrs Urmstone had seen Mrs Haffisidge smile. She turned in her chair while at cards and observed Lady Vyrrington had departed the table, and had stanced herself at the parlour window. She approached her.

"I bid you all the blessings of the Christ-tide, My Lady Oliviera," she said with a solemn undertone, standing beside the Countess at the window, "I fear we will both feel our respective losses quite heavily this year."

"I fear so, Elspeth," returned Lady Vyrrington, continuing to stare out the window, "'Tis a pity my husband seeks to grieve in private as he always has. That he should have some small alleviation from his suffering as I am permitted this night."

"We shall not see His Lordship then?"

"He would be here by now if he were coming at all," sighed Lady Vyrrington, her disappointment being spoken gravely through an otherwise warm visage, "I know Judith-Ann was relying on him to bludgeon any would-be intruders tonight."

They both turned away from the window to observe their friend at whist with Mrs Warwick and Misses Osborne and Gwynne. She was laughing one minute, concentrating another, then perhaps having a mouthful of mackerel another.

"I do not believe Mrs Haffisidge has any need for any protection this evening after all, My Lady," said Mrs Urmstone, "This is the most at ease I have seen her in weeks."

"That's good," returned Lady Vyrrington, "I regret that I cannot be at town more often to occupy her. I have been very selfish and cloistered in my grief."

"We bid you no ill on that score, My Lady Oliviera; on that I promise you!" Mrs Urmstone exclaimed sharply, "And tonight we make merry as we always have."

The hours seemed no longer than minutes for before the ladies knew it, for all their tale-telling, card-playing, drinking and eating, the clock in Mrs Haffisidge's parlour was soon striking twelve, chiming in Christmas Day.

Garbing themselves in their thickest furs, shawls and hooded cloaks, they were met at Mrs Haffisidge's gate by Zephaniah Gussage, who had, prior to the party been looking after his landlady and colleague Mrs Rudgerleigh. He was there to escort the ladies to the church, where they would light candles to send a blessing and a remembrance to those whose absence they were feeling at this festive time. For Mrs Urmstone, it was her husband; for Lady Vyrrington, her sons Felix and Augustus. This ceremony was but a short one, accompanied by a couple of quiet carols, before they were again supervised home by Mr Gussage. Mrs Urmstone, satisfied she had helped ease Mrs Haffisidge's angst with a great festivity, accepted her invitation to stay at her house until the morning.

Chapter XXIII
Melancholy of the Master

LORD WILSON WAS NOWHERE TO be seen in society at all that night. An hour or so after his wife had left for the party, he was asleep at his desk in his study. His appetite had all but disappeared, and his mouth was becoming ever-slowly more lined with blood. He only woke when the study door opened quietly. He had to blink several times before he could clearly distinguish the entrant to the room: his wife, Lady Vyrrington. Though his vision was not quite so clear as to see it, her face spoke several volumes of anger and exasperation.

"Ah, my dear," Lord Wilson began, "Forgive me, I appear to have been too long at work in here."

"I had to ask Zephaniah Gussage to escort me up to the front path of this house tonight," she said, her tone bereft of humour or sympathy, "If that were not enough, then at least you should recognise the sheer *discourtesy* with which you have conducted yourself to Elspeth and Judith-Ann. Two of our longest and closest friends, to whom you promised your attendance. In the morning, after Mass, I bid that you pay them both considerable apology."

"Again, pray forgive me, My Lady," Lord Wilson remained quiet, unable to argue with his wife, "Love, honour and *obey* I vowed to you once – thus it shall be tomorrow. I… have no excuse." He was breathless, and scrunched a handkerchief in his hand, out of the Countess' view, before he could not help coughing into it. The force with which he spluttered shocked Lady Vyrrington somewhat, but her annoyance with her husband was such that she could not pay him any sympathy. Instead she merely approached him and placed a hand on his shoulder, kissing his forehead.

"I'm far too vexed with you to say very much right this minute. But I do love you, Lord Wilson Vyrrington." He looked up at her. Even in the mere glow of the dying firelight, she was a strikingly beautiful woman. He put his hand upon hers, still on his shoulder, and caressed it a little.

"I don't deserve you, My Lady. At all."

"Indeed, sometimes I think not," she returned acidly, moving back towards the door. He watched her as she went to leave.

"Do not remain in here too much longer, sir," she said, before opening the entrance to the study. Whitlocke was there, with a tray of a light supper and a glass of brandy. Lord Wilson watched as the Countess whispered something to the butler; she disappeared in one direction while Whitlocke came in and set the tray down before his master.

"What did My Lady say to you out there, Whitlocke?" he enquired curiously. Even he was aware of the fractious relationship between his wife and his butler.

"She told me to ensure you went to bed in the next half-hour, sir," Whitlocke replied.

"And what did you tell her?"

"I have to follow orders, My Lord."

"Hmmm, well. And what is that, Whitlocke?" Lord Wilson asked, inclining his head at the tray.

"It's Christmas Day, sir," the butler replied, "And this is the first meal I've seen served to you in the last twenty-four hours. I know you don't feel like eating, milord, but if you want to put on a good deception, best at least *look* healthy and eat a little." Lord Wilson smiled slightly. Whitlocke's pandering to his current state of mind and yet remaining sympathetic reminded him of what a loyal servant he was.

"Eat with me, Whitlocke," he said – all the coughing had reduced his voice to a croak, "Stay with me. It may not be for long, I think."

Whitlocke was taken aback.

"I could not do that, sir. 'Twould betray all statutes of the house, sir."

"Who lays down those statutes, Whitlocke?"

"Why, you do, My Lord."

"And it is your job to see they are executed *without* fail. So don't be a fool; sit down and share this meal with me."

Nervously, Whitlocke pulled out the chair from the other end of his master's desk.

"You have always known the cross I bear, Whitlocke; this I know," Lord Wilson continued, and he began to pick at the small meal in front of him, "I cannot deny my family their livelihood, but I cannot own it to them either that it's entirely my fault that all others must suffer to maintain it. The number of people I must have virtually thrown in the workhouse, just to keep us in fine clothes and food. As though I dumped them at the doors myself. You have no idea."

"My Lord, you punish yourself. With all due respect."

"None due, Whitlocke. I relinquished the right to any respect from my servants a long time ago. And that from my children. And from my tenants. Even that from my wife."

Whitlocke looked up at him. He had stopped eating; his head was to one side and staring into nothing. Almost as though he had fallen asleep without closing his eyes.

"They all adore you, sir," Whitlocke returned, "Now I think it's time for bed, My Lord, or Lady Vyrrington will have both our heads!"

"I will be along presently, Whitlocke; I will not risk causing trouble between you and Lady Vyrrington," Lord Wilson replied, chuckling, "But you go on. Thank you for listening to my drivel."

"Not at all, My Lord. Good night."

"And merry Christmas, Whitlocke."

Chapter XXIV
Adeste Fideles

CHRISTMAS DAY MASS WAS NOT to begin until the Vyrrington family all arrived to church, which, given the patriarch's delicate state of health at present, was later than usual. Nevertheless, the rest of the congregation waited on His Lordship's convenience and stood once his figure stepped through the church doors. He was arm-in-arm with Lady Oliviera, who could only caress his forearm as they made their way down the aisle towards the front pews, reserved especially for them. Lord Wilson coughed intermittently, though with increasing severity to a point where the Countess started to grow concerned. After a piece-by-piece retelling of the Nativity, the Reverend Helton announced that they would sing *Adeste Fideles*, at which point Mrs Urmstone, who was seated behind Lady Oliviera, next to Mrs Haffisidge and Mrs Warwick, tapped her shoulder. The Countess wanted to ask her what she wanted, but the singing had begun:

"[1]Adeste Fideles,

---

[1] O Come, All Ye Faithful, Joyful and triumphant; O come ye, O come ye to Bethlehem; Come and behold him, Born the King of Angels

Læti triumphantes;
Venite, venite in Bethlehem;
Natum videte,
Regem Angelorum..."

The first chorus began, during which Lady
Oliviera then tried to regain the attention of her friend.

"...²Venite adoremus,
Venite adoremus,
Venite adoremus
Dominum...!"

"Elspeth, what is it? Can it wait until after
Mass?" the Countess whispered.
"That depends entirely on whether Lord Wilson
keels over before then!" she returned.
Lady Vyrrington's eyes widened at the reply.
"Keel over? Don't be so melodramatic, Elspeth!"

"...³Deum de Deo,
Lumen de lumine,

---

² *O come, let us adore Him, O come, let us adore Him, O come, let us adore*
Him, Christ, the Lord

³ *God of God, Light of Light, Lo, he abhors not the Virgin's womb; Very*
God, Begotten, not created

Gestant puellæ viscera;
Deum verum,
Genitum, non factum..."

The chorus began again, and The Countess regained her friend's attention.

"He just has a frog in his throat – it's nothing."

"It seems a very aggressive and persistent frog. Have Doctor Street examine him."

"It's Christmas *Day*, Elspeth. Now *really!*"

"...[4]Cantet nunc hymnos
Chorus angelorum,
Cantet nunc aula cælestium,
Gloria, gloria,
In excelsis Deo...!"

Again, the chorus was sung, and this time, it was Amethyst who spoke to Lady Oliviera.

"Milady..." she said quietly, "...Mr Whitlocke said he had business to discuss immediately after the service."

---

[4] *Sing choirs of angels, Sing in exultation, Sing all ye citizens of Heaven above, Glory to God In the highest!*

"Business indeed! Well! At least he has the good grace to wait until Mass has finished..." she turned her head slightly to eye Mrs Urmstone, "...Tell him I said, 'very well'."

The fourth and final verse began:

"...[5]*Ergo qui natus*
Die hodierna,
Jesu tibi sit gloria;
Patris æterni,
Verbum caro factum!

[6]*Venite adoremus,*
Venite adoremus,
Venite adoremus
Dominum!"

The congregation all sat after the sounds of the church organ faded. After the final readings had been

---

[5] *Yea, Lord, we greet thee, Born this happy morning, Jesus, to thee be glory given; Word of the father, Now in flesh appearing!*

[6] *O come, let us adore Him, O come, let us adore Him, O come, let us adore Him, Christ, the Lord!*

made and the collection had been taken, the church emptied from the front pews to the back.

This was convenient for Lady Oliviera's discreet meeting with Whitlocke, as they could both easily lose Lord Wilson, as well as her children and Mrs Urmstone.

Lady Vyrrington quickly made her way to the opening of the church cemetery, knowing full well that Whitlocke was following her closely.

She stopped, and when Whitlocke neared, turned around sharply, her face expressing vehement emotion.

"So, what do you want of me, Whitlocke?" she spat, "This had better be important!"

"Of course it's important. Do I look like Mrs Urmstone to you?"

"Much as that statement rings true, Whitlocke, mind your place."

"My master is ill, milady."

"Oh for Heaven's sake; don't you start!"

"Been coughing a little much for the start of a cold, do you not think?"

"Lord Wilson ran into a burning building to save a man's life – he probably breathed in a little too much smoke and his body is just expelling the poison. Plus he smokes those dreadful cigars – I suppose I could put a stop to that."

"Could you at least persuade him to visit the doctor once Christmas passes?"

"*If* he is still ill come seventeen-ninety-four, which he *won't* be, I will insist upon it. Will that suffice for you, *sir*?" she looked him up and down, "Now, *please*, let us go home before we freeze to death."

Book Seven
LORD WILSON'S DECLINE

Chapter XXV
For Love and Lust

L ORD VYRRINGTON'S HEALTH CONTINUED TO
depreciate as the earlier months of 1794 passed.
But rather than keep her word to Whitlocke, the
Countess did not insist on any doctor's attention, and
Lord Wilson retained his cigars. Her Ladyship was in
total and utter denial of his worsening condition, and
all the while, Lord Wilson began to withdraw his
attention to his wife and children, remaining confined
to his study for lengthy periods of time, not even
emerging to eat on some occasions. In fact, he was quite
as he had been months before, despondent and silent
toward all.

Though at last there came a time where even Lady
Vyrrington could not hide herself from the truth any
longer – she noticed when she discovered herself
breakfasting alone more and more often. On this
occasion, she had received a letter from her cousin, the
Countess of Styridge, informing her of the death of her
husband, and that the funeral would be a week hence.
Although Lady Vyrrington was adamant that she was to

attend *with* her husband, she sensed there was little chance of that actually happening, for so little of Lord Wilson had been seen that she almost did not know where to look for him, or if she would even find him alive.

In the afternoon, after perusing the haberdashery in town for any fashionable mourning pieces, the Countess returned home to find her husband playing with their two youngest, Spencer and Edward, in the nursery. It was not an uncommon thing; they had resolved very early into their marriage that they would not be one of those society families who only saw their children once or twice a day, otherwise leaving the child raising duties to a governess. It surprised yet nonetheless gladdened her that she should find Lord Wilson there. He stood up immediately upon seeing her, and only acknowledged her presence by looking at her briefly. She would not accept this, thus she stood her ground and blocked his exit from the nursery.

"My love, what has caused this rift between us these past days?" she asked him, "One minute you are all loving and attentive, the next you are hollow and unfeeling."

"There is no '*rift*', as you put it. I am merely enjoying my own company and relishing my privacy."

"And only seeing our children when I am out of the house?"

"Let us not quarrel in front of them."

"No, let us! Or you will go skulking back to your study without another word for the rest of the day."

"Oliviera, what is it that you want?"

"My cousin Riva wrote to me today. Lord Stephanus has passed..."

Lord Wilson looked aside, being careful not to display any emotion at the news, regardless of how grievous he actually found it. The late Lord Stephanus Styridge had been a distant kinsman of his.

"...The funeral is next week; should we attend?"

Lord Wilson did not need to give his answer any thought whatsoever.

"*You* may attend, My Lady," he said, "But you'll excuse me if I do not."

Shutting her eyes and bowing her head, she moved aside to let him out of the nursery. She ran to her children, sitting on the carpet by them, and holding them both close to her. A single tear trickled down her cheek. And as she had expected, Lord Wilson returned to his study, and locked the door.

His manner and tone were far from how her memory served of him, when she first met him at a society party given ten years before. At the house of the late Lord Stephanus and Lady Riva Styridge, attended by most among their acquaintance: Lady Vyrrington and her four sisters; Mrs Urmstone, then known as Miss Elspeth Hawthcourt, and her elder sister Juvelia; and Lady Vyrrington's cousin, Abel Stirkwhistle. The Countess remembered looking across the well-embellished drawing room from the table she shared with her sisters and cousins, and saw a fine, straight-backed, upstanding, flat-stomached officer in uniform aged a couple of years older than she, and being able to think of nothing else thence.

Abel introduced them and within a month, he had written to her inviting her to the town of his seat – Berylford St. Barbara – where she had remained ever since. Seven children of whom four remained, and a marriage endowed with no real love or affection for a long time. Around the time of the death of their firstborn – Isaac Vyrrington – she first noticed. Her husband's heart was rendered bereft of any warmth or love, replaced by impenetrable grief and sorrow. And it was at this time that her mind then turned to a footman she herself had had installed onto *Beryl Court*'s household staff; like her father Lord Ensbury Isaacs, she was inclined to tokens of charity, and through circumstances known only between the two of them, Jesse Blameford was brought to Berylford. A happily-married woman was she at the time, and so it was a cordial yet cautious camaraderie that pre-existed between the two. But upon her son's death, when Lord Wilson was no longer able to express the love that she required to comfort her, Jesse Blameford took his place.

As she sat there on the rug, holding her two sons so close to her that she might have smothered them, her thoughts remained fixed on that young footman. His middle-height but attractive build, and lush, thick auburn locks, his strong arms and broad shoulders. She missed even his presence about the house. If they passed in the corridor, he would often wink at her subtly in a display of his own cheeky impudence that he knew he could get away with, employing a mere flash of his smile. She dared not think back upon what he would do to her behind the closed door of her bedchamber, only that she wished it could happen again. Her lips alternated between smiling and frowning, the former for her happy remembrances, and the latter for they would not continue as she sent him away. To protect him from suspicion of a crime he did not commit.

That was something that had remained unanswered. The disappearance of Joshua. A creature of little consequence or worth to anyone, only to the household he served. That someone of such insignificance should rend the order of so many lives asunder, was an impenetrable mystery to the Countess. She feared to own it, as she had told Blameford before, but she wondered if it was divine intervention. That God was giving her reason to doubt and, therefore, to stop her liaison with Blameford. But they had not stopped. Instead they continued, adding again and again another sin of lust to the list for which she had to repent. Thus, God intervened again, and had her fall down the stairs. At first, she thought she had been pushed, but now she was not so sure. Providence had dealt her another blow, one that may have cost her life. She survived, but Lady Vyrrington wondered if she was due to witness another ill turn. One that would finally spell an end to her atonement, and the absolute forgiveness for her sins from The Almighty. The ill turn, she now dreaded, would be the sickness of her husband, unto the ending of his life. And with that thought, she wept, cradling her two youngest for any lasting comfort they brought her.

Chapter XXVI
The Cross He Bore

I N SUCH DESPERATE TIMES, WHITLOCKE was willing to go against the statutes set down not only by the household, but by all manner of rank and status. He had defied a convention he would have dared never go against at any other time. He entered His Lordship's study while his master was not within. If Lord Wilson was to be talked around, and persuaded to consult a doctor on his sickness, it would be in that room, and it would be Whitlocke doing the persuading.

Standing behind the desk of his master, the butler waited. He was not eager or enthusiastic about his purpose there, only intent on fulfilling what he had set out to do, though nonetheless apprehensive about the confrontation that may ensue. While he knew he shared a close confidence with Lord Wilson, the line between master and servant was not so blurred that it may be crossed lightly. Indeed, he had to inhale sharply when the earl came into the study and wheeled around to find him there. Whitlocke observed his master's eyes were wide open with confoundment.

"Good Lord!" Lord Wilson exclaimed, "What is the meaning of this, Whitlocke? What do you do here?"

"You once told me, milord, that I knew the cross you bear. I do, such as it is."

"What I may have said once upon a time does not explain how you happen to be here in my private quarters at such an unconscionable time, Whitlocke."

"I bid that you hear me out, sir. Please."

Lord Wilson sighed deeply and impatiently.

"Very well. But mind my words, Whitlocke; you are already dangerously close to crossing a threshold. You'd do well to tread carefully, or you will have reason to regret it."

"You fear displaying your own weakness, or that which you believe to *be* weakness," said Whitlocke, "The young Lordships dying, and now Lady Vyrrington's own brush with death and seeing her swift recovery. All under your nose and powerless to stop it. I implore you, My Lord – please do not punish yourself anymore."

Lord Wilson coughed hard three times, and wiped his lips with his handkerchief, which he put down on the desk in front of him. It was visibly stained with blood. He otherwise remained silent, his expression indifferent.

"Are you finished, Whitlocke?" he then asked coldly, "or have you anything further to say?"

"Yes milord. No milord," the butler replied, already fearing, if not knowing, he had said too much.

"Then there you are, I've heard you out. Now get out."

Whitlocke did not dare speak again. He let himself out, and collapsed against the wall outside, breathing deeply. Lord Wilson was not to remember himself this time. 'But there will be a next time…' Whitlocke thought to himself, '…this cannot be the future for this household.'

*

Later on, in the evening, when supper was being served in the dining room at the usual time, Whitlocke and Amethyst both waited outside the study door, a dinner tray in Amethyst's hands.

"My Lord?" Whitlocke called through the door, "We've brought your dinner *to* you, My Lord."

There was no answer.

Whitlocke tried the door, and it was open. Edging in, the butler called again. Amethyst followed him. Lord Wilson was not in there.

"What do you two do?"

They turned around and found His Lordship behind them, the opposite side of the door.

"My Lord," said Whitlocke, "We –"

"For what reason have you entered my *study*?" Lord Wilson barked, "*Answer me!*"

Amethyst shuddered and whined in fear.

"Have *you* something to say, Miss Cheshill?" Lord Wilson glared at her, and grabbed one of her wrists, "*Well*? *Have you*?"

The maidservant became more and more frightened, to the point at which she screamed, leapt away from her master and dropped the dinner tray and that which rested upon it. The crockery smashed upon impact with the floor.

"You *stupid, foolish bitch*!" Lord Wilson growled at Amethyst, "You–"

Whitlocke stood in front of Amethyst as she hysterically picked up the pieces of broken crockery off of the floor. She had cut her hand on a jagged shard of a plate.

"My *Lord*! Calm yourself!" Whitlocke said firmly in a raised voice.

"Do you *instruct me*, Whitlocke?" returned His Lordship with a snarl.

"What on Earth is going on out there?" Lady Vyrrington appeared at the end of the corridor leading from the dining room and rushed toward the scene. The cook, Mrs Trudgedawes, also ascended from the kitchen. She came into the study, knelt down by Amethyst and assisted her, as did Lady Vyrrington.

"I *swear to you*, Whitlocke..." Lord Wilson hissed, "...that if you do so much as *dare* speak in my presence again, you and that little scamp down there will be out of this house quicker than the news can reach your common little *brains*!"

"*Lord Wilson!*" Lady Vyrrington protested on the floor, "Can you not *see* what you have *done*?" Whitlocke had backed to the edge of the room to survey what transpired before him, watching closely his master. Lord Vyrrington looked down and saw Amethyst kneeling by the remains of the dinner he had been brought, her head buried in her hands in fear of him. Whitlocke observed that His Lordship appeared to know not what he had said or done.

"Mrs Trudgedawes, have Amethyst's hand seen to," Lady Vyrrington instructed, "Mr Whitlocke, see to it that my husband retires to our bedchamber."

"No," returned Lord Wilson, his voice quavering in the shock at his own actions, just as Whitlocke had proceeded to approach, "No, no, it's all right. I can go myself."
The butler instead stood by Lady Vyrrington, and they watched her husband ascend the stairs. His eyes were still wide, his expression stricken by utter shock.

*

After dinner, around an hour after all the chaos had ensued, Whitlocke was resolved, despite what felt like an age wrestling with his personal disliking for her, to confide once again in his mistress regarding Lord Wilson. And this time, knowing she had witnessed such an out-of-character display of temper from her husband, the butler knew the Countess would not so lightly brush aside his concerns.

Lady Vyrrington sat alone with her thoughts in the sitting room as was often her habit of an evening these days. With his intent laid crystal clear in his mind, Whitlocke entered.

"Yes, Whitlocke?" the Countess said calmly. She did not look up at him.

"I was wondering if I could tell you something important, My Lady?"

"Something *important?*"

"About Lord Wilson."

"His behaviour earlier is inexplicable," Lady Vyrrington returned, "And unforgivable. Amethyst dares not exit my room. She is inconsolable with fright. The intensity of the anger on his face and in his voice, it will haunt her for the rest of her life. All to redolent of events in her past that she would sooner die than recollect."

"My Lord is *ailing*, My Lady. In some way, I know this. And I fear for his health."

"He appeared not to know where he was. No less did he seem to remember what had happened. Though it shames me to own it, I should have listened to you in the first place, Whitlocke. I shouldn't have been so blind."

"May I suggest something, My Lady?"

"Yes, Whitlocke?"

"Why not you go to him?"

"What makes you think he'll *see* me?"

"Maybe the lack of the other's presence in your lives is what has driven you apart. I insist that it can only be for the benefit of Lord Wilson's health."

Lady Vyrrington observed that the mantle clock had struck the ninth hour. As it chimed its ninth chime, she got up from her armchair.

"Accompany me, Whitlocke," she said to him, "I believe I will only succeed in this... if you are with me."

"And I can assure you, My Lady, in spite of our enmity; we can put it aside while we care for Lord Wilson. Can I rely on your agreement to that?"

"Yes, Whitlocke. You can."

She walked out of the sitting room and ascended the stairs, Whitlocke following her closely. They both approached the door to Lord Wilson's room. Whitlocke walked before her, and knocked on her behalf. She took a step back. When no answer was received, Whitlocke tried the doorknob, and held the door open for Her Ladyship to enter. The butler observed as his mistress approached the bed of her husband, and quietly shut the door. Leaning against the wall, he sighed deeply, thinking that for once: he and Lady Vyrrington had seen eye-to-eye.

Chapter XXVII
A Manifestation of Ailments

INSTANTLY UPON ENTERING LORD WILSON'S bedchamber, the Countess saw that her husband's appearance and disposition were far from their usual, even relative to recent months. He had lost all colour in his face, bearing a sallow, almost lifeless complexion; his eyes seemed to be tinged with yellow, as if clouded by a haze of sulphur; the edges of his swollen lips were stained a dark red with dried blood.

He lay beneath his soft linens, his arms placed by his sides on top of the bedclothes. Lady Vyrrington walked over and slowly and quietly sat on the bed beside her husband, taking one of his hands in hers. It was quite cold to the touch; if she did not know any better, she may have mistaken him for a corpse. But to her even greater surprise, he squeezed her hand gently and held it.

"Oh my dear..." she said quietly, "...my dear you are far from yourself. Why did you not express your sickness?"
He merely coughed and gave no verbal reply.
"Why did you tell no one?"

He looked at her with his ashen eyes. His lips did not seem to move much when he spoke the word:

"Weakness."

The Countess closed her eyes and shook her head a little.

"You are a fool, Lord Wilson Vyrrington," she said *sotto voce,* "We have buried three children and endured a great deal in our years together. I think I know you to be among the *strongest* and *stubbornest* men in my acquaintance."

The Lord Wilson Vyrrington in the best of health would have found this amusing and would have quipped something witty back at his wife; suffice it to say he attempted to chuckle but instead choked and spluttered again. Knowing not what else to do, the Countess put a hand on her husband's face and caressed it softly with her thumb. Before she had a chance to say anything else, Whitlocke entered the room, and immediately walked over to her.

"Now do you believe me?" said the butler, "He is *blatantly* sick."

"Indeed, and this has gone far enough," returned Lady Vyrrington, "For Heaven's sake then, man! Make haste and fetch Doctor Street!"

"Right you are, milady."

As he made his exit, Lord Wilson spluttered again and suddenly clutched his wife's hand. His voice was hoarse.

"Will I survive this, Oliviera?"

"Oh yes of *course* you will!"

"Where–" he coughed once more, "–where is Amethyst?"

"She is too frightened to come out of my room, my dear."

"Know this..." Lord Wilson huskily continued, "...I saw merely a vague image. A blur. I could not see her..."
He looked away for a moment, gazing blankly at the bedchamber wall.

"...Not that any of that excuses my actions. To own the truth, my Lady Vyrrington, I have not the slightest notion as to what stroke of evil, whatever devilry possessed me to visit such wrath upon that poor girl."
He coughed thrice more and groaned in agony, clutching his side.

"There will be a time for forgiveness, My Lord," said Lady Vyrrington, continuing to hold her husband's hand as he continued to cough intermittently, "Just hold on. Help will be here soon."

Doctor Street took little time in arriving. Lady Vyrrington waited outside of the room, with Whitlocke standing by, until a diagnosis had been made.

"My Lady Vyrrington..." Doctor Street said once he had exited the bedchamber, "...I have been here more times than I care to remember in recent years. And now I find myself speaking in a similar vein as I have before, it grieves me to say."

"Is my husband going to *die*, Doctor Street, or is he going to *live*?"

Doctor Street sighed deeply.

"Lord Wilson is suffering from a *manifestation* of ailments," he said, "A calamitous cornucopia of difficulties, the most prominent of which that I can define are asthma; cataracts in the left eye which is now affecting the right, and now *dropsy* as well. Your husband also complains of a lack of sleep. Insomnia will further the effects of the three aforementioned maladies and will make him prone to an irascible disposition and aggressive outbursts."

"Cataracts you said?"

"Indeed."

"Lord Wilson became very angry with my lady's maid last evening. And just now he claimed that he could not even see her. It was a very sudden vehement occurrence in his behaviour."

"I see."

"I do not wish to prove a *nuisance* to you, good Doctor, but I cannot avoid informing you that you have *failed* to answer the question I *put* to you. Will Lord Wilson *die*?"

Her voice became more husky and trembling with each sentence.

"That remains to be *seen*, My Lady," returned Doctor Street, "I can recommend that you have the cook embellish Lord Wilson's food with basil. I can furnish you with a quantity now. And some lavender for his bed – that will alleviate the insomnia, at least. In time, the effects of his other illnesses might fade if he gets suitable rest, and thusly he should live..."

Lady Vyrrington smiled and gasped in relief.

"...But I do *insist* that he remain confined to his bed..." continued Doctor Street, "...Until his health has improved. Not all patients rally, but I find the soldiers and *former* soldiers the most stubborn against disease. I will return within the next few days to observe any changes."

On his way out with the Countess, the doctor went on.

"Your husband's numerous afflictions have severely weakened him. He will need assisting with regard to any movements *necessary*, though limited they should be. Obviously, his eyesight is failing, which cannot be cured. And the dropsy will make movements painful. Your servants shall see to the easing of that, no doubt."

"Of course, Doctor, thank you for your good attention as always," returned Lady Vyrrington.

Chapter XXVIII
A Turn About Berylford

DOCTOR STREET MADE VISITS TO *Beryl Court* every three days thenceforth, keeping a hawkish eye on any waxes or wanes in Lord Wilson's health, of which there were few. Lady Vyrrington had been unfailingly obedient to the prescriptions the good physician had given to her. The lavender he had brought from the apothecary had succeeded in allowing Lord Wilson to partake of several hours of sleep. He would neither wake nor rise unless in a case of the utmost necessity.

With her husband incapacitated, Lady Vyrrington had since written to her cousin, the newly-widowed Countess of Styridge, informing her of the recent events:

My dear cousin Riva,

It pains me to a greater dimension than you can imagine that I find myself unable to support you at the funeral of your late husband. I am currently plagued by the incommodious business of the health of my own spouse, who finds himself marred by a variety of maladies and oncoming blindness.

I again send my condolences with this letter, and only hope that you can understand that Lord Wilson is too weak and sick to attend the funeral with me and my leaving him alone at this time would be an act of deplorable character.

Begging your forgiveness most humbly, and welcoming any request you would put upon me to ease you in your mourning.

Sincerely yours,
Your otherwise devoted cousin,
Oliviera

Days passed; March turned into April and Lady Riva had not yet sent a reply. Indeed, upon the passing of a week after Lord Stephanus Styridge's funeral, Lady Vyrrington had begun to expect one less and less.

While the study was at most times Lord Wilson's private quarters, his Countess adopted it for her own at times where the sitting room would not suffice for an atmosphere for concentration. Amethyst was in there attending to the housekeeping at that time, and much as her work was always silent and efficient, Lady Vyrrington still deemed her too much of a distraction.

She sat at a small mahogany bureau in a westerly corner of the generously-sized room, writing a correspondence to her sisters in Dover over the subject of Lord Wilson's health. She had to look up from where she was sat a moment, rubbing her neck, now stiff and sore from the length of time she had had it pointed down to the paper. It was then she saw something she had never noticed before: a small painting, depicting her husband as a child no older than their youngest daughter Lady Minerva, or so the gilt plaque reading *Wilson, Viscount Beryl, 1761* would have her believe. She stood up and caressed the little boy's cheek.

From behind her, she heard the study door open. Her eyes allowed a couple of tears out, and she sniffed.

"Not now, Whitlocke," she murmured. Her eyes remained fixed on the portrait.
Footsteps were heard coming closer, and Lady Vyrrington turned around.

"Whitlocke, I said–"
She stopped upon not seeing Whitlocke, and smiled when she saw the figure of the slightly dilapidated Lord Wilson.

"My Lord?" she gasped happily, "My *dear!*"
Tears still dripped down her cheeks. She ran to him and they immediately kissed and embraced.

"You are well? You are *well!*" she said to him as he held her in his arms.

"I am *better*, Oliviera. And as stale a thing it is to say, I can only put it down to seeing you."

Lady Vyrrington chuckled.

"It *is* a *very* stale thing to say indeed. But I am happy that you have said it nonetheless."

They both laughed – it must have been the first time in weeks, if not months for Lord Wilson, as it took his breath from him and he coughed as a consequence. His Countess placed her hands about his chest and back.

"My Lord, are you quite sure you *should* be out of bed just yet?" she said, her voice endowed with acute concern.

"I have been bereft of appetite these last few weeks," he returned, "And now my strength comes back to me, so does my desire for food. Fetch Whitlocke and have him tell Mrs Trudgedawes I would like a magnanimous elevenses, or as much to that effect she can achieve on such short notice!"

It was as though a stranger had possessed him. Lady Vyrrington almost did not recognise her husband, not for his greyed and beleaguered aspect but for his undeniable and ineffable happiness. His contentment with his state of mind and health were probably alien even unto himself. The Countess had to pause for a moment to think on the notion, but when she had returned to herself, her husband was gone, though the sounds of frivolity had ascended up the stairs, and a truly unfamiliar sound followed. It was the sound of children's laughter; to be more precise: that of their youngest children, their sons Spencer and Edward, who, still in their bedgowns were now under one of the arms of their father each, and being brought down the stairs at great speed, to their sheer delight. Her cast-iron countenance was waning fast; Lady Vyrrington knew not how to react.

'Go and find Whitlocke and have this elevenses seen to', she thought. She knew that the butler too would be overjoyed to see his master restored.

Lady Vyrrington knew her way about downstairs well enough. Quite unlike the rest of the house, which to call it labyrinthian would be an understatement, it was a simple, linear set of corridors. And since there were fewer than ten servants on the *Beryl Court* payroll these days, finding the most senior among them was not too trying a task. There he sat at the head of the kitchen table, as a lion surveying his pride; as lordly as one in his position could aspire to become, peering down his nose through narrow eyes at a fiefdom of his own administration. A poor fiefdom it was, too. A man employed as both groom and coachman, to maintain the horses when they were at the stable and whip them roundly when at the carriage. Then there were the two housemaids, both of whom were neither able to read nor write – indeed if either of them could say their own names properly, it would be thought miraculous – who attended their duties alongside Amethyst, who was in many ways their direct superior, though she never asserted as much. Amethyst herself made four; Mrs Trudgedawes, the sole authority of the kitchen domain now was five, and the sixth: George Whitlocke. The other servants, including the cook stood from the table when Lady Vyrrington entered. Whitlocke took his time about it.

"Pray don't let me disturb you," the Countess said quite sweetly, taking all her staff aback, "Please go on."
Unsure if this were a trick or not, the servants all obliged her slowly. Whitlocke remained stood, which was just as well, as it was he she had come to see.

"What is it, My Lady?" he asked her, a note of worry astride his voice.

"Lord Wilson has risen," the Countess returned, "He's going to *live*!"
Whitlocke breathed in very deeply in half-surprise, half-joy.

"I am speechless," said he.

"Well *there's* a thing indeed!" replied Lady Vyrrington, "George Whitlocke speechless – have this

day noted for the history books, Mrs Trudgedawes."
She laughed loudly with the cook, who was astounded
at being permitted to have a joke at the butler's expense
on Her Ladyship's permission. After coming back to
herself, the Countess went on:

"His Lordship has requested a large breakfast
for the family, if you please, Mrs Trudgedawes.
Whatever you can scrape together at the last minute –
we would be most obliged."

"Certainly, My Lady," returned Mrs
Trudgedawes, "I'll rifle through the pantry and see
what can be spared."
As she went to waddle off, she curtsied to Lady
Vyrrington, a tear in her eye.

*

The late breakfast was served in the dining room that
day in celebration of this joyous occasion. Mrs
Trudgedawes had been responsible for making the jams
in the late-autumn and early-winter months since the
still room maid had been dismissed. She had placed a
pool of raspberry jam from the October before in one
silver bowl, and another contained a pool of orange
marmalade. There was toasted bread, and across the
other end of the table was a plumb cake, a plate of eggs,

a plate of gammon, plus fillets of mackerel and pancakes of beetroot.

The Lord and Lady Vyrrington sat together with their children – the youngest, Edward, sat in his mother's lap at the foot of the dining table, sucking on a piece of bread that had been dipped in a little raspberry jam. Spencer – Lord Wilson's heir apparent – was seated on his father's knee at the head of the table, doing the same. The two daughters – Lady Venetia and Lady Minerva – were sat along the vertical edges of the table. After finishing and swallowing a mouthful of bread and jam, Lord Wilson wiped his lips with his serviette and then said:

"I was thinking, my dear, that while the children are in the nursery, Minerva and Venetia could assist Amethyst in the garden."
Lady Vyrrington looked up at him.

"And *who* will look after Spencer and Edward in the nursery?"

"Ah, yes. Well, then they can *all* assist Amethyst in the garden. Should you all like to do that, children?" There was a buzz of indistinguishable excitement from the young family.

"For what reason do you not think Amethyst can cope on her own? And why won't *we* be in the nursery?" Lady Vyrrington enquired, somewhat perplexed.

"Well, actually, I intended for us to walk into Berylford. Let Mrs Urmstone cease in her rambles that my health is for the last and show them that I am still alive."

Lady Vyrrington laughed.

"Elspeth has been almost unending in asking me when *mourning clothes* will be necessary again!"

He laughed with her.

"So that is an agreement, is it?" he asked her, "You will accompany me at Berylford?"

She was too far down the table to caress him or embrace him, but her eyes and her smile spoke volumes. For the first time in ages, Lady Vyrrington felt happily married once again.

Dressed in a plum frock coat and silver waistcoat, Lord Wilson looked better than he had done in weeks. His hair, nonetheless, had greyed and thinned in places. His Countess was also dressed in purple, right down to the hat she wore and the parasol with which she equipped herself.

They joined arms and walked into Berylford, which was already lively with the townspeople going about their everyday business.

The first people to notice them were Mrs Rudgerleigh and Zephaniah Gussage. Lord and Lady Vyrrington smiled and said a quiet "hello" to both of them. At first, Mrs Rudgerleigh and Mr Gussage had not quite recognised who was walking with Lady Vyrrington; upon realising, Mrs Rudgerleigh turned around open-mouthed and jabbed Mr Gussage in the side.

"There you see, Zephaniah", she said to him "I *told* you Lord Wilson would pull through!"

"You did *not!*" Mr Gussage argued, "I told *you* that! Once a soldier, always a soldier – there's my opinion. Lord Wilson's stronger than half the men in this town together."

They next walked past the haberdashery, and waved to Miss Osborne, who was putting up new displays in the window. She, like Mrs Rudgerleigh, did not quite realise who it was until she looked a second time. She then called and beckoned Miss Gwynne over, as Lord and Lady Vyrrington had stopped to converse with Mrs Urmstone and Mrs Haffisidge directly outside the shop window.

"Mrs Urmstone..." Lord Wilson addressed her, "...My Lady has informed me as to your supposing my sickness would prove fatal..."

Mrs Urmstone looked at Lady Vyrrington as if she understood not what Lord Wilson had put to her. He coughed briefly.

"...And that *mourning clothes* would be necessary soon," he continued.

"Oh!" Mrs Urmstone suddenly comprehended, "Merely facetious humour on my part, My Lord. I meant no malice in it. No malice at all!"

"No *malice at all!*" Mrs Haffisidge repeated, laughing nervously.

Lord Wilson coughed again and groaned in slight anger.

"My dear, perhaps we should go in the tea shop and converse with my friends," said Lady Vyrrington, caressing his shoulder, "I fear we have let the good air wreak havoc on your lungs, sir."

"Please, My Lady, make no fuss on my account," said Lord Wilson, "I am quite well. It is merely a tickle."

But he coughed more and more, and clutched his sides as he had done before, and then placed a hand on his heart. He tried to breathe as he normally did, but felt that his breath was laboured as he did so.

"My dear?" Lady Vyrrington continued to say, and when his knees gave way, the three ladies all tried to hold him up. Eventually, his weight became too much for them to endure, and they let him to the ground as gently as they could.

Miss Osborne and Miss Gwynne exited the haberdashery.

"We will send for two able-bodied men to help him back to the house," said Miss Osborne.

"My Lady..." Miss Gwynne took Lady Vyrrington by the shoulder as she stared down at her husband's unconscious body, "...You *must* come *indoors!*"

"Yes, My Lady Oliviera. We *insist* you come into the haberdashery with us. Let us take *tea*," Mrs Urmstone said.

"Tea?" Lady Vyrrington shrieked, "*Tea* at a time like this indeed, Elspeth! And while my husband lies here maybe we shall put a few sugar cubes down his throat to *choke* the final hours of his life away!" She collapsed to her knees beside him, burying her face into his chest and whispered

"Don't leave me now. Don't leave me alone."

Chapter XXIX
Wrought in Silence

VERY SOON AFTER LORD WILSON had been brought back to *Beryl Court*, he had been hauled to his bedchamber and put into his bed. His breath was laboured – more of a pained wheeze than anything else, and much interrupted by bouts of coughing. Doctor Street arrived soon after Lady Vyrrington, Mrs Urmstone and Mrs Haffisidge, who had convened in the sitting room on the ground floor.

The servants had been confined to downstairs quarters; even Whitlocke had been shut out of the sitting room. This was not enough to hinder him, thus he, along with Amethyst and Mrs Trudgedawes stood by the sitting room door, eavesdropping into the woes of their superiors. They neither flinched, nor removed themselves when Lady Venetia and Lady Minerva both walked past them to enter the room, where their mother had placed herself on a small settee, gazing blankly into nothingness. Her eldest children kept asking her if their father was going to be all right, and similar questions, though Lady Vyrrington could only be silent to them, for she knew not how to explain to her daughters that Lord Wilson was *not* going to be all right.

Mrs Urmstone and Mrs Haffisidge both emerged from the adjacent dining room, bringing brandy for Lady Vyrrington. The children ran to them.

"My Lady?" Mrs Haffisidge said, "My Lady, where is Doctor Street? What has he done with Lord Wilson?"
Lady Vyrrington was silent to her as well.

"I believe she is in a trance," Mrs Haffisidge turned and said to Mrs Urmstone, whose sides were being clung to by the distressed Vyrrington daughters.

"No, merely asleep with her eyes open," returned Mrs Urmstone, "Hence why she cannot answer. Lady Venetia, Lady Minerva, go to your other godmother a minute."
The girls immediately ran to Mrs Haffisidge and embraced her. Mrs Urmstone sat beside the vacantly-expressed Countess, and placed their hands together.

"Disturb her *not*, Elspeth!" expostulated Mrs Haffisidge, "She might *need* her sleep!"

"I am aware of that!"
Before an argument between the two ladies could ensue, Doctor Street came in. Mrs Urmstone stood again, and Mrs Haffisidge sent the young girls along. The doctor waited for the children to be out of earshot.

"Please be seated, ladies," he finally said, approaching Lady Vyrrington and also sitting, before going on:

"My Lady, I told you when I first gave my diagnosis that asthma was one of the many maladies from which Lord Wilson was suffering. It appears it has been affecting him for a lot longer than I first believed..."

Lady Vyrrington remained blank.

"...Due to the lack of attention given to *smoke inhalation* when your husband saved a man from the burning barn at Cox Farm, his lungs have endured several months of aggravation."

At last some expression appeared in Lady Vyrrington's face. She half-smiled, albeit still while staring into the wall.

"He refused to permit anyone to examine him after that incident," she said *sotto voce,* "He insisted there was nothing to worry about."

"I must lament, My Lady..." Doctor Street continued, "...but I now know that the irritation of Lord Wilson's lungs has extended to such a severe dimension that it has affected his heart as well. It is my belief that pneumonia has set in, My Lady."

She looked up at him.

"*Pneumonia?*"

"I am truly very sorry, Lady Vyrrington, but I can now do nothing else for your husband. Time will be the doctor now. I cannot predict for certain how long he has left to live."

Standing up he placed a hand on the Countess' shoulder and, in a tone imbued with as much sympathy as one in his position and occupation should be expected to give, said:

"I advise you to prepare yourself."

It took some moments of deadly silence, but soon Lady Vyrrington burst into tears, burying her face into the shoulder of the adjacent Mrs Urmstone, who even herself let go of her cast-iron emotional strength and shed a few of her own tears.

As Doctor Street was about to exit, Miss Osborne and Miss Gwynne arrived at the door. He held it open for them, but only nodded in a sombre greeting. The haberdashers both walked into the sitting room slowly, and bowed their heads when they saw the expressions on their friends' faces.

"Has he gone?" Miss Gwynne said, quietly.

Mrs Haffisidge inhaled deeply.

"Not yet Agnes, no..." said she, "...But 'tis only a matter of time."

Lady Vyrrington looked up at the two ladies.

"Miss Osborne, Miss Gwynne, can I put myself upon your mercy please?" she asked them.

"Of course My Lady. *Whatever* you require," returned Miss Gwynne.

"The girls: Lady Venetia and Lady Minerva. And my two sons. Might they go back with you Elspeth, Judith-Ann, to the haberdashery? I cannot bear to have them see their mother suffer."
Mrs Urmstone took out a handkerchief and wiped her eyes.

"Should you not like someone to stay with *you*, My Lady Oliviera?" she asked.

"I shall be well enough by myself," returned she, "I insist that you go."

They agreed without further question. Spencer and Edward had been put to bed in the nursery, where Miss Osborne and Miss Gwynne found them. Mrs Urmstone and Mrs Haffisidge both departed in tears, and once she had been left alone, Lady Vyrrington approached the sitting room door, leading out into the hallway, where Whitlocke, Amethyst and Mrs Trudgedawes were still stood; none of the others entering or exiting the house had even noticed them there. Lady Vyrrington appeared at the door and held it open for them, inclining for them to enter. They did so very hesitantly.

"Will you all sit down?" Lady Vyrrington said softly.

It was one thing to be invited into upstairs quarters like the sitting room, but another thing entirely to be asked to sit *with* Her Ladyship. The three servants acquiesced slowly after a few seconds. None of them dared speak out of turn and ask what had happened.

"It transpires that Lord Wilson is afflicted by pneumonia..." she began to explain.

Whitlocke immediately bowed his head. Lady Vyrrington continued:

"...I am no surer than the doctor as to how long he has to live. But as you can imagine, it will be a short time only. Lord Wilson's condition is still yet to worsen, and I find I am unable to see him like that. As much as I would like to do that, my emotions disable me."

"If you please, My Lady..." said Whitlocke, who stood up again, "...might I suggest that *I* go in your place?"

"That was to be my request Mr Whitlocke."

"I understand. And be assured you can rely upon me."

"I thank you."

Chapter XXX
The Departure of Lord Wilson Vyrrington

THROUGHOUT HIS MANY YEARS OF servitude in the Vyrrington household, George Whitlocke had never once been encumbered by the thought that he would walk to the bedchamber door of Lord Wilson for the last time. Perhaps he thought he would predecease his master, or maybe he always supposed the room would be occupied by a living Lordship – even if the current occupant were to die, in Whitlocke's mind at least, the heir apparent would have been of age to take the room on thereafter. But little Spencer Vyrrington was not yet five, so by the time he would take over the earldom, Whitlocke believed he himself would be long dead. Thus, there the butler was, approaching slowly and silently the door of his master's bedchamber, knowing this would probably be for the final time. He was very much afraid of what lay behind it. Wasting no time on contemplation and speculation, he decided to just have done with the whole abhorrent issue.

Lord Wilson was lying awake in his bed. He was breathing with difficulty; all the colour was drained from his cheeks. A corpse who had not yet been granted the privilege of eternal rest. His yellowed eyes turned to a squint, and then he smiled.

"Whitlocke?" he wheezed.

"Begging your pardon, milord, but My Lady sent me in on her behalf. She fears that seeing you will distress you both too much," said Whitlocke.

"I understand that she should not wish to see me in a condition such as this," returned Lord Wilson, "Besides I have a matter I would convey only to you. Come here and sit down."

Whitlocke was slightly taken aback by his master's request, but he accepted.

Lord Wilson tried to lean over in his bed to face the butler, managing after a lot of uncomfortable fidgeting.

"Whitlocke..." he said hoarsely, '...My Lady would not like to hear me say this... to *her* ears at any rate. So, I shall say it to yours instead."

"Do not strain yourself, milord," returned Whitlocke.

"No, 'tis important that you hear it. Now, do you remember when I told you of my mother, the former Countess of Vyrrington Lady Adeliza?"

"I think I recall."

"I told to you that she had squandered most of the estate before I inherited it, did I not?"

His breath became more and more desperate.

"Erm – yes, *yes* you did, milord. You did say that," returned Whitlocke, panicking slightly.

"The money left in the Will to My Lady to be passed onto my son when he inherits is–"
He was interrupted by a fit of coughing, and then a groan of inner pain. His next words were peppered with irregular pains in his chest.

"–It is not *sufficient* to allow Her *Ladyship* to retain the servants and the *house* together! She can– (more coughing)– she can *only keep you and Amethyst*!"
Whitlocke continued to nod in accordance with his master's revelations, maintaining the otherwise stoic cast of countenance for which he was known not only at *Beryl Court*, but in Berylford.

 His Lordship went on:

"I permit you to propose marriage to Amethyst, so that she will keep her place no matter what happens!"
Panting quickly and in agony, Lord Wilson grabbed Whitlocke by the collar and pulled him in closer, before he had any time to contemplate that last sentence.

"But you – *you must promise me* this, Whitlocke!"

"Yes, My Lord," returned he.

"You must..." Lord Wilson spoke hoarsely and slowly, his strength diminishing more and more,

"...You *must stay* with Her Ladyship after I am gone. No matter what happens!"

Whitlocke did not answer. It was a promise about which his thoughts were twofold: to accept this promise and spend his remaining years in service to a woman he deplored, or to decline a dying man his final wish.

"Of course, My Lord," he said, "I promise." Lord Wilson shut his eyes, and his breath became deeper. In a long exhalation, he formed a breathless question:

"Did you push her down the stairs?"

Whitlocke's eyes whitened at the words, but as he opened his mouth to answer, he beheld his master's eyes as they stared into the nothingness of death. A thin crimson ribbon of blood lined the corner of his lips. Whitlocke clutched at his own throat, not for want of air, just to choke out any possible betrayal of emotions that may afflict him. His mouth hung ajar; the thought that had incommoded him only the once had been realised – he would go hence from this room, never to enter it again. Lord Wilson, the fourth Earl of Vyrrington and lord presiding over Berylford St. Barbara, was dead.

PART 3
THE **RETURN**

Book Eight
THE COUNTESS EMBRACES WIDOWHOOD

Chapter XXXI
Death's Bitter Reality

L ADY VYRRINGTON WAS SAT HALFWAY down the
corridor, on the settee by the window, her gaze
fixed rigidly on that bedchamber door. She had
had a mind to press an ear to it and listen, but did not
for two reasons. Firstly, she believed that was behaviour
too redolent of that of her dear friend Mrs Urmstone,
and would decidedly not be party to such things;
secondly because she was afraid of what she might hear
– she had sent Whitlocke in there on her behalf for a
reason, after all.

What felt like a lifetime passed, not once did her eyes deviate from that door, until it opened and Whitlocke emerged therefrom, whereupon they met with his as he approached her. He only shook his head.

She knew what he meant, for it was a gesture with which she was all too familiar. She had first witnessed it with her elder sisters sat beside her, when she saw the family doctor in Dover inform their father of the death of his wife, her mother Lady Regina Isaacs. Then twice again in more recent times, on both occasions committed by Doctor Street, when reporting that deplorable news, the deaths of her sons. When she was too young to know or understand death, she did not recognise what she felt as pain. When her firstborn Isaac Vyrrington died, she thought her own life force was bound to that of her son and would soon pass with him, such was her utter anguish. But, though her heart broke, her soul endured. On the third instant, her pain was wrought in ice, stone and steel; cold, hard and silent. And now, it was her husband whose death was heralded by a mere, solemn shake of the head from her butler.

The Countess immediately stood up and walked around the corner leading to her own bedchamber. As the bitter reality of her husband's death hit her, her walk turned into a run for the final steps to her door. As soon as she had entered, she leant up against it, breathing quickly. She knew not whether she was distraught beyond all measure or utterly relieved. Her husband was dead. Suddenly there was this hole in her existence. Though at only thirty-seven years of age, while she was still entitled the Countess of Vyrrington, she had the word 'widow' attached to her, wherever she walked. When her son Spencer came of age (at seventeen), she would hand over Lord Wilson's estate in its entirety. The house and the money. Until then, she thought, it was hers by right, and she knew not where to begin imagining what to do with it.

Before she could contemplate for too long over it, a slow and somewhat indecisive-sounding knock came at the door. The Countess blinked several times and wiped away the tears that lined her eyelids.

"Come in," she said hoarsely.
Seemingly as hesitantly as he had announced his presence behind it, Whitlocke opened the door and entered his mistress' bedchamber.

"You appear to sound *shaken*, Whitlocke," Lady Vyrrington said.

"My master just died before me, My Lady," he replied, "It is not something I am used to."

"I should hope not," returned the Countess, "Though in recent times one does expect to get used to Death ingratiating Himself with one's household. And yet still He can shock you."

"'Tis not Lord Wilson's passing that perturbs me so, but his words to me before his death."

He stopped. Lady Vyrrington looked up at him.

"*Well*?" said she.

Whitlocke had to think hard about his next sentence. He remained silent.

"Whitlocke, I have been frightened enough for one day. I beseech you, *speak* to me!"

"Lord Wilson gave to me a brief description of what his estate consists," he finally explained aloud, "He told me that his mother Lady Adeliza was – in the nicest possible way – *extravagant* with the money she had prior to Lord Wilson's inheriting the Earldom. He was left with little."

"I see," Lady Vyrrington replied throatily, her eyes filling up, "Go on."

"After your sons died, Lord Wilson was forced to dismiss nearly half the staff here at Beryl Court in order to acquire funds enough to pay for the funerals. I opposed that decision, though that is immaterial now. But there, as my master lay dying, I listened to him tell me that the remainder of the estate will only have enough to keep two servants as well as the house. You and the children too will be supported on the income brought by the interest to the estate and, obviously, the tenants as per usual. That is all, My Lady. The remaining maids and footmen, even Mrs Trudgedawes; they will all have to go."

"Even Amethyst?"

"Amethyst is to stay. She will take on all duties previously undertaken by Mrs Trudgedawes, as well as the other kitchen and housekeeping staff. And I am to remain as butler."

"That is what Lord Wilson wanted, Whitlocke," replied Lady Vyrrington, "And I shall not delay you in resuming your duties. You had best break the news to Mrs Trudgedawes and the other servants. And I must write to my cousin Abel. He will want to know of Lord Wilson's death."

"Will the servants not be allowed to stay for Lord Wilson's funeral?"

"I will retain Mrs Trudgedawes until she finds a decent position. I will *not* see a woman of her age and talents thrown in the workhouse. But the others will have to go immediately. If what my husband told you is *true, Whitlocke,* I have not money enough to support them even now. I am sorry Whitlocke, but that is my final word."

"Very good, milady."

He left the room.

"And Whitlocke…" she called.

He had not left the other side of the door. It was ajar enough for her to know he was still there.

"…Thank you."

Even though she received no answer, she knew he had appreciated it, for once in their relationship.

Chapter XXXII
A Solemn Occasion

ESPITE THE LOOMING THREAT OF dwindling finances, the Countess wasted no time in arranging her husband's funeral. Her children – particularly the youngest two, Spencer and Edward – all required fitting for mourning clothes, with which Miss Osborne and Miss Gwynne were more than happy to oblige her.

Having not received a reply to her last letter to Lady Riva Styridge stating her reason for not attending Lord Stephanus' funeral, Lady Vyrrington thought it prudent to send another, in case the first had not reached its addressee. This next correspondence she wrote was in a more formal tone – in the voice of a widowed noblewoman, as opposed to a member of extended family.

Dear Lady Styridge,

Upon these last few weeks, I found myself troubled that I had not received a response to my last letter, addressed to you regarding the attendance of your late husband's funeral. My purpose for writing this letter is threefold.

On the first account, I wish to reiterate my sincerest apologies to you for my failure to attend the aforementioned event, and that my reasons for that failure remain just and valid.

On the second account, I wish to reassure you that no harm on your feelings neither emotional nor personal was intended by the aforementioned failure, and that I offer nothing but friendship here in Hampshire whilst you remain in widowhood.

On the third and final account, I have mournful news of my own to convey, My Lady, for I now have lost my own husband Lord Wilson Vyrrington.

Even though I expect nothing from you in this regard Lady Styridge, I offer you the information that my husband's funeral will take place a week from Tuesday. I would appreciate the same courtesy that I did to you by informing me by letter as to whether or not you can attend.

Sincerely yours,
Lady Oliviera, Countess of Vyrrington

Her Ladyship had kept to her word with regard to the servants. While Mrs Trudgedawes had been gently informed that her position as cook at *Beryl Court* would be imminently terminated, Lady Vyrrington had done her best to ensure her comfort while a new position was sought for her. In the meantime, she was being paid to tutor Amethyst in the ways of the kitchen.

The other servants, however, had not been so fortunate. Those that had been retained by Lord Wilson following the deaths of Their Lordships Felix and Augustus a few months since, had all been thanked sincerely by Lady Vyrrington, and had exited Berylford for good. Meanwhile, Whitlocke had settled into his additional duties – now they were only a family of five, it was not too strenuous an undertaking in doubling as a footman.

The Tuesday of Lord Wilson's funeral seemed to have arrived sooner than expected, in spite of it having been three weeks after his death. Until then, the Countess had not felt at all nervous. It was only upon that Tuesday that her stomach began to quaver. Whitlocke and Amethyst were both arm-in-arm waiting by the front doors of the house. Mrs Trudgedawes exited from her downstairs room, at the same time as Lady Vyrrington was descending from her dressing room upstairs. Mrs Trudgedawes had a handkerchief in her hand, and was already dabbing at her wet eyes.

"Mrs Trudgedawes," Lady Vyrrington spoke sympathetically, and walked over to console her, "You must not weep yet. The funeral has not even commenced."

"Pay me no mind, milady," returned Mrs Trudgedawes, "I'm merely being foolish. But Lord Wilson was always such a wonderful person. I knew something was queer when he lashed out at Amethyst when he did. He was always of tranquil temperament; even as a boy."

"I did not know you knew him when he was a child."

"This is why I find it so hard to face it!" Mrs Trudgedawes spoke through her tears, "The fact that I can still see him as clear as I see Master Spencer or Master Edward. They're both so much like him. And yet, he's gone and I'm still here!"

Lady Vyrrington struggled to hold off her own tears. She placed a hand on Mrs Trudgedawes' shoulder, and caressed it.

"I do appreciate you letting me stay for his funeral milady," she continued, "I wanted to be here. To say goodbye to the boy I knew."

"Mrs Trudgedawes, walk with *me* when the train begins. I will ensure that you do not weep alone."

The cook wiped her eyes again.

"I thank you milady, for that gesture," said she, "If you please, though, before the others arrive, I shall wait with Mr Whitlocke and Amethyst outside to receive them."

Beryl Court seemed all the emptier, and Lady Vyrrington began to notice the dominating presence that the late Lord Wilson used to have. There were only three black-clad servants lined up beside the door, and Lady Vyrrington stood opposite them with her two daughters and two sons.

The first carriage pulled up, containing Mrs Urmstone, Mrs Haffisidge, and Mr and Mrs Warwick. Mrs Haffisidge and her nephew-in-law were both making their usual dagger expressions to each other while the other spoke.

Mrs Urmstone bustled up the gravel path and surveyed the three servants up and down.

"Really, My Lady Oliviera were these three *all* you could retain?" she said. Amethyst and Mrs Trudgedawes both presented their own respective attempts at curtsies. Amethyst's was a clumsy downward kneel, and Mrs Trudgedawes, who was squat in stature, made what appeared to be a mere small bounce.

"I am afraid so," replied Lady Vyrrington, "I see Mr Warwick was more than happy to be invited."

Mrs Urmstone turned around to observe Mr Warwick's facial expression, which showed a man reluctantly attending a solemn and formal event when he could be at the same time drinking in *The St. Barbara's Arms*.

"Indeed," returned Mrs Urmstone, "And Judith-Ann is having no nonsense from him today either. He put to her a criticism about her mourning bonnet as she was fastening it before we left, and she could well have taken a hand to his face. You were unfortunate to have not seen the look in her eyes though. She would have stabbed him there and then if she had had a knife to hand!"

Lady Vyrrington's eyes widened.

"Really?" said she.

"Oh indeed, My Lady Oliviera," Mrs Urmstone continued, maintaining the quick pace of her speech, "Mrs Warwick and I *both*, as we were sat together already prepared on one of Mrs Haffisidge's nice settees, had to suffocate our laughter until Mr Warwick had left."

Mrs Haffisidge approached Lady Vyrrington.

"Judith-Ann..." Lady Vyrrington kissed her on both cheeks, "...Elspeth has been informing me of your latest conflict with our disinclined guest Mr W."

"What *he* should be disinclined for is beyond me!" Mrs Haffisidge did not whisper, and looked around to make sure Mr Warwick could hear her, "I put it to him as firmly as I could that 'it is the least you can do: to bear courtesy to the memory of the man who risked his life in order to save yours!' If you don't mind me saying, My Lady, I wish he'd left him in that barn to burn."

"Mrs *Haffisidge*!" Mrs Urmstone said, chuckling, "Do not tempt fate."

Mrs Warwick, practically dragging her husband with her arm in his, walked up beside her aunt.

"I bid you our condolences, My Lady," she said, "And my husband has his own piece to convey, don't you Luke?"

He stood up straight, and breathed deeply. He spoke slowly, mainly to annoy Mrs Haffisidge.

"Your husband was a gallant man, Your Ladyship..." he said, "...And he was gallant in terms of risking his life to save mine."

"That was his *profession*, Mr Warwick," returned Lady Vyrrington, "As a soldier; he considered it his *duty* to save another man's life."

"*Have you no respect for the dead*?" Mrs Haffisidge vehemently hissed at her nephew-in-law, "*If not for them, at least those left behind! You had not even the courtesy to convey your condolences without mocking somebody!* My Lady, I apologise for my niece's husband's lack of conduct. I hope that one day he –"

"Auntie Judith *please!*" Mrs Warwick quietened her aunt, before returning her address to Lady Vyrrington, "I also apologise for my *aunt's* lack of ability to keep her less-than-desirable feelings toward my husband at bay on this solemn day."

Mrs Haffisidge only held her tongue, as did Mr Warwick. Lady Vyrrington was not sure how to feel, either amused by Mrs Haffisidge's outburst, or offended by Mr Warwick's mockery of her husband and disregard of her feelings. She found no more time to think about it, for Miss Gwynne, closely followed by Miss Osborne, came up the path. They conveyed their own condolences, and were followed then by Mrs Rudgerleigh and Zephaniah Gussage.

While Mrs Rudgerleigh followed suit with her friends with regard to expressing her sympathies, Mr Gussage took Lady Vyrrington's hand.

"My Lady, I know I'm not a man of society myself..." he began, in his thick West Country drawl, "...And I did not know your husband in society. But I knew war and he knew war. And so we both know or knew bravery when we see or saw it. And I'll never forget his bravery when the barn at Cox Farm burned down. He was going to rush in again before the explosion and collapse. I would not have been able to manage that."

"Mr Gussage..." said Lady Vyrrington, "...I really know not what to say."

"It seems a bit much to say it but, I treat that experience as a service with your husband. And I will say to you, My Lady, that it was an *honour* serving with Lord Wilson that day."

He said no more and went and stood with Mrs Rudgerleigh who, along with her other friends looked at the next carriage, which was like nothing that had been seen in Berylford before. Who it contained however, was another matter.

She exited with a black lace parasol in her hand, the silver handle exquisitely formed into a J shape. Her dark hair was tied back tightly. Mrs Urmstone's mouth hung open. The lady was Juvelia, Mrs Urmstone's sister. She was even more astounded to find that she was accompanied by a gentleman. His gait suggested that he was of frail health. He appeared at least twenty years older than she.

"What are you about returning on *this* solemn occasion?" Mrs Urmstone ejaculated at her sister, who with her gentleman friend was approaching the party, "Why not my *own* husband's funeral?"

"I apologise for not having been here at such a time, Elspeth," returned her sister, "I was suddenly asked to journey to Italy. It was awfully mysterious, but I accepted nonetheless. I was abroad for some years and then I visited Wales. Which reminds me..."

She brought forward her gentleman friend, placing her arm in his.

"...This is *The Honourable* Blatchford Ullswell. The first cousin to the Earl of Merrylton..."

She surveyed the party, who all looked at her intently.

"...And my husband."

Mrs Urmstone gasped and brought her sister close.

"Now *Juvelia*! Remember where you *are*!" she whispered into her ear, "You are at the funeral of a dear friend of ours' *husband*! What business do you have presenting your *own spouse* to her?"

"It amuses me to see your behaviour and intentions have become so much more pragmatic. Married life and widowhood have changed you Elspeth…"

Mrs Urmstone grumbled, but did not form actual words in doing so.

"…Does it not *please* you, though?" Mrs Ullswell continued.

"Hmmm?"

"To be the sister of a woman with a *title*? To be the sister-in-law of the cousin of an Earl?"

Mrs Urmstone did not answer, and Mrs Ullswell knew that this was her sister's way of conceding defeat without having to verbally announce it.

"But how did you know of the Lord Vyrrington's passing?" Mrs Rudgerleigh asked, "None of us in Berylford knew of your present address."

"I received word from Abel Stirkwhistle. We met briefly in Italy, you see. Only last fortnight, as it happens. He should be here soon, I wouldn't wonder."

Another carriage drew up at that point. The parties expected Abel Stirkwhistle to exit, but they were wrong to do so. Instead Lady Vyrrington's sisters the Ladies Lavinia, Clementina, Diana and Georgiana Isaacs appeared out of it. They all approached her one-by-one, kissing their sister on both cheeks. Lady Diana, who was Lady Vyrrington's favourite sister and closest sibling, stood with the Countess while the other three kissed their nephews and nieces.

Then the hired pallbearers arrived, as the coffin of Lord Wilson had been kept inside in order to be buried within the Vyrrington family mausoleum.

The coffin was opened before the assembly, the women of whom were all weeping. Even the likes of Zephaniah Gussage and Whitlocke were struggling not to betray their emotions.

The reposed and restful body of Lord Wilson – dressed appropriately for his burial – was brought out in his coffin and into the mausoleum, in order to be gently placed into one of the empty stone tombs, which, on the front, had the words engraved:

HEREIN LIETH THE MORTAL REMAINS OF

LORD WILSON,
THE FOURTH EARL OF VYRRINGTON
AND FOURTH VISCOUNT BERYL

WHO WAS BORN UNTO THIS WORLD ON THE
SIXTH DAY OF FEBRUARY OF THE YEAR 1754

AND DEPARTED THIS LIFE AND WAS TAKEN UNTO GOD ON
THE TENTH DAY OF APRIL OF THE YEAR 1794

After a few minutes of silence, Lady Vyrrington stepped forward and placed a rose into the tomb with the corpse of her husband, before the pallbearers sealed it by placing its heavy stone lid on top. The Reverend Helton stood at the centre of the congregation, and sombrely spoke the lines of the Requiem Mass chosen by Lady Vyrrington herself. As he spoke, many heads – those of Mrs Trudgedawes; Mrs Urmstone; Mrs Ullswell; Mrs

Haffisidge etcetera – were bowed to hide away their tears:

> *"[7]Requiem ærternam dona eis, Domine*
> *et lux perpetua luceat eis.*
> *Te decet hymnus Deus, in Sion,*
> *et tibi reddetur votum in Ierusalem.*
> *Exaudi orationem meam;*
> *ad te omnis caro veniet.*
> *Requiem ærternam dona eis, Domine*
> *et lux perpetua luceat eis."*

"*Amen*," were the sadness-smothered whispered words of the assembly. The Reverend Helton held up his hand with his index and middle fingers held together. He made a cross in the air in front of the mausoleum, and said:

> *"[8]Pie Jesu Domine,*
> *Dona eis requiem. Amen."*

---

[7] *Eternal rest grant unto them, O Lord And let perpetual light shine upon them. A hymn becomes you, O God, in Zion, and to you shall a vow be repaid in Jerusalem. Hear my prayer; To you all flesh shall come. Eternal rest grant unto them, O Lord And let perpetual light shine upon them.*

[8] *Lord, all pitying, Jesus blest, Grant them thine eternal rest. Amen.*

Once again, the attendees reiterated the final word; the more devout among them made a cross on themselves with their hands and kissed their fingers. As she turned to go back towards the house, the Countess looked up to behold, however blurred by the tears veiling her eyes, that handsome, wiry figure she knew so well. That of Jesse Blameford.

Her first impulse was to smile broadly (the first time she had smiled properly in weeks) and run straight to him, but she knew only too well where she was and the nature of the occasion. Thus it was that she remained remote and silent and much aggrieved, merely acknowledging his presence with a slow nod of the head and a mere flicker of a smile. His time with Abel Stirkwhistle had taught him a degree of *savoir-faire*; he sensed immediately her restrained reaction to seeing him and followed suit accordingly, returning her gesture almost identically.

The Countess then approached him – she decided she would test and tease him. She stood to the side of him as she passed him, allowing him to murmur:

"I bid you my condolences, Lady Vyrrington. Lord Wilson was the most respectable employer I have ever had. *One* of the most."

She half-smiled, again not entirely facing him, and her gaze pointed at an upward diagonal.

"Thank you, sir."

The bait was set, and Blameford was biting. He bent forward and kissed her hand. She gave a short, sharp curtsey in return and bid him good day.

Chapter XXXIII
Mrs Urmstone Speaks Plainly

THAT GESTURE REALLY RUBBED SALT in the wound for him. Jesse Blameford has never known Lady Vyrrington, or any woman he had been with (of which there were an indeterminate number) for that matter, to be so unreceptive to his charms. He mulled over the thoughts of what he had done wrong or differently to make her act so, but justified it as 'it's a funeral, she's obviously just not thinking clearly' or 'You've been gone for six months, she's in shock if anything else at the sight of you'.

He straightened up again, and watched her walk away to mingle about the other attendees in the drawing room, not realising he himself was still not altogether alone.

"No doubt My Lady was often in your thoughts while you were abroad, Mr Blameford?"
He wheeled round – Mrs Urmstone was stood a short way behind him.

"Of course," he returned politely, "I was gone half a year; my thoughts often turned to home."

"May I speak plainly?" she seemed to ignore his response, intent on arriving at her point forthwith. Among her many attributes, which could be listed in short as querulous, fastidious, temperamental, shrewd, irksome and unforgiving and at the same time mercurial and prone to moments of profound wisdom (though she was by no means a stupid or unintelligent lady), impatience was another quite synonymous with Elspeth Urmstone.

While polite in her way, she was unfortunately of that class of lady who – quite unlike Lady Vyrrington and Mrs Haffisidge, both of whom had been raised to appreciate and assist the poor and less-fortunate as they had the means with which to afford it – was set in her ways to be dismissive of those who ranked beneath her in society, and dignify conversation with such people as little as possible. Blameford knew from the first time he had served her tea when he joined the *Beryl Court* staff that he was one such individual; Mrs Urmstone had almost recoiled from his presence in an abhorrence one associates usually with spiders or other repellent creatures.

Since her tone was sharp and bereft of courtesy, Blameford returned likewise:

"As if you need my permission to speak plainly. I've never known you to speak in any other manner."

"Indeed," she muttered contemptuously.

"You don't care for me very much, do you Mrs Urmstone?"

"My feelings toward you are immaterial, Mr Blameford. My feelings toward My Lady Oliviera and your *relationship* with her – that is what is material."

"Oh really?" he returned, rolling his eyes, "How so?"

He knew too well the sort of woman Mrs Urmstone was. Even amongst servant classes, her reputation preceded her. A lady who endowed herself with the belief she needed to know everyone else's business and affairs, believing it to be her duty to protect them if necessary.

"It will not *do*, Mr Blameford, since we *are* speaking plainly!" she said austerely, "You desire a thing you cannot possibly possess for yourself."

His tone turned from deliberate defiance and indignance, to arrogance. Just for the sake of provoking this woman even further, to cause her to embarrass herself as she inevitably would.

"Stranger things have happened than the youngest daughter of an Earl and a former servant coming together," he said.

"Not in *Berylford*, there has not!" Mrs Urmstone dismissed the idea sharply, "I can say nothing of the *former* servants for you are the first to *return* to the town after being positioned overseas. But I know this – My Lady Oliviera Vyrrington's widowhood does *not* sever her marriage to Lord Wilson. She will remain matrimonially bound to his *memory* rather than risk scandal with a match that far from befits her class and social duty."

"I won't be *just* a servant forever, Mrs Urmstone. You have no idea how well-paid my position with the Stirkwhistles was."

"So, you'll be a *rich* former servant and that will make you more eligible a match for Lady Oliviera than the Earl of Vyrrington, will it?" she scoffed at him, "I think not, Mr Blameford. Indeed, I think we will end this discussion; I fear we will struggle to find common ground here. I bid you a good afternoon."

While he bowed, again intent on showing her up as the disrespectful party in this, she merely pursed her lips and peered down her nose at him, and walked away. Having enjoyed himself, since he had never before been in a position to trade barbs like that with a woman as close to his former employers as Mrs Urmstone, he smirked as he watched her find Mrs Haffisidge and Mrs Rudgerleigh and begin conversation with them, 'no doubt, about me', he thought to himself.

Quite amused, he surveyed the goings-on in the drawing room, for an indeterminate amount of time; it felt like seconds but it could well have been minutes, until all of a sudden he felt a brush of something on his back and a hand stroke his shoulder.

"I need you to come to my room. *Now!*" the dulcet voice of Lady Vyrrington said to him, *sotto voce.* Whether correct or not, he had an idea of her intentions and so he followed her, managing as he did so to eye out Mrs Urmstone again, just to see the incredulous disapproval on her face.

Chapter XXXIV
Upstairs, Downstairs, in My Lady's Chamber

IT WAS AN IMPENETRABLE MYSTERY. The Countess, whose mind was already utterly besieged by emotions of every kind – amazement, grief, desire, guilt, then paranoia – had also been plagued by curiosity. Provoked upon seeing her former lover, for she had *not* seen her cousin Abel, into whose employment she had sent Blameford in the first place. Even Mrs Ullswell had mentioned seeing him in Italy, yet she was here and Blameford was here, yet no sign of Abel whatsoever. She said none of this while making the long, labyrinthian journey through *Beryl Court*'s corridors, merely keeping an astute and silent lookout the entire way there and even after once she and Blameford were in the privacy of her bedchamber.

"You have come alone, Mr Blameford?" she said, immediately approaching the window, which had among the best views of the gardens.

"I often travel alone, My Lady", he returned, remaining stood by the door after ensuring it was shut properly, "What of it?"

"I mean without my *cousin*. Abel Stirkwhistle! I wrote to him informing him of the date for the funeral. How is it that you received tidings of this event when he did not? Or if he did, how is it that you attend without him?" Her tone was frantic, angry and grief-stricken. Sensing her distress, Blameford disposed with all polite moral, religious and social codes and embraced Her Ladyship, stroking her ebony hair as her head met his breast.

"I have not been in Mr Stirkwhistle's employ for this last month, My Lady," he replied calmly and gently.

"Were you dismissed?"

"Yes, but not by him."

"How do you mean?"

"Mr Stirkwhistle was very pleased with my work. His sister, Miss *Rebecca* Stirkwhistle was not so much."

"She always was disagreeable even as a girl. So, *she* dismissed you?"

"Yes. Mr Stirkwhistle was called away on urgent business in Venice, but would not be gone long enough to need my attendance, so I remained in their rooms in Verona. When he was not there to protest and overrule her, Miss Stirkwhistle did away with my employment. But upon arriving back in England I read of Lord Wilson's death in the newspaper. So, I am come unto you. To give you comfort and solace. And we can finally be together."

"Don't talk so absurdly. On today of all days – for goodness' sake."

"No – don't you see? Your husband's gone. There's no one for Whitlocke to tell and no one else knows."

"We can't be sure of that. The walls have ears; you know this!"

"Let them hear what they want to hear."

"And I was attacked. Out there. In that very corridor. Thrown down the stairs by God-knows-whom. This is all to punish me for something. For this. For us. For *you!*"

She tried to free herself from his arms, but only half-heartedly, as, though she was reluctant to own it in her grief, it was exactly where she wanted to be. As such, he held her strongly, and she found herself exactly as she had been, with her head on his burgeoning chest. Her ear met his heart, which was pounding rapidly.

"I am come unto you to protect you," he whispered smoothly, "And after months apart from you, I want to come *into* you as well."

Lady Vyrrington looked up at him. His lips found hers, and as he kissed her, his tongue lapped her upper lip softly. She closed her eyes to enjoy it, but only for a second. This was her husband's funeral, she remembered. This time she freed herself from his embrace.

"Not today, Jesse," she said, "You could have me any other six days to Sunday such as your desire dictates. But not on *this* day. Today I buried my husband."

"And he's buried. He won't be leaving that mausoleum any time soon."

It was obvious he would not be easily deterred, whether or not Lady Vyrrington had any choice in the matter, for before she knew it, he had taken her strongly by the shoulders and pinned her down on the bed, sitting over her as he began to undress and unbuckle the belt to his breeches. She was powerless – never did she think she would *not* want to have sex with Blameford. Thankfully, they were interrupted. A knock came to the door.

"Wait a minute please," the Countess called quickly, allowing her time to push Blameford off her and regain her composure, mouthing at him "Are you mad?" He cursed under his breath and walked to the window. After ensuring before the looking glass she did not look as though she had been ravaged even slightly – not a lock of hair out of place – she went to the door and opened it slightly; she found Whitlocke stood there.

"My Lady? Is everything all right?" he said.

"I'm sorry Whitlocke – I was suddenly quite overwhelmed by emotion down there. So many people, and Mr Warwick and Mrs Haffisidge have been arguing, and... I came up here to collect myself and get away from it all for five minutes."

"I quite understand, My Lady," Whitlocke returned, bowing slightly, "If you are up to it, the lawyer Mr Jackdawe wants to speak with you."
Lady Vyrrington sighed deeply – the family lawyer was a tiresome and often rude man whose company was relished by very few – but also knew it would be a quick escape from Blameford.

"Yes, very well, I will see him," she returned, exiting the room and making her way down the corridor, taking care not to look back and concentrating completely on getting away.

Chapter XXXV
The Dismissal of Jesse Blameford

"I WILL BE BEHIND YOU presently, My Lady," Whitlocke called after her. Of the many things in which he was most efficient, deceit was certainly one of the higher-ranking. Waiting until she was out of eyeshot, rather than follow her, the butler instead skulked outside the bedchamber door as if he were a skilled poacher waiting to ensnare a brace of pheasants.

Mere minutes later, Blameford, unsuspecting of any danger, came out, at which point Whitlocke pounced. He grabbed the former footman by both broad shoulders and pinned him against the wall, holding him in place with one forearm across his throat.

"What the fuck do you think you are doing?" Blameford choked, resisting powerlessly against the deceptively strong Whitlocke.

"I could very well ask the same of *you*, sir," the butler returned, "But we both know the answer to that question, don't we? Have you no respect for the dead, Mr Blameford? Lord Wilson is barely cold in the tomb. And you want to make free with his marital bed, do you? Or supplant his place in it?"

Blameford said nothing, just gritted his teeth and struggling as he tried to release himself from Whitlocke's grip.

"I think you can take this as your *official* dismissal, Mr Blameford. If you had time to unpack, I wouldn't have bothered if I were you."

"You can't dismiss me."

"Quite sure about that, are you?" Whitlocke quipped in reply, "You see, actually, as butler, I have the authority to dismiss and eject any servant from the house in any manner I see fit. Especially when it concerns inappropriate behaviour towards the mistress of the house. That gives me ample grounds. So be gone from here within the hour or a constable will be summoned to ensure that you are. Clear?"

Desperately, Blameford bit Whitlocke's arm. In the shot of pain that followed, the butler was forced to let him go. Not looking back, his face flushed crimson with rage, Blameford stormed away.

Whitlocke looked down at his arm. His livery had not torn in Blameford's teeth, nor had any blood been drawn, but the bite marks were visible. He had half a mind to pursue the former footman, but decided that, being the funeral of his beloved employer Lord Wilson, a scene would be the last thing any of them needed.

Covering his sleeve with his other hand, he went back in the direction of the stairs to return to the ground floor.

Chapter XXXVI
Lord Wilson's Will

MR JACKDAWE, WHO COUNTED MRS Urmstone among his clients as well as the Vyrrington family, was a short and stocky man whose hair almost looked as though it did not fit the rest of his head, often cropped too short on the one side. Were it not for his impressive credentials and qualifications, and the reputation for efficiency that preceded him, his ill-kept appearance would bely his being a lawyer in any manner imaginable. He stood in the hallway at the foot of the stairs, awaiting Lady Vyrrington, who – graceful to the last, regardless of her grief – glided down the staircase to receive him. His lips, which always looked swollen to a point whereupon they would have belonged more becomingly on a fish than on a man, formed as close to a smile as thought possible.

"My Lady, my condolences..." Mr Jackdawe was brief in giving his sympathy; Lady Vyrrington expected nothing more.

"Ah, Mr Jackdawe. You *have* just missed the service," said she.

He seemed to condone this, and continued as if she had not spoken.

"...Your husband's Will and Testament requires reading tomorrow."

She did not answer immediately – the Countess had not yet reconciled herself to the idea of Will readings and the like. In fact, she barely knew the contents of her own. Law in general bored her, and paperwork and documentation were chores that she had always been happy to let Lord Wilson get on with. Now she was the *de facto* head of the household until her son Spencer came of age, matters of notary, amendments, codicils and revisions were the least of her worries. Accounts, ledgers, bookkeeping and estate management, in the absence of the funds to employ someone to do all this on her behalf, were now her duty. And if tomorrow was to be Lord Wilson's Will reading, she would find out for herself, despite Whitlocke's prior warning, just how abysmal her financial situation really was. Her thoughts had diverted her attention for what felt like a considerable amount of time, her expression was bereft of emotion, wrought to a completely blank stare. It was the first time Mr Jackdawe appeared to be endowed with a glimmer of concern.

"My Lady?" said the lawyer, "is something amiss?"

"No, nothing," she replied, "I am merely tired, I expect. Will you partake of some refreshment, Mr

Jackdawe? My cook and her pupil have excelled themselves with cake. Or perhaps just a glass of wine?"

"Thank you, Lady Vyrrington, but I must decline," Mr Jackdawe replied, "I must go into town. I have to acquire for myself a room at The Saint Barbara's Arms for the night so that we can convene tomorrow."

"Ah, very well then sir. As you wish."
Lady Vyrrington smiled and walked him to the front door.

"I can't think where Whitlocke must have gone," she remarked at the butler's absence.

"Think nothing of it, My Lady, I'll see myself out. Actually, that reminds me – Mr George Whitlocke and Miss Amethyst Cheshill are to attend the Will reading tomorrow as well."

"For what reason? Are you suggesting that they too are mentioned?"

"There are one or two complicated clauses in your husband's Will that require the attention of all three of you."

"I understand. Now, you will take that glass of wine won't you, Mr Jackdawe?"

"Thank you, My Lady. I suppose *a* glass of wine cannot do me too much harm."

During the gathering following Lord Wilson's funeral, Mr Jackdawe made several less-than-subtle attempts to persuade Lady Vyrrington to allow him a room for the night. She did not give in, and so he was forced to hire a room at *The St. Barbara's Arms* after all.

They reconvened the next day in what was now the Countess' study, although she did not even touch any of the documents or books of Lord Wilson's, and left them as they were.

Whitlocke and Amethyst were both seated either side of Lady Vyrrington by her desk, while Mr Jackdawe stood and presented the contents of the Will. It was a large and well-drawn piece of documentation, written in excruciatingly twisted cursive hand that, despite her best efforts, Lady Vyrrington could not decipher upside-down.

"As you are aware, Lady Vyrrington, your husband bequeaths that *'the house and estate of Beryl Court in Hampshire and all properties and possessions therein'* are yours for the duration of *your* lifetime and are to be divided between you and Spencer Aloysius Vyrrington, currently the Fifth Viscount Beryl and the heir apparent to the title of the Fifth Earl of Vyrrington, as well as the Vyrrington Earldom in its entirety when he comes of age at seventeen years."

"What about the other children?" asked Lady Vyrrington, "My daughters? Minerva? Venetia? And Edward, my other son? What does my husband leave *them*?"

"As you are *also* aware, My Lady, your daughters are, by law, *unable* to inherit their father's estate unless one of them marries the heir apparent. And *incest* requires that all bequests within the Earldom of Vyrrington be *broken*. And so, unless your sons both die before they come of age, the Ladies Minerva and Venetia will not garner the Countess' coronet within the Vyrrington Earldom."

"I see. So no money for any of them?"

"Oh no, there *is* money, Lady Vyrrington. Each of the children is left an income of a thousand pounds per year, which will become available to them when they marry. That *includes* the aforementioned Spencer Vyrrington, who is entitled to that income in addition to the rest of the estate."

"That *is* a relief."

"Now this is where the Will becomes complicated, My Lady. Your husband's mother – the former Countess Lady Adeliza Vyrrington – was less-than-*mindful* with regard to her expenditure prior to your husband's inheriting the estate and the Earldom. As you may have already been told, you are only left enough money to support yourself, your children and probably only one or two servants. The incomes for your children following their marriage are being kept in separate accounts within 'Mullens and Cooke Finances in London'. Accounts which you – My Lady – are unable to access according to your late husband's Will."

"I am unable to access the accounts of my own children?"

"A precaution His Lordship and I agreed with Mr Mullens and Mr Cooke as the overseers of the Vyrrington estate money; Lady Adeliza's – shall we call it – spendthrift nature – was exacerbated primarily in times of grief and distress. You may consider Lord Wilson overcautious there and 'tis not my place to judge you, My Lady. But in the interests that your children may have something to live on after your death, this *is* the best course."

"I understand. My butler Mr Whitlocke has informed me of Lady Adeliza's extravagance. I have already dismissed the majority of my staff. I will be retaining Mr Whitlocke and Miss Cheshill here, and I am keeping my cook Mrs Trudgedawes within the house on low pay until my sisters leave for Dover; she is to go with them as their new cook."

"And now *regarding* the complexly-natured clause that I was given reason to mention yesterday to My Lady," Mr Jackdawe recommenced, "This particular amendment to the Will expresses Lord Wilson's desires to see that Mr Whitlocke and Miss Cheshill suitably waged in spite of the finances retained in the inheritance."

"And how may I ask is that such a difficult thing to comprehend?" asked Lady Vyrrington.

"It is the reasons for *why* he wishes to see them suitably waged that is the complicated matter. He wishes to see them…"
The lawyer paused.

"…*Married.*"

"*Married?*"

"Indeed. He writes that '*in order to ensure that Mr George Edward Whitlocke, butler to my household, and Miss Amethyst Judith Hazel Cheshill, my Countess' lady's maid, remain both financially secure and do not separate should the estate collapse, I hereby express the desire to see them matrimonially bound, and bequeath to them the sum of five hundred pounds with which they may use to pay for such an arrangement.*' That is the clause in the words of Lord Wilson himself."

"I am not sure how to respond to that, Mr Jackdawe. Are there any other mentions? My cook Mrs Trudgedawes?"

"Sadly no. That is all there is to convey to you in Lord Wilson's Will. A copy has been drawn up for you. In the meantime, My Lady, I can only advise that husbands are found for your daughters in order to secure them with the money left to them."

The four of them stood up, and Whitlocke opened the study door, holding it open for Mr Jackdawe to exit. The lawyer turned in the doorway and bowed to the Countess.

"As ever, your humble servant," he murmured; Lady Vyrrington had never known Jackdawe to be a humble anything, but nevertheless received the gesture graciously, and watched him narrowly as he left her sight.

Chapter XXXVII
Marital Prospects

AFTER THE LAWYER HAD DEPARTED, Lady Vyrrington watched Whitlocke out in the hallway. He was clearly hesitating about re-entering the study.

"Is he gone, Whitlocke?" she asked.

"Yes, he's gone!" he returned after a moment of pause.

"Then come back in here – I need to speak with you."

She had never known him to dawdle over anything before, regardless of how awkward the matter may be. He usually relished an opportunity to exacerbate her temper (or so she was convinced). After a few seconds though, he did eventually return to the room, if only for the lack of choice. The butler remained stood before his mistress at the desk. Amethyst had remained seated.

"Did you know about this, Whitlocke?" the Countess asked the butler sharply, "This marriage plan?"

He shuffled uncomfortably.

"Lord Wilson did mention it, yes."

"And you neglected to inform me, why?"

"Seemed in poor taste to disclose a thing like that to someone so recently widowed, My Lady, if it comes to that."

"Oh no you don't. Don't pretend to have any regard for my feelings in this matter. You were afraid I would say 'no'!"

"Do I have reason to think otherwise?"

"Now you watch yourself, Whitlocke!" she pointed a long, slender finger squarely at him, and her nostrils expanded as though steam or smoke were to billow out with her slowly flaring temper, "Lord Wilson is gone now. If there's any good to come of it, it will make dismissing you that much easier…"

Amethyst squeaked, and the Countess turned to her; whatever her maid had attempted to say or wanted to, she had obviously reconsidered, as her face was now directed pointedly at the floor. While Whitlocke was the perennial thorn in her side ever there to exasperate her and provoke ire whenever possible, Amethyst was the calming influence that counteracted it. And to see Amethyst fear her was evidence that Lady Vyrrington had failed her again and again; she may as well have left her in the workhouse at the mercy of the cruel wardens there. The Countess closed her eyes with this thought in mind, and said gently:

"…Such as it is, I have not yet decided what I am going to do."

Whitlocke looked confused.

"My Lady?" said he.

"You may go back to work," Lady Vyrrington told her servants, "Irrespective of His Lordship's words and wishes, *I* have the final say in this matter."

"My Lady, please –" Amethyst began, but once again she thought twice and quietened herself.

"You may postpone dinner; tell Mrs Trudgedawes I will have a cold supper on a tray in my room, Amethyst. At around six, if you please. I will not require either of you again until then."

They bowed and curtseyed respectively before leaving Lady Vyrrington to her thoughts.

It was a match she had opposed since first she saw its conception. A week into her accommodation in Berylford, when she was a guest in the house of Mrs Haffisidge, Lady Oliviera Isaacs as she was then, was invited for an interview with Lord Wilson one morning. It was her first visit to *Beryl Court* and, rather than have a carriage drive her and arrive by way of the front drive, she took the West Stairs, which were a steep uphill climb that actually led into the gardens. It was there that Lady Oliviera met the man that was to become her husband, and unfailingly loyal, Amethyst arrived shortly afterwards, serving as chaperone, since the acquaintance with Lord Vyrrington was otherwise a secret. Amethyst met Whitlocke, who was but a footman back then, and was taken immediately. Age and stress had not been kind to his looks; two decades ago, Whitlocke was a strapping young man with broad shoulders and a flat stomach, and his hair curly in places rather than the lank, straw-textured state it possessed these days. Between those hulking, brutish, thuggish beasts of workhouse wardens who beat her and those limp, emaciated, wretched creatures of fellow inmates who were beat with her, Amethyst had never before beheld a handsome man, let alone one who looked upon her with warmth and kindness in his sapphire eyes. In their faux-sisterly conversations around the mirror as per their usual ritual, these were the unusually poetic spells of near-Quixotry that Amethyst found herself divulging, to both Lady Vyrrington's amazement and disturbance. She had never found Whitlocke to be anything Amethyst described. As cold and distant as he was toadying and almost unnaturally loyal to his master. A faithful dog would probably be more likely to commit betrayal than Whitlocke to Lord Wilson. And yet, all the same, by rights he had. The day Whitlocke had first discovered her liaison with Jesse Blameford he could have done it. Revealed all to the late Lord Vyrrington and done away with his two enemies in the household in one fell swoop.

The Countess had to wonder to herself the reason why Whitlocke had not, even though deep down she knew the answer. She had threatened him with it often enough – of this too she was quite aware. Amethyst was the reason.

To get rid of Lady Vyrrington would be to get rid of Amethyst: the one woman Whitlocke loved more than anything. All hope of being with and marrying her would be dashed if the Countess were to be ousted from *Beryl Court*. Lady Vyrrington knew it herself – Amethyst was her insurance and her saviour.

'I can't repay her that in any other way,' the Countess thought to herself, drumming her fingers on the desk in contemplation, 'She loves him. Much as I despise him, she adores him. For all she's done for me – failing that, though I am loath to admit it – for all *both* of them have done for me, can I really deny them their chance at happiness? When it has even been decreed as a final wish of My Lord husband? Does my hatred for George Whitlocke outweigh my love for Amethyst? The man who could well have seen to it that I was thrown to the ground, my reputation rent to shreds, my livelihood all but spent, my sins laid bare for the satisfaction of the gluttonous gossips of society and my amoral deeds exposed to the most unforgiving creatures to walk the earth. Lord knows the Martyr Himself would hesitate to show me mercy and absolve me for the things I have done. And the woman who was little more than a wretch when first I laid eyes on her, whom I have loved and protected like a sister. I can deny him his happiness, but not without denying her hers. I do not have that right. I have that power, but I do not have that right.'

She placed her head in her hands. Had she the strength, she felt like clawing her eyes out, just to spare herself the consciousness of what she was about to do. Make George Whitlocke the happiest he had ever been. To reward him for his loyalty.

BOOK NINE
Arrivals and Departures, Unexpected

Chapter XXXVIII
A Character Reference

WITH LITTLE DELAY, AS SOON as permission from Her Ladyship had been given, arrangements were made with the Reverend Helton and Whitlocke and Amethyst were married within the fortnight. There was little frivolity or fuss; no magnanimity or grandeur. It was the wedding of two servants, after all – regardless of whose servants they were. However, affording Amethyst one gift for her day, the Lady Vyrrington had requested from the reverend that the bells be swungen, to mark the day as one of jubilation and joy. But being as it was, a servants' wedding, it was attended by few. The Countess herself and Mrs Trudgedawes looked on as witnesses. The latter stayed only shortly afterwards, before (following a tearful farewell to her mistress, who had always treated her with the greatest respect and compliments) left Berylford to accept her new position at *Vellhampton Park* in Kent with Lady Vyrrington's sisters.

Time can be deceitful at times: in some instants, wherein little occurs in the lives of folk, hours can feel stretched out to feel as long as weeks. In others, when chaos and calamity befall, the opposite is true. Two months passed, though Lady Vyrrington would have sworn blind that she had only buried her husband but a week thence. Time had performed its cunning dance and she came to realise she had stopped writing to her cousin Lady Riva Styridge, still in want of reply to her now-numerous letters. Though to be eternally bound in blood, whether either party liked it or not, their friendship was broken; all that connected them were the branches of the family tree. With virtually no servants and very little for which to entertain, life at *Beryl Court* became very quiet, and a lot of the recent events faded into distant memory. No one saw hide nor hair of Jesse Blameford, and whatever shred of hope there was that Joshua would be found, dead or alive, was all but gone forever.

The Countess was therefore surprised to receive an invitation to take tea with Mrs Rudgerleigh one afternoon, as the two were not prone to socialising without other members of their social circle such as Mrs Haffisidge or the Misses Osborne and Gwynne. Mrs Rudgerleigh owned a house with several rooms that she let out to lodgers. It was quite central to the town, at the beginning of Elxham Road. The square had a schoolhouse at its centre, and so Mrs Rudgerleigh, the schoolmistress, and Mr Gussage, the schoolkeeper, who was also one of Mrs Rudgerleigh's tenants, did not have far to walk to work. It turned out that the reason that Mrs Rudgerleigh had asked Lady Vyrrington to tea was to pursue a conversation regarding one of her more recently-acquired tenants.

"Thank you for taking the afternoon to see me, My Lady," Mrs Rudgerleigh said, once she had shown Lady Vyrrington to the upstairs sitting room, which was nicely kept and simply furnished.

"Is there something you wish to discuss, Mrs Rudgerleigh?" Lady Vyrrington asked.

"I was not sure if you were aware..." returned Mrs Rudgerleigh, "...that I took Mr Blameford on as one of my lodgers."

Lady Vyrrington choked on her tea. She had not seen Blameford since the day he showed up unannounced at her husband's funeral. She had also never asked Whitlocke after him, for she had no reason to – she knew nothing of his dismissing him, whether or not she even regarded him as still on *Beryl Court*'s payroll – she could not have retained him now, even if she had wanted to. Recalling she was in company, Her Ladyship could not contemplate long over this. Recovering herself quickly, she looked up at Mrs Rudgerleigh, whose face spoke volumes of concern.

"Excuse me," Lady Vyrrington said quite calmly, despite her inner emotions playing all instruments to the contrary, "You took whom? Mr... *Blameford* did you say?"

"Indeed. I was quite surprised to find that he required accommodation as I was given to understand that he held hitherto a position in *your* household. As a footman?"

"He did. Once upon a time. Might I ask what business this is of yours, Mrs Rudgerleigh? No offence intended."

"And none taken, to be sure, milady," returned Mrs Rudgerleigh, "Mr Blameford is seeking a new occupation, as, from what he tells me, service was one undertaken ill-advisedly. For some reason, Mr Blameford seems *averse* to the idea of asking you for a reference. I was surprised that you did not provide him with one prior to your dismissal of him."

"Forgive me, Mrs Rudgerleigh, but you have been misled in this regard," returned Lady Vyrrington, "I engaged Mr Blameford as a manservant to my cousin, Mr Abel Stirkwhistle on a trip abroad. I regarded him as an employee of the Stirkwhistle household thenceforth. There was no dismissal of which *I* was ever aware. So this is why you have invited me here? To request a reference for your tenant?"

"Indeed, My Lady. In short."

"My cousin Mr Stirkwhistle was an absentee from my husband's funeral. He has not written to confirm as much, which, I admit is unusual, but I must assume he has stayed on in Italy. As Mr Blameford's next-most-recent employer, I suppose I can oblige you, Mrs Rudgerleigh. I shall have my butler Mr Whitlocke bring it to you within the next couple of days."

The door was heard opening at that point, and lo, Mr Blameford appeared. His absence these last months had rid Lady Oliviera's memory of his figure and stature – he looked broader and more handsome than she had remembered. However, his expression bore no such attraction to her.

"Good day Mrs Rudgerleigh..." he then nodded curtly to Lady Vyrrington, "...My Lady. I have had a word with the carpenter regarding those beams for the schoolroom, Mrs Rudgerleigh. He will have them planed for tomorrow."

"Thank you, Mr Blameford. Lady Vyrrington was just giving me the reference I require for you." Blameford was indifferent to the statement.

"Was she? Indeed – I hope all is to your satisfaction?"

"I trust you gave no reason for it not to be?" Mrs Rudgerleigh chuckled in response.

"No indeed," returned Lady Vyrrington, her eyes fixed on Blameford, somewhat hurt at his bitterness towards her.

"Well, in that case, I will repair to my room. Good day."

He then disappeared upstairs.

Had she been alone, she would have gone after him. The Countess may not have recognised the months that passed to have been months, but she realised nearly every day of his absence from her life, she had yearned for his attention. But, again, since she was in company, Lady Vyrrington had to regain her self-awareness and pay heed to Mrs Rudgerleigh's further conversation.

"Just the particulars of his employment, and those of his character will suffice if you please, My Lady." she said.

"For that I am relieved," sighed Lady Vyrrington, "I have known Jesse Blameford since he was nineteen years of age, so almost ten years. I would be unlikely to recall the majority of that time in great detail as I'm sure you'll appreciate?"

"Indeed not, My Lady – as I say, the basic gist of it all will suffice. He seems of a pleasant sort, at any rate. I fear I shall have no trouble from him. But formalities are formalities."

Lady Vyrrington merely smiled in return and, believing this line of conversation could only hold out for so much longer, stood up.

"Well thank you, Mrs Rudgerleigh; I will have that written up and brought to you forthwith..."

She turned to go back down the stairs so as to leave the house, but returned to Mrs Rudgerleigh a moment longer.

"...Actually, if you'll forgive me..." she said, "...please pass my compliments *on* to Mr Blameford. I fear I may have offended him when last I saw him. It was at Lord Wilson's funeral. His arrival was quite unexpected, and I believe I may have acted quite rudely towards him. The emotion and all that, but that should be no excuse."

Mrs Rudgerleigh once again bore an expression of deep concern, and also a fleck of perplexity.

"But of course, My Lady," she returned.

"Just inform him I wish him the best of luck, and that if the House of Vyrrington may still be of use to him in future, he need only ask."

These were words she herself hardly believed she would be saying to another person. 'Lord only knows what she must think of me right now,' the Countess thought to herself, observing Mrs Rudgerleigh's increasingly-confused expression.

"As you wish, My Lady. I bid you a good afternoon."

A dismissal was welcome, lest she should embarrass herself further. Lady Vyrrington took that as her bye to depart. Overwrought with her own confused feelings about Blameford, she had no choice but to make back for *Beryl Court*, and stifle them in her solitude.

Chapter XXXIX
The Fate of Mrs Rudgerleigh

BERYLFORD WAS NOT A LARGE town in which goings-on of note were common; not enough to appear in the printed presses at any account. But by way of the mouth or pen of the seemingly constantly-to-hand Mrs Urmstone, events worth knowing about were usually common knowledge about the town within hours of their happening. Such was the case when Lady Vyrrington received a letter from Mrs Urmstone, no more than five days following her visit to Mrs Rudgerleigh's house, informing her of their dear friend's sudden and unexpected passing. As usual, the Countess was at breakfast when perusing her correspondences, and was so profoundly shocked by reading Mrs Urmstone's letter that she dropped her butter knife mid-spread attending to her toasted bread, causing a clatter down the dining room that alerted Whitlocke's instant attention. When he questioned her on what was amiss, Her Ladyship found herself barely able to answer, wrought to breathlessness in her utter astonishment and sadness.

My Lady Oliviera…

…Mrs Urmstone's letter read…

…You will forgive me for not delivering this news in person but time is simply an indulgence of which we are all bereft. Thus you will further excuse me if I am brief.

The simple fact of the matter is – Clara Rudgerleigh is dead…

That was the offending passage that had rendered the Countess utterly spent of all other directions of thought.
'I saw the woman less than a week ago, alive and well!' her mind spoke 'What on Earth can have happened?'

After asking Whitlocke to fetch a clean knife, she continued to read:

…There is little I can report since the only witnesses were her pupils, from whom the truest account of the incident is unlikely to be acquired, and Zephaniah Gussage, who was to hand at the time when it occurred, but from whom an intelligible explanation cannot be gained through the thick veil of tears. I have seen widows and widowers young and old who appear to have been in better states than him. Mr Gussage is in the most

extreme maelstrom of grief to which I have ever borne witness.

I think any attendance on him may be appreciated at this time.

Yours most faithfully,
Elspeth Urmstone

She had decided what she was to do even before reading Mrs Urmstone's instruction. The Countess would return to Mrs Rudgerleigh's house, and pay her respects to Mr Gussage. It would be the day following, however, for the custom in Berylford was to wait at least a day to visit a person in mourning – a custom lost on the ravenous need for information of Mrs Urmstone - but, indeed, at noon the following day, Lady Vyrrington found herself back where she had been just days before, except that she found herself conversing with a deeply-grieved Zephaniah Gussage instead.

His aspect, which was often dilapidated and dishevelled, posture slumped to one side somewhat, the grizzled hair on both his face and head unkempt, his clothes appeared ill-fitting and were patched in places. The one thing that stood out from all of this were his eyes, which were the brightest shade of blue. It was easy to imagine, not just to Lady Vyrrington, but to many ladies of the town, that in his youth, he would have been quite a handsome man. Except these eyes, which still glistened their aquamarine colour, like crystal over water, were lined and veined with threads of red; those which tell of a man exhausted, bereft of sleep and whose happiness seemed all but spent. Lady Vyrrington knew not where to begin their conversation; Mr Gussage ended up commencing himself:

"She was so well that morning," he said to the Countess, a hand half-clasped upon his face, "Nothing out of the ordinary whatsoever. Dear Clara. Dedicated to her pupils was she. Adamant that she would teach them to go beyond this little market town. Those poor creatures. They had to see that. She was up there, in front of her students. She was writing on the blackboard; she turned to me and she says 'Zephaniah, I think I've stood up too quickly. I've come over all aquiver. Could you open the window?' I does as she says, but while my back was turned, I heard this thud from behind me. Like a sack of potatoes being dropped from a great height. I turned again and saw no Clara by the blackboard; just an arm on the floor from behind the desk. I had to run over of course and I knew what had happened even before I felt for her heart. She was gone before she hit the floor, I wager. Doctor Street said it was a stroke what killed her."

He buried his face in a dirty handkerchief. Lady Vyrrington, still reduced to silence upon seeing Mr Gussage like this – the very opposite of the man she knew – looked at him and, in the first useful gesture she had made that afternoon, offered him her lace handkerchief. He declined it.

"No, My Lady, I must not," he said, "What would anyone else think? A crying man taking a handkerchief off a *lady*?"

"Let them think what they like, Mr Gussage," replied Lady Vyrrington, at last finding something to say, "*They* are not the ones in *mourning*. Now go on, I insist that you take it."

Thus he obeyed, wiping his eyes. However, upon the door suddenly opening, he clutched it in his fist and turned around to see who had entered. Lady Vyrrington was indifferent as to seeing it was Mr Blameford. They briefly exchanged glances, before he exited again.

"Forgive me, My Lady," said Mr Gussage, "Allow me to see your handkerchief washed."

"I will not hear of it, Mr Gussage," she replied, "I will see to the laundering of my handkerchief. There is no need for you to undertake such duties. The duty you *will* need to undertake is the arrangements of our dear Clara's funeral."

She stood up, and he followed her.

"Ah, Mr Gussage, I had forgotten..." Lady Vyrrington placed her hand in her reticule, in order to find a written reference for Mr Blameford she had prepared for Mrs Rudgerleigh. However, considering their current relationship, and the frailty of Mr Gussage's own emotions, she took her hand out again.

"I'm sorry, My Lady?" said Mr Gussage. Lady Vyrrington chuckled, her eyes looking at Blameford's door.

"...And I appear to have forgotten again. How my memory grieves me, Mr Gussage."

"Of course, My Lady. I did forget to mention, were you aware that someone had moved in opposite Jeremiah Devonshire's?"

"I was *not* aware."

"Three. One of them appeared afflicted. A stroke I th–"

He then realised what he had said, and sat back down, placing the handkerchief to his eyes once again.

Chapter XL
The Stirkwhistles

THOUGH SHE WAS RELUCTANT TO **leave Mr Gussage** in such a state, Lady Vyrrington exited Mrs Rudgerleigh's house and immediately was met by Mrs Urmstone and Mrs Haffisidge in the street. Both ladies seemed agitated and out of breath; Mrs Urmstone's cheeks puffed out as she stopped to curtsey to Her Ladyship.

"You appear to have been running, Elspeth!" Lady Vyrrington observed, "Be careful who sees you, now. You don't want to get a reputation." She then looked at Mrs Haffisidge, who managed to hide a smirk, knowing the Countess had been deliberately ironic.

"Your butler up at Beryl Court told us where you had gone, My Lady Oliviera," said Mrs Urmstone, sounding anxious and between deep intakes of breath, "And so we came directly. Are you aware of what has happened opposite Devonshire's?"

The Countess was somewhat perplexed – Mrs Urmstone was prepared to inform her of Mrs Rudgerleigh's death by letter but insisted on delivering news of a new arrival in the town in person. It made no logical sense, even for her.

"Mr Gussage mentioned a family of three had moved in…" she returned, her perplexity clear as crystal within her voice, "…which I suppose is newsworthy because no one has occupied that house for six, *seven* years?"

"Indeed, My Lady," returned Mrs Haffisidge, "Mr Devonshire was asked if he might take it on, but since he is here so very seldom these days, he thought it would not be worth the added expense."

"*Returning to the point!*" Mrs Urmstone interjected, sounding exasperated, "My Lady Oliviera, you were correctly informed. A family of three *has* arrived in Berylford.

"But you will not believe *which* three!" said Mrs Haffisidge, expressing an equal amount of disquiet.

"Mr Gussage also mentioned a stroke," Lady Vyrrington said as she walked quickly with her friends towards where Jeremiah Devonshire had made his house into a rag-and-bone shop, "His emotions are so frail at present. It brought him to tears at the mention of the malady."

"Just wait, My Lady Oliviera, just you wait!" Mrs Urmstone returned, "You will be equally as shocked as Mrs Haffisidge and I!"

She rapped upon the door knocker and let herself into the newcomers' house; an action that only added to Her

Ladyship's confusion. Mrs Haffisidge followed her into the hallway, and then both ladies stood aside to allow the Countess to precede them in the doorway.

"You must go in first, My Lady," said Mrs Haffisidge.

"Am I acquainted with these people?" replied Lady Vyrrington, "Is *Berylford* acquainted with these people?"

"*Very* well acquainted, My Lady Oliviera," returned Mrs Urmstone, "This is why it came to us all as such a shock."

The Countess was still just as confounded as to whom her friends could be referring. Nevertheless, she turned, inhaled deeply, and walked in.

Her eyes immediately met a figure slumped in a chair. It was a man she felt she knew, but did not recognise. Zephaniah Gussage had been correct in saying he exhibited the look of a stroke sufferer. His entire left side appeared sunken. Behind his chair was stood a spindly dark-haired woman whose presence gave off an unsettling air. She had a hand pressed on the back of the chair, her fingers like the talons of an eagle. They appeared cold and as if made of steel. Her hair was arranged highly, much the same as Lady Vyrrington's, and although the same colour, the locks appeared as wires, stretched to their longest and tied very tightly.

She was, if anything, a wingless harpy, or perhaps a creature whom, if one believed such things to be possible, would go abroad of an evening to hunt a child to eat. The very air around her was encumbered by neither warmth nor love.

Mrs Urmstone and Mrs Haffisidge edged into the room behind Lady Vyrrington, who stared open-mouthed at the dilapidated figure before her in the chair. She finally knew who it was.

"Abel?" she said hoarsely.

"My brother has not the energy to speak at present," replied the spindly woman.

"Oh, dear me. Is that Miss Rebecca Stirkwhistle?" Lady Vyrrington exclaimed, "I would never have recognised you. You were but a babe in arms when last I saw you."

"A quarter-century has passed since then," returned Miss Rebecca, coldly.

"Your brother may have mentioned me? My name is Oliviera. The Countess of Vyrrington. I am your second cousin. Our grandmothers were sisters?"

"My brother frequently mentioned you, My Lady, albeit you were known as Lady Vyrrington and there was no 'second cousin' about it. I was never taught to recognise distant family. Growing up in such a *tight-knit* clan as the Stirkwhistles of Iverleigh Warren."

Miss Rebecca's voice was as hollow as she appeared. There was naught but ice contained within her words. Lady Vyrrington could now imagine her crouched over a cauldron like one of Macbeth's witches, concocting and conjuring to her heart's content, if such a thing existed within her. She was unsettling to all three ladies. The citizenry of Berylford – male and female – were known for their warmth and hospitality. It was easy to see that Miss Rebecca Stirkwhistle would never uphold such a position.

"I suppose that should explain why no one wrote informing me of your coming. Abel was always so diligent in contacting me well in advance of any visits he made here."

"He has lost the use of his writing hand, along with his speech so even a dictation was not feasible," returned Miss Rebecca.

"Tell me, how did this happen?" Lady Vyrrington asked Miss Rebecca, and then she finally realised that both Stirkwhistles were wearing black.

"You cannot have heard – no. You could not have known – you *did* not know!" Lady Vyrrington referred of course to the death of Mrs Rudgerleigh.

"Abel was to travel to Italy," explained Miss Rebecca, seeming to ignore the Countess' remarks and perplexity, and moved slowly from behind her stricken brother's chair, "Our father had recently consigned himself there for the remainder of his retirement. His health began to dwindle and Abel feared that he would die. By the time we arrived at Verona, our father had indeed departed this life forever. His lawyers were based in Venice, so Abel left me to arrange our father's burial while he attended his estate. A few days later *I* received a letter from Venice reporting that the heat had had a dreadful effect on Abel's health. His brain had been exhausted – the physician said – and that the burial of our father would have to be committed here in England so that Abel could leave Italy. The physician told us that Abel was fortunate to have survived his stroke."

"And so your father is buried in England?

"Back at our ancestral home with the rest of the family in Kensington. Abel had often spoken of Berylford as a place to live following our father's death. Nevertheless, I took him to Wales first to allow him some repose from all that has happened. There, he was fortunate enough to have found love. With the woman we employed as his nurse. Would you come in, my dear?"

From the room adjacent emerged the figure of a small and markedly thin woman with wavy golden blonde hair and a somewhat prominent nose. She could have easily been mistaken for the scullery maid, such were the state of her clothes and apron, much-stained with soot and gravy. She did not look comfortable to be in a social situation, despite the best efforts of Lady Vyrrington to bear a kindly expression.

"Lady Vyrrington..." Miss Rebecca continued, "...This is Liza: *Mrs* Abel Stirkwhistle."
The Countess turned back to Abel, who was unable to return with any expression.

"So, you are married, Abel," she said quietly.

"Is it likely that Mr Stirkwhistle will regain the use of his speech?" asked Mrs Haffisidge.

"Oh I do–" Mrs Stirkwhistle began, but stopped when Miss Rebecca cleared her throat ostentatiously.

" –Rather, *we* do hope so," she corrected herself, "Though I am not yet aware as to when he could start talking again. It may be days; weeks; months?"
Lady Vyrrington and Mrs Urmstone both were still rather unsettled by Miss Rebecca's icy and unpleasant nature. The former smiled at Mrs Stirkwhistle.

"Well, the sooner the better, I am sure," she said, "It was good to meet both of you."
She walked over to Abel and bent down to kiss him upon his forehead. Before she could do so, Miss Rebecca hissed at her:

"You must not kiss him! You may hold his hand."

Mrs Haffisidge and Mrs Urmstone looked at one another, astounded. Their shock was doubled however, when Lady Vyrrington, in spite of being of higher rank and authority, did as Miss Rebecca had said. Silently, after she had done so, all three ladies saw themselves out.

Immediately, Mrs Haffisidge and Mrs Urmstone moved in front of Lady Vyrrington and blocked her path.

"Really, ladies, we might take tea up at Beryl Court if you rely on my company *that* much," she said, and carried on walking.

"My Lady Oliviera, what just occurred in that house?" asked Mrs Urmstone.

"We have just paid a visit to our dear Mr Abel Stirkwhistle and his family."

"I meant with *Miss* Stirkwhistle!"

"Elspeth is referring to your taking a command from someone of lower class than yourself!" said Mrs Haffisidge, "I have never seen such a thing happen in Berylford before!"

"We will not condone it!" added Mrs Urmstone.

"And what was I to say to a young woman who has suffered aplenty in recent times?" returned Lady

Vyrrington calmly, "Do you not think *I* would be *condoning* her suffering if I rebuked her for instructing me against affecting the welfare of her brother?"

"My Lady, close your eyes to my impertinence..." said Mrs Haffisidge, "...but have *you* not endured a lot in these recent months also? Are you truly so selfless that all other members of society's problems are superior to your own?"

Lady Vyrrington did not answer right away.

"I believe that I have suffered enough to know what conflicts and disputes can arise from such situations," she finally said, "I believe that it does not do well for one's place in society to assert said place, and I would rather alleviate the suffering of others. So yes. I am that truly selfless, Mrs Haffisidge. Because it is the better thing."

She turned on her heel and walked back towards her house. The two ladies followed her, Mrs Urmstone calling out:

"My Lady! Is the offer of tea still open?"

Chapter XLI
Lady Vyrrington Has Questions

LADY VYRRINGTON KEPT TO HERSELF that evening, staying in her bedchamber. After Amethyst had ascertained if she needed anything else following her dinner service, she sat alone by the fire, a glass of wine clutched in one hand, drumming her stiletto-long fingers on the arm of her chair with the other. Solitary was her existence at this time, and that was just how she desired it. Her dinner of roast mutton had given her little satisfaction – her appetite was practically nonexistent, owing to her preoccupation with another matter. She was contemplating over a thought that had been haunting her since learning of Mrs Rudgerleigh's death, and of Abel's stroke. These incidents both had only one individual in common – the Countess' former lover and servant, Jesse Blameford.

She could not confess or confide any of this to Mrs Urmstone or Mrs Haffisidge, for neither could really be trusted with matters of secrecy – Mrs Urmstone's excitable nature loosened her tongue at the slightest potential scandal, and Mrs Haffisidge could only keep it from her friend for so long. Amethyst would be more trustworthy, though what she relayed to her husband Whitlocke, Lady Oliviera would not dare risk, if only to deny Whitlocke the pleasure of being right about Blameford all along. And as for Abel, whether she was a Countess or not, it was clear that Miss Rebecca paid no mind to status in the Stirkwhistle household, and Lady Vyrrington would not be welcome there. The Countess was resolved eventually to pursue only one course – to confront Blameford personally, and she would do it that night. Any further procrastination on the matter would only rob her of more peace of mind than it had already extorted from her, and her sleep accrued.

Still in the heart of mourning Lord Wilson, black was a convenient colour at this time, her furs – pelts of dark-coloured animals – glittered and glistened in the candlelight as she dressed for her venture abroad that night. She let herself out, the dagger-sharp heels of her high black boots clacked against the hard, wooden floors of *Beryl Court*'s entry hall, alerting Whitlocke, who had been seeing to his duty of decanting new wine for the week. He watched his mistress narrowly through one of the sitting room windows; though she appeared but a silhouette, there was no mistaking the glittering sheen from her moonstruck fur collar. He was tempted to follow her, but then thought again – now his master was dead, whether or not he was married to her lady's maid, the Countess held all the power over staffing the household until Lord Spencer came of age. If so much a toe came out of line for Whitlocke, he would be dismissed without time for quarrel or qualm. He snorted angrily to himself at conceding defeat. 'For now,' he thought.

*

The Countess paid meticulous heed to where she was walking on her way down to town. The streets of Berylford were not well-lit even when the aligning gas lamps were aglow. They were as will-o'-the-wisps in the enveloping darkness, a haunting image to behold as they lined the roads to be followed. For a person of a weak cast of countenance, it was not a neighbourhood visited lightly at night, but Lady Vyrrington was a strong and stubborn creature. Her course had been set and she was resolved not to deviate. However, wanting to emphasise the urgency of the matter, she slammed on Mrs Rudgerleigh's door intent on waking someone within.

"Mr Gussage? Mr Gussage! Please come to the door, sir." She rapped on the door again and repeated her call. As she went to iterate a third time, the door opened, where she beheld not Zephaniah Gussage, but the quarry she had sought out in the first place – Jesse Blameford, stood before her in a loosely-worn nightshirt, dishevelled having obviously been woken from sleep. She expected him to be angry, but his expression told otherwise – a mixture of confusion and concern.

"Have you any idea of the time? What are you *doing* here? Come inside before someone sees!" and he ushered her in swiftly.

She looked around the downstairs and found it empty, and dark but for the one candle held by Blameford.

"If you've come to see Zephaniah, he's not here. He goes out most nights – sometimes I don't see him at all. Typical landlord, really," said Blameford.

"Do you really think I would venture abroad at this time to visit Zephaniah Gussage?"

"With all due respect, Lady Vyrrington, I didn't think *you* would venture abroad at this time to visit *anyone*. But you're here now – I presume it was I you wished to see?"

She kept her lips pursed. She did not want to come right out and accuse him of what she suspected – she was looking him up and down, though her expression was not demonstrative of the fact, she was enjoying what she was seeing, remembering she knew what was under the nightshirt.

"Well?" Blameford pressed her.

The Countess blinked a few times, as if to regain her self-awareness. She thought she would keep him stewing a little longer.

"I don't know where to begin; it seems so unthinkable," she murmured, deliberately dramatically, making her way up to the sitting room. He had followed her, and began lighting the lamps at the sides of the rooms.

"I'm not an educated man, milady," he said as he carried out his task, "but I'm told the beginning is usually a good place to start."

She watched him from the window, her lips remaining pursed, intent on remaining apparently unamused.

"Your wit was never appreciated, even when you worked up at the house," she quipped.

"That's not true," he returned, impudently.

The Countess chuckled, but withdrew immediately as she recalled her purpose there. If she continued to wrestle with her emotions and questions, which were tied tightly in a stranglehold in her mind, she would have no choice but to flee from the house, and forget the whole thing. The fact was she did not want to ask the questions lest her fears be realised, but she knew she would not have a peaceful night again until they were answered.

"Did you -? I mean-" she stammered and stuttered and shilly-shallied until she had to sit down. He continued to stand, waiting for her to speak fully.

"I can't sleep for wondering," she finally said coherently, "Knowing what I know about you. How it was you came to be in my service, and all besides. For years nothing happened but then that poor servant boy disappeared. I sent you *away* so that you would never be suspected in having anything to do with it."

"I *had* nothing to do with it."

"Shut up, *please*, and let me finish or this will consume me until my dying day."
Blameford sat down slowly on the settee beside her, his eyes fixed on Lady Vyrrington.

"Once you had returned, you came here and within weeks, my poor friend Clara was dead. And then my cousin Abel, not dead but close to it, by the looks of things. The only thing that any of this has, right at the heart of it, is *you*, Jesse Blameford."

"What is it you're telling me, Lady Vyrrington?" Blameford replied after a long pause, "That you think I killed Mrs Rudgerleigh, and tried to kill Mr Stirkwhistle?"

"And that little boots boy! And, after all that, why not add your family? – from whose deaths you were only acquitted because they did not find enough evidence to convict you."

"Because there was no evidence to find!" Blameford snapped in response, "I *didn't* kill them, and you knew it. You *still* know it or we wouldn't be having this conversation. You would never have pitied me as you did; you would have seen me as all others did – a wretched creature whose *shadow* the dregs of society would have deemed unworthy to breathe!"

"You were close to death, Jesse," Lady Vyrrington returned calmly, "Someone had to be The Good Samaritan. In that instance, I suppose it had to be me. And all the good it's done me. A widow with four children and half an income, a house I can only just afford to keep, and two servants, one of whom despises me. I have been punished by God the second I took you into my household, let alone my bed. I ask myself if it was worth all this suffering if you were guilty all along." Blameford stood again.

"What would you have me do, Oliviera?"

"Don't call me that."

"Is it not your name?"

"The name my mother gave me, but I have never heard it from you before, and I cannot even now."

"If you think I am guilty I shall leave this town and never be seen again under pain of death, if it's what you ask of me. But I am not guilty. The death of my family, I cannot explain; Joshua did not disappear on my watch or else we would have found him, and Mrs Rudgerleigh's passing was nothing more than a tragic turn of fate."

The Countess stood up, and looked Blameford in the eyes straight-on.

"And Abel?"

"I assure you Mr Stirkwhistle was in the best of health when he left. He was in Venice when his sister dismissed me."

She approached him slowly, her gaze unwavering from his. She caressed his face with one of her hands.

"You did none of this," she said, her voice trembling, "I can't tell you how overjoyed I am." The Countess pulled his face to hers and their lips met. He hoisted her up and she wrapped herself around him, and they carried on kissing.

Within what felt like mere seconds, they were in his room and half-dressed on Blameford's bed, having barely stopped for breath in the midst of all the kisses and caresses. After a lot of clumsy fumbling of belt buckles and petticoats he was inside her, and the Countess could not remember the last time a man had entered her with such passion and power. Even in the latter, better days of her marriage, she had done most of the work for Lord Wilson (much to her well-hidden consternation at the time). She smiled and licked her lips as he continued to ravage her, his lips and tongue cascading up and down her neck as he did so. She hooked her hands onto his muscular shoulders and dug her nails in so hard it was a wonder she did not draw blood. Blameford hissed in agonised pleasure and kissed her again. They looked each other in the eyes as intently and intensely as they had downstairs minutes before in the final throes of their intercourse, as their pleasures reached a powerful crescendo. The Countess bit her lover's ear as she felt her own climax, before feeling a warmth beneath her that indicated his. She was fully sated, and she released Blameford's shoulders, sleepily flinging her arms above her head and resting them there. Her eyes were shut – had she known any better, she would have said she had dreamt the whole encounter.

Chapter XLII
The Scheming Strangers

A RGUMENTS BETWEEN MRS HAFFISIDGE AND Mr Warwick were a regular feature of a Berylford evening, so much so that they had started to cost Mrs Haffisidge quite a bit of money replacing all the crockery she had undoubtedly thrown in her despicable nephew-in-law's direction. A lady of organised income, though she insisted on keeping it all in hard, physical cash form – from her widow's annuity, all the money her late husband Captain Upholland had bequeathed her upon his passing, and the instalments of her own family's money she had insisted were made available to her periodically, otherwise under the care of the well-reputed financial institution *Mullens & Cooke Finances in London* – she had laid aside a few shillings for such a purpose. A few pounds a week for food, given there were now four mouths to feed, plus refreshments for when she entertained Mrs Urmstone and the Misses Osborne and Gwynne (guests of an especial quality such as Lady Vyrrington would be catered for with extra funds); her travel costs to and from society gatherings and soirées only cost shillings since she was friendly with the drivers; and the remainder was for indulgences at *Osborne & Gwynne's Haberdashery*, and the presents for the baby Paul, on whom Mrs Haffisidge felt duty-bound to dote. Aside from the few shillings that were to accommodate the broken crockery.

These outbursts were the only displays of temper for which she had ever been known. In Berylford, Mrs Haffisidge was recognised to normally be a woman of sanguine temperament and calm disposition, especially when paired with the querulous and easily-excited Mrs Urmstone. But since her run-ins with Christopher Tratsly, and the attack on Lady Vyrrington in her own home, she had become almost paranoid that there was some force that wished ill upon her and her house. Who should be the one to exacerbate all manner of stressor and provoke her blood to boil for his own amusement, and relish every opportunity to do so? – only Mr Luke Warwick.

The latest contretemps occurred as a result of Mr Warwick's indignance towards his aunt-in-law's referring to his son Paul as her grandchild, which Mrs Haffisidge justified as true enough since she was the closest the baby would ever get to a grandparent. Mr Warwick's response involved something along the lines of calling Mrs Haffisidge a failure as a woman for never having mothered a child of her own, and in a fit of pique, Mrs Haffisidge flung a cast iron pan at her nephew-in-law, after which she drove him from the house, proclaiming him banished thenceforth. The part of the scene that occurred outside the house, including Mr Warwick's kicking the door after it had been slammed in his face, was witnessed by Miss Rebecca Stirkwhistle, who had been stood in the doorway of her own abode, wondering what all the commotion was coming from. Mr Warwick, in no mood for any attention whatsoever, shot her a dirty look and spat "What are *you* looking at?" in her direction. Miss Stirkwhistle cared not to answer, merely half-smiling with amusement and tilting her head upward slightly to stare down her narrow nose at him as he swaggered away towards *The St. Barbara's Arms* tavern.

He was in there often enough not to merit asking what he wanted to drink by the barman when he arrived. Instead, Mr Warwick merely sat on a stool at the bar, slightly hunched with his eyes directed firmly at the floor, seething and fuming silently and solitarily. The barman left a tankard of ale by him, and such was his anger and exasperation that he did not even notice it for some time. Even when he did finally realise he had been served, he only sipped at the vessel contemplatively, bent on committing some further nastiness unto his aunt-in-law, without risking endangering his wife and son, both of whom he was actually fond of, though his personality would not demonstrate as much. Being not one of the sharpest minds in Berylford, or England for that matter, when Mr Warwick contemplated, it took a while for anything particularly clever to enter his mind. Really, his chain of thought consisted of question after question: 'How can I get my revenge on the old bitch?' 'How shall I be rid of her?'

"Penny for your thoughts, friend?" a voice came from behind him.

"Piss off," replied Mr Warwick, abruptly, believing the voice to belong to the barman, "And mind your own business."
There was a brief silence, before a hand of long fingers clawed themselves onto his right shoulder and a figure came and sat next to him.

"What d'you want?" he asked, a little startled, "Who are you?"

"As I just said, I'm a friend," replied the fellow. He was dishevelled of dress and unkempt facially – one could have been forgiven for mistaking him as a tramp or a vagrant.

"If a penny won't pay for your thoughts, then perhaps another one of those will?" he continued, and pointed at Mr Warwick's tankard.

"Why should you want to help me?" Mr Warwick returned, "You don't know me. Or anything about me."

"Perhaps that's true," replied the stranger, obviously intent on revealing nothing about who he was, "Or perhaps I know *enough*, to know we have a common enemy. Judith-Ann Haffisidge."
Mr Warwick scoffed.

"I can hardly bear to hear that old cunt's name right now!" he said, drinking his ale down, "Believes herself to be so good and wise. Undermines me, looks down that beak of hers like she's someone of noble birth. It's a wonder she can see anything over that thing for the size of it!" He snorted, and drank again. "They built the gutter *around* her family, I bet. And she knows I know it. I see through her and it drives her mad, so she attacks me out of spite. I would leave Berylford just to be rid of her, but my wife is devoted to her." He finished his tankard and slammed it down on the counter, before demanding another from the barman. He breathed deeply and calmed down, noting that the stranger had listened to every word, and remained silent.

"What did she do to you?" he asked him, "How do you know her?"

"That is not important," replied his new friend, "I put it to you that I have a way to destroy her. And have her out of your life as you say."

Mr Warwick smiled.

"I'm listening."

"Does the name 'Juliette Harrowsleigh' mean anything to you?"

Screwing his eyes shut, Mr Warwick had to contemplate again; his memory for names was on par with the rest of his ignorance, in that he had very little memory for them at all.

"Not sure it does, no."

"Well, that's no matter. I will tell you."

"I'm Luke Warwick."

"Christopher Tratsly."

They both grinned, oozing evil as they did so, and shook hands, before concocting their vile scheme.

PART 4
THE <u>LETTERS</u>

Book Ten
ASPERSIONS AND INTERCESSIONS

Chapter XLIII
Miss Stirkwhistle is Offended

WITH THE TURN OF SUMMER now quickly upon them, Miss Osborne and Miss Gwynne's shop was overrun with the newest seasonal stock, and thusly the two proprietresses expected to be equally swamped with the seasonal customers looking for the latest influx of styles of daywear, eveningwear, haberdashery and millinery. In a bid to ensure their new merchandise would attract all of Berylford's citizenry, for the shop catered for men as much as women, favourite benefactors of theirs – not only those that spent the most across the year, but who gossiped the most about their purchases – had been told that they had a 'special priority viewing' of the summer stock before it was unveiled to the rest of the town. This, of course, meant Mrs Urmstone and Mrs Haffisidge, neither of whom were prone to keeping secret what they had bought from the haberdashers and how much they paid for it.

Also, among the invitations were those to Lady Vyrrington and military wife Mrs Knyveton, both of whose social positions could potentially attract custom to the shop from the upper echelons of the circles in which they mingled. However, both had declined the invitation in favour of pre-existing engagements. The Misses Osborne and Gwynne had sent further invitations to Miss and Mrs Stirkwhistle, the former of whom had come to form an albeit cautious camaraderie with the haberdashers – probably the only people among the citizenry to have formed such a relationship with Miss Rebecca. Because of her brother's position in society and that of her family as a whole, Miss Rebecca Stirkwhistle was considered on the same rank as Mrs Urmstone, and thusly superior to both Miss Osborne and Miss Gwynne. A pleased customer, even one of such crocodilian temper as Miss Rebecca, would pay them in spades if they gave a satisfied recommendation.

In order to not arouse suspicion from any wandering eyes that were only too abundant among the Berylford townsfolk, the ladies who had been given their priority invitations were required to arrive at the haberdashery at eight o' clock in the morning. Mrs Urmstone, whose home was only a few doors down from the haberdashery on Portchester Road, was first to arrive, whereas Mrs Haffisidge had turned up with Mrs Liza Stirkwhistle and Miss Rebecca at the same time – having met the two women on the way out of her own house. Mrs Stirkwhistle was dressed in very plain clothes and Miss Rebecca was – as always – dressed like a sorceress from a fairy tale, entirely in black. They all felt obligated to keep their conversation *sotto voce*, lest they should wake any neighbours or attract other townsfolk with their innate vulture-like dispositions to their private engagement.

It had been decided that the guests would be served breakfast as a form of refreshment. The Misses Osborne and Gwynne had their living quarters set up behind their shop, in which the parlour doubled as a dining room. In light of the fact they entertained rarely, as theirs was a business premises, it was not a room grandly or proudly decorated. Simple, plain magnolia walls from which hung a couple of pictures and a looking glass, and well-worn furniture, on which the upholstery was discoloured, frayed and even patched with the odd pool of dried candle wax. It was clear that the bookkeeping for the shop was done in the parlour too. It was not a room of leisure.

This all being said, the dining table was well-presented, showing off barely-touched ceramic crockery, which was edged in gold; and gleaming hallmarked silverware. Tureens of small tomatoes – each carefully cut in half – were placed generously about the table, as were racks of slices of lightly-toasted, buttered bread. Another pair of tureens appeared to contain scrambled eggs. There were also little bowls of jams of both strawberry and raspberry. Glasses of water had been poured at each place. In the centre, a pound cake had been placed on a silver stand. It was obvious the Misses Osborne and Gwynne entertained very irregularly; they had presented their table as though they were receiving royalty.

Each lady took their time in serving themselves, as if they were waiting upon one another to give permission to the rest. They partook in all but complete silence – the only noise made were the clattering of cutlery against crockery.

Mrs Urmstone was soon unable to endure the lack of conversation any longer and became fed up of waiting on any of the other ladies to begin a discussion, and so took it upon herself to do so as she usually did.

"Are there many novelties in the summertime fashions this year Miss Osborne?" she asked quietly.

"Indeed..." replied Miss Osborne, placing her cutlery down and tapping her lips lightly with her serviette, "...We are very colourful this year. Scarlets and crimsons and burgundies, and several shades of blue."

"Miss Stirkwhistle's sense of dress and colour will be quite revolutionised," Miss Gwynne piped up jokingly.

Mrs Haffisidge choked on her glass of water, and Mrs Stirkwhistle gasped in shock. Miss Rebecca looked across with wide eyes to Miss Gwynne, who had sat back in her seat and resumed her breakfast – realising she perhaps had said more than she should have.

"What are you trying to say Miss Gwynne?" Miss Rebecca asked, her voice quavering in a mixture of disquiet and anger.

Miss Gwynne did not reply, acting as if she had not heard.

"Agnes!" Miss Osborne nudged her cousin from beneath the table. Miss Gwynne placed her cutlery down.

"Merely, Miss Stirkwhistle..." she returned, dabbing at her crumbed lips with her serviette, "...That I consider your constant colour scheme of black and blacker to be mournful. Such a dress sense ages you. I know you to be twenty-or-so years younger than your brother and yet with the way you dress you present yourself to be the same age as him!"

There was an abominably awkward silence around the breakfast table. Not one of the ladies made a sound – even the cutlery was still.

"Have you quite finished throwing offences at me Miss Gwynne...?" Miss Stirkwhistle said surprisingly calmly, "...Or do you intend to twist the dagger further?"
Miss Gwynne hesitated in answering.

"I can assure you Miss Rebecca that I have no such intention."

"Then let that be the end of it..." Miss Stirkwhistle replied, wiping her own lips and placing her serviette upon her still-half-empty plate.

"...I shall take my leave."
She walked out. Miss Osborne pursued her in order to see her out, while the other ladies stared in awkwardness and embarrassment at their plates, lips sealed lest they should do any more harm to the situation.

Utterly insulted beyond all measure, Miss Rebecca remained deliberately ignorant to Miss Osborne's continuous calls after her through the shop. However she managed to catch her at the door before she had exited; as the shop was closed for business, it had been locked again after their priority guests had arrived.

"Miss Stirkwhistle I hope you will accept a heartily true and sincere apology on behalf of my cousin," Miss Osborne said, breathless after pursuing her quarry so vigorously, "She can be rather unfeeling on occasion and I wish you to know –"

"You are at liberty to hope as much as you like my dear Miss Osborne," returned Miss Stirkwhistle in her usual cold manner, "Yet you will find me – not only as an individual, but as a member of The Honourable Stirkwhistle family – to be rather disobliging to such pleas."

"Please, I beg of you-"
Miss Rebecca held a hand up as an indication she wished to hear no more from Miss Osborne.

"If you would be so good as to unlock the door, Miss Osborne, I wish to leave now," she said, her voice bereft of any emotion, her eyes directed upwards, away from the proprietress. She held her head high; her pride unshaken as, Miss Osborne, silent, embarrassed and

ashamed, unlocked and held the front door for Miss
Rebecca to exit.

*

Her pace quickened as she crossed Berylford's square.
Miss Rebecca was vexed enough when she had first
heard Miss Gwynne's disparaging remark – whether
any humour had been intended or not, she was resolved
not to find it – but as she had had time to mull over it
en route down Portchester Road, her vexation escalated
to fury and rage. It was one sin of which she knew
herself to be frequently guilty. She could not help it,
though. Her education, under the tutelage of nuns in
the same Catholic institutions that had moulded her
brother, had taught her the importance of not straying
into sin, but the holy sisters' own harsh demonstrations
of the sin of wrath had sown a seed in Miss Rebecca that
had taken root deeper than any other. It had endowed
her with neither the patience nor the mercy to suffer
indignance or insubordination by anyone she deemed
beneath her. Hitherto their encounter today, the Misses
Osborne and Gwynne had strived to satisfy Miss
Rebecca as a customer as her reputation could be
profitable to them in the long run; it was a contrived
friendship on the part of the haberdashers, whereas for

- 297 -

Miss Rebecca it was little more than them knowing their place.

Reaching Kellford Road, where her brother's house stood, her anger had not quelled. She hurtled through the front door so fast and vehemently that it clattered against the adjacent wall. A disturbed and curious head popped out from the parlour door. It was that of her brother, Abel. Since his coming to Berylford, which was decidedly a permanent one, Abel Stirkwhistle had made the most markedly astonishing recovery from his stroke. Not only had his speech returned, but most of his movement with it. A slightly slumped posture, awkward, crab-like gait accompanied by a permanent limp for which he now required a cane; and a stiff, crooked neck that caused his head to be tilted diagonally to the left, were all he had to show for the terrible malady that nearly killed him. Miss Rebecca was in no mood to see him, recovered or otherwise, when she observed his presence in the hallway.

"Did nothing enchant you sister?" he asked her, sardonically.

"Enchant, no. Insult, yes," she said huskily as she pushed past him to sit in the parlour. He followed her and went and sat in the dining room. It appeared he was still partway through his breakfast.

"What do you mean 'insult'?" he asked, through a mouthful of turtulong, "Though it will explain why you came storming into the house at such a time."

"Miss Agnes Gwynne had come to the rather strange conclusion that it was her place to cast aspersions on my sense of dress!"

Abel could be heard chuckling. Miss Rebecca, her current mood unwavering from its incensed course, widened her eyes and peered through to the dining room where she could see her brother.

"Did you hear what I said?" she asked, shrilly.

"What did she say?" Abel continued the conversation on.

"What matters it what she said? The matter is that she forgot her place in society. I do not take kindly to being mocked by someone socially inferior to me."

"There are few in this world that do, Rebecca," returned Abel, "But you must remember that Miss Gwynne is used to equality among social circles in Berylford. Did Miss Osborne say anything?"

"Oh what do *you* think, Abel? She had no qualms in defending Miss Gwynne, of course," Miss Rebecca replied disdainfully, "People of such a low class always band together!"

"I do think you have taken the matter a little too much to heart, sister."

"Not so!"

"Very well then. What do you intend to do?"

"I intend to retaliate with force tenfold!"

"How? Set the haberdashery shop on fire?"

"Don't tempt me, Abel."

"Oh, go upstairs, you ridiculous woman," her brother dismissed her, carrying on with his breakfast and opening a newspaper beside him, "You know as well as I do that you're all talk."

Her nostrils flared in fury, like a great dragon about to exhale Hellfire. She stood up as swiftly as she had done in receipt of Miss Gwynne's remark earlier that morning and, intent that this would not be the last of the matter, whether to Miss Osborne and Miss Gwynne, or to Abel, cloistered herself in her room to calculate her revenge further.

Chapter XLIV
A Confession and a Request

IN THE MEANTIME, AS THE priority stock viewing ensued, the haberdashery shop counter went untended. Miss Gwynne was in a state of unmovable anxiety; in fact, she had not left her seat at the breakfast table since the incident with Miss Rebecca had occurred. Miss Osborne had given their other guests leave to peruse the store without them, all the meanwhile attempting to bring her cousin and business partner around. At this point, to no avail. Miss Gwynne remained where she was, an elbow on the table and her hand clasped over her mouth, staring blankly at one of the parlour walls, not even appearing to recognise Miss Osborne sat next to her, attempting to get her to engage.

Mrs Urmstone, followed closely by Mrs Haffisidge and Mrs Stirkwhistle, had returned to the parlour to find this scene.

"Miss Osborne?" Mrs Urmstone said *sotto voce,* "I wonder if someone could attend the counter downstairs? I would like to pay for my purchases." Neither of the proprietresses spoke immediately, or made any noise at all, save for one small cough from Miss Osborne as she cleared her throat. A woman of occasionally-sharp tongue, even relative to one such as

Mrs Urmstone, she may have been stifling a less-polite response than the one she finally gave.

"Just… write down what it is you intend to take," she eventually said, "I will… draw up the totals and send you a bill to settle on your next visit." Mrs Urmstone was stunned, and looked around at Mrs Haffisidge and Mrs Stirkwhistle, both of whom returned the perplexed expression.

"Well… as you wish, Miss Osborne."

"And if there's anything we can do for either of you, we are at your service," Mrs Haffisidge interjected. If anything, it drove out some of the awkwardness. However, there was still a pause and the atmosphere in the parlour was still as grave as it had been before.

"I think, Mrs Haffisidge, if you'd be so good as to leave a sign in the shop window stating we're closed today, that would be most prudent," Miss Osborne whispered, quite calmly.

"No Julia, we cannot. We *mustn't!*" Miss Gwynne finally spoke, to everyone's surprise.

"You are in no state to work, Agnes," hissed Miss Osborne in response, "All of Berylford cannot see you like this!"

"All of Berylford will see us both in the *stockade* or worse by the time Miss Rebecca is through with us!" returned Miss Gwynne anxiously, almost to a point of delirium, "You know well of her temper, Mrs Stirkwhistle! You know it to be true!"

Mrs Stirkwhistle, who was stood closest to the doorway, backed away slowly and timidly; it was clear she feared any retribution for speaking ill of her sister-in-law, whether it was the truth or not.

"Mrs Urmstone, Mrs Haffisidge, I fear we must take you into our confidence," Miss Gwynne continued, and beckoned her friends closer, "The truth is our shop is in great financial difficulty…"

Miss Osborne scoffed and stood up, placing a hand at her forehead and massaging her temples as if suffering from a headache. This was not a conversation she had planned to be having that morning.

"…Should Miss Rebecca seek… revenge… against me or us as a business, we will be ruined," Miss Gwynne went on, "She will persecute any who come near these premises again. And I could not endure the shame of bankruptcy, and neither, I think, could Julia."

"We shop here too much as it is, Miss Gwynne," said Mrs Haffisidge kindly, "I fear *we* would be ruined if we offered any more patronage than we already do!"

"I'm not asking you that, Mrs Haffisidge. I am asking you to go to Lady Vyrrington and ask her to have a word with Miss Rebecca. They are family after all. Ask her to have Miss Rebecca see reason and that what I said meant no real malice."

Mrs Urmstone and Mrs Haffisidge looked at one another again, in a rare moment of uncertainty and hesitance.

"We can but try, Miss Gwynne," returned Mrs Urmstone impulsively, "I don't think reason is something Miss Rebecca readily recognises. But in the esteemed and wise presence of My Lady Oliviera, I think we may be better assured of a successful intervention."

It seemed like the first time in years that Miss Gwynne had been seen to smile. Indeed, it looked as though it pained her lips and jaws to create the expression.

"We will go forthwith," Mrs Urmstone continued, "I should advise you to open for business soon. 'Tis nearly ten!"

She curtseyed to both women – Miss Osborne was still stood, gazing painedly into the looking-glass on the wall – and went downstairs.

*

In the shop, Mrs Stirkwhistle was nowhere to be seen.

"She has probably gone back to report," Mrs Urmstone muttered to herself, then turned to Mrs Haffisidge outside the shop as they exited it, "Will Lady Vyrrington be awake at this time, do you suppose?"

"Well she couldn't come this morning for a reason. But she has the little ones to attend to. We may catch her in," returned Mrs Haffisidge, "But we had best make haste. She may have twenty engagements this afternoon."

They treated this as recourse to run, as much as they could at any rate, to *Beryl Court*. Steep was the gravel path leading to the front entrance. It was meant more for carriages than travelling on foot, and for ladies in their early-forties, as Mrs Urmstone and Mrs Haffisidge were, this made for exhaustive exertion. They were both quite out-of-breath by the time they reached the front door; it was just as well Whitlocke neither needed to announce them to Lady Vyrrington, nor inquire as to their business, so often were their visits.

"Sitting room," he stated quite straightforwardly at them, and did not follow them as they made their way in there.
The Countess was sat in an armchair with a cup of tea, reading a letter. She looked up when she saw her friends in the doorway, trying to catch their breath.

"Elspeth! Judith-Ann! What an unexpected surprise; I thought you'd be at Osborne and Gwynne's trying on hats and bonnets until at least noon," she joked, inclining to the other two to sit down, an invitation they readily obliged.

"You appear to have been running, ladies," Lady Vyrrington observed, her tone turning curious, if a little sardonic, "I suppose it must be urgent. What news?"

Mrs Urmstone had regained her breath while Mrs Haffisidge was still catching hers, so she spoke.

"We knew you were not long for your pre-existing engagement, My Lady, which deterred you from attending the scene that occurred at the haberdashery this morning over breakfast. To cut a long story short, Miss Gwynne – as a passing comment *only* – may have said something mildly disparaging of Miss Rebecca's mode of dress."

Lady Vyrrington's expression did not alter.

"What 'mildly disparaging' comment did she say exactly?" the Countess asked.

"Something about her always wearing black and blacker," Mrs Haffisidge finally had the energy to interject, "And that she looked mournful."

Lady Vyrrington huffed:

"More like an evil queen from a child's tale." She stood up and paced the sitting room. Clearly her view of Miss Rebecca's temper was the same as the other townswomen.

"Miss Gwynne now fears for the continuing success of the haberdashery given Miss Rebecca's… reputation," Mrs Urmstone went on, "and she humbly requested that we ask you to intercede on her and Miss Osborne's behalf to calm the waters, so to speak."

The Countess could not help but laugh. Mrs Urmstone and Mrs Haffisidge looked at each other.

"My Lady?" Mrs Haffisidge said, perplexed.

Her Ladyship was still chuckling.

"You have met the woman of whom we all speak, my dear friends," she remarked, "And you are well aware of her opinion and regard for me, or the lack thereof as the case may be. What on *Earth* makes you suppose I can make a difference?"

"Nothing at all, My Lady," returned Mrs Urmstone, "Miss Gwynne was the one who requested, I could not dare deny her and watch her despair. Miss Rebecca may not be a reasonable woman, but I believe we would be in with a better chance of success *with* you than without you."

Lady Vyrrington turned again and looked out of the sitting room window, which looked out onto the back gardens and then by extension the town below.

"I will pay Abel a visit this afternoon," she said, though uncertainty was prevalent in her voice, "And I will attempt to smooth this over. As long as you are both assured that if I fail, I *cannot* be held accountable for Miss Rebecca's actions, nor the fate of Miss Osborne and Miss Gwynne's business."

"We understand, My Lady," returned Mrs Urmstone.

"Very well then. You nearly killed yourselves coming here, you may as well have a cup of tea." She sat back down, and called for Whitlocke from the next room.

Chapter XLV
An Unappreciated Intervention

STAYING TRUE TO HER WORD, **following her engagement** with a highly-appointed and august personage, namely the Dowager Marchioness of Wrexhall, Lady Vyrrington found time to visit Abel Stirkwhistle and his sister. She did not know why she was bothering to go – she knew this would end in anger and strife. No encounter with Miss Rebecca was going to pursue a calm, pleasant course. And she had been wrong in saying she would have no accountability for *Osborne & Gwynne's Haberdashery* – a portion of their income went directly into hers by way of the Vyrrington estate of which she was the current keeper. Miss Rebecca would be treated very severely indeed should she jeopardise that income wilfully.

In that case, why did she not just turn on her heel and go back to *Beryl Court*? The Countess could not help it – she had been put up to something, she intended to follow it through. Even if it was to start an argument with Miss Rebecca she would not necessarily win. Rank meant nothing to Rebecca Stirkwhistle, so Lady Vyrrington was powerless even to use that as a shield in her defence, or as a mark of her own authority. Thinking over all of this had taken time, time enough for her to all of a sudden be outside the Stirkwhistle house on Kellford Road.

Prior to her decidedly subtle exodus from the shop, Mrs Stirkwhistle had bought a new dress during the private viewing, leaving as instructed by Miss Osborne a piece of paper detailing her purchase, and was wearing it when she came to answer the door. She smiled so widely, it almost seemed false, as though some invisible force where holding a stiletto to her back, and she would strive to look happy under pain of death. Lady Vyrrington observed the garment Mrs Stirkwhistle was wearing, the one she had purchased, was a burgundy party dress with gold trim around the sleeves, a dress considered far too formal for the time of day. All the same, she smiled sweetly and greeted Mrs Stirkwhistle likewise. As the Countess entered the hallway, Miss Rebecca emerged from the parlour, a fiery, almost draconian expression in her eyes.

"What do you think you're wearing?" she hissed at her sister-in-law.

"The dress I bought at Osborne and Gwynne's," returned Mrs Stirkwhistle, "Seemed a shame not to wear it!"

"A party dress?" Miss Rebecca whispered incredulously, "More to the point – a party dress from *that* wretched establishment? You will do well to change into your regular grey dress. Lady Vyrrington will not mind, will you?"

Lady Vyrrington was not used to being asked a question in such a manner and only answered when she realised whom Miss Rebecca was addressing.

"Erm no – no of course not..." she said initially, but then she observed how Miss Rebecca was looking at Mrs Stirkwhistle and how crimson her face had turned. She decided to play Miss Rebecca at her own game.

"...But that being said, I think burgundy suits you Mrs Stirkwhistle. There is no need to change on my account; I believe you should keep it on. Miss Rebecca won't mind, will you?"

"Forgive me, Lady Vyrrington, but I'm afraid I will mind very much! I am insistent that my sister-in-law change out of it. It is not suitable for an occasion like this afternoon visit."

This was something else that the Countess was not used to: being argued with by another woman. And more to the point, she was not going to let Rebecca Stirkwhistle – the youngest granddaughter of an Italian countess – defeat her. However, she used the simplest technique to overthrow her: – by smiling astutely and saying superciliously:

"Believe me – I have seen society women dressed in much worse – that garment is more than suitable. Please lead the way in Mrs Stirkwhistle."

They smiled at one another; while Miss Rebecca stared daggers at Lady Vyrrington.

Abel was sat in the parlour reading a newspaper; he placed it down swiftly and stood up, however slowly and awkwardly such was his disability now, to greet the Countess. She sat down.

"Liza," Abel said, "See to tea for Her Ladyship." Mrs Stirkwhistle dared not argue with her husband and disappeared away to the kitchen. Miss Rebecca came and sat opposite Lady Vyrrington, glaring at her when Her Ladyship's gaze turned elsewhere.

"To what do we owe the pleasure of your sole company this afternoon, Lady Oliviera?" Abel asked, "Rumours have been flying round that you've been recently seen in the company of one Jesse Blameford..." His face was well-hidden behind the newspaper, which expressed as broad a grin as his stricken face could make, "...Thinking of marrying below your station this time, cousin...?"

Lady Vyrrington could not be sure if he was being serious or not – in truth, she had not been to see Blameford in days, though it was not for the lack of wanting to. Fortunately, before she could respond, Abel continued, though this time he addressed Miss Rebecca.

"...You see, sister, I did tell you, our cousin Lady Vyrrington has more chance of falling for the charms of Jesse Blameford than you ever will..." he once again turned to the Countess and murmured jovially, "She had a bit of a thing for him when we were in Italy." Lady Vyrrington had never seen Miss Rebecca look so vehement; she looked ready to screw up Abel's newspaper and stuff it down his throat to choke him.

"For shame, Abel, you disgrace us!" she spat, "You do me a disservice in front of Lady Vyrrington!"

"You must excuse me, Abel," Lady Vyrrington interjected, dousing the fire wildly being fanned between the two siblings, "but my being here actually hails from a matter concerning Miss Rebecca."

"Oh?" Abel said, his tone darkening "What matter would that be? What's she done?"

"I suppose she will have told you of her exchange with Misses Osborne and Gwynne a few hours ago?"

"I did," Miss Rebecca said, sounding irked, "But I see no reason why that should concern *you* in any way Lady Oliviera."

"Rebecca!" Abel hissed in a mixture of anger and embarrassment, "My Lady I must apologise. And so must she!"

"I shall most certainly not apologise!"

"You will change your mind when I've finished with you!" Abel growled, "Retire to your room. This instant!"

Lady Vyrrington was mortified. Had she been in possession of such a thing, Miss Rebecca looked prepared to unveil a pistol and shoot her brother square between the eyes. Before any party could speak again, her lip curling, she shoved past her sister-in-law as she rose and went upstairs. Tea had spilled, and stained the new dress, and Mrs Stirkwhistle merely looked at her front in shame. Lady Vyrrington rose and took the now-empty teacup from her.

"It won't come out," Mrs Stirkwhistle said hoarsely, "It's the best thing I've ever owned and now it's ruined."

"I shall pay for a replacement," returned Lady Vyrrington, "Walk out with me."

"My Lady I implore you to forgive my sister," Abel said, standing up, "I know not what can have afflicted her behaviour so."

"Please Abel be not so apologetic," Lady Vyrrington replied, "I came here at the request of Mrs Urmstone and Mrs Haffisidge to sort out the falling-out between Miss Gwynne and your sister."

"She shall still face a consequence for speaking to you the way she did. I will deal with her in due course."

"In her absence *and* as you are the head of your household, may I have your assurance that, given the circumstances, Miss Rebecca will not... *persecute* the Misses Osborne and Gwynne or in any way pose their business any threat? It will be perilous to those two ladies and by extension will do the Vyrrington estate no good either."

"You mustn't worry, Oliviera," replied Abel, "My sister will not be permitted to do any such thing. And even if she does, I will overrule her. And I will write forthwith to Miss Osborne and Miss Gwynne to dispel them of their anxieties as well."

"Oh Abel, you are too good," returned the Countess, clutching her cousin's hand and kissing his cheek. She then went to his wife.

"Mrs Stirkwhistle, change into a regular daytime outfit and then accompany me to the haberdashery." She took her by the arm and led her to the stairwell, where she ascended.

Her small room was next door to that of Miss Rebecca's, whose door was ajar; its occupant sat on her bed, her lip still curling vindictively, and her teeth gritted. She had heard every word between her brother and The Countess. And she hated them both.

Chapter XLVI
Advisements in the Street

HER OWN ANGST ABOUT THAT entire affair now put to rest, en route back to *Beryl Court*, Lady Vyrrington passed Chine Road – one of the four main roads in Berylford – that on which Jesse Blameford's current lodgings stood. In light of what Abel had remarked, regardless of whether or not he was just annoying his sister, she toyed with several ideas and conversations in her head, reluctances and excuses for why not to go there. She would have to make a decision quickly if she did not want to look suspicious – such a thing would be all but suicidal with the prying eyes of Mrs Urmstone or Mrs Haffisidge potentially at any street corner. Having lingered long enough, she approached Number Five, the late Mrs Rudgerleigh's former abode, and rapped on the door.

Blameford was slow to answer; he had clearly not been expecting callers, especially Lady Vyrrington. When he first saw her, it looked as though his immediate impulse was to shut the door again and not say a word. But he relented and let her inside. And once they were there, they could not resist each other any longer. Their passion was rekindled as soon as the door closed. He wrapped both of his arms around her and kissed her neck from behind, and she panted as he did so, running her long fingers through his thick locks. His kissing turned to licking, and her panting turned to crying out in pleasure. He then turned her around in his arms to face him and kissed her lips repeatedly.

"I want you," he said in between kisses, "I never stopped wanting you."

"I've missed this…" she returned, "I have missed you. I've been so alone."

"Let's not wait any longer. Let me take you now!"

"No, I cannot."

He kissed her again and slid one hand up her outer thigh. The sensation was tempting her to change her mind.

"No, I cannot!" she repeated.

"I want to fuck you. Right here."

She did not think about it. She did not have time. The Countess' impulsiveness overwhelmed her.

"Tonight, Jesse! *Tonight.*"

"Here?"

"No, at Beryl Court. In the gardens – no one will see or hear us there."

"Are you sure?"

"I know it…" she said, clasping her hands behind his neck and kissing him again, before whispering in his ear: "You've waited weeks to have me again. You can afford a few hours more."

He exhaled raggedly.

"Only just. My Lady," he sighed, smirking impudently thereafter.

*

She left his house at just the most awkward moment, for as she stepped over the threshold and back out of Chine Road to turn toward Kellford Road, she came across Miss Rebecca again, only this time the Countess only acknowledged her cousin with a polite nod of the head, which in turn was not reciprocated. Too proud and self-respecting to extend the encounter any further and lower herself to Miss Rebecca's level, Lady Vyrrington carried on her way back to *Beryl Court*. Or so she would have done, had she not heard the all-too-familiar cries of "My Lady? My Lady?" from behind her. The ever-peripatetic Mrs Urmstone came running to catch up with her.

"Elspeth, my dear, I had not expected to see you again so soon," she said.

"How did it go?" Mrs Urmstone asked eagerly.

"Not well, to own the truth," replied Lady Vyrrington, "As I professed to you and Judith-Ann in the first place, my interference would not be appreciated. And I was right. But Abel assured me he will write the Miss Osborne and Miss Gwynne informing them he intends to overrule any decision his sister makes against them. Should it come to that, which I don't think he will allow it to."

She smiled at Mrs Urmstone, who had, for once, remained silent. However, it did not appear she was interested in Lady Vyrrington's talk with Miss Rebecca anymore.

"What?" asked Lady Vyrrington, confused.

"You have been visiting Mr Blameford, it would seem, My Lady?"

"Yes, it would seem so, Elspeth. What of it?" Mrs Urmstone smiled; she clearly did not wish to give offence where it may appear.

"You know Berylford well enough by now, My Lady Oliviera, to know that no secret goes untold for too long. And rumours fly everywhere. One has been circulating that you and Mr Blameford have been seen together a number of times recently."

"They are falsehoods, Madam," Lady Vyrrington did sound offended, despite Mrs Urmstone's best efforts, "And, if I may speak plainly, with whom I socialise and the nature of that society is my own business."

"Just be aware, My Lady, society may not understand, should you... 'shack up' with someone in a lesser echelon to yourself."

"'Society'? Yourself, you mean?"
Mrs Urmstone knew now she had said too much.

"Need I remind you, Elspeth, that the first time I met Jesse Blameford, he was little more than a living corpse," the Countess went on, "Wronged by every fleck of society that still draws breath. I saved him from a wretched fate and worse, and as such I consider myself duty-bound to watch over him. Even then, he's an honourable man, Elspeth, and I personally think you treat him unfairly, and always have…"
This time, Lady Vyrrington felt she had perhaps spoken a little too harshly, so she took her friend's hand in hers.

"…I *know* you are looking out for my welfare, Elspeth, as my friend, and I love you dearly for it. I readily admit I do not always look to the wider aspect of a situation where society is concerned. But as your friend, I need only say – I know what I am doing."
Mrs Urmstone smiled again, albeit nervously.

"As you say, My Lady. I know you to be a wise and honourable Christian woman. I should never doubt your integrity. I will bid you good evening."
She curtseyed and made her way back in the direction of her own house.

'See – there's the reason this entire thing was a mistake!' Lady Vyrrington thought to herself immediately after turning back to walk in the direction of her house. Assailed by all manner of emotions for innumerable people – lust and desire for Blameford, anger and spite for Miss Rebecca, relief and joy for Abel and his goodness, pity for his downtrodden and neglected wife Liza, and now fear and unease – not to mention very deep conflict – for her dear friend Elspeth Urmstone. 'What if she doesn't believe me? Elspeth talks to people. What if someone confirms her suspicions? Whether by design or inadvertently.' The conflict struck, and she could not bear to doubt Mrs Urmstone so. 'No. Of course she wouldn't do that or think that. Elspeth is one of my oldest and dearest friends. She wouldn't dare speak or think ill of me like this. I am most certainly safe.'

The Countess half-turned around, as if to make for Chine Road and call off, or at least postpone, the tryst with Blameford in the garden that night. She could not bear to do that either. 'I want him too much. We have been risking ourselves every time. It didn't worry us enough then – why should it do so now?'

That was it – she was resolved. Everything would go ahead as planned, and by the time she had finished thinking over and over, she beheld her own front door.

"Abroad late this day, My Lady?" was Whitlocke's sardonic greeting to his mistress as he received her in the entrance hall.

"So you see, Whitlocke," the Countess returned with equal sarcasm, "Do I detect a criticism lurking behind your words?"

"Only that the children were asking after you and I knew not what to tell them. It gives me no pleasure lying to children, My Lady, especially yours and Lord Wilson's."

"But you mean not to presume any need to know where I was or why I was out so late?"

"Correct. Unless you should give me a reason to?"

He raised his head and looked at her down his nose. She squared up to him, doing the same.

"You listen to me, Whitlocke," Lady Vyrrington said slowly and menacingly and approaching him in an alike manner, her index finger pointed straight at him like a sharp, slender dagger, "I will never give you the *right*, let alone the *reason*, to know anything of my affairs, much less the right to *question* them!"

"Your affair is what brought us here in the first place. My Lady," Whitlocke replied insolently.

The Countess' eyes whitened in anger, her head surveying him up and down in a sharp and *staccato* manner, her mouth ajar. Whitlocke stood his ground, to her expectation.

"You will do well to remember your place, Whitlocke. You hold no power over me. Be my guest. Tell anyone what you want of me and Mr Blameford. No one will ever believe you, and if they do I will discredit you – because you're a servant! But be assured that if you do, you won't spend another day in this house."

"And what of Amethyst? We're married now, remember? Would you risk her happiness to save your precious reputation?"

"Without me, Amethyst would be dead or close to it in the workhouse. And the two of you would never have met. Pay heed to that fact, Whitlocke; Amethyst is more-than-well aware of it. Now if you'll excuse me, I'll have my supper brought to my bedchamber."
The butler glared at her as she ascended the stairs. She did not look down at all.

Book Eleven
SHORT CORRESPONDENCES

Chapter XLVII
In the Garden in the Small Hours

T HE MOON WAS A GRAND, giant pearl of striking, eerie, silver luminescence; a haunting sight to behold suspended motionless amid the black, starless sky, as though it were a ghostly ship abreast great waves of purple and smoke grey cloud. A singular great streetlamp of spectral aspect almost lighting the path to another world. A beacon of the ether, summoning home the spirits of the dead and dying. Apart from the moon, the night was black – it was perfect for an illicit and concealed passionate encounter.

Lady Vyrrington crept down the stairs barefoot, so as to not alert Whitlocke, who, officious to the last, was prone to carrying out his duties at such an hour. Carefully and silently, she unlatched the door and managed to exit to the gardens without making a conceivable sound.

Behind a tree in *Beryl Court*'s garden, she found her lover waiting there, sat on the grass. A white shirt, cut low at the chest, tight-fitting brown breeches and black boots were all in which he was clad. She approached and straddled him. They kissed immediately and, despite the winter cold, wasted no time in undressing each other roughly, until Blameford's shirt only loosely hung off of his well-muscled body, his breeches unfastened and down to his knees. Lady Vyrrington was bare to the waist and clung to Blameford as he lowered her to the ground, kissing her breasts as he did so. He then pressed her arms either side of her head, linking hands with hers as he entered her. His tongue went inside her mouth at the same time, silencing her cries of pleasure. He began to thrust harder and faster, and her moaning began to reach a *crescendo*. But at the one moment where she opened her eyes, Lady Vyrrington saw something from the corner of the garden. A bush rustling, and a shadow behind it. She tried to ignore it, but the shadow soon disappeared – she knew it had been cast by something. Or, much worse, someone. Her mind deviated from her pleasure.

"Stop!" she whispered.

"What?" he panted, continuing to ravage her.

"Stop for Heaven's sake! We are betrayed!" she slapped his back, and he withdrew. He groaned angrily as he rolled onto his back – his still-erect prick held loosely in his fist.

Wrapping herself in a fur shawl, Lady Vyrrington got up to investigate where she thought she had seen the shadow. She found nothing there. She turned around and saw Blameford had not moved.

"Let's go again," he said.

"Shut up for Heaven's sake! Someone is there."

"I'm coming inside you tonight if it kills me!"

"You may have to hold that thought, my dear," the Countess replied, "We're not safe. This is not safe."

"It could have been a hedgehog for all you know! Come! Sit on me!"
He tried to pull her down to him, but she resisted.

"I must insist, Jesse. It was a mistake doing this. We should never have arranged it."

"You're scared of something. And I don't know why!" he growled at her. He readjusted his breeches, put his shirt back on, and walked off without another word. Her common sense prevailed in not calling him back and inviting him into the house to continue their tryst. It was just as well, for Blameford was gone quickly. Now very cold and despondent, the Countess returned to the house. After locking the door again, she surveyed the ground floor and saw nobody there, so she had not disturbed her servants – to her knowledge, at any rate. She would not sleep easily that night though, she knew too few of her own enemies, and if they did exist, what they may have seen would undoubtedly destroy her. However, as she started her ascent up to her own bedchamber, she was received by Whitlocke, armed with a lantern, only roughly dressed in his livery. He looked both suspicious and bemused.

"My Lady?" he exclaimed, "Whatever are you about at this hour?"

"A little fresh evening air, Whitlocke, if it's any business of yours," she replied, snidely, "I find I am having trouble sleeping of late; I find a walk helps alleviate that."

Whitlocke allowed her inside.

"Very good milady, I meant no offence. Since Zephaniah Gussage went missing, we're all a little on-edge around here. In case he arrives on one of our doorsteps."

"I beg your pardon?"

"Zephaniah Gussage has disappeared. Or so they're saying around town."

"Elspeth – Mrs Urmstone, that is – told me he had gone to stay with a relative in Somerset."

"Gussage has no relatives to speak of," returned Whitlocke, "So Lord-only-knows where he has gone. And if he will ever return."

The Countess sighed exhaustedly. That news was too much to consider when her thoughts of Blameford and the suspicious shadow in the bushes were already occupying her mind enough.

"How long have you been awake?" she asked Whitlocke, hoping to reduce the conversation to small-talk, so that she would be given a bye to retire.

"Not very long, My Lady – I heard a disturbance in the gardens, or so I thought. It must have been you, but I thought I would investigate all the same."

"All right, Whitlocke. Thank you; you may return to bed. There was nothing untoward in *our* garden at any rate. And if Zephaniah Gussage *does* grace our doorstep, we should send for the doctor to be on the safe side."

"Understood, milady. Good night."

She ascended the stairs quickly lest he should question or seek further conversation.

'It had to have been him in the bushes; it *had* to!' she thought to herself, 'Whitlocke is the only one who would know where to look. If not Whitlocke, then whom?'

She continued to think and overthink as she almost mechanically followed the labyrinth of corridors and entered her own bedchamber.

'Whitlocke was only half-dressed when he received me at the door. If he was going to spy on us, why take the trouble to exit and re-enter the house?'

Her hands clasped to her lips to stifle a gasp, she sat on her bed.

'It *can't* have been him. It defies all logic. Elspeth, perhaps?'

She was mortified at herself for even daring consider that notion. Mrs Urmstone was not a lady who crept about at night spying – Mrs Urmstone's stories and claims were often unfounded and victims of her own embellishments and exaggerations, so to spy for evidence would be totally out-of-character. And even if she *were* to be abroad at a late hour doing such a thing, she was not sufficiently subtle to carry out the task effectively.

'Who on Earth could it have been, then?' the thought contrived to plague Her Ladyship's mind further. She laid back and placed a pillow over her face, as if in an attempt to suffocate herself.

'Maybe I'm being paranoid. Perhaps Jesse was right – it was just a hedgehog, or a fox.'

On that wave of thought, she began to relax, but her mind did not focus there long, and once again became embroiled with worry and fear.

'Or maybe, another enemy. One I did not know I had!'

Chapter XLVIII
The Morning Summons

GIVEN HER BROTHER'S HITHERTO DANGEROUS condition, Miss Rebecca Stirkwhistle had had to sacrifice luxuries like a soft mattress and a sizeable bedroom-cum-study. Her room was around the size equal to that of their kitchen, enough to contain a small bed, which was appropriate given her spindly build; a small writing desk and chair, and a wardrobe that was twice the size sufficient to contain all her clothes. Miss Gwynne's comments had indeed rung true; most of Miss Rebecca's garments were black, but far from the sepulchral mood she was accused of carrying, it was more indicative of the darkness of the hole that took place of her heart. Far from a mournful woman, she was instead irascible, stern and icy, endowed with no humour or *savoir-faire*, but also lethargic and seemingly old beyond her years. Though she was only in her mid-twenties, her tightly-fastened hair aged her by at least two decades, to a point she may have been mistaken for Abel's elder sibling, when in fact Abel was, as Miss Gwynne had pointed out, considerably the older. All this was exacerbated by her impenetrable lack of sleep, provoked by the ill quality of her mattress. She could feel the springs beneath the fabric with every toss or turn, and the woollen sheets, at this time of year, made her intolerably hot. It could reach the small hours of the morning by the time she was just so exhausted that her body could permit her no further consciousness and she was contrived to sleep, and even then, it was a hollow and dreamless slumber, encumbered by no fantasies or wild imaginings. It better resembled a repeated death than a night's rest, but it was the only rest she had.

So, when her sister-in-law awoke her quite early that next morning, saying that her brother had "summoned" her to the parlour, she was incensed. It was just as well for Mrs Stirkwhistle she had not entered the room, for she was liable to have something large thrown at her in response. In the hope that she was tired enough to return to sleep after she had humoured Abel in whatever annoyance he had planned for her, she, albeit irately, obliged. She put on a black satin dressing gown and went downstairs with the intent of protesting profusely to her brother.

"You 'summon' me?" she said to him as she entered the parlour, her eyes screwed into a squint in her disgust and her nostrils flared draconianly, "And pray, who are you to presume to 'summon' me, Abel Stirkwhistle? What am I? A dog?"

She then saw that her brother was stood, with a woman around his height with her back turned wearing a rather outward-bearing dress and a thick fur boa held astride her shoulders.

"Your wife did not mention to me we had company!" Miss Rebecca cried in both embarrassment and shock, "Forgive me, madam for being so incorrectly disposed."

The woman turned around, revealing herself to be Lady Vyrrington. Miss Rebecca's discomfiture doubled.

"Abel! Why did you not tell me Lady Vyrrington was here?" she screeched at him.

"Because I knew that if I did, you would not come down," her brother replied. His sister detected a definite tone of fierceness in his voice.

"And would it be so bad if I had refused? What can Lady Vyrrington possibly need to see me for?"

"Rebecca Stirkwhistle hold your tongue. You owe Lady Oliviera a sincere apology for your behaviour the other day and you are not leaving this room until you have given it."

Lady Vyrrington quietly attempted to intervene:

"Abel, I think –"

"Please allow me to deal with this, My Lady," her cousin abruptly interrupted her.

"I deeply and sincerely apologise to you Lady Vyrrington," Miss Rebecca hid her inner disdain for both her brother and Her Ladyship very well as she spoke, "The way in which I spoke to you the other day was entirely unacceptable."

"There Abel, she's apologised. Now may she leave?" the Countess spoke up again, "The poor girl must be mortified with embarrassment."

"Indeed. Go and get dressed," Abel commanded his sister. Her lip curled, and she turned and exited, quickly ascending the stairs. Upon reaching her room, she sat in front of her mirror and started brushing her dark and wiry hair.

"The 'poor girl'," she muttered to herself disdainfully, "'the poor girl' indeed. As if you care." Scowling midway through attending her hair, she turned around and went outside into the hallway.

It was a dark passageway, only receiving light at all from downstairs during the day, or in the rare event of one of the upstairs bedroom doors being opened. It was just as well as the decoration was nonexistent. Fading white walls, mottled black about the corners with damp and mould, and some patches greyed with age and neglect. The skirting boards were dusty and splintered in places. The walls did possess one sole decoration, which came in the form of a small, framed silhouette of Abel. In the fit of pique from which she was suffering, Miss Rebecca, still in *déshabillée*, silently unhooked the picture from the wall, took it back to her room and, in a brutal display of anger, smashed the frame against her wardrobe, where it broke into pieces, the glass shattering. After examining her hands to ensure she had not been pierced in any place, she threw what remained of the image into the wardrobe.

The truth was Miss Rebecca deplored her brother. Jealousy, spite, malice and rage ruled her every action towards him, ever since she had been old enough to recognise such emotions. Being thirteen years her senior, Abel had been quickly established in the household of her childhood as her superior, but also in many instances, a makeshift caregiver. Neither of these things, Miss Rebecca willingly recognised. She was stalwartly against not being in control of her own affairs or actions. Her brother had always wielded considerable influence over, not only their immediate family – presenting himself as a pragmatic, wise, educated and shrewd judge of character and situation, and always having the ability to know exactly what to say or do – but to all circles in which he moved. Miss Rebecca thusly felt a prisoner to her brother's will. Following the death of their father, Abel went away and consequently suffered his stroke, whereupon Miss Rebecca finally had her chance. To usurp her brother's position as head of the household and seize his control over their family and social circles – especially in the hitherto likely event that the malady would kill him.

But Abel did not die, and now his sister had to suffer the added annoyance of Lady Vyrrington, a woman who, despite her admissions, Miss Rebecca knew very well indeed. It was true that, prior to the death of her and Abel's father, and the arrival of Jesse Blameford into their household, that Miss Rebecca had never met the Countess or had any reason to recognise her as close family, as Abel did. But now she had encountered her on several occasions, on all of which, she found another to bow, scrape and defer to. Descend from sleep when summoned. Apologise when ordered to. 'What right did she have to any of this?' Miss Rebecca's thought, 'Who does she presume to command in their own home? Manage their household? Instruct their sister-in-law what is acceptable to wear and not wear?'

She arranged herself at her desk, beginning her morning's correspondence, all the while hating those two people more than she deigned ever imagine.

Chapter XLIX
A Letter to Lady Vyrrington

IN BERYLFORD, THERE WAS THE usual regular post service that delivered correspondences to all addressees early in the morning. But with the presence of the Farthing-'Twixt-'Em-Cottages, just down the road, it was common that a number of young urchins – the few who survived through infancy and the first couple of years of childhood – from that wretched outskirt of the town would find quick employment as messengers, to deliver letters at a moment's notice. They depended on the money, so they could not afford to swindle the members of the citizenry who paid them for their services. Thus it was that, around two in the afternoon, a boy who may have been ten, though was ill-fed enough to still look six or seven, ascended to *Beryl Court* via the road that carriages arrived and departed the grounds on.

Whitlocke had taken advantage of his spare time, given there was no household to manage anymore, and had gone down *The St. Barbara's Arms*. Only Amethyst was around to answer the door to receive the young creature. The boy did not speak to her; only handed to her the envelope and ran – it was probable he could not read the name of the addressee and had only been given a description of where he was to deliver the message. Thinking nothing of it, as correspondences from Mrs Urmstone or Mrs Haffisidge were often delivered in such a way later in the day, Amethyst observed the addressee of whatever was within the envelope – Lady Vyrrington – and took it to her.

Her Ladyship was in Lord Wilson's study, which she had now claimed as her own. Amethyst knocked quietly but confidently – she was a greater deal relaxed and calm when in the sole presence of Lady Vyrrington. After being permitted entrance, the maidservant placed the envelope on Her Ladyship's desk as she was writing.

"A boy left you this, milady," Amethyst said. Lady Vyrrington did not look up, concentrating on what she was writing.

"A boy? Which boy? Do we know him?"

"Only a small brick-maker boy. He did not give his name. In fact, he didn't speak at all."

"All right Amethyst. That will be all."

"Very good milady."

She exited, and as soon as she had Lady Vyrrington signed the correspondence she had been writing and took up a bejewelled letter opener her father Lord Ensbury Isaacs had bequeathed to her at his death. She sliced the top of the envelope open and unfolded the paper to read the words:

You are a filthy slut. I know what you've done.
Who will I tell? Unless you pay…

She was immediately taken aback by what lay before
her. She flipped the paper backward and forward,
looking to see if the threat was extended anywhere else
upon it. There was nothing, and it was anonymous. She
put it back in the envelope and locked it in the lowest
drawer of her desk. She knew it would be safer in there,
as burning it could always leave small remnants, which
would be observed by Whitlocke when he came to
empty the grate. The Countess' heart was pounding,
almost clattering inside her, shaking her entire being
that she may have felt as though she were having a
seizure. She remained at her desk, eyes darting left and
right and left and right, until so overexercised that she
had to close them. Then a headache came on, and she
massaged her temples as she thought and questioned
and contemplated. Who was the only one who knew of
her only secret: her affair with Jesse Blameford? Who
had always threatened her with exposure so long as the
liaison ensued? And who had the means and motive
with which to blackmail her? George Whitlocke
himself. But once she had convinced herself that
Whitlocke was in fact the sender – the culprit, this vile
blackmailer – she knew at once what she would do. As

much as she did not feel threatened by the letter, Lady Vyrrington knew that she would have to bring her rekindled affair with Blameford to an end once more.

It was not a task she took much pleasure in performing, but with Whitlocke out, she did not need to give any explanation or assurance as to where she was going. If tongues were already cocked like pistols regarding her visits there, the Countess had no qualms about being seen publicly to go to Mrs Rudgerleigh's former house. The street, on this instance, was in fact deserted, so she entered and went upstairs. Blameford was lying on his bed, which was where she expected to find him. She was carrying a reticule, within which was the letter. It was difficult to focus on her objective when, as soon as she had entered his room, and as soon as he had seen her, he had jumped to his feet and pinned her up against the wall and escalated down her neck with kisses.

"I do hope you're here to finish what we started last night," he whispered to her passionately, as his lips moved down to her breasts.

"Well if you listen to me first, maybe we can," she returned, fighting the urge to let him continue. He groaned with intense frustration.

"Oh, fine. What's the matter?"

"Please sit down."

He did as he was told – if he was getting fucked that afternoon, he would do whatever it took to ensure it happened.

Without speaking, she took the letter out as she sat down beside him on the bed and showed it to him. His reaction to its words practically mirrored hers, though there was an added note of perplexity about his expression, one that did not warrant any words.

"I received that earlier today," Lady Vyrrington said.

He hesitated in his reply.

"And have you any idea who sent it?"

"No."

"You have no idea who knows about us?"

"As far as I was aware, we were the only two", Lady Vyrrington returned somewhat sardonically, "Unless you've said something to someone?"

"Don't be stupid!"

"All right, Mr Blameford. Don't forget you are *still* in the presence of a Countess!"

Her lover sighed deeply, rubbing his face with his hands vigorously and looking away from her in thought.

"Well we know Whitlocke knows," he said, "Lord knows he would like to see us both disgraced."

"Yes, that's true," returned Lady Vyrrington, standing up again and pacing, "But I have leverage over George Whitlocke, Jesse. He loses his one prized possession – Amethyst – if he does anything to me. Plus, though I am loath to own it, this isn't his style. He would be more direct if this was him."

"Mrs Urmstone? She hates me."

"Elspeth *adores* me! And I her."

Blameford scoffed.

"You won't even consider the possibility?" he retorted.

"No, I will not, Jesse! It's utterly out of the question. It would make no sense."

"Then maybe it's just gossip. A rumour for the sake of a rumour."

"It isn't unheard of. Drawing-room talk is taken more seriously by some than by others."

He walked up behind her and wrapped his arms around her waist, nuzzling her neck. She moaned quietly.

"Let me fuck you then," he whispered in her ear.

"I want to," she replied, "Lord *knows* I want to. But Jesse, I can't take the risk of this being more real." He released her and swivelled her around to face him. She kissed his lips.

"So, what then?" he said, unamused, "You're ending this?"

"Not ending it, no; I don't want it to end!"

"Then let's not hide anymore. Then they have nothing to blackmail you *about*!"

"I can't do that Jesse, you *know* I'm not at liberty to do that." She walked away from him towards his door, "We must both lay low until this storm passes. I *promise* I will see you again when I am assured these threats are of no real danger!"

Then she left, before he could protest, and before she could change her mind.

Chapter L
The Ladies Contemplate

RUMOURS ARE A MALIGNANCE; FESTERING and venomous, existing purely for the sake of ruining another party or parties' reputation. In Berylford, they were not a commonplace occurrence. Even the exaggerated tales of Mrs Urmstone were at least initially based in fact. But the vicious, slanderous words written to Lady Vyrrington were exemplary. Especially where they were broadcast to more than just one recipient. The Countess herself had ruled Mrs Urmstone out as a suspect (indeed it was only Blameford who suspected her in the first place), and it was just as well, for she too had received a letter. As had Mrs Haffisidge. One letter to the person it concerned is a threat of blackmail. Upon involving third parties, it becomes a conspiracy, as quickly as a quiet zephyr escalates to a ferocious hurricane.

Mrs Haffisidge had received hers, which read:

> *Lord Vyrrington – the cuckolded husband.*
> *Lady V. whores herself in our midst.*

Such vulgar language. Even to a lady who lived under the same roof as Mr Warwick. Mrs Haffisidge could not bear giving any of what she read credence. It was shocking enough to see such words against Lady Vyrrington, but the mention of the late Lord Wilson as a cuckolded husband disgusted her. The anonymous sender clearly had no respect for the dead, or the truth, as far as Mrs Haffisidge was concerned. Shortly after its arrival came that of Mrs Urmstone, who also came with an opened envelope, in a similar hand. The two ladies looked at one another in a mixture of confusion, abhorrence and terror, and made their way into Mrs Haffisidge's parlour.

They put the two thin sheets of paper on the tea table before them, and beheld them only reluctantly. As though they were both boxes, under which some repellent creature lay concealed, loath to be touched or disturbed lest they should attack and devour. Mrs Urmstone's letter said:

The wise, noble Oliviera V. – the bed-mate of servants

Sipping her tea quickly and nervously, Mrs Haffisidge eventually broke the silence:

"Well there's no doubt as to what they're suggesting."

"I would scarcely know a dignified way of confirming it, Judith-Ann."

"We need not confirm it! It isn't true. It *can't* be!"

She stood and snatched up both pieces of paper. On the mantlepiece, there lay some matches, one of which she struck and lit a candle on the mantle. She then held each letter, one-by-one to the flame, where it quickly consumed the paper and the vile words they held. She tossed each burning slip into the grate.

"There. We may never read them again," Mrs Haffisidge muttered, returning to her seat and her tea. She looked at Mrs Urmstone, whose head was low in contemplation.

"Elspeth? What is it?"
Mrs Urmstone started and shook her head, as though she had just been woken from sleep.

"I was just thinking," she returned.

"About?"

"When we went to that party at Griggsden Manor. Lady Hilda Albion said something about Lady Vyrrington 'being the guest head on more than one pillow' or some such nonsense. Such a sentence does not even constitute feasible English!"

"*But*?" Mrs Haffisidge exclaimed, pressing Mrs Urmstone to continue.

"Well I dismissed such slander and of course scolded Lady Hilda accordingly. But now upon seeing these letters, in a hand I do not recognise, I cannot help but think."

"I advise you against this line of thinking, Elspeth," replied Mrs Haffisidge, "I think it makes little sense that one such as Lady Hilda Albion, who cares to know neither of us, would seek out our addresses to discredit Lady Oliviera."

"Then whom, Judith-Ann? Who would dare commit such a toxic betrayal?"

"I don't know, my dear. And whom is Lady Vyrrington even alleged to have been cuckolding Lord Vyrrington with?" She scoffed. "Jesse Blameford, do you suppose?"

Mrs Urmstone cleared her throat uncomfortably.

"No, I think not," she murmured, "My Lady Oliviera has already assured me *personally* that her relationship with Jesse Blameford is nought but one of friendship. It is not a friendship I necessarily approve of – a Countess and her former servant socialising however privately – but I trust Lady Vyrrington to act in her own wisdom."

Mrs Haffisidge merely smiled and nodded, her fingers steepled in her own deep thought. Mrs Urmstone's comments about the party at *Griggsden Manor* had led her to recall deplorable memories – those of her encounter with Christopher Tratsly – and then tried to justify how a man like him could be the culprit behind these letters. But what motive would he have to ruin Lady Vyrrington? There was no motive, and Mrs Haffisidge knew it. It was an easy way out of a difficult question, and thus her theory ended.

"We are left with one final decision, Judith-Ann…" Mrs Urmstone continued, "…Do we inform Lady Vyrrington of this?"
Mrs Haffisidge inclined her head back towards her fire grate.

"Tell her of what, Elspeth?" she returned, almost coldly, "The letters never existed, and the words on them will never be repeated. Not between us, nor to Her Ladyship. As her two closest friends, our duty is sacred – to protect her at all costs!"
Mrs Urmstone looked almost bemused by her friend's vehemence.

"I agree wholeheartedly, my dear Judith-Ann," she replied nervously.

"Now, if you'd like to take luncheon together, I must go to market. I'll just be upstairs to fetch some money."
Mrs Urmstone sat upright in her chair.

"Do you keep no money in your reticule?"

"To own the truth, I appear to have been miscalculating a lot these days – it pays to know exactly how much I have if it is all in one place, and I can take out how much I need for each time I go into town. A couple of pounds should afford us a decent luncheon." And with that, leaving Mrs Urmstone continuingly bemused, she went upstairs.

Chapter LI
Mr Warwick's Realisation

IN TRUTH, MRS HAFFISIDGE HAD not miscalculated her money at all. She had, however, underestimated the odious actions of her nephew-in-law Mr Luke Warwick.

He, too, knew of the one place in her house she opted to keep her money, and, in a rare moment of cleverness for him, had had a second key made for the bureau in which her banknotes were kept, so he could make free with her finances whenever he chose. Or rather, whenever Christopher Tratsly demanded or instructed. While not a learned man, basic arithmetic was not unknown to Mr Warwick; his co-conspirator Mr Tratsly had already acquired four or five sums of ten, sometimes fifteen pounds at a time.

It was lucky that her late husband's estate left Mrs Haffisidge considerable funds to live on, to a point where the odd ten or fifteen pounds going missing *could* be dismissed as an error. Mrs Haffisidge dared never deal with banks or other institutions; those such as *Mullens & Cooke Finances in London,* whose clients included the Vyrrington family. She never wanted to come to ruination through such vessels of unscrupulousness, she often professed. But by having all her money aside in physical form, it was ripe for the picking in Mr Tratsly's extortionate ways.

All Christopher Tratsly had to do was ask Mr Warwick if he wanted the key to destroying Mrs Haffisidge once and for all. Mr Warwick would pay to show much he wanted it, and Mr Tratsly would promise to deliver it, once he had received further information from his so-called 'source', on a few of 'the subtleties of the case'. And Mr Warwick dared never question him – he could not afford to believe his quarry was not totally vouchsafed to him.

His hopes were as high as his anxiety when he had received an invitation from Tratsly to meet at *The St. Barbara's Arms* – in the private backroom where they always conducted their business. Another ten pounds had been taken from Mrs Haffisidge's bureau for the power to destroy her, the notes scrunched coarsely into Mr Warwick's pocket and thumbed repeatedly, agitatedly, with one hand, while the other drummed upon the table before him, awaiting Tratsly's arrival. The fellow Mr Warwick knew to be Christopher Tratsly did indeed enter the backroom moments later, but his appearance had changed drastically. From the shabby, dishevelled creature with whom Mr Warwick normally did business, the man who sat across the table this time was dressed in his finest, an embroidered frock coat, waistcoat with dazzling brass buttons, a silk cravat fastened tight enough to strangle around a starched collar enveloping his throat. These were not rented clothes. These had been paid for, and recently.

"I feel underdressed," Mr Warwick quipped, "Are you off somewhere?"

"I hope you'll forgive me, Warwick old friend, but I must away to London," Tratsly replied.

"To *London*? What for?"

"Only all the more to benefit the *case*, of course! Why else?"

"You look like you have a few society parties and maybe an opera on your list!"

"This is for appearance's sake, Warwick! I can't very well go making inquiries in our glorious capital if I look like I woke up in an alley this morning, now can I?"

Mr Warwick sipped his ale, admitting to himself that it made sense.

"There is a vital piece of information that will be the *true key* to bringing about your meddlesome aunt-in-law's downfall, I promise you," Tratsly continued, "But we can't go about stating these things without proof. Or else we'll both be done for slander. Want that?"

Mr Warwick shook his head.

"I ride for London today to *acquire* that proof. Which reminds me – ten pounds will cover the travel I should think." He eyed Mr Warwick's pocket, in which his hand was still placed, fingering the screwed-up banknotes. Almost reluctantly, Mr Warwick pulled the notes out and placed them on the table. Tratsly tutted at the state of them, and straightened them out one-by-one as he counted them.

"You don't pay much heed to appearances, do you, Warwick?" he sighed, folding the banknotes and placing them in his coat pocket.

"I do wonder if it is *all* for appearances and you have no information at all!" replied Mr Warwick.

"I should be insulted."

"Could you at least tell *me* what this 'vital piece of information' is? With or without the proof?"

"Of course I could. Do you swear you won't tell another soul until I have said proof?"

"Just tell me, damn you!"

"Not here!" returned Tratsly sharply, "There are too many ears that might be listening. Ears that may be more loyal to Mrs Haffisidge than they are you!"

"Where then?"

"Follow me outside."

They both stood and walked out of the tavern to a neighbouring alley. Tratsly was looking about cautiously at the entrance to the backstreet for any would-be listeners – almost as though he had arranged a brief public tryst with a whore. Warwick watched him turn to face him, and that was the last thing he remembered seeing. Then it was just black.

*

When he next saw light, he was being stood over by his wife and his aunt-in-law Mrs Haffisidge – both of whom were giving him looks of blatant disapproval – as well as Jesse Blameford, who seemed to be trying to hide his amusement. He offered Mr Warwick a hand up. Once on his feet, his hand straight away felt for his left temple; he felt as though he had been struck.

"If you have to get drunk during the day and engage in a tavern brawl, Mr Warwick," Mrs Haffisidge hissed at him, "At least have the decency to not disgrace *me* or *Alicia* any further, and *win*!"
She then turned and walked off, and was followed closely by Mrs Warwick.

"You don't normally get *in* brawls, Luke!" said Blameford, "What happened?"
Mr Warwick's mouth hung agape with the realisation. Christopher Tratsly had gone to London – God only knew where exactly – with Mrs Haffisidge's stolen money.

"The money. The man!" he stuttered, "He stole the money. *My* money."

"You've been robbed – that's what you're saying?"

Mr Warwick's expression did not change.

"I've been robbed of so much," he gasped, barely able to breathe.

Chapter LII
A Rumour from the Cook

A FORTNIGHT PASSED, AND LETTER after letter and note after note, each all more threatening than the last, had arrived at *Beryl Court.* Threatening the Countess of Vyrrington with her own downfall should a payment not be received. Not willing to ransom her own reputation for the benefit of someone too cowardly to hate her in person, Her Ladyship would not bend to her written assailant's demands. Instead, she decided to visit her sisters at their ancestral home *Vellhampton Park* in Dover and would be accompanied by her children. If anything, it was to protect them from reading something they may or may not understand.

They started at first light, for it took many hours to eventually reach the grand old house that was the home of Lady Vyrrington's childhood. They were received in the gardens in the late morning of the following day by the other four Isaacs sisters – Ladies Lavinia, Diana, Georgiana and Clementina. They were all tall women, like Lady Oliviera, but now all in varying degrees of middle age, the dark hair prevalent in the Isaacs family was now streaked with threads of silver. Indeed, to Lady Vyrrington, it was a sight that provoked a conflicting sense of both relief and dread: relief that she was still in possession of her however-waning youth, and the dread that her sisters were as her reflections, should she look in a crystal ball to see herself ten years hence.

After being allowed a moment to see their rooms, Lady Oliviera and her sisters took tea together, while the children had been permitted to explore the gardens and grounds, with the guidance of a couple of the *Vellhampton Park* servants. Amethyst was also on-hand and had been assigned as a supervisor to them.

Following tea, Lady Vyrrington made her excuses to her hostesses, and surreptitiously directed herself downstairs. Even though she had not lived in the house since she had arrived in Berylford, she knew every corridor and passageway as well as she had when she was a child, when she would demand extra pastries from the kitchen staff. There, she was reunited with Mrs Trudgedawes, who was both astounded and overjoyed to see her. They agreed to share a conversation in the kitchen after the ladies of the house continually boasted about the number of social visitations *Vellhampton Park* had been subject to in the past month or so – particularly Lady Jacqueline Rhésel-d'Ivre – the French noblewoman notorious for her overly exclusive diet.

"It is a pity you did not bring your daughters," she said to Lady Vyrrington, "I would very much have liked to have seen how well they've grown."

"Their beauty exceeds mine when I was their age."

"I'm sure that's not true milady."

"Oh it is. They remind me often enough..." she sighed deeply, "...In fact society itself is beginning to notice, I have discovered."

"You oughtn't to pay them any mind milady. I may have been a cook all my life, but I've learnt that socialites think what they like to think. And it isn't always the truth they're thinking about."
Lady Vyrrington did not respond to the comment, leading Mrs Trudgedawes to continue the conversation on the same subject.

"As it happens, I have heard something that might interest you," she said.

"Something in society?"

"Indeed."

"How did you–?"

"I hear things milady. And this was a couple of weeks back during the visit of Lady Rhésel-d'Ivre."

"The one with all the allergies?"

"That's the one milady. A terror to try and cook for – I can tell you."

"What did you hear, Mrs Trudgedawes? Pray tell!"

"I don't know much milady, but she was talking to Lady Diana about something that had been said in society. Something scandalous in nature. About you." Lady Vyrrington's eyes merely widened, and she blinked a few times.

"About me?"

"Apparently a rumour has been circulating throughout London society. Someone's out to tread your name in the dirt milady, and if you want to know any more, I'd speak to Lady Diana."

Chapter LIII
The Favourite Sister

THE COUNTESS' MIND WAS UTTERLY besieged. Lady Jacqueline Rhésel-d'Ivre, of all people, had heard a rumour regarding her. 'This is not good...' Lady Vyrrington thought to herself as she ascended back upstairs, one hand clung to the bannister, the other was clasped around her mouth, '...What if Diana or any of the others have asked people questions? What if they have discovered the truth about me and Jesse?'

While all five sisters had grown up very close, the Countess enjoyed the confidence of Lady Diana the most, and the two favoured one another. They both held liberal views, were kind to servants and took pity on the poor and wretched – things that their late father had encouraged. But in Diana's spinsterhood, she kept almost constant company with her other sisters, and as such, Lady Vyrrington knew that difficulty would arise in getting her favourite sister away from the other three. There was only one thing for it – she would have to visit her later at night.

*

It was executed entirely to plan. Lady Diana sat alone in her room brushing her hair in front of her mirror when Lady Vyrrington knocked on her door and opened it, standing in the outside hallway.

"Oliviera dear, you have caught me at an inconvenient moment," Lady Diana said, "Whatever it is I'm sure can wait until morning?"

"No, not really Diana. I need to talk to you alone." She walked in and sat on her sister's bed.

"And you cannot do that in the morning?"

"Dear sister, you and our other three siblings are nigh inseparable in the daytime. This is why this conversation must take place now."
Lady Diana sighed.

"Well very well, what is it you wanted?" She returned back to brushing her hair, only half-listening.

"You and Lady Jacqueline apparently had a conversation while she visited you recently."

"Of course we did, dear; she was a guest in my house."

"A conversation concerning me."

"This was your house too if you can remember that far back."
It was obvious that Lady Diana was avoiding the topic.

"Apparently there has been a rumour about me in society," the Countess said straightforwardly, "And Lady Rhésel-d'Ivre spoke to you about it."
Lady Diana sighed once again and turned to face her sister.

"Now before I continue, please know wholeheartedly I do not give any of this credence. And neither do any of the others. Do you understand that?"
Lady Vyrrington nodded anxiously and vigorously.

"Please, sister. What has been said?"

"Lady Jacqueline received some sort of intelligence from an anonymous person that you have allegedly committed to a man outside of the matrimonial bond."

The Countess had prepared herself for the worst, but at the same time did not expect her fears to be realised. To send threats to Her Ladyship was one thing. To her closest friends Mrs Urmstone and Mrs Haffisidge (though she still knew nothing of this) was already a definite conspiracy. But to send such a thing to Lady Jacqueline Rhésel-d'Ivre – a woman who had only the year before fled the terror of the French Revolution, the grip of Robespierre and the blade of the guillotine, and whose company Lady Vyrrington had only kept across opposite ends of the same drawing-room – was an unfathomable, impenetrable mystery. What did her anonymous antagonist intend by involving such a distant acquaintance?

"That's ridiculous!" Lady Vyrrington denied vehemently to her sister, "Lord Wilson was my one and only love! I would dare never betray him!"

"Sometimes after a man has been dead for some time, a lady's passions find themselves wanting."

"And just what would you know of a lady's passions?"

"Do not be so quick to judge your sisters, Oliviera! The four of us may have remained unmarried while you found someone who would keep and support you. That does not mean to say that we ignored all men in society."

"You said you would not believe this? You will condone this as a slanderous slur to my name?"

"Give me a reason not to, Oliviera," returned Lady Diana, "You made yourself perfectly clear that you would never betray Lord Wilson."

"And I stand by that."

"Then I will destroy this as well..."
She opened a drawer in her dressing table and took out an envelope.

"...we were sent this message shortly after Lady Jacqueline's visit. One each. I cannot say what the others have done with theirs, but I kept mine if ever you came to visit. We believe this to be related to the rumour of which Lady Jacqueline spoke."

She took out a slip of paper from the envelope and showed it to Lady Vyrrington.

It read:

Oliviera Vyrrington – countess upstairs, whore downstairs

Her Ladyship immediately recognised the handwriting as that of her anonymous blackmailer. It narrowed the possibilities of the perpetrator's identity. It could not have possibly been Whitlocke now. He did not know the address of *Vellhampton Park*, much less that of the apartments of Lady Jacqueline Rhésel-d'Ivre; even Lady Vyrrington herself did not know the latter.

Vellhampton Park's address was kept in her private address book. She had to think: who could possibly hate her so much to want to expose her? Enough to seek out her sisters' address?

She watched as Lady Diana tore the slip in two and threw it in the fireplace.

"I thank you for having faith in me, Diana," she said.

"You are as much my sister as the rest of them. You are family, Oliviera. It is our sacred bloodline duty to have faith in one another."

"I know. And once again, thank you."

*

Returning to her own room, Lady Vyrrington found Amethyst arranging her dressing table.

"Thank you, Amethyst – I will not require you anymore tonight."

"Very good milady."

Without argument Amethyst left her mistress to her thoughts:

'I have no enemies. It can't have been Whitlocke. Jesse would gain nothing from exposing us. But to contact my family! And strangers in the city! Who is capable of so much spite? Of so much contempt of me?' she thought continuously. The words then struck a mutual chord. Spite. Contempt. They fit only one person's description that Lady Vyrrington knew – other than Whitlocke, of course.

'Rebecca Stirkwhistle?' Lady Vyrrington continued to think, 'But she does not know of Jesse and me. Or does she? Has she found out somehow?'

Her thoughts then returned to her small-hour tryst with Blameford those nights ago, and the disturbance that had cut it short.

'Can it have been her in the bushes? Or a spy of hers, no doubt.'

Her paranoia doubled with every second her mind dignified it with credence. But in her heart, she knew herself to be correct.

'There is no other explanation. No other possibility. It has to be Rebecca Stirkwhistle.'

Chapter LIV
The Family Name in High Esteem

THERE WAS NOT EVEN TIME for one last breakfast with her sisters before they left. The children were readied, the luggage was packed and, after quick goodbyes to her siblings, and no time for qualm or question, Lady Vyrrington's carriage sped from *Vellhampton Park* at the fullest extent of the horses' power.

She could not risk an overnight stopover on the way back to Hampshire; rather than impose upon the hospitality of friends who lived in Chichester, they changed horses there instead. While she arranged food for her children, Lady Vyrrington could not eat. She was too anxious and too angry.

It was later into the evening by the time they came up the dusty gravel path that led to *Beryl Court*. Whitlocke was there to receive her and help her down from the carriage, but to his surprise, she swiftly turned to go back in the direction she had come, on foot.

"My Lady?" the butler called after her, as he helped Amethyst assist with the children, "The carriage can be sent on to wherever you need to go?"

"Thank you, Whitlocke, but that won't be necessary," she returned, continuing her present course and not turning to face him in replying, "I have business in Berylford that must be attended to immediately. We have not eaten for many hours so have some supper served to the children. Whatever you can find that's suitable."

She had disappeared from sight by the time the butler looked back to question her further.

*

Her destination was the Stirkwhistle house. The Countess' expression was vehement, and her steps filled with anger. However, she would have to relent and lighten her disposition to be seen about town, especially since Mrs Haffisidge lived directly opposite; the slightest glimpse of anything untoward in Her Ladyship's manner would undoubtedly spark tongues wagging. She concealed not her feelings when knocking on the Stirkwhistles' door – three sharp raps of the cast iron knocker were all the courtesy she afforded them. She heard footsteps, and she was ready to launch a vicious tirade at Miss Rebecca, when, to her utter astonishment, she beheld Abel there before her. It sometimes surprised her to recall his miraculous recovery.

"My dear Oliviera," he said, "This is an unexpected surprise. We did not expect you home so soon from Dover. How are the family?"

"They are quite well," she returned, following him inside, "They rarely vary. You look much stronger, Abel. Every time I see you, it assails my mind to see you so recovered, given the circumstances."

"For the most part, indeed, and thank you," replied Abel, "Movement is still difficult and painful, but the pain is a beast and I intend to conquer that fellow all the same."

He led her into the study and closed the door, which perturbed her.

"Is Miss Rebecca home?"

"Upstairs attending to personal correspondence. Which reminds me…"

He limped over to the desk and took a folded piece of paper from it. He handed it to his cousin.

"What do you think of this?" Abel said, quietly. Lady Vyrrington had to feign ignorance of the fact she knew of the nature of the contents of the folded slip in her hands. Though Abel was among her closest and more beloved living relatives and theirs was an especially cordial relationship, even she was not immune to his formidable presence. She was compelled to open the paper, lest she should inflame his temper.

Oliviera V. – she lies with servants

She shut her eyes in dread that Abel had read those words and potentially believed them. Especially if it were but his own sister's poison.

"It's utter nonsense, of course. Clearly someone is out to discredit me," she muttered.

"What is the meaning of it?" Abel returned, not sounding amused. The Countess looked him in the eyes square-on.

"There is *no* meaning to it, Abel," she replied, matching his tone, "Though it gives further fuel to the reason for my being here!"

"Please don't mistake me, Oliviera. I do not believe with a single inch of my being that you have done anything *unbecoming* of someone in your position."

He approached her and placed a hand on her shoulder.

"Thank you, Abel."

"But be under no allusions," he continued, his tone now quite sinister, "I hold our family's name in the highest esteem."

"As do I, Abel!"

"Thus you will comprehend that I would not react well were I to learn that you *had* done anything to bring it into disrepute."

The Countess stood upright, with an air of indignance.

"Have you forgotten who I am, cousin?" she reacted hoarsely, "Am I a Countess? *The* Countess of Vyrrington still? Or am I one of those French harlots whose company you relish?"

"You watch yourself!"

"Of all the members of my family, the one person I thought I knew would never doubt me was you. I thought the strength of your good opinion would not be so easily swayed by such a thing as a piece of paper. Bearing nothing but the poisonous twistings of your own blood."

Abel's eyes were white and glaring.

"My own blood? Who?"

"As if you really need to ask."

He directed his head upwards (as much as he could, anyway) and muttered "I'll kill her."

"Just ensure that no more of these letters go around."

"'No more'? How many have been sent, besides this one and the ones Mrs Urmstone and Mrs Haffisidge received?"

Lady Vyrrington had to sit down, her eyes white with mortification.

"Elspeth and Judith-Ann as well?"

"To my knowledge, we're the only three. But you obviously know of more."

"My sisters. All four of them. And even that wretched Lady Jacqueline Rhésel-d'Ivre. I tell you if *she* received one, half of society thinks... I 'lie with servants'. That I'm a '*countess upstairs*' and a '*whore downstairs*'. Not to mention all the threats I have received personally. In the same handwriting. Demanding payment under pain of exposure. Well here we have the exposure, Abel. I'm thankful my reputation has survived this!" Her hands clasped themselves over her mouth, though they made their way down to her throat, as if in a subconscious attempt to strangle herself, and spare herself any further indignity.

"Please tell me you believe me, Abel," she whispered.

"I do, Oliviera. Now, if you will excuse me, I must see my sister."

Chapter LV
Malice is for Malice

AWKWARDLY, ALMOST AS A CRAB would, Abel staggered out of the study and up the stairs. His sister Miss Rebecca was sat at her writing desk, eyes fixed firmly on the correspondence before her, over wire spectacles. Her brother stood in the doorway; she did not dignify him with the courtesy of looking at him, though she knew of his presence.

"Yes?" she said, continuing to write.

"You know we have always been at war since you were old enough to believe you could think for yourself," Abel returned, "And by now I thought I would have learned every trick in your book. It appears I underestimated you. In terms of how vile and malicious a creature you have grown into. And how vile and malicious your capabilities!"

Again, such was her arrogance towards him, she did not look up from her letter.

"Oh Abel, spare me the theatrics. What are you blithering on about…?" her voice then lowered into a mutter under her breath: "…I swear that stroke did more damage to your wits than we first feared. That will teach us to hire a Welsh woman to be your nurse!"

"I just thought I would let you know – I know what you've done."

"Is that so? Would you care to elaborate?"

"I hardly think that's necessary. But also be aware that there is a *price* to pay for any mode of disgrace – attempted or otherwise – to our family name."

This time, Miss Rebecca did turn in her seat, but more to rid herself of her brother's presence than out of any intimidation or curiosity.

"One hopes you will soon arrive at some sort of point, Abel? Or else, leave me in peace."

"As I said, much as I have known you have always been an evil bitch, sister, I never thought you would sink to such cowardice as poison pen letters. I dignify you with more credit than you're due, clearly."

He took the key to his sister's door from out of the keyhole, and he saw her watch him as he did so, for once a twinge of fear struck her steely and arrogant countenance.

"What is the meaning of this?" she asked hoarsely, starting to stand up.

"This is to ensure no further correspondences leave this house without my say-so," he returned darkly, "*This*, dear sister, is the price you pay for such an attempt on the credit of our house. As 'nothing is for nothing', so it is with 'malice is for malice'. A maxim I intend to uphold and demonstrate and execute forthwith."

As she stood to protest, he stepped backward out of her room, slammed the door shut and locked it from the outside, taking the key out and placing it in his waistcoat pocket. She was slapping and slamming on the door and screeching from behind it at him, but no real words were totally audible, other than the cries of "Let me out" and "You cannot do this to me", plus numerous curses to her brother, some of which may have made the likes of Mr Luke Warwick blush crimson.

"You will cool your heels in there for a few days, sister, until you learn respect for the dignity of Lady Vyrrington's seat and authority here. And to hold our family name in the esteem it warrants. Do so and I may even honour you with some bread and cheese."
He heard her spit at the door, and in response merely smiled evilly as he ambled back down the stairs, patting the key to his sister's room in his pocket.

Lady Vyrrington was stood in the downstairs hallway, watching him in a mixture of relief, appreciation and fear. If imprisoning his sister in their own house was how far he would be willing to go for writing a poison pen letter or three, the Countess only wondered what on Earth her cousin would do to her if he ever found out that what the letters reported was true.

As he passed her, his expression lightened and warmed.

"Fear not, Oliviera," he said, "I don't think any malicious words will arrive at your doorstep anymore."

"Oh Abel," she fell into his arms and he embraced his cousin, "It has been a nightmare. I cannot know what possessed her to do this. My intervention with the Miss Gwynne affair was overstepping my bounds, I'll admit, but-"

"Hush now, Oliviera," Abel returned, "You will drive yourself bereft of your wits if you ever try to seek reason behind my sister's foul deeds. Some devilry infected her heart and corrupted her mind long ago. But she will pay the price for what she has done. And be released in due course, with humility and contrition accrued."

They both looked up the dark stairwell again. It was silent.

"What do you think she will do?" the Countess asked, still anxious, "Shout that I'm a whore who sleeps with servants from her window?"

"Then I'll gag her…" returned Abel straightforwardly, "…Beat her senseless. And scare anyone who will believe her poison into thinking otherwise. I will do whatever I must to stifle the lies, My Lady."

He kissed her hand.

"Go home to your children, Oliviera. They need their mother, and they need her at peace with the world and in mind."

Lady Vyrrington found for the first time in weeks she could smile without masking some inner terror. She kissed her cousin's cheek, and left him, not at all looking back up as she did so on the window of the prisoner who, there, lay within.

Chapter LVI
The Betrayal of All Common Sense

S HE WAS LOATH FOR THE notion to enter her mind, but with her blackmailer under lock and key, the Countess was now at liberty to visit Blameford without cause for fear or dread. Number Five Chine Road was within eyeshot as she crossed the square at the centre of town. Her proper mind and more astute judgment would have advised her to carry on walking without a second thought, but she was so relieved by the thought of Miss Rebecca languishing in her room with no means by which to torment her any further that she became complacent. She felt as though there was no force that could harm her. She betrayed that common sense and wisdom for which she was so extolled and renowned in town; turned down that road and once again entered that house.

Blameford was smartly dressed. It was surprising; he had found work as a joiner but his trappings were more those of a banker. He looked well in a waistcoat, tightly laced at the back, which only complemented his well-muscled physique. He turned when the door closed and beheld the Countess there. He was surprised to see her.

"What happened to laying low?" he said, an eyebrow raised. Lady Vyrrington was eyeing him up and down, enjoying what she was seeing.

"Did you inherit a peerage while I was gone? Or become engaged to a Marchioness?" she asked him. He laughed.

"I should be so lucky!" he returned, "I had a meeting with some investors regarding a proposal I have been planning."

"What proposal?"

"The machine that caused the disaster at the barn last Christmas. It was an early model."

"And caused the deaths of four men," said the Countess sharply, "Severely injuring two others. Such instruments have no place in the future of this world."

"They do if they are improved upon."

"You have the answers to that, do you?" she scoffed, "A former footman and a joiner?"

"Who was employed in factories where these things were developed prior to… other unfortunate events…" Blameford returned, smirking, "…it turns out this experience was welcomed. Mr Devonshire at the rag-and-bone shop knows someone who knows someone who was involved in the initial invention of the machine in question. And they required my advice on how to move forward."

Lady Vyrrington was quite shocked.

"Well!" she said, "I am quite overcome."

"Which means I am likely to come into quite a bit of money if I impress. I will have a name for myself, and increased status…"

The Countess looked him in his eyes. His expression changed from enthusiastic to bemused.

"…What?" he said.

"I can see where you are going with this."

"Tell me it's not feasible."

"Very well then – it is not feasible."

"*Damn it*! My Lady, what can I do to ensure we are together?"

"You can't, Jesse – it's out of the question. I didn't come here to quarrel with you about this." She quickly changed her motives for coming there. If his proposed success was as imminent as he made out, she could not risk proving those who had believed the rumours about them correct, nor incurring the wrath of Abel for deceiving him. Or Miss Rebecca, for the part the Countess had played in sealing her fate.

"So why have you come here?" Blameford asked her.

"Well I thought it would be obvious. Our arrangement cannot possibly continue."

"Why should it not?" Blameford snapped back, "Because someone knows about us?"

"No, there will be no further letters. That was Rebecca Stirkwhistle's doing. Abel has dealt with it in his own way."

Blameford looked away and laughed. Lady Vyrrington was at a loss as to what he found so amusing.

"What?" she asked him.

"Nothing; it's just not all that surprising, that's all," returned Blameford.

"One almost believes you're going to enlighten me," the Countess pressed him to elaborate, "Was there something between you and Miss Rebecca when you were in Italy?"

"*No*! Well, she *imagined* there may have been. She thought I was attracted to her as she was to me. After Mr Stirkwhistle left for Venice to confer with their father's lawyers, she made an advance to me, which I rejected. She told me she was in love with me and threatened me with my position if I refused to oblige her in her requests."

"Dear *God*! She's more insane than I gave her credit for!" Lady Vyrrington exclaimed, "And so she dismissed you when you rejected her?"

"That's correct. Mr Stirkwhistle had no hand in it – I believe he was impressed with my work. No doubt she told him some other story."

"Perhaps. It matters not now, anyway. He has locked her away. In her room. Just for sending those letters. She cannot harm us anymore."

"Then why should we hide?" Blameford approached the Countess again, "Don't you understand? Your husband's dead now! You no longer have the obligation to remain faithful!"

"Jesse, it does not diminish the fact that, despite how much I enjoy being with you, every day I *miss* Lord Wilson!"

"No, no, it's more than that; it's *always* been about more than that! I realise what this is. It's all to do with class! You're ashamed to be with me is what it is!"

"Don't be stupid," she muttered, standing up in order to leave, "Do you think I would have done half of the things we've done together if I was ashamed to be with you?"

"You're worried that if you are discovered with me, your place in society will be ruined!" Blameford continued.

"Could you cope with the disgrace? I may be a widow Jesse, but I am not married to you either! It's an illicit and illegitimate relationship and is equally as scandalous!"

"I don't believe this. You justify ending what we have because you want to stay at the top of people's invitation lists!"

"I think we should end this discussion," Lady Vyrrington went back towards the door, "I fear it isn't a subject on which we are likely to agree."

Blameford ran over to her, grabbed the Countess by the shoulders and pinned her up against the wall, kissing her lips passionately. She was both aroused and frightened, eventually having to claw at his shoulders to get him to release her.

"Let me go, Jesse, please!" she hissed at him.

"No!"

"I beg of you, sir, release me!"

"Say you'll see me again."

"It's out of the question, Jesse. This must end once and for all."

"Then give yourself to me one last time."

"There will never be 'one last time' if I let you have me now," she sighed, stroking his face, "I must go."

He did then unhand her and watched her out of the corner of his eye. His expression was fierce and angry.

"When you get home…" he said, unusually calmly for someone looking so vexed, "…You should speak to Whitlocke."

"About what?"

"Joshua."

A chill, more potent and powerful than the bite of the coldest winter wind, shot through her entire being as though it had been a bullet released from a flintlock pistol. After almost a year since the disappearance, Lady Vyrrington had long considered the necessity of hearing that wretched child's name again all but spent. Especially in connection with either Blameford or Whitlocke.

"Talk to Whitlocke? About the boots boy? What knows he of this? Beyond what was said at the time?"

"You should go, My Lady, as you said," returned Blameford, his voice now bereft of both the passion and the affection it had hitherto possessed.

Chapter LVII
An End to All the Mystery

THE SIGHT OF THE DEVIL Himself leading the forces of Hell into battle would not have cast half as fearsome a visage as that of Lady Vyrrington ascending the steps to her house. There was naught in her heart and mind but fury, rage and grief. A force of bitter wind followed the Countess as she finally entered *Beryl Court* again, her pace did not dissipate as she came through the doorway. Even Whitlocke was perturbed as witness to her ire; he stammered and stumbled after her attempting to speak as she continued to move.

"I would like to speak with you, Whitlocke. *Privately.* In the study."

"Yes, of course, milady. But your hat? Your gloves? Your coat?"

"Pay no heed to them, sir," Lady Vyrrington returned sharply, entering the study and allowing him to follow her, "Shut the door behind you."

"I spied you leaving Mrs Rudgerleigh's old place," he said, quite calmly as he did so.

"Oh! Here as I live and breathe: George Whitlocke, the eternal all-seer", returned Lady Vyrrington acerbically, "What was I doing then if your intelligence extends so far? And more to the point, what business is it of yours?"

"I know that Mr Blameford lives there now."

"Now don't be absurd Whitlocke and remember your place. I thought we were past this!"

"No, I warned you, milady. I told you that if the affair were to continue I would take action against you."

"And – I repeat – what business is it of yours if it were to continue?"

"You are being disloyal to Lord Wilson! To my master!"

"You really are a toadying little bastard aren't you, George Whitlocke! Lord Wilson is dead! Let me put it to you that if you sought companionship in another woman if anything ever happened to Amethyst I would not judge you. Or blame you. If anything, I would advise it!"

"And that's your justification is it? For your disloyalty to the memory of your own husband?"

"No one deserves to live alone!"
Whitlocke merely stared at her vehemently.

"Nevertheless," the Countess went on, "I have taken recent affairs into account and so I have ended it once and for all."

"Milady?" Whitlocke enquired, taken aback.

"I went around to Mr Blameford's residence to put an end to our arrangement."

"I see."

"Now if you will excuse me, I have questions for you!"

Whitlocke was almost afraid to speak again, lest he should provoke Her Ladyship's impending wrath. He could not help himself in the end.

"I've seen you angry, Lady Vyrrington, with all due respect," he spoke quietly, in case she should interject with another vitriolic tirade, "I've seen the maids in this house weep for deliverance after a display of your temper. But this fury is beyond all contemplation."

"What is beyond contemplation, Whitlocke, is how *sick to death* I am of being *lied to* all the time!" the Countess replied hoarsely. Her anger had exhausted her, in truth, to a point where she had to sit down.

"Who has lied to you?" Whitlocke replied, after a cautious moment of silence.

"The list is too long, but we can start with *you*!"

"Me?"

"Yes, *you*, Whitlocke. You, the vessel of deceit who presumes to rule my household. All this started when that little boots boy disappeared. *Tell me what happened that night, Whitlocke!*"

"What makes you think I know?"

"I can hardly believe one as efficient as you would allow a child that young to just vanish…" again she was exhausted and had to calm herself, fanning herself with her hand. He merely watched her, mouth ajar and at a loss as to how to satisfy her inquiries.

"…Whitlocke. I *know* you know…"
Her temper waned, and it was probably the kindest she had ever looked upon the butler at that moment.

"Please…" she whispered, her eyes now closed, "…I want an end to all the mystery."

Whitlocke observed tears under his mistress' eyelids, and he bowed his head.

"Very well," he murmured, "Whether or not you were aware of this is no longer relevant-"

"Is the child dead?" Lady Vyrrington interrupted.

"That is *also* no longer relevant."

"It is to me!"

"Then yes. Yes, he is."
The Countess shut her eyes. It was not the answer she had hoped for.

"Go on, Whitlocke."

"As I was saying, it doesn't really matter if you knew at the time, Joshua saw you and Blameford one night."

"He saw me and-?"

"Together. Yes. Only a couple of days after you buried Felix and Augustus."

"Dear God."

"You say 'dear God'. You should be thankful the boy came running to tell *me* and not Lord Wilson. Joshua didn't know the significance of what he had seen. I knew everything already, of course, and so I had the choice – either report it to Lord Wilson, or not."

"And you chose 'not'," returned Lady Vyrrington, "Why?"

"It was not a choice of what I had to gain from the situation but rather what I had to lose. If Lord Wilson learned of your infidelity, he would divorce you and banish you from this house. I would be lying if I said that isn't what I wanted."

"But?"

"But Amethyst," he replied, "If you were gone, there would be no need for a lady's maid in this house until the young Ladyships were old enough. I could not risk Amethyst being sacked or sent away with you, for all possible chance of marriage to her would be rent to nothing. I had no other choice – Joshua had to be silenced. Young necks aren't very difficult to snap." Lady Vyrrington winced at the idea.

"How did you bury him? Where?"

"Oddly enough, Mr Blameford helped me. He lies behind one of the tombs in the mausoleum."

"What about the attack on me here, in this house?"

"I hope you will believe me when I say I truly know nothing about that."

The Countess averted her gaze, staring blankly into nothing in particular.

"You really put your love for Amethyst before your hatred for me?" she said quietly.

"Yes, I did," he replied slowly.

"I would never have thought you capable of such admirable sentiment," she said, "It was this entire *stupid* thing with Jesse that has caused all this pain. It is my punishment, I fear."

"My Lady, I-"

"Go to Amethyst, Whitlocke. I shall not require you again this evening."

"Very good, milady."

"And Whitlocke?" she said as he turned to go out the door, "Thank you."

He was in every sense as much indebted to her as she to him, and, without anything further to say, carried on his way.

Chapter LVIII
What Else Whitlocke Knew

DOWNSTAIRS WAS QUIET. NOW THAT they were the only servants in the house, the Whitlockes had moved their marital and sleeping quarters down there. All servants had hitherto worked downstairs and slept in the attic. But there was a sizeable bedchamber adjacent to the butler's pantry, which now belonged to the Whitlockes.

This domain was all theirs. It felt to the Whitlockes as close to their own kingdom as any of their class dared ever hope for. Whitlocke found his wife sitting by her small dressing table in their bedroom. He leant over and kissed the top of her head gently and sighed deeply in relief.

"George?" she turned around and said, "What's the matter?"

"It is done," he sighed again in reply, "She knows."

"And that is everything? We still live here? *Work* here?"

"As long as certain other things remain unknown to her," he returned.

"Such as?"

"I think you know."

Amethyst stopped questioning and just stared at her husband, waiting for him to elaborate.

"I know it was you that pushed her down the stairs that night..." he said.

She then turned back around and looked at herself in the mirror, her hands clasped around her mouth.

"...I just need to know why?"

"Why do you think...?" she replied sharply – it was the first time he had seen or heard her display temper. He remained silent.

"...I did it for you."

Whitlocke looked perplexed. It was not the response he had been expecting from his mild-mannered wife.

"For me?" he repeated, knowing not what else to say.

"Of course, for you. Lady Vyrrington threatened to sack you that night. I don't know why or when or whatever else. But the idea that My Lady would come between me and my *happiness* in such a way to satisfy her own ends; it made me angrier than I ever thought possible of myself. And I just lost control. But as soon as I had shoved her over that top step, I came back to myself. I would be long dead were it not for her father and I would not have risen to the position I have now if it wasn't for her! I carry the regret of even *wishing* harm on her, let alone *causing* it, every single day. It will haunt me forever..."

She looked up at the mirror and saw in the glass that Whitlocke was sat on the edge of the bed, listening and understanding.

"…How could you ever love someone who would do such a terrible thing?"

"Are you mad? I'd be the worst hypocrite living to condemn you with the things I've done!" he replied, "That you would go to such an extent to defend me only makes me love you *more!*"

He knelt beside her at the dressing table and kissed her lips.

"We are married, and you are my wife, Amethyst Whitlocke," he said to her, "And that means we share in everything. Including our deepest, most awful secrets. We will conceal them from the world together, so long as we don't conceal them from each other."

She chuckled a little and smiled broadly.

"I love you, George."

"And I you, my dearest," he returned.

Then a bell could be heard ringing from out in the hallway.

"That's probably Her Ladyship now," murmured Amethyst, "She'll be wanting her dinner, and the children too no doubt."

She rose from her seat in front of the mirror and kissed her husband again.

"Thank you," she said, before walking off to attend her mistress upstairs.

Chapter LIX
The Vows of the Stirkwhistle Siblings

SEVEN DAYS PASSED, AND BERYLFORD had unknowingly acquired itself a resident vulture. Watching over its goings-on hawkishly from her bedroom prison was Miss Rebecca Stirkwhistle. While she barely knew most of the citizenry, she hated them all the same, as she hated all other creatures. None more so than her brother.

The wretched, sunken, stricken man who, in spite of all his evil, spite and cruelty and a slight dance with death, wielded such power, such control, such mastery over all who dared cross him. Even she, his sister, who, though she maintained it herself, was a force few dared oppose, had been thwarted and vanquished by him. As there she sat, drumming her stiletto fingers on the windowsill, each bladed fingernail rat-a-tat-tatting on the rotting wood rattled it like a hag's old bones.

She continued to survey, and noticed Mrs Haffisidge walking past, arm-in-arm with her niece Mrs Warwick and Mrs Urmstone. She watched them as a great bird spies a rabbit in a heathland, awaiting its opportune time to swoop and capture its prey. Her lips were no more than a mere line, before her attention was diverted by the twisting and turning of the lock of her door. It swung open, and there she beheld the severe countenance of her brother Abel.

They stared at each other in silence for a few moments.

"Well?" Miss Rebecca eventually said; she was encumbered by neither patience nor energy at this time.

"Come out. Downstairs and eat," Abel returned coldly.

It had been days since she had had a full, substantial meal. If she never had to look at another plate of stale bread, a slither of cheese and – if Abel was feeling merciful – half an onion again, it would be too soon. Miss Rebecca stumbled feebly out past the threshold, glaring endlessly at her brother, who reciprocated the expression. As she passed him, he seized her by the throat and held her by the wall. She had not the strength to resist him.

"I will only warn you once. If you *dare* speak against me, or *Lady Vyrrington*, or *any* member of our family again…" he whispered at her, sinisterly as if he had become some Hellish daemon, "…or do anything that would bring us disrepute, I'll fling you from that bedroom window – do you understand?"

"For what you have done to me, I would have readily done it myself, if only it would not prevent me from exposing you to be the *monster* you truly are!" she returned, "To spite you, I am resolved to live! I would like to claw your eyes out and serve them to your wife, brother! But thanks to your starvation I do not have the energy."

"Perhaps you did not hear me. Though you know I *abhor* having to say things more than once. *Do you understand?*"

"Yes!" she responded through gritted teeth, "Now let me *go*, damn you!"
Abel released his sister, and she fell to her knees in exhaustion. He went down the stairs. As soon as she was certain he was out of earshot, she muttered to herself:

"I vow this, Abel. With God as my witness I vow this. Your time smiting your way up and down this town, this house and this family will not be long, I think! Whether by my own hand or another's. But I will have my revenge for what you have done to me. I will have my revenge on you. *And* Lady Vyrrington. Both this house and hers will end in Hellfire by the time I'm through. I curse thee, brother, that even after I am dead you will be plagued and haunted, tormented by my memory, even unto the ending of your own life…"

She finally found the strength to stand but had to go back into her own room a moment and sit. Such was her exhaustion that even rising to her feet had rendered her dizzy. Massaging her temples, she continued on thinking aloud:

"…As for Lady Vyrrington, I have had my successes. My vengeance on her will be exacted much sooner. She is your right hand, brother, and you are hers. And you will both suffer a fate worse than death once I'm done with you."

She did not know how she would do it. These were if anything the mindless ramblings of an overtired, malnourished young woman with an axe to grind for her brother and all others whom she deemed responsible for her plight. Once she had a satisfying meal inside her, she would be able to approach realising her curses and executing her revenge with greater, deadlier conviction.

Chapter LX
A Secret Invitation

*M*Y VERY DEAR COUSIN, OLIVIERA,

No doubt you will be thankful to be in receipt of a letter from my house not in any way dealing out wanton disparity or vicious slander. Whilst on the subject, I must confer upon you the news that I have released my sister from the confinement of her bedchamber. As I vouchsafed to you, she emerges humbled and much contrite, with a greater deal of respect and recognition for your authority in this town, and in our family.

At the advice of Reverend Helton, she has decided to devote more of her time to improving the lives of those around her, and as such she has taken the late Mrs Rudgerleigh's place as schoolmistress here in Berylford, as it is our intention to remain in the town indefinitely. With the return of Zephaniah Gussage looking all the more unlikely, I have decided I shall assist her by serving as schoolkeeper.

I intend to install myself as a prominent figure among the citizenry here, so that, when the time arises, I may stand as candidate for Lord Mayor of Berylford, in

which I would be most grateful for any assistance and
support you can offer.

> *Sending love to you and your children,*
> *Abel Stirkwhistle, Esq.*

This was a letter Lady Vyrrington received a fortnight
following her last visit to her cousin's house. Since his
imprisonment of Miss Rebecca, she had dared not go
over there, lest Miss Rebecca should break down the
door and attack her with a carving knife. Her paranoid
thoughts had turned almost to deliria of ridiculous
proportions.

With all the news conveyed in the correspondence, first
she was perturbed by Abel's statement that he had
released his sister, then highly amused to imagine that
Miss Rebecca should be allowed anywhere near
children, let alone teach them, and then intrigued at
Abel's political ambitions. He had while living in
London had some interest in working in the Foreign
Office, and their cousin Lady Riva Styridge's late
husband had made certain arrangements for this to
happen. A Mayoral seat would be much more suitable
for Abel at this time, with his health still so recently
afflicted. His energies to campaigning and delivering
speeches and manifestos would not be so easily
exhausted.

And while she wanted to devote her attentions to that part of the letter, the Countess was much more fixated on the first paragraph, concerning the release of Miss Rebecca. The only real enemy she knew, given Whitlocke was, at the moment, in her favour. She would have to cut the head off the snake before it bit again and sunk its venom in so hard and potently that escape from death would be futile.

She repaired to the study and began a letter of her own. She did not waste time on pleasantries and did not attempt any falsehood by composing it with any warmth or affection.

To Miss Rebecca Stirkwhistle,

This is a cordial invitation to come to tea at Beryl Court at three, tomorrow. You are under no obligation to attend, but be assured that, should you not, I may send a few short letters of my own, revealing some of your own secrets. Those which I <u>*know*</u> *to be true.*

I look forward to seeing you.

Yours,
Lady Oliviera, Countess of Vyrrington

She wrote on the envelope: *Private and Confidential*, to ensure their meeting would be a secret one, even from Abel. Lady Vyrrington could not run the risk he would intercept all of Miss Rebecca's letters. She did also not await or expect to receive a reply – she could definitely be sure that Abel would check the content of any outgoing post.

The Countess contented herself with the knowledge that she had the upper hand over her enemy, despite what she perceived Miss Rebecca to know and what she wondered she would threaten her with. Lady Vyrrington possessed an influence that Miss Rebecca did not – the power to sway opinions in society and wield control over Miss Rebecca's acceptance therein. As such, she did not dread her arrival.

Indeed, punctual to the last, Miss Rebecca was received at the front door of *Beryl Court* as the clock finished striking three. The invitation was a secret, so even Whitlocke had not been informed as to her coming; he was surprised to behold her there across the threshold.

"I have come to see Her Ladyship?" Miss Rebecca addressed the butler snappily.

Whitlocke held her in about as much esteem as the rest of the town, even daring to look down his nose at her a little, and silently let her past him.

He led her in the direction of the sitting room, where Lady Vyrrington was waiting.

"Miss Stirkwhistle," Whitlocke scornfully announced, as the woman entered and stood before Her Ladyship. Lady Vyrrington regarded her coldly, looking up but not smiling, nor did she incline for her guest to sit.

"See about some tea, Whitlocke, if you please," to the butler she said. He nodded and obliged, leaving them both alone.

They were like two great queens, at opposite ends of a chess board. Miss Rebecca had no pawns or rooks, no bishops or knights at her disposal; the Countess had these in abundance, counting Miss Rebecca's own brother among them. But neither were there to protect a king. They were there to save one another's reputation from being checkmated.

"Are you going to invite me to sit?" Miss Rebecca breathlessly finally broke the terrible silence. The Countess continued to leer up at her.

"I think not," she replied icily.

"You invited me here."

"You were not obliged to come."

"Under pain of my secrets being *exposed*?" returned Miss Rebecca incredulously, "Forgive me, My Lady, but yes I *was* obliged to come!"

Lady Vyrrington scoffed, then opened her mouth to reply with some sort of acrimonious response. She held her vitriol, to allow Amethyst into the room to serve tea, waiting until her maidservant was gone and out of earshot before continuing.

"No doubt it is unsettling to have a secret and someone who knows it," Lady Vyrrington calmly went on, "Especially when the one who knows it, threatens to profit from it."

Miss Rebecca breathed deeply, contemplating an equally-calm response.

"I have paid the price for that. I believe my brother advised you of that fact," she said.

"So he did. A question that continues to plague me is how you found out about my... arrangement... with Mr Blameford at all."

There was silence. Miss Rebecca had shut her eyes, biting her lips. She was obviously reluctant to answer.

"It was you, wasn't it?" Lady Vyrrington went on, "Who spied us in the garden together. You who disturbed the bushes."

"It was very dark; I nearly tripped on something," returned Miss Rebecca, "But I saw all I needed. More than sufficient, actually. And you?"

"I beg your pardon?"

"How did you find out *my* secrets, My Lady? Was it Mr Blameford himself? Or was it that *devil* my brother?"

The knowledge that the Countess knew at all, and that it was the truth, was enough to torment Miss Rebecca.

"Abel alerted me to the possibility. Mr Blameford apprised me of the details. When I was trying to justify your motives for the letters. They were a means of spiting both of us."

"Yes," Miss Rebecca quietly and hoarsely replied.

"Come and sit here, girl," Lady Vyrrington commanded, pointing at an empty seat next to her. Her enemy had no choice but to acquiesce, slowly and disdainfully. The Countess continued:

"Henceforth, silence will be exchanged for silence – do you understand me?" she said, *sotto voce* and sinisterly, "You will forget all about my liaison with Mr Blameford, which is at an end at any event, and I will forget yours. If you do not, I will deal out more pain and punishment than you can possibly comprehend – to the extent you will wish you were imprisoned at your brother's hands."

Miss Rebecca sat back in the chair, her face further stricken by fear of Lady Vyrrington's vehemence.

"I- I understand, My Lady. I'll not cross you again," she stammered.

"Good," the Countess at last smiled, "Now get out."

PART 5
THE **TRIAL**

Book Thirteen
THE TRIAL OF JESSE BLAMEFORD

Chapter LXI
Constables at Berylford

I T WAS A LITTLE-SECRETED fact that George Whitlocke, prior to his taking employment under Lord Wilson Vyrrington, was a member of the Stirkwhistle household in London. His father had been butler at *Iverleigh Warren* – the ancestral home of Abel, his sister and their numerous cousins. As such, Whitlocke had gained much of his experience in service, but also a well-honed view into the inner workings of society, by way of Abel. The two were something of close, if cautious, friends; Abel often affording Whitlocke more courtesy than he may be due between such a class divide. Since Abel's recovery, they had made a habit of meeting once a week in *The St. Barbara's Arms*, where they were free to discuss and converse over topics Whitlocke would otherwise have to keep to himself. Politics, Lady Vyrrington, war, Lady Vyrrington, Abel's foreign travel and Lady Vyrrington, were some of their oft-discoursed subjects. And while Whitlocke had been sorely tempted many a time, he had never told Abel about the Countess' affair with Jesse Blameford. Such wanton destruction would sooner be desired on the steps of Hell than that which Abel would visit on his cousin in the event of his discovering her extramarital liaison, besmirching their family name irrevocably. But Whitlocke knew just as well that Abel would be just as unforgiving to a man who had concealed the fact from him for many years, usually for self-serving reasons.

On their way back from one such visit, just as they were preparing to part ways, Abel's attention was arrested by three gentlemen, all walking side-by-side, carrying an air of authority in every stride.

"What is it?" Whitlocke asked him; the men were walking in the opposite direction, towards the town square.

"Constables," Abel murmured in reply, suspiciously, "What's the meaning of *this*, I wonder."

He started back in the same direction, pursuing the three constables. Whitlocke had no time to dissuade him, so ran after him instead.

"I say, gentlemen?" Abel called to them, "Is that Constable Marris by any chance?"
The man stood central of the three stopped and turned around. He looked perturbed to having been recognised.

"I am Marris, yes," said he, "Mr Stirkwhistle, correct?"

"And where were you off to in such swift stride?" Abel continued, "There are no thieves, bandits or murderers here, I can assure you. Just rogues like myself." He chortled, but Constable Marris did not reciprocate the humour.

"No thieves or murderers you say?" he returned, with a deadpan expression, "That remains to be seen." He then turned to continue on his way but Abel grabbed his shoulder firmly and swivelled him around again.

"You need not involve yourself, Stirkwhistle," Marris continued, "It'll be the worse for you if you do."

"What did you mean by that? 'That remains to be seen'?" Abel was now deeply suspicious, "There's no one in town worth enough to be stolen from, and no one worth murdering for there to be any murderers."

"If you stop impeding me in my duty, perhaps all shall explain itself."

Marris then shrugged Abel's hand off his shoulder and, with the other two constables now guarding him from behind, followed his previous course.

"Abel, don't-" Whitlocke began, but it was too late. Abel had already limped off in pursuit of the lawmen again, intent on satisfying his curiosity; Whitlocke had no choice but to follow him.

They saw the constables had stopped outside a house, on the door of which Constable Marris was knocking. They had forcibly entered before Whitlocke and Abel beheld it was Mrs Rudgerleigh's old house, and by the time they arrived, Constable Marris was outside it again, allowing his two colleagues to bring an angry, struggling Blameford out into the streets. They threw him to the ground.

"What is the meaning of this?" Abel shouted, running over.

"For the last time, mind your own business, Mr Stirkwhistle," Constable Marris did not even look at Abel in his reply, "Jesse Alexander Blameford, you are hereby arrested for murder."

"This man is a former employee of mine and by extension the house of Vyrrington; I make it my business, Marris," Abel hissed at the lawman, who once again remained unimpressed. Abel was surprised;

Constable Marris was one of very few indeed who did not view him with fear.

"And just who am I supposed to have murdered?" Blameford groaned from the pavement. One of his eyes was black, his face scuffed and bruised, and a thin ribbon of blood trickled from his nose.

"In *this* town? I am arresting you for the murder of your landlady Clara Rudgerleigh, and that of your colleague in your former employment: a Joshua – no surname ever given. Constables you may take him away."

"Marris, this is outrageous," Abel protested.

This time Marris turned and approached Abel intently, looking him dead straight in the eyes. He was not a man of any great stature, but he was prepared to assert his authority as much as he could.

"If you insist on intervening, Stirkwhistle, have a word with the prosecutor Mr Ickrell. In the meantime, once again, allow me to do my duty. Take the man away, constables."

Abel was truly shocked. A mere glint of anger in his eyes had given opponents, belligerents and general annoyances full regret for any action against him in the past. Constable Marris was a match for him, but then perhaps this Mr Ickrell was not. As Blameford was hauled to his feet and dragged away, he cried out for help to not just Abel, but Whitlocke too, whose thoughts were so besieged he knew not how to even move or speak. Though by no will or action of his, this was happening to Blameford – a man whom Whitlocke had mutually despised since the first moment they met. And now the butler was in two positions; he could let his enemy hang and be done with it forever. All of them, including Lady Vyrrington, could move on with their lives, without looking over their shoulders. Or he could be weighed down by the knowledge he let a mere accomplice to a crime he otherwise solely committed himself die. He would have contemplated over this dilemma longer, but before he knew it, Abel had taken him firmly by the shoulders, trying to acquire his attention.

"Whitlocke! *Whitlocke*! I must go to the assizes. You must convey yourself back to Beryl Court and tell Lady Vyrrington."

The butler remained speechless and in shock but did manage to muster a nod of the head in agreement.

Chapter LXII
The Grand Old Judge

THE ASSIZE COURT RESPONSIBLE FOR meting out justice in criminal and civil matters in Berylford and its neighbouring towns Hinxstone and Wraxhill-on-the-Test, was situated in Andover, just an hour's ride from Berylford itself. While a number of judges sat there, the most revered, famed and renowned across the bench was an awfully thin man in the earlier stages of being elderly, by the name of Sir Joseph Ezrington. Recently made a baronet by the grace of His Majesty, he presided over his court with a splendour unsurpassed by any of his peers, with a deep, resonant and commanding *basso* delivery, a constantly somewhat-smug half-smile, an easily-provoked ironic and dry sense of humour, and an equally-quick and combustible temper. Conversely, his cloak and ermines loosely hung across his scarecrow-like shoulders to the extent that he looked dishevelled when seated in his courtroom. Through all of this, his fellow judges, the barristers and attorneys, the clerks, bailiffs and scribes all uniformly named him "The Grand Old Judge".

Moving in the circles he did, which included the House of Commons, Judge Ezrington had come into the acquaintance of Abel Stirkwhistle, when a career in the

Foreign Office had attracted him and the late Lord Stephanus Styridge had been trying to garner for him a place. As such, The Grand Old Judge seemed to be the better person to approach to intervene in Blameford's case than the stranger, Mr Ickrell. As the opposition, Abel's encounter with Ickrell would likely be hostile and counterproductive. With Judge Ezrington, Abel would keep his manner professional and respectful.

Ezrington's name was the first that Abel was speaking when he entered the courthouse, demanding that they speak before the next session commenced. The next assize was not due to start for another hour, or so a lawyer standing in the foyer informed Abel, before directing him to the judge's chambers, only to also advise there was a clerk to get past first before an audience with His Lordship would be granted. Abel, insistent that time was of the essence, took the steps up to the judge's chambers on the next floor two at a time and paid the clerk with a banknote of indeterminate value – it must have been a great figure for the clerk merely laughed and abandoned his post – leaving Abel at total liberty to enter uninterrupted.

In the interests of not angering the judge, and by extension jeopardising his entire purpose there, Abel knocked and waited for a summons from His Lordship before entering. Every respect need to be shown for the dignity of his office.

A low "Come," was heard, and Abel obliged.

The Lord Ezrington was not garbed in any robe or wig; instead a simple suit with a waistcoat and gold pocket watch, which he was checking as Abel entered. The Grand Old Judge looked surprised at whom he beheld.

"What is the meaning of this?" he asked, quite calmly, "I took you to be my clerk."

"There was no one on the door, My Lord," returned Abel, "You may or may not recall who I am, sir?"

"I do, Mr Stirkwhistle. There are few who mingle with House of Commons people as arrogantly as you did. You made yourself quite a laughingstock back then."

"A lesson well-learned, Lordship, I can assure you. Tried to run before I could walk," Abel returned, smiling with his self-deprecation, "I thank you for granting me an audience on such short-notice."

"I haven't granted you anything, Stirkwhistle. You entered by my permission, but I was not aware whom would be entering…"

He went and sat behind a great mahogany desk, put on a pair of spectacles, took up a quill that he dipped in some ink and began to write. Abel watched him.

"…But you are here now. You must have had the audacity to pay my clerk off for something of reasonable consequence?" Ezrington went on, "Or would you like me to have some officers clap you in irons for wasting a judge's time and… contempt of court… for my trouble?" He looked up over his thin, silver spectacles; Abel could see clear as crystal he was not joking.

"Indeed, My Lord," returned Abel, in a very rare moment of fear for his own being. He had not been invited to sit, so did not do so.

"You may have a man brought before you later today or possibly tomorrow, My Lord. A man named Jesse Blameford. Arrested wrongfully for murder."

"I am not the only judge seated here at these assizes, Stirkwhistle: Judge Cresswell could be presiding over the case or… Judge Saquidge. Judge Trumpford."

"The man was formerly in *my* employment, and that of Lord Wilson and Lady Oliviera Vyrrington. As such, it is a criminal matter that needs to be dealt with in a manner of decency and discretion."

"For what reason?" said another voice, one that did not bother knocking before entering.
Abel turned around and saw another man, who looked to be even thinner than the judge – as if such a thing were possible. His abundant, oily hair had been combed upwards, his face was scarred and well-lined, his lips

swollen and cracked, and his eyes very far set into his skull. He did not display a very trustworthy aspect.

"Ah, Mr Stirkwhistle, I introduce you to Mr Ickrell, one of the chief prosecutors here," said Ezrington. The two other men regarded each other down one another's noses; they did not shake hands.

"And is this gentleman the attorney for the defence?" Mr Ickrell said quietly and with an air of undeniable arrogance.

"I am not, sir," returned Abel, "The accused has no lawyer at present."

"He should see about that, really," muttered Ickrell, "Not that I'm sure it can do a lot of good. The accusations are quite damning, as are the witnesses I have brought to testify."
Abel turned back to the judge.

"See here, My Lord, I beseech you. Does Mr Blameford not have the right to have an attorney brought for him?"

"He does, Stirkwhistle. Though you have failed to answer Mr Ickrell's question as to why we should handle this case with any more delicacy than any other, and by extension why it *deserves* such treatment?"

"My Lady Vyrrington, I am sure, would *appreciate* it!" returned Abel, and he raised both eyebrows at the judge.

"Appreciate it, *how*?" Ezrington said slowly and deeply, "Mr Ickrell, I will converse with you presently. You may wait outside."

The prosecutor left, yet not without exchanging another condescending glance at Abel. They waited until they could be sure he was not listening at the door before recommencing their conversation.

"I will agree to hear Mr Blameford's case…" said Ezrington, "…though a quid pro quo comes attached to this generosity."

"What sort of quid pro quo?"

"You seem to wield a lot of influence over Lady Vyrrington?"

"Not influence necessarily. But she is my cousin. Favours are regularly called in from her to me as I to her."

"Perhaps you could persuade her as to a recommendation in the House of Lords," the judge murmured quietly.

"For herself?"

"For me."

Abel's eyes widened. In the interests of bribing a judge, this was not at the extreme he had been anticipating.

"For you? Merely a recommendation?" Abel repeated, incredulous that the price should be so low.

"An elevation in position is all I require, in exchange for hearing this man's case."

"Then I must go directly to Lady Vyrrington. She knows a trustworthy attorney!"

"Stirkwhistle, you must be under no allusions…!" the judge called after Abel as he went to depart, "…I make no promises that… the worst should not happen. If the jury finds Mr Blameford guilty, I will not intervene and acquit him. I hope that's understood?"

"I ask for no more than your hearing his case, sir."

"Then be quick about it and fetch this man a lawyer. His case will appear before me two days hence."

Chapter LXIII
Indictment and Trial

LADY VYRRINGTON HAD BEEN INFORMED by Whitlocke as to Blameford's arrest per Abel's instructions, and was immediately overwrought by fear. First it was Whitlocke's threats, then it was Miss Rebecca's letters; now by no human force, but by the law would her secrets eventually become public knowledge. And with it, her deceit, her hypocrisy and her cowardice would be brought to bear before her family, her friends and her tenants.

Flight was her first instinct, but she could not. It would spell out guilt of her own sins without question; besides, she could neither leave Amethyst, whether she was married and happy with Whitlocke or not, between them without their wages, they could not afford to keep *Beryl Court* on their own; nor her children, who would have no place in society if her scandal was proven to be true. Old sins cast long shadows, and those shadows often engulf the children of the sinners, paying the price over and over again in their turn thereafter. Too easily does society punish the children for the crimes of their parents. Such wanton destruction would be brought about if the Countess absconded now.

Her first letter was to her own lawyer, Mr Jackdawe, seeking his assistance at a moment's notice. His offices were in Andover, close to the assize court, so his response dictated it would be to Lady Vyrrington's better convenience to attend him there. She brought with her Whitlocke, whose testimony into Blameford's character would be warranted, as well as his knowledge of the disappearance (and alleged death) of the boots boy, Joshua. Lady Vyrrington had, in fact, not been informed as to the charges on which Mr Blameford was arrested, only that he had *been* arrested. Whitlocke had decidedly omitted the fact that he had heard from Constable Marris' own lips that Blameford was arrested for having murdered both Mrs Rudgerleigh and Joshua, even if neither thing were true.

The Countess and Whitlocke beheld Mr Jackdawe, who was stood outside the courthouse with Abel, as they exited Her Ladyship's carriage. They greeted each other, and, entering the courthouse, Mr Jackdawe began his explanation:

     "It will begin with the indictment…" he said, "…And a statement of the charges against my client."
     "Charged with what?" asked Lady Vyrrington.
     "Murder, My Lady!"
The Countess was astounded.

"*Murder*?" she repeated, "And *whom* exactly is Mr Blameford supposed to have murdered?"

"Well I have had a word with the prosecutor – a Mr Ickrell. They're concentrating on two persons who died in suspicious circumstances in Berylford in the last year…" returned Mr Jackdawe, "…One Clara Rudgerleigh, and a young boy called Joshua, no other name given."

Lady Vyrrington scoffed, looking sharply at Whitlocke as she did so.

"Clara Rudgerleigh died of a *stroke* – plain and simple. A tragic accident that took a lady from this world before her time. As for the young boy-"

"I think it best that we don't discuss it out her, My Lady," Mr Jackdawe interrupted her, indicating and reminding her they were not in private quarters, but rather the foyer of the assize courts, surrounded by attorneys and other men in court dress.

"You will be called to give evidence as to Mr Blameford's movements on the night of the boy's disappearance," Mr Jackdawe went on to the Countess, "Mr Whitlocke here will reinforce your statements, and Mr Stirkwhistle will then advise as to the defendant's character. I have also listed Doctor Jonathan Street to speak to the medical particulars of Mrs Rudgerleigh's death, and also – though I know not why I was possessed to think this a good decision – Mrs Elspeth Urmstone – dreadful woman."

"*Elspeth*?" Lady Vyrrington gasped, "What on Earth for?"

"Mr Blameford insists he was with her when Mrs Rudgerleigh died. It will quash the argument Mr Ickrell intends to bring for means to murder her."

"Doctor Street can refute that, *surely*?" cried the Countess, "How does one go about deliberately causing another person to have a stroke?"

"You said, Jackdawe, they were concentrating on these two murders?" Abel interjected before Lady Vyrrington drew too much attention to them, "Indicating that there are more?"

"Mr Ickrell told me that Mr Blameford's past is… complicated…" returned Mr Jackdawe, "…that he may have been acquitted of five other counts of murder a few years ago. But they intend to use it against him."

"Do you know of this, Oliviera?" asked Abel. Lady Vyrrington held her tongue. She did know, for the circumstances thereafter were what led to Blameford coming into her service in the first place.

"I think I know what this Mr Ickrell plans to ask me," she said breathily, "I fear I will be more hindrance than help in this case. I should not have come."

"My Lady, you have been called as a witness for the defence. And if you choose not to attend, Judge

Ezrington will hold you in contempt of court, and Mr Ickrell will just subpoena you so that you *have* to testify," Mr Jackdawe was speaking politely but firmly. An usher was heard, announcing the court was now in session. All four of them were led in.

*

Many monumental events in local history had taken place in that very courtroom – criminal and civil alike. Cast iron prosecutions foiled and guilty parties spared the noose, and likewise the most impregnable defences rent asunder. Criminals and recidivists of varying notoriety and infamy had been brought to justice within those four walls, all at the word of a number of upstanding members of the citizenry – the jury – and the judge, the great arbiter of the law. Besides the priest, one could argue the judge was as close to God as any mortal could presume to become: should he consider a defendant innocent, he could grant back a life. He was also as much Death as he was God, for he could take the life equally without qualms, if he decided them guilty.

The suspected perpetrator of the five child abduction-murders over two decades ago had been sentenced to death in that room – this vast hall of varnished wood and carven stone with ceilings so high they could touch the Heavens. A mass of black robes, powdered legal wigs and scrolls of paper detailing affidavits, statements and testaments were visible from the public galleries above. Now it would be the place that would mete out Jesse Blameford's fate.

Lady Vyrrington, with Abel and Whitlocke behind her, could see across the great room to distinguish the jurors, who would be ultimately responsible for deciding Blameford's guilt or innocence. To her left, and the jurors' right, on a singular, wooden chair so large it was like a throne, sat Judge Ezrington, now fully garbed in his judicial dress and ermines. Opposite him, appearing in another gallery, flanked at either side by a constable, was Blameford. Lady Vyrrington had not seen him prior at his apprehension; she was thus shocked to see him so badly beaten.

Ushers were calling for silence and order in the court as proceedings were to begin. Below all of them, Mr Jackdawe and Mr Ickrell stood opposite each other. As the room fell silent, a bailiff called out:

"On this day, the twentieth day of August on the year of our Lord seventeen-ninety-four, Jesse Alexander Blameford is hereby indicted that he did commit the murders of Mrs Clara Harriet Rudgerleigh of the parish of Berylford Saint Barbara, and the presumed murder of one Joshua, no other name known, *also* lately of the parish of Berylford Saint Barbara. The accused has pleaded Not Guilty to these charges, m'lud."

"Mr Ickrell, if you please, you may deliver your statement to the jury," Judge Ezrington said. Though he was calm at this time, his voice was resonant throughout the courtroom.

"Thank you, My Lord," returned Mr Ickrell, "Gentlemen of the jury, we bid that you are not deceived by this man Mr Blameford's charm, or his wit, or his charisma. They are all a masquerade. A veneer, behind which is concealed the dark, twisted and poisonous mind of a very dangerous man. Who has been before a court on a separate occasion on such charges…"

Lady Vyrrington felt an impulse to speak out and object at Mr Ickrell's last sentence, but Abel gently restrained her.

"…He was found not guilty. This is true…" the prosecutor went on, "…But I will be presenting Mr Blameford as a recidivist. A man not only guilty of the two murders of which he stands accused today, but of those for which he was acquitted seven years ago."

This time, the Countess did not move but did watch Mr Jackdawe as he stood up to object. However, Mr Ickrell had stopped speaking, and so his opponent took his cue to make his own statement in Blameford's defence.

"You will find from the witnesses we will present to you that such frightful deeds are *utterly* uncharacteristic of Jesse Blameford. *That* is why he was released of his charges before. My client is not by any means a recidivist, as my learned colleague would have you believe, but merely a recurrent victim of ill judgment. This day, we aim to end that."

Mr Jackdawe stood down, and Judge Ezrington spoke.

"Very well, you may call the first witness to attest for the defence," he said.

"The defence calls Mr George Whitlocke to stand before Your Lordship," returned Mr Jackdawe.

Lady Vyrrington looked to her butler, who had hitherto remained silent during all the proceedings. She made eye contact with him and nodded somewhat. It was all she could do despite actually feeling like falling to her knees and beseeching him to speak the truth of what had happened to Joshua, but for what purpose? Blameford had assisted Whitlocke in disposing of the body, not to mention concealed the fact for the last ten months. If Whitlocke confessed, two men would be condemned, not one. And while it would certainly rid the Countess of an adversary, even though hers and Whitlocke's enmity had been intermittent of late, it would rid Amethyst of her husband and her happiness.

All this Lady Vyrrington considered, as she watched Whitlocke appear in the witness box below.

"Mr Whitlocke," Mr Jackdawe began, "You were the accused Mr Blameford's direct superior at Beryl Court during his tenure there?"

"I was, sir," returned Whitlocke.

"And what did you make of Mr Blameford as an employee?"

"Highly competent sir, if he had had better application in his duties, he may have been considered for succession to butler in his turn."

Lady Vyrrington tilted her head up to think on that statement. Whitlocke had never spoken highly of Blameford once, his knowledge of their affair notwithstanding.

"And as to Mr Blameford's character? What would you say to that?"

"He liked to be charming to all women – upstairs and down. He could be impudent, arrogant, outright disrespectful at times."

"You disliked him?"

"I still do, I won't deny it."

"But you kept him on your staff when it was well within your power to dismiss him?"

"I did. Because Beryl Court runs on efficiency. And Mr Blameford was a very efficient worker."

"I beg your pardon, My Lord…" Mr Ickrell spoke up and stood as he did so, since he was addressing the judge, "Riveting as I am sure we are all finding this, I fail to see where we are going here."

"Mr Whitlocke is currently testifying as to the accused's character, Lordship," Mr Jackdawe sharply interjected, "If Mr Ickrell would be patient, we will turn to the night of the disappearance of the boy Joshua."

"Be quick about it, Mr Jackdawe," returned Ezrington.

"Mr Whitlocke, you were still on duty the night of the disappearance of Joshua, the boots boy – am I correct?"

"You are, sir, yes."

"Could you recount the events? – I appreciate it was ten months ago or so."

"As best as I remember, sir, My Lady had gone out for dinner on another invitation, so it was only His Lordship, my late master Lord Wilson Vyrrington and the children to attend to that evening. The boy Joshua had caused a little trouble that evening – he had caused a tray to be disrupted. Just clumsiness becoming of a child of his age and energy. I sent him to his room; told him I would speak with him after dinner service had finished. When I came back at around ten, his room was empty. After searching the usual places, I concluded he had gone missing."

"You say 'the usual places'?" said Mr Jackdawe, "Was this not an uncommon occurrence?"

"Not entirely, no, sir," returned Whitlocke, "Joshua was often in trouble downstairs and prone to hiding when due punishment."

"So, his disappearance may have been merely an extension of his hiding. He just ran away?"

"I believe that to be the case. If he's alive or dead now, I could not say."

Up in the gallery, Lady Vyrrington shut her eyes in silent relief. Once again, Whitlocke had served her faithfully.

Mr Ickrell was seen to stand up, to conduct his own questioning.

"What was Mr Blameford's relationship with Joshua like?" he asked.

"Sir?" Whitlocke replied.

"You have testified in great detail your knowledge of the events of the night the boy disappeared, yet you have neglected to attest to the relationship between the accused and the deceased."

"*Presumed*-deceased, sir. I did not believe it to be relevant. I do not regard Mr Blameford to be guilty of any crime, because I cannot be certain a crime was even committed."

The prosecutor fell silent.

"Mr Ickrell? Have you anything further for this witness?" Judge Ezrington pressed him.

"It is not for you to decide what is relevant, Mr Whitlocke," Mr Ickrell finally spoke again, "Nor is it for you to decide whether Mr Blameford is guilty – we have a jury for that."

"Yes, sir."

"Please answer my question, then."

"Well, since you asked, Mr Blameford was frequently exasperated by Joshua, often angered…"
The prosecutor turned away and smirked somewhat.

"…But if that is a motive for murder, then you had best arrest and charge *me* and fourteen others for the same thing," Whitlocke went on, "Had he not been an orphan with no hope of anything but the workhouse to fall back upon he would not have remained in the household much longer."
After another long pause, which was dominated by a low hubbub of discussion from the jury and the gallery, and silenced by a call of order from the bailiff, Mr Ickrell turned to the judge and said:

"No further questions, Lordship."

"Then may the next witness be called?"

"We call Lady Oliviera Vyrrington to testify."

'God in Heaven, deliver me,' was the Countess' immediate thought, a silent prayer that she should not now be responsible for Blameford's fate, 'I have not served thee well of late, but I beseech thee now for one last salvation. Endow me with the power to save this man's life, rather than condemn him with my words.'

She left the gallery and was escorted by an usher to take to the witness box. The courtroom was even more vast and daunting from down on its lowest levels – Judge Ezrington, the paragon of justice, was seated at such a terrible height as if in place of the Martyr on the crucifix in a great cathedral – and the jurors, like a chorus of angels seated at her right. She did not dare look behind her at Blameford. She could not bear it. Before she could consider over any of this further, she was instead beholding the forbidding aspect of Mr Ickrell, with his dark, reptilian eyes staring right back at her, his lips pressed into such a frown they appeared as little more than a line on his pitted and scarred face.

"My Lady, as your butler Mr Whitlocke attested, you were absent on the night of this boy's disappearance?"

"Yes sir, that is correct."

"Then how is your testimony at all necessary and, at the risk of effrontery, relevant today?"
The Countess chuckled softly.

"I have been contemplating that very question myself, Mr Ickrell," she returned, hoping now that he would make a mistake that would harm his own case.

"Well I can enlighten you a little, perhaps," said the prosecutor, "Mr Jackdawe, the attorney *you* supplied the accused, Mr Blameford, has you here to act as a further character witness so that the jurors may deem the defendant totally incapable of murdering an innocent child. Much less a townswoman who had given him board and lodging. Whereas I am here to ask you – how long have you known Jesse Blameford?"

"Since he was nineteen," replied Lady Vyrrington, "Seven years ago."

"At about the time he was acquitted for murdering, let me see, five members of his family? First reportedly pushing his stepmother out of an upper-storey bedroom window, then shooting his father and three siblings?"

The Countess had been right about what she had supposed Mr Ickrell would ask her. She exhaled very deeply, before answering with great confidence:

"Shortly thereafter, sir. Though I had taken an interest in the case, and I had read that there was little evidence to convict him, leading to his acquittal. But after that, he was still tarred with the brush of murderer. No one would employ him or accommodate him. Mr Blameford was little more than a corpse when I took him into my service."

"You nursed him. You raised him back from the dead. Would it be fair to say you have a maternal feeling towards him?"

Lady Vyrrington was not expecting that. She had never once had the feeling of being motherly towards Blameford, not that she could let Mr Ickrell know that. His misconception let her off the hook. He could not accuse her of having an affair with Blameford if he thought their relationship to be familial. She answered straightforwardly:

"It was nothing more than my sacred Christian duty, sir. To help another in need, when he had been otherwise shunned by the world," she responded firmly and emotively, "I did not behold a murderer then and I do not behold one now. The boots boy Joshua ran away as orphans and children do. Clara Rudgerleigh died of a stroke."

"As any mother would say of their child, so a lady of maternal instinct would say of one for whom they share that feeling. I have nothing further for Lady Vyrrington, My Lord."

Mr Ickrell stood down.

"Mr Jackdawe, do you wish to question My Lady Vyrrington at this time?" the judge's voice resonated, "I rather think Mr Ickrell spoiled your fun by telling us what you were going to say."

"There will be no need, My Lord. I think Her Ladyship has satisfied my argument to the jury for the moment," returned Mr Jackdawe.

Abel was then called as a third character witness, describing Blameford's time in his employment, which Mr Ickrell attempted to argue conveniently started shortly after Joshua disappeared. Knowing the truth of that matter – she *had* sent Blameford away for his own protection in case he should be suspected – Lady Vyrrington felt like clutching at her neck. The tension was suffocating her.

The judge and the attorneys had grown weary of the lines of questioning regarding Joshua, and so the case turned to the second supposed murder – that of Mrs Rudgerleigh.

"Doctor Jonathan Street is called, My Lord," Mr Jackdawe said.
Lady Vyrrington watched as Berylford's perpetually sombre-faced physician appeared below them.
"Sir, were you called to attend to the deceased Mrs Rudgerleigh when she was initially taken ill?" asked Mr Jackdawe.

"I did. I was called to the schoolhouse – a boy summoned me stressing the urgency. I arrived shortly thereafter and concluded upon my examination that Mrs Rudgerleigh died of a stroke. Her brain was starved of the air it needs to function. Plain and simple."

"Prosecution's witness, Lordship," and Mr Jackdawe sat down, satisfied. Mr Ickrell rose.

"Doctor Street – you are considered eminent in your field, are you not?" he said.

"I cannot attest to people's opinions," returned the doctor, remaining indifferent to the prosecutor's cloying tone.

"Tell me, can physical force, or the application thereof, *contribute* to a stroke?"

"How do you mean?"

"I mean if someone were to say – *strangle* – another person, would that potentially lead to a stroke?"
The physician seemed reluctant to answer.

"Strangulation… in *very rare cases* can, or has been known, to cause internal injury that could restrict the flow of air… to the brain."

"Thank you, Doctor Street."

"I had not finished, sir," the good doctor went on, "I do not believe any such thing happened to Mrs Rudgerleigh prior to her death. There were no signs of force about her neck that would indicate an attempt of strangulation. Or else I would have reported the death as suspicious at the time."

Mr Ickrell's expression did not change. He looked incensed that a testimony that may have scored him some points with the jury had then been so quickly put asunder.

"Thank you, sir, you may stand down," he told the doctor coldly.

"Any further witnesses, either of you?" asked Ezrington, sounding weary and exhausted.

"The defence summons Mrs Elspeth Urmstone to testify, Your Lordship," returned Mr Jackdawe.

Lady Vyrrington looked around and saw that, to her great amazement, Mrs Haffisidge had joined her in the gallery. After embracing quickly, the Countess and her friend returned to the edge of the balcony to watch as Mrs Urmstone, looking unimpressed with all that lay around her, was walked to the witness stand.

"Mrs Urmstone, would it be fair to say you are a hostile witness here?" asked Mr Jackdawe.

"Not least for my contempt of *you*, Mr Jackdawe, but I hold the accused in no high regard either," she returned caustically.

"Then why are you here?"

"I know the man is innocent. In murdering Clara Rudgerleigh at any event."

"How so?"

"Much as I don't care for the man, I had heard Mr Blameford had acquired for himself some reputation as a competent joiner. My house is old, sir, and I required such work, so I thought it would be backward to hire someone from out of town when Mr Blameford was at liberty."

"And why is this relevant?"

"He was working for me at the time when Mrs Rudgerleigh died, and late into the evenings on the two days previous to that. If Mr Blameford had strangled Mrs Rudgerleigh and left enough time for her to suffer the stroke that killed her, his arms will have grown long indeed!"

"I have no further questions. The defence rests its case."

"I actually have one final witness, Lordship, if you'd entertain that?" Mr Ickrell spoke up.

"You do not wish to question Mrs Urmstone?"

"What you will hear from this witness should refute Mrs Urmstone's testimony, along with those of my learned colleague's other witnesses, My Lord."

"In your *opinion*, Mr Ickrell. Who is this witness of yours?"

"The prosecution calls Mr Zephaniah Gussage to the stand."

The Countess started, and turned to Mrs Haffisidge, then to Abel and Whitlocke, before looking down again at the courtroom below. Mrs Urmstone was being led away and replaced with the dishevelled and shabby reality that was Zephaniah Gussage's presence. She then looked across at Blameford for the first time in a very long time. His head was in his manacled hands, locked in despair.

"Mr Gussage, you were the former colleague and tenant of the late-departed Mrs Rudgerleigh?" said Mr Ickrell.

"That'd be true," returned Mr Gussage, his West Country drawl garbled and slurred amid the forest of grizzled whiskers surrounding his lips.

"And shortly before her death, Mrs Rudgerleigh took in the accused, Mr Blameford, is that correct?"

"Aye, that'd also be true. He came with a reference from Lady Vyrrington, no less."

"Well we have heard enough from Lady Vyrrington on her opinions of the accused, sir. Now when you brought this case before us, you said you could say with certainty that your late colleague was murdered by Mr Blameford. Could you enlighten the court as to how you can be so certain?"

"I overheard an argument between them, sir. An argument about something Mrs Rudgerleigh had read about him. Something about his past. And his family. And that if he wouldn't tell her the truth she would turn him out. And then there was the sound of choking. A lady choking."

Lady Vyrrington shut her eyes very briefly, and looked directly across at the jury, who were all murmuring between themselves. She then glanced again at Blameford, who had not moved since she last looked at him.

"Choking, as if being attacked, Mr Gussage?"

"I would say so."

"The *prosecution* rests its case, My Lord," and Mr Ickrell sat down for the final time.

Mr Jackdawe stood up again and looked around at Ezrington.

"Permission to question this witness of whom I was unaware, My Lord?"

"Granted. But be quick about it, Mr Jackdawe – we would all like to have dinner soon!"

There was a tremor of laughter from the gallery.

Mr Jackdawe was seen to face Mr Gussage, who looked dilapidated in his seat in the witness box.

"If what you say is true, Mr Gussage, and you overheard Mrs Rudgerleigh – your colleague, your landlady, your *friend* – being attacked, why on Earth did you not intervene…?"

Mr Gussage opened his mouth to speak but only stammered and slurred in response.

"…And indeed, when you brought this case to the constables, it took you several months after the event had actually occurred. Because in truth your grief reduced you to a love of drink, didn't it, Mr Gussage. You have not been seen in Berylford for at least three months, and one could argue you have been drunk that whole time. One could argue you're drunk even now as we speak."

"I have no other love left," Mr Gussage mumbled, "He rid me of that."

"Who did?"

"*Mr Blameford!*"

"I must ask you to pacify the witness, Mr Jackdawe!" Judge Ezrington raised his voice, "Or stay this line of questioning."

"He threatened to kill my Clara if she kept asking her questions. She ran in fright."

"Why should we take the word of a drunk, apparently long bereft of his wits?" Mr Jackdawe asked contemptuously.

"My Lord!" Mr Ickrell objected.

"That was a rhetorical question, Lordship. I have nothing further."

"Then we will adjourn for today," said Ezrington, "The jury will convene in the morning to decide over a verdict. Mr Blameford will remain in the custody of the court."

The bailiffs called for all to rise as the judge stood up, and the commotion began. Lady Vyrrington stayed where she was against the balcony of the gallery, watching helplessly as Blameford was led away by the constables. Full of regret that she could and should have done more to protect him, she shed a tear, her mouth hanging ajar.

Chapter LXIV
The Innocent's Despair

BLAMEFORD SAT ALONE. HE HAD been spared chains and manacles whilst confined to his cell, but the dank, damp and darkness, save for a single candle, which was little more than a stub of wax. It was going to be a long night. Full of regret for the things he had not done in his life, which he was utterly sure would be over, sooner rather than later. His time was running out, and he had asked for a pen, ink and paper to be brought to him.

He penned a long effusion regarding the truth of the deaths of his family – not a confession, but the truth of the matter as he knew it to be, and that, as Mr Jackdawe had surmised, he had been the victim of ill judgment. The only member of his family left alive must have been responsible for the demises of the rest, and his acquittal was based on the lack of evidence on the part of the prosecution at the time. As he was coming to the end of this part of his writing, footsteps were heard coming from down a nearby corridor. It was the clack of a lady's shoes, followed shortly after by the heavy steps of a man's boots. In the dim light, he regarded the tall silhouette of a lady whose shape he knew very well, supported by a shorter, upright-standing man.

The lady was of course Lady Vyrrington, whose face Blameford beheld as the light from a second candle, which she was carrying herself, cast a soft amber glow on her dark eyes. She was flanked by Constable Marris, the man who had arrested Blameford in the first place.

"Just call when you wish to leave, My Lady," said Marris, who then walked back whence he came.
Lady Vyrrington approached the bars of Blameford's cell and crouched to meet his level.

"I'm not sure if I'm glad to see you or not," he said breathily, "I never wanted you to see me here in a place like this!"

"I would never have thought to," she returned, "This is wholly unexpected. But now we know why. Zephaniah Gussage. That treacherous drunken wretch! Though I don't know how he knows about the boy."

"It doesn't matter, My Lady."

"But I know the truth of that, Jesse! It wasn't you – it was Whitlocke!"

"I just told you it doesn't matter."

"What doesn't?"

"Any of it. All of it…"

He stood from the bench on which he had been writing and started pacing the cell. Lady Vyrrington rose.

"…I have decided to confess."

"*What?*" she replied hoarsely, "But you can't! You have done nothing wrong!"

"I have done sufficient," he returned, "And I am trapped. I cannot flee from this anymore. I will be running from my past even more so now that I have these two accusations on top of the five I had before. I only wanted to give *you* a life you wanted and deserved."

"Me?"

"We will never be safe. We can never be happy. It is out of the question, as you yourself have said to me. No – here at the end of all things, My Lady, my life is at last as clear as I see you now before me. I will confess to murdering Mrs Rudgerleigh. Let the truth of Joshua's disappearance go with me, you and Whitlocke to the grave. And we will *both* be free. You can live the rest of your years without fearing for your life or reputation."

"I cannot condone this. The prosecution's case is flimsy at best. The word of a drunk, and the rest of the evidence is circumstantial."

"I've already told you: it doesn't matter. I want it all to end. And so it will."

He sat back down on the bench and began writing again.

"Would you send for Mr Ickrell when you leave here. I will be amending my plea of course."

He did not look up as he heard her silently walk off.

In the second part of his document, he wrote the confession he intended to give. That he had persuaded the boy Joshua to abscond from his employment at *Beryl Court* under pain of death, and that, when Mrs Rudgerleigh questioned him about his past, and the death of his family and the role he played in it, including details of the trial that found him not guilty, he throttled her in a fit of pique. Her death from the stroke over the days that followed was just a delayed result, a by-product of his violent display of temper, that achieved his original end.

Again, as he finished his paragraph, footsteps were heard returning, and again, by candlelight, he looked upon the face of he to whom the steps belonged. The scar-faced prosecutor Mr Ickrell stood there, and as the last remnants of Blameford's own candle melted and the cell fell engulfed in darkness, Blameford uttered the words, "I am guilty. I killed that woman."

Chapter LXV
Jesse Blameford's Last Visitor

THE COURT CAME TOGETHER AGAIN the following morning as arranged. It was brought into uproar when Judge Ezrington declared that the accused had amended his plea to that of guilty of the murder of Clara Rudgerleigh.

Judge Ezrington himself did not seem wholly convinced as to the confession itself, which he professed in his closing verdict, saying that most evidence given had favoured him. As such, he would grant an extended "clemency period", as he called it, a courtesy which the Grand Old Judge had been prone to affording defendants for whom he felt an especial sympathy, of an additional week next to the three Sundays the law stipulated. It was time that the judge stated Blameford could use to organise his affairs. Otherwise, a month hence, in the prison in which he would last reside, Jesse Blameford was sentenced to hang by the neck until dead, for the murders he had, in whatever truth existed there, not committed.

*

Following his sentencing, Blameford was bereft of emotion for he knew not how to feel. Was he relieved that the outcome he had sought had been finally delivered? Was he afraid that now his death was impending? Was he satisfied to know that his lover Lady Vyrrington would be free of him and at liberty to love where she pleased again?

The work he had written that night and again in the small hours of the morning, once a new candle had been supplied to him, had culminated into a packet, and it lay beside him on the bench that served as both bed and writing desk. That was when he received one final visitor. He had hoped it would be Lady Vyrrington; for one final time he would like to look upon that face, so pale and icy in complexion contrasted with the dark eyes and hair, the bewitching gaze, the slender neck, and what he knew to be further down. Instead his eyes met those of George Whitlocke, who for the first time looked upon him with an air of sympathy.

"*You* came?" exclaimed Blameford.

"I can go if you'd rather."

"It's up to you: I can't exactly go anywhere."

"Were you expecting Her Ladyship, perhaps?"? Blameford looked away, his gaze directed towards the cold and damp stone floor.

"I thought…" he stammered, "Maybe… perhaps-"

"Lady Vyrrington has gone *home*, Blameford," returned Whitlocke, "These proceedings have overwhelmed her. And even if that weren't the case, her being here poses great risk to the both of you. I was surprised your little liaison was not revealed during the trial."

"Why should it? It has nothing to do with anything. And besides, it's over."

"As you say."

Blameford looked back up at Whitlocke. He was not being helpful.

"I am a man about to spend his last month in manacles and squalor, Whitlocke. By my own election, I grant you-"

"Doesn't have to be so," Whitlocke interrupted, "You could tell them the truth of what happened. You could have thrown me under the cart a hundred times over and I would be sat there instead."

"I helped you, Whitlocke," said Blameford, his voice now little more than a whisper, "You would be here *beside* me, not *in place* of me. This way is easier."

"Why?"

"Because with my death, Lady Vyrrington is free. Free from the threats to her life and livelihood that our being together posed. Free to live her life without looking over her shoulder. Free from your hold on her."

Whitlocke stood upright.

"I had my reasons."

"You take the moral high ground, but you killed to protect her secret."

"I didn't do it for her."

Blameford scoffed and looked away from him.

"Do right by me, just his once, Whitlocke please?"

"You're going to your death in place of me, Blameford. What do you want?"

"Give this packet to Her Ladyship."

He passed the folded series of papers through the bars of his cell and Whitlocke took them in both hands.

"What is this?" the butler asked.

"Something only for My Lady's eyes to read. But it's all in there. Past, present and future. Promise me you will give it to her?"

Whitlocke looked down at the packet, and then at his long-time enemy once again.

"I promise," he murmured.

Blameford said no more and watched as Whitlocke walked away silently, knowing that he would receive no more visitors again, and that his only encounters thenceforth, would be those with his gaolers, and with his executioner.

Book Fourteen
EXTRAJUDICIAL PROCEEDINGS

Chapter LXVI
The Cruelty of Abel Stirkwhistle

*D*EAREST COUSIN ABEL,

 I HOPE *you will humour me in never requiring me to attend a trial again. Such deplorable events, with their attorneys and judges so loquacious and eloquent, yet whom actually seem to say very little after the fact, and their proceedings so tiresome, drowning in paperwork and documentation. And all for what? The guilty plea and impending death of an innocent man. No matter what says he, Jesse Blameford is innocent. Insane, but innocent.*

 The events of the last few days have left me quite overwrought, so I have decided with immediate effect to take some time away from Hampshire – I am visiting my sisters again in Dover for a few days. Mine and my late husband's former cook has taken ill – at her age, it is reasonable to expect the worst, so I would like to ensure I see her should she die. She was a very faithful servant and I was fond of her in her time at Beryl Court.

Whitlocke shall be alone in the house as Amethyst and the children are to accompany me, so feel at liberty to employ him as you see fit in my absence. Ensure he does not shirk his duties – you know what they say about cats and mice, after all!

Upon my return, I should like to invite you and your wife to dine with me regularly every Tuesday if you would find that agreeable. If nothing else, it will give you a few hours' solace away from your sister (and you may tell her I said so, if you don't think it too internecine a decision).

> *All hope for as little scandal as possible in my absence,*
> *Affection,*
> *Oliviera*

Whitlocke presented that letter to Abel in person on his doorstep, before complaining at great length about how redundant he was feeling. It was Sunday, and most of Berylford was at Mass, including Mrs Stirkwhistle and Miss Rebecca. Abel, despite having grown much stronger in his recovery, still found the walk to the Church of St. Barbara too tiring and overwhelming, due to the steep acclivity one had to endure to get there. He loathed public transport, so hiring a carriage or even a sedan chair was out of the question. And besides, it was Providence who had put him in this position, he believed, and because of this inconvenience, Providence would have to visit him and not the other way around or else would have no right to complain if He was displeased with Abel's lack of worship. To visit such a catastrophic malady on one who believed himself to be so righteous and devout: Abel had lost much of his love for God, and it would take a great and empowering visitation to install that faith again.

While the ladies of the house were out, and Whitlocke was waiting on no one, Abel invited him in for a drink. A small glass of port had to suffice in lieu of ale, since there was none in a household run by two women. In the midst of their conversation, which had covered such subjects as the state of the management of the Foreign Office and by extension, the ministry of the Right Honourable Mr. Pitt, and also the state of warfare between England and the French revolutionaries, some commotion was occurring just down the road.

Berylford and its neighbouring towns were mostly untouched by the recent declarations of war, but a select number had received orders from their regiments to go to France. One such was the long-time officer Captain A. H. Knyveton – who had for some months been in candidacy for a promotion to Major, having proven his worth in command during both the Anglo-Spanish and Anglo-Dutch wars.

Such wanton death and destruction he was sure to have witnessed on the battlefields therein, and his mind was plagued as such that the Captain had, over the years, developed a problem regarding his indulgence in alcohol. Whilst on leave and awaiting his orders, he frequented *The St. Barbara's Arms* from its earliest opening hours, and often returned to his house, his wife and his children – two sons, Arthur who was six and Zachariah, only still an infant, with only half of his senses intact. The result: a quick and cruel pair of hands, which – at the Captain's worst – became clenched into fists. On the occasion that Abel and Whitlocke had overheard from within the Stirkwhistle house, Captain Knyveton was at his worst.

It was a relief to many that neither Arthur nor Zachariah were at the scene, for they too may have fallen victim to the drunken rage of their father. While it was unclear how the situation had begun, much less how it had been set ablaze as it had, the general consensus among the citizenry who bore witness was that Mrs Knyveton had gone to *The St. Barbara's Arms* and attempted to force her spouse to come home. The Captain had apparently tried to assault his wife physically while still in the tavern, only to be impeded by the barman and ordered to leave. The confrontation between husband and wife continued out in the street, which culminated with Captain Knyveton taking his poor wife by her hair and throwing her to the floor with such a force it was a wonder to many how her hipbones remained intact. No one – man or woman – dared intervene. They could but only watch as this heavily-built upstanding military man, of inflamed temper only the worse from drink, slap and strike this innocent and defenceless woman. Her face was bruised, and her nose was bleeding.

By this point, Abel and Whitlocke both had exited the house and followed the noise of the event to its origin. Captain Knyveton had a tight grip on his wife's hair again and was slurring something to her in a malevolent whisper. Another's hand grabbed his wrist with such speed that the Captain instantly had to release Mrs Knyveton's hair, at which she fell with her face to the pavement, sobbing in pain and fright. Whitlocke approached her and helped her to her feet. It was Abel who had dared take hold of the Captain, who looked at him with one eye open, his lips screwed into a disgusted scowl.

"Who the Hell do you think you are to handle *me*!" he said, his voice garbled.

"A bystander who will send for the constables if you continue," returned Abel, "You have beaten your wife."

"Many a man beats his wife. What else are they for if not for good sport?"
With surprising force, especially for one of such limited mobility, Abel launched his left knee into the Captain's gut, winding him and causing him to fall to the ground, bereft of breath and unable to speak.

"Captain Knyveton, if you weren't aware of it before, you certainly will be this day: there is a price to pay for assault in this town."

"I do not remember a point at which you were placed in a position of *power* in this town Stirkwhistle," replied the Captain breathlessly, "Had you served in the army for fifteen years, I'm sure you would know how it feels to be in a position of power!"

"You are a captain, sir. A junior rank is it not?"

"I was going to be a *major*! As of the next month!"

"Not if your superiors hear of what has happened here. And they will sir, don't worry. Because it was *I* who elected myself the *judge* of moral correctness in this town. And I hereby judge you guilty of assaulting your wife in public, condoning that you may or may not have been temporarily insane with drunkenness!"

Abel grabbed Knyveton by the back of his neck and pulled him up to his feet.

"I sentence you to public humiliation and *ostracism* from this town."

"You can't *do* that! You have no *legal authority*!"

"Miss Osborne, Miss Gwynne?" Abel addressed the haberdashers, who were also present at the scene; they approached slowly and nervously, "Please take Mrs Knyveton into your shop and send for the doctor to tend her injuries. I will deal with her husband."
He went to drag Knyveton with him, but the captain resisted and pulled back, so Abel struck him across the face again, where the officer fell back onto the pavement, unconscious.

"Lay him flat on his back Whitlocke, and fetch a second able-bodied man. I need a wooden board and some rope too."

"What are you going to do?" Whitlocke asked, now somewhat fearful of the formidable Abel.

"I'm going to carry out the Captain's sentence like any respectable judge would."

"But the Captain was right, Mr Stirkwhistle. You aren't a judicial figure here!"
Abel approached him and he nodded his head as he spoke his next sentence.

"I can tell by the quavering in your voice, Whitlocke. You're just as afraid of me as the Captain was. And I have not even threatened *you*! So how much ease do you think I'll have in striking the same fear into the people of this town; to exhort their respect for me as Berylford's moral arbiter?"

Knowing that Abel had been correct in every word, Whitlocke did not reply, and did as he had been instructed. He returned with Mr Warwick of all people, who, he confessed, was only interested in helping when offered money. Within minutes, the unconscious Captain Knyveton was strapped by his wrists and ankles to the wooden board Abel had requested and lifted across the town to the main square, stood up in front of the townsfolk Abel had gathered to witness his procession:

"Today this man you all know as an officer in the Second Hampshire Infantry Regiment of the Army of King George the Third – the Captain A. H. Knyveton – committed a violent act upon his wife before you – the citizens of Berylford Saint Barbara."

The townsfolk all groaned and growled disdainfully at the comatose Captain.

"And such a deed cannot go unpunished, can it?" Abel asked the crowd, "And so we provide this to carry out said punishment!"

While Whitlocke and Mr Warwick kept Knyveton's board upright, another two men handed out pails containing rotten fruit, which had been given by the farmer's wife Mrs Early.

"Have at him!" Abel commanded, and the townsfolk did so. Their leader watched sadistically, his lip curling as he saw the rancid flesh disperse across Knyveton's face, his chest and his abdomen.

A rotten tomato hit his face and bits of the flesh travelled in all directions, onto Whitlocke and onto Abel. Maggots had already gnawed their way through, it appeared, as Abel discovered as he flicked one off of his cheek.

They had only just run out of ammunition at the point where Knyveton woke from his unconscious state. He was disorientated and took a few seconds to work out why his movements were so restricted. He gritted his teeth and fought against the strong ropes that were keeping him bound to the board.

"We hope you had a nice dream, Captain!" Abel shouted at him, playing to the crowd, "Because you'll find that the next few hours of your life will be one of your worst nightmares!"

He nodded to Whitlocke and Mr Warwick, who let go of the board and allowed it to fall backwards. Knyveton gasped in pain.

"Oh gentlemen, *gentlemen*, that was so very careless!" Abel said, feigning disappointment, "Help him back upright."

They did as they were told, actually unsure of Abel's true intentions. From his pocket, Abel took a penknife, and cut through the captain's bonds. Once Knyveton was able to stand properly again, Abel grabbed him at the back of his neck.

"Now I *swear* to you, *Captain...*" he whispered sinisterly in his ear, "...that if you *dare* set foot in Berylford again while I'm still living here, it will be your throat this knife will cut. And believe me; I'll have no qualms in making it painful! All the more enjoyment for me!"

He pushed Knyveton to the ground.

"Now *get out of this town while you can still walk*!"

The crowd all hassled the Captain to his feet and in the direction of the town gates. In the meanwhile, Abel faced the crowd again, who were struck silent under his devilish gaze. No one dared speak, blink, even breathe.

"Pay heed to these words," he articulated powerfully, "I vouchsafe unto you all that I shall prosecute any and all who fall astray of their civic duty. Let Captain Knyveton be an example to all husbands that would raise a hand to their wives and children…"

He continued to survey the congregation before him. His wife and sister he spied at the back.

"…I am hereby announcing my intent as candidate for mayor of this town, as soon as the next term begins," he went on, "And I promise that if I am successful, under my mayoralty, the stain of vice shall be washed clean out from our very walls."

He then turned on his heel and walked away from the crowd who, behind him, erupted into applause and cheers. Miss Rebecca, with Mrs Stirkwhistle in tow, had made their way to the front of the crowd and eventually caught up with Abel.

"You are a total hypocrite, Abel Stirkwhistle," Miss Rebecca muttered to her brother, "You speak so eloquently of ridding this odious town of men who beat their women, but they won't think so much of you when they see what you do to *me*!"

"You're no woman, dear sister," Abel quipped in response, "You're a gorgon. Don't spend too long before the looking-glass or you're likely to turn to stone!" He carried on walking, with his wife following him closely, however fearfully. Miss Rebecca slowed her pace, her expression ire-stricken and hateful.

Chapter LXVII
The Unravelling of the Plan

S TOOD, UTTERLY UNABLE TO MOVE, exactly where he had been when he had been bribed into participating in the banishment of Captain Knyveton, Luke Warwick's mind was encumbered by only one thought. Being as feckless and benighted as he was known to be, he had hitherto neither had the capacity to recognise authority nor the fear or appreciation of it.

Since the display that had ostracised and disgraced a decorated military officer, Mr Warwick now knew the one figure in Berylford that he realised he feared: Abel Stirkwhistle. The devil that punished devilry, the Hellish creature who claimed to have descended from Heaven. A man who appeared to be so well-humoured, wise and sociable with people of all classes, who was at home as much in a tavern or brothel as he was in a ballroom or drawing room. He was, behind this veneer, a man of sheer sanctimonious cruelty and malice, a law unto himself who zealously relishing the pain of those who ran afoul of his temper and self-righteousness. And the greater their pain, the greater he relished it.

Mr Warwick began to think deeper than he knew his mind able. If a public humiliation, with the defendant strapped down on a board for all to see and at the mercy of the townsfolk with their rotten fruit, was what Abel did for a simple case of a husband beating his wife in a drunken rage, what would he do to persecute a man who had wilfully stolen money from his wife's aunt, all the while conspiring to discover and reveal a long-concealed secret?

And that was only half of the problem. He was already aware of Abel's connection and friendship with George Whitlocke (who had since left the scene), and he knew the butler was not one for forgetting things easily. As such, he still would carry with him the knowledge that Mr Warwick had attempted to rape Amethyst, just minutes after his own son had been brought into the world. Whitlocke had quite deliberately not spoken a word about the event at Amethyst's insistence, not Mr Warwick's. If one deplorable act were to come to light, it was likely the second would follow it.

It was the most, if not the only intelligent decision Mr Warwick had ever made. He was resolved in that moment to carry out an act of desperation. To avoid the same punishment and ultimate fate of Captain Knyveton, should Whitlocke reveal the long-held secret, he had decided to flee Berylford, abandoning his wife and son. He knew that by doing so he would put Mrs Warwick in the same position as Mrs Knyveton – a husbandless wife to bring up their child virtually alone. But then when was there a moment that Mr Warwick put others before himself? The question he was asking himself was 'When would be the most convenient and subtle moment to disappear?'

He made for his house, in his haste not taking care where he was going. As such, he rammed shoulders with another gentleman walking in the opposite direction; Mr Warwick's panic was such that he quickly and nervously pardoned himself and carried on his way. However, the gentleman he had collided with pursued him, and dragged him into a nearby alleyway. Mr Warwick had not had time to react but found himself facing a person he knew. He did not know him well, but he knew him enough. He was gazing once again at Mr Christopher Tratsly.

"*You!*" Mr Warwick hissed, utterly stunned.

"We do have a habit of meeting down these alleys, don't we, Warwick?" Tratsly said sardonically.

"Fuck me! What are *you* doing here?"

"I am coming for what I am owed. Five hundred pounds for months of *relentless* research. I trust you can oblige?"

"*Five-hundred what?*"

"You keep your voice down or I will gut you like a fish," Tratsly's voice became soft yet sinister. Mr Warwick felt a point press against his stomach. He dared not look down, but Tratsly had the blade of a dagger held straight at his gut.

"If I do what you ask, she will discover everything. That's the old bitch's life savings."

"What do you care? Were we both not in this to destroy her?"

Tratsly took a step back and returned the blade to his inside jacket pocket.

"You're not finally acquiring a conscience, are you Warwick?" he asked.

"A lot can happen in the space of a few months. I thought you had disappeared with the money forever."

"I would be lying if I did not call you an instrument in my grand design. A design that has taken – it's true – more years than you know, to realise. But it is a design whose results are mutually beneficial. I get her money; you see your dear Auntie Haffisidge's reputation set ablaze forever."

Mr Warwick looked away, his mouth ajar contemplating his next move.

"So will you bring the money?" Tratsly pressed him.

He did not speak, merely nodded slightly, after which Tratsly silently left him.

*

It took no time at all to find Mrs Haffisidge's money. While subtlety was not a skill at which Mr Warwick was adept, the months of practise had given him full knowledge of his aunt-in-law's habits and hiding places. Even a lady as shrewd as she was victim to a little foolishness; keeping all her money in one place was not among her cleverest decisions.
Such a large amount of money was difficult to conceal should the wrong eyes be looking, and when the unsuspecting Mr Warwick handed the packet of banknotes to his associate over a table in *The St. Barbara's Arms*, he came under the eye of George Whitlocke from the other side of the bar.

He observed Tratsly leaving, observing that Mr Warwick was sat still in his seat, nursing the tankard of ale before him. Whitlocke decided there was no time like the present and approached him, though it was not to be a conversation to be had in a tavern. He grabbed Mr Warwick firmly by the shoulder.

"Let's go outside, shall we?" he murmured, not giving Mr Warwick much choice in the matter and leading him out of the pub into the street.

"What is the problem, Mr Whitlocke? I have had enough of conversation for one day, quite frankly! Come to think of it, you said I would be paid for helping you and Abel Stirkwhistle!"

"I saw you in the tavern and thought 'it's unlike Luke Warwick to be sitting with a pint alone and drinking it so slowly'. But then I noticed you *weren't* on your own; you were handing off a rather large number of banknotes to, for my part, a total stranger. And so then again, I thought, 'that's a lot of money for Luke Warwick to have on him. I don't see how he came by *that* on his own'! So, *'come to think of it'*, you don't seem to require payment of any sort. You seem to be doing quite well for yourself…!"
Whitlocke's tone turned menacing and threatening, his expression had turned deadly serious. Mr Warwick was quite surprised at how nervous he felt.

"…You didn't come by it on your own, did you?" Whitlocke went on, "You stole it from your wife. Or maybe Mrs Haffisidge?"

"What's it to you how I came by it?"

"It's nothing to *me*, at all," Whitlocke returned, turning his tone back to facetious and jovial, and yet still sinister all the same, "But I can't say I'd care to imagine how Mrs Warwick would react when she learned the truth. Or Mrs Haffisidge. Or... Abel Stirkwhistle, for that matter..."

Then it hit Mr Warwick; stunned into silence and eyes wide with fear, he was all but paralysed, he could not help but listen to Whitlocke continue.

"...You were there today, Warwick. You saw what he did to Captain Knyveton. That was for striking a woman – his wife, come to that. Now I can't say I know what he'd do in the event of a theft – probably just report you to the authorities and have done with it – but *attempted rape...*?"

It was as though the Devil himself had opened a cage and all of Mr Warwick's horrors were engulfing him at once like a stampede. These were all the words that he had dreaded to hear; even after such a long time had passed, his attempt to have his way with Amethyst the afternoon after his son's birth had still gone unforgotten by Whitlocke. And now here he was, dangling that mistake in front of him.

"...Let's just say it would have even the hardiest of men shitting themselves in fear," Whitlocke concluded.

"This is all about her!" Mr Warwick could remain silent no longer.

"All about who?"

"My wife's aunt. The bitch. Makes my life a living Hell; she enjoys it. Go ahead and tell anyone – tell *everyone* – but the man I paid in the tavern just then gave me all I need to bring her down for good. If I am banished, even executed in the street, then so be it. It'll be worth it if she's destroyed too!"

This time, it was Whitlocke who was speechless. He had no choice but to turn on his heel and make for Abel Stirkwhistle's house.

Chapter LXVIII
An Unexpected Return

TO HIS DISMAY, WHITLOCKE WAS received by an as-usual-disgruntled Miss Rebecca Stirkwhistle at the door.

"Servants may go around the back," she said to him coldly, peering down her nose as was her habit, "You may work for the Countess, butler, but that does not diminish the fact of what you are."

"I thank you for that acknowledgement, Miss, but I am here not in my capacity as a servant, but in order to speak to *Mr* Stirkwhistle on a pressing and urgent matter." His voice was hurried and anxious, things which Miss Rebecca appeared to find amusing.

"Well!" she exclaimed, mockingly, "You can't! He isn't here! He was called away at very short-notice to Andover. Or maybe it was Southampton. Do you know – he quite neglected to tell me. I shall tell him you stopped by!"

And she shut the door in his face.

Whitlocke knew a losing battle when he was fighting one, so he decided there would be little for it but to return to *Beryl Court* and let the events play out. Much as he knew them well in that they were frequent guests of Her Ladyship, Mrs Haffisidge and, most probably,

Mrs Urmstone, would place little credence in Whitlocke if he told them of Mr Warwick's intentions directly. It was hopeless, yet at the same time he was not duty-bound to meddle in the affairs of his betters.

As he came upon the house, breathless after scaling the great acclivity that led to the front door of *Beryl Court*, his perplexity was instantly provoked by the presence of a great, ostentatious carriage outside. One that he knew to be Lady Vyrrington's, which he also knew to have left the day before.
The butler ran inside.

"My Lady? *My Lady*? Amethyst?" he cried. The Countess' presence, glimmering in purple and crimson garments, appeared in the sitting room doorway.

"Whitlocke, I presume you were at Abel's house?" she said calmly, "Stay your troubled mind, I have been quite able to pour myself a cup of tea."

"I was not expecting you back today – you only left yesterday."

"It would appear Fate had other plans. One of the horses is lame. There is no honour among aristocrats these days! We limped back to a house in Emsworth, but they were going to charge us an *inhuman* amount to borrow one of their own horses for the length of time. I found the day-and-a-half's ride to Chichester and back just as weary and tiresome as that entire trial proceedings. I'd sooner suffer another assize!"

She laughed to herself, sipping her tea in between. She then looked up again and placed her tea to one side. She had noticed that Whitlocke was not laughing; indeed he looked and felt still very disquieted.

"What, Whitlocke?" she said, now also worried, "Did they take away Mr Blameford's clemency? Is he to die next week? Or did Abel die? Is Abel dead?"

"No, milady, nothing like that. Forgive me, I have no wish to alarm you."

"Then out with it, man!"

"I don't know what mischief he intends to make with it, but-" and here, the butler felt he needed to be creative with the truth, "I overheard Mr Warwick in the tavern, saying something about having discovered something about Mrs Haffisidge. Discovered 'her disgrace', I think he said."

"I see," the Countess replied, contemplating for a moment. She had not enlightened Whitlocke of the fact, but she had been present the night Mrs Haffisidge found the cryptic *Remember: Juliette Harrowsleigh* message pinned in her berry bushes.

"And did he care to enlighten as to the nature of this 'disgrace'?" Her Ladyship went on.

"No, milady."

"Then there's nothing more to be said about it. You merely heard the ravings of a drunken imbecile. Come now, Whitlocke, you know better than to listen to Mrs Haffisidge's reprobate nephew-in-law!"

"I saw him paying a man. It did not look to be a small amount of money."

"Would it satisfy you if I paid Mrs Haffisidge a visit tonight?"

"And do what?"

"And do *nothing*, sir. Merely a social call, observe Mr Warwick's behaviour. If my suspicions are struck, I'll merely mention what you heard. Will that suffice?"

"I'll come with you, milady?"

"You will do no such thing, Whitlocke. There are four other Vyrringtons, and your *wife*, who depend upon you this evening."

Chapter LXIX
Mrs Haffisidge's Secret

SHE DID NOT KNOW WHY she was humouring him.
'Since when did Whitlocke believe what he heard
in the tavern?' the Countess asked herself. And
yet, she did not turn back and deny Whitlocke the
goodness of her time. Even though she had made a
pointless trip to Chichester and back and was much
fatigued from the stress of recent events. She could not
help but think, though, 'Would Whitlocke *really* have
bothered me with this if it were a trivial matter?' His
accusations had to be of some consequence, or the
butler would never have confided in her.

Now there was the question of how to go about the next
step: relaying the accusation. To Mrs Haffisidge, it
would be easy, since she would readily entertain any
notion whatsoever that her nephew-in-law was a good-
for-nothing wastrel, a stain on the fabric of her
household, and capable of surprising feats of malice. In
front of her niece, Mrs Warwick, however, confronting
the situation – cutting the head off the snake before it
bit, so to speak – would be a more delicate task. One
that Lady Vyrrington would not feel it her place to
carry it out, notwithstanding the regard her friends had
for her and her opinions.

Once outside that beautiful house with the neatly-kept garden in Kellford Road, the Countess' time to think of what to say was sliced, for Mrs Haffisidge, who had obviously seen her coming up the garden path, appeared at the door.

"Oh My Lady, I am so glad you've come – unexpected as it is, all the same," she spoke with a spritely air to her voice, as though an event that merited great joy and glee had occurred, "It has been quite a spectacle, really! Come in! Come in!"

"Whatever has happened, Judith-Ann?" returned Lady Vyrrington, at a loss as to how to act at this time.

"The very best of news, My Lady. And at the same time, the very *worst*!"

"Pray explain what you mean!" the Countess pressed her friend, following her into the parlour, where she found Mrs Urmstone sat on the settee, her arms wrapped in a tight embrace around Mrs Warwick, who was almost purple in the face in a state of seemingly impenetrable distress.

"Mr Warwick has *absconded*!" Mrs Haffisidge went on, "Vanished with naught but a little note to my dearest Alicia saying he was never meant to be married.

"'Chained to anyone'!" Mrs Warwick sobbed, "That's what he wrote. '*Chained*'! As if he were my prisoner!" She then buried her face into the shoulder of Mrs Urmstone, who was, for once, at a loss as to what to say.

"Do you know, he did not even *mention* his son!" continued Mrs Haffisidge, "That poor child who will now grow up fatherless. Not that I deemed Mr Warwick a worthwhile figure on which Paul should model himself. But *nevertheless*!"

"Many a dissolute man has usually absconded *with* the child as though it was his property," returned Lady Vyrrington, "At least Mr Warwick had the decency-"

"'*Decency*'! Indeed!" Mrs Haffisidge gasped, "Forgive me for speaking out of turn, My Lady, but such a word will only be attributable to Mr Warwick upon his death!"

The Countess decided she would tread with care; it was clear the temperament in the house stood upon the edge of a knife.

"Did the note say anything else?" she reverted to her original purpose for calling and would examine if Mr Warwick had revealed anything about this alleged secret to his wife.

"No," returned Mrs Warwick, "He just said he was leaving and that was the end of that…" She stood up and ran to Mrs Haffisidge.

"…You were always right about him, Auntie. That creature I married."

"Love is blind, my dearest girl," her aunt consoled her, stroking her hair, "So often the faults are right under our noses."

"I would say so too," another, familiar, voice entered the room.

The ladies all looked around and beheld that Mr Warwick was stood in the parlour doorway, with, to Mrs Haffisidge's apparent horror, Christopher Tratsly a short way behind him.

"How dare you presume to enter this house again!" Mrs Haffisidge hissed at Mr Warwick like an oriental serpent, "I demand you leave at once. And *you*!" Her finger was pointed about Mr Warwick's shoulder between Mr Tratsly's eyes like a dagger.

"We shall both be leaving soon enough," Mr Warwick returned.

"But there's no sense in hiding the truth anymore, Mrs H.," Mr Tratsly piped up, stepping in front of Mr Warwick and proceeding into the parlour, "You can keep your secret no longer, madam."

"What is he talking about, Judith-Ann?" Lady Vyrrington asked, hoarsely, sitting down into an armchair slowly, keeping her eyes on Mr Tratsly, in case he was to make a sudden move against one of her friends.

"Would you like to tell the tale, Mrs Haffisidge? – I know you pride yourself on being quite the storyteller!" Mr Tratsly said mockingly. Mrs Haffisidge was stunned silent.

"Very well! We will do the honours. Mr Warwick – if you'd care to begin?"

"Oh, what can he possibly know of anything?" Mrs Haffisidge muttered disdainfully.

"I pray you will be silent, Mrs Haffisidge – it'll be the worse for you if you are not," Mr Tratsly threatened.

"Well it did not strike me until I was going through some old belongings a few months ago, and I found mine and Alicia's marriage certificate…" Mr Warwick said, and he pulled out an old and well-folded document, "…It lists her name as 'Alicia Haffisidge'. And that struck me as strange because you, *Mrs* Haffisidge, have always said that was *your* maiden name. And so, therefore, that of your sister's as well, correct?"

"What of it?"

"I didn't understand it, but Mr Tratsly has told me since that, Alicia wouldn't have *had* the surname Haffisidge at birth, unless her father was… not known." Mrs Haffisidge closed her eyes.

"…That's the truth isn't it?" Mr Tratsly pressed her firmly, "Your beloved niece, your adopted daughter. Actually a bastard with no true knowledge of her parentage."

"We did not suspect my sister had much say in the… conception," Mrs Haffisidge murmured, breathless, "We came from a good, Christian family. Juliette would *never* have just *given herself* to a man."

"Regardless of the circumstances, as if that were not scandalous enough, I scoured certain records…" Mr Tratsly went on, "…And found that your sister Miss Juliette Haffisidge had contracted a case of the clap. By way of the girl's father…?"
Mrs Haffisidge was remaining silent, but she nodded, reluctantly and regretfully.

"…When that took hold; when the clap began slowly claiming Miss Haffisidge's mind and wits and gradually dragging her into a quagmire of madness, and her grip on reality began to dwindle, you and your late husband, Mrs Haffisidge, made the decision to adopt the baby for yourselves, and conceal your sister from the world."

"You told me she had taken Holy Orders," Mrs Urmstone commented.

"I had to conceal *her* shame from the world," returned Mrs Haffisidge, "The world would not see her as a victim but would brand her a whore, or much worse."

"But in the end, even that became too difficult for you to endure. Your husband persuaded you to have your sister committed to a sanitorium. The *Harrowsleigh* Sanitorium, in Havant."

"'Remember: Juliette Harrowsleigh'," Lady Vyrrington muttered, "That was the message we found in the bushes. You left it there!"

"A bit of fun, really," returned Tratsly impishly, "A cryptic message, I grant you, but nonetheless a means to alert you to the fact I was coming for you, Mrs Haffisidge."

"Why? I have never met you before!"

"Oh, my dear madam – you insult me! You have. You required my services once upon a time, and my silence for the rest of your *lifetime*. You see: discretion was required in transporting your sister to Harrowsleigh. I was in their employment back then as a cart driver, charged with taking inmates in, and delivering their *remains* when the time came. And you paid me *two sovereigns* to keep my mouth *shut* about the matter. I assured you I would never remember enough to breathe a word again."

Mrs Haffisidge half-smiled.

"If you say so."

"Let him finish," Mr Warwick said.

"When Harrowsleigh was closed a year or so later, I was left without employment, so I made the best of the devices open to me and stole some of the records of the inmates. These included the names of the family members who had requested or recommended their incarceration. You are just the next name on the list, Mrs Haffisidge – a list of people who have made me very rich over the years."

"You have blackmailed the families of sick people, who wanted nothing more than for them to be well!" Lady Vyrrington said, her voice shuddering with disgust.

Mr Tratsly nodded his head nonchalantly.

"You would think they were doing the right thing, but society isn't all that understanding, is it, madam?"

"That's *'My Lady'*, to you!" Mrs Urmstone spat hoarsely.

Mrs Warwick stood up and approached her husband, before slapping him hard across the face. The sound echoed through the hallway.

"And you, Luke, you helped him do it?" she whispered to him, her voice quavering with imminent tears, "Were you always as monstrous as you have become?"

"Perhaps. Had we not come and live here under the roof of that *witch*, perhaps I may have been a better husband."

"Don't bring my aunt into this! No, not my aunt – my *mother*! The only real one I've ever had! No, Luke. I took it all in good humour and with a pinch of salt when I had the mind to, but I don't anymore! I banish you from this marriage. I banish you from this house. I disown you. And your son will never know you. Lord knows he will be all the better for it."

"Couldn't agree more," another man's voice joined the room.

Whitlocke was now present. Lady Vyrrington stood up, her eyes white with fury.

"Whitlocke, what is the meaning of this?" she ejaculated, "I told you to remain at the house."

"I do apologise, My Lady, but since secrets are all coming out, I thought I may as well add to the party."

The Countess clutched at her throat. Surely not now, after all this time, and with Blameford facing imminent execution, Whitlocke was not going to reveal her own disgrace.

"On the day of the birth of your son, Mrs Warwick, your husband tried to have his way with my wife, Amethyst," said Whitlocke straightforwardly.

Lady Vyrrington's eyes were whiter than the moon and looked like to eject from her skull, such was her utter shock.

"*What*?" she gasped.

"She swore me to secrecy, My Lady. I could not tell you at the time. But Mr Warwick is not a man worthy of protection. You will see how he does not deny it."

The room was silent for a moment, but then the ladies descended into cries and gasps as Mrs Warwick, presumably overwhelmed by Whitlocke's information, collapsed to the ground unconscious. After helping her niece to lie on the settee, Mrs Haffisidge, along with Lady Vyrrington and Mrs Urmstone enclosed around Mr Warwick.

"If you are ever seen anywhere *near* this *town* again, so help me Mr Warwick, I will not be held responsible for my actions," Mrs Haffisidge hissed at him.

"I will be writing to Judge Ezrington directly," added Lady Vyrrington, "And arranging a warrant for your arrest, for the attempt of rape."

"*And* conspiring to blackmail!" Mrs Urmstone piped up.

"You will be given this grace period to flee from Berylford now," continued Mrs Haffisidge, "You will not say goodbye; you will not take with you any money or belongings. You will *just go*."

Mr Warwick bit his lip, beholding all three of them with contempt. To Lady Vyrrington's surprise, he turned and went in the direction of the door. Whitlocke stopped him and murmured to him:

"If Abel Stirkwhistle gets to you before the constables, expect worse than what he gave Captain Knyveton."

Mr Warwick appeared to listen, before slowly walking out the door.

From in the parlour, there then came the creak of furniture being passed. The ladies turned around and found Mr Tratsly was still there – they had quite forgotten about him.

"I will be on my way, Mrs Haffisidge," he said, "I have done what I set out to do."

"You have not blackmailed me very efficiently, sir," Mrs Haffisidge observed, "You have made no demands of payment."

"I have had my payment, thank you," he returned, patting about his breast. But as he went through the parlour doorway, Whitlocke stopped him also, but instead of threatening him as he had Mr Warwick, he merely struck him across the face, causing the ladies to cry out. Mr Tratsly fell to the ground, knocked out.

"Whitlocke, have you taken leave of your--?" Lady Vyrrington questioned, but cut herself off as she observed her butler's actions, "What are you doing?"

Whitlocke was rifling through Mr Tratsly's jacket, and pulled out an envelope from one of the inside pockets, and in standing up, handed it to Mrs Haffisidge.

"I think this might be yours, Mrs Haffisidge," he said, "I think he had it from Mr Warwick, and I have no doubt he had more from the same place."

"You had noticed money was going missing, Judith-Ann," Mrs Urmstone whispered, "It was Mr Warwick all along!"

"I am always right in the end, I think," returned Mrs Haffisidge, "Thank you, Mr Whitlocke for your services."

The Countess then approached her butler, her lips contrived into a smile, yet looking nevertheless severe.

"You have some explaining to do when we return to Beryl Court, Whitlocke, do you hear me?" she said, "But I echo Mrs Haffisidge's thanks. And will admit readily: you were right about Mr Warwick."

The butler merely half-smiled in response, and, in a surprising display of strength, pulled the comatose Mr Tratsly over his shoulder.

"I'm going to make a delivery to the police," he said, before leaving the house.

After all sighing very hard and very deeply, the ladies all resumed their seats in the parlour; the very places where they had been the first time Mrs Haffisidge had seen Mr Tratsly's silhouette in the window. Mrs Haffisidge had a hand pressed up against her face, as though she were trying to gouge out her own eyes.

"Judith-Ann, are you quite well?" Mrs Urmstone asked her.

"I never thought to hear that terrible story again," she returned, "Much less did I expect you, my dear, dear friends to be there to witness it. My utter shame brought to bear before me. I can only expect our acquaintance must end forthwith."

"I have no intention of doing that," said Lady Vyrrington straightforwardly, "Society will never hear a word of that man's allegations, and even if they do, *we*, who know the truth of the circumstances, can never condemn you."

"You did it all to protect her," Mrs Urmstone interjected, and all three ladies looked across at the unconscious Mrs Warwick, still lying on the settee.

"It shall be she who bears this the worst," Mrs Haffisidge said, "I fear she actually loved that deplorable husband of hers."

"No longer," returned Mrs Urmstone, "Good riddance to him."

"This should be a day of celebration, not one of remorse," the Countess said rousingly, "I shall away to Beryl Court and return with my best port. We shall toast this new age in your household, Mrs Haffisidge. One without the stain of Mr Warwick's presence."

Mrs Haffisidge sat back in her armchair and breathed another great sigh of relief.

"Do not be gone long, My Lady," she said, exhaustedly.

Chapter LXX
Dinner at the Judicial Palace

I T WAS 14TH SEPTEMBER, ONE week before the execution of Jesse Blameford. The summer had waned, and the equinoctial changes in the climate were becoming all the more apparent. The Harvest would soon be upon the citizenry of Berylford, as would the beginning of the school year, under the new mistress, Miss Rebecca Stirkwhistle. Her brother Abel had installed himself as the schoolmaster with a mind to keep an eye on his tyrannical sibling, but also as a means of securing him position as a pillar of the community, which would benefit his mayoral candidacy all the more. The incident with Captain Knyveton notwithstanding. He had instilled fear in most of Berylford's public, but for the few who knew him personally, and Mrs Knyveton, who had felt obligated to appeal to the Stirkwhistles for money, given her own source of income had been banished from the town indefinitely.

Upon hearing of his candidacy for the mayoralty, and with the sentence of Jesse Blameford soon to be carried out, Judge Ezrington had written to Abel inviting him to dine at the judicial palace, in which several rooms were taken by His Lordship for his residence. It was not palatial in the vein of Versailles or Sandringham; more on the scale of a place inhabited by a bishop or archdeacon. Nevertheless, for an unmarried and middle-aged gentleman like Ezrington, it was more than sufficient.

His dining room was long and seemingly remote; as though the sound of a mere drip of water could resonate throughout and shake the entire house. Had there been music, the room may have felt warm and inviting, a place of life and frivolity where grand dinners could be held. But in this cold and silent chamber, there would be more revelry seen in a mausoleum. Large portraits with gilt frames occupied the walls, bearing the likenesses of Judge Ezrington's more revered and prevalent predecessors in the judicial seat. All of their faces were humourless and severe, and their eyes painted to bear piercing gazes, which appeared all the more ghostlike in the dim light. There were candelabra lit at all corners of the room, and at regular intervals down the dining table, which could happily have seated and was set to serve at least a score of people. This night, however, it was only Abel and the judge. The guest waited quietly on his host as Grace was spoken, Abel carefully observing Ezrington in case he should notice that he was not participating in the prayer. With the Lord thanked, the two men commenced their repast.

Abel was a well-travelled, shrewd and educated socialite with no small degree of *savoir-faire,* for which he was renowned, but when it came to Judge Ezrington, he was utterly stumped as to what to say. He might have waited on His Lordship to begin the conversation himself, but the Grand Old Judge appeared quite contented eating his cutlets. His plate was quite empty – his thinness did not come as much of a surprise; he ate very little. At last, he set down his cutlery, sipped his wine, and then turned to Abel, who had been regarding him hawkishly throughout their meal thus far.

"I heard a troubling report some days ago…" the judge said calmly, "…that a certain highly-decorated officer, soon to be promoted to Major, had an unfortunate encounter before his fellow townspeople."
Abel decided to feign ignorance, already disliking the direction of the conversation.

"Really?" said he, wanting to drink some of his own wine, but hesitating in case it was a giveaway to his nervousness. Ezrington did not look amused. Abel knew already he had seen through him.

"Indeed," the judge continued, "By name, one Captain Knyveton? Is he known to you?"

"I think you know the answer to that question, sir, with all due respect."

"You aren't the first man to put a wife-beater in the stockade and have the townsfolk have at him with rotten fruit, Stirkwhistle, and I daresay you won't be the last. But strapping him to a board? And banishing him from the town under no authority but your own – that which exists in your head? Really! – what were you thinking of?"

"Something had to be done at the time, My Lord," returned Abel, confidently and righteously, "I instinctively acted as I saw to be fit for Captain Knyveton's transgressions. Berylford is no place for such creatures."

"That is *not* your place to decide!"

Abel sat upright, his head staring down at his plate. He knew he was to be in receipt of a tirade, or at least a lecture, from the Grand Old Judge.

"We judges take little comfort in the actions of a man meting out justice however he sees fit without, at least, recourse to us. It is not only insulting to the dignity of the office we uphold but will end in its redundancy. One débâcle upon another and the floodgates of extrajudicial chaos and anarchy will be opened, until a lawless society will be unleashed."

"Yes, sir."

"I am given to understand that you have undertaken to be considered for the local mayoralty?"

"Yes, sir."

"Such actions will not reflect well upon your candidacy from those who control the election."

"Yourself, you mean?"

"I may be among those who hold that power, yes."

"What is it you would have me do, My Lord?"

"Ensure that your cousin Lady Vyrrington sees to an elevation in my position – a Viscountcy if she can."

"My Lady Vyrrington is quite preoccupied at present," returned Abel, starting to eat again, "The man you tried – Jesse Blameford – was an old friend of hers."

"And a murderer."

"I don't believe that. And I'm not sure you do either."

"True," said the judge straightforwardly, "But if a defendant, regardless of how innocent he may be, decides to confess – my hands are bound. Mr Blameford made his choice – his reason for that, he will take to his grave."

Abel remained silent; soon the only sounds echoing throughout that vast room were the scrapings of his fork against his plate. He looked out of the corner of his eye and noticed the judge was watching him narrowly.

"Lordship?" he said.

"Why did you come to *me* that day?" returned Ezrington, "You thought I could be paid off, didn't you? A lighter sentence in exchange for a bribe?"

"Not at all, sir," said Abel, "But in certain circles you have a reputation for being lighter on sentencing, and often overruling juries. I thought Mr Blameford stood a better chance of acquittal under your presidency."

"I wanted to acquit him, Stirkwhistle. The evidence shown to me by Mr Ickrell was speculative at best, apart from that damning witness Mr Gussage who, by all accounts, appears a half-mad, grief-bent drunkard."

"Whom Mr Ickrell believed all the same. It was Zephaniah Gussage who brought the case to the prosecutor, correct?"

"He did."

"How did he know *anything* about the boy? The orphan who Blameford allegedly killed? Gussage was never in the employ of the Vyrrington estate!"

"I know, and Mr Jackdawe attempted to bring that question before me, and *would* have ripped Mr Gussage's testimony to shreds if he had had the opportunity. But Mr Blameford pleaded guilty – the case is dismissed and with it, the jury. There is nothing I can do."

Abel sighed, his frustration decidedly remaining dormant.

"As you say," he murmured.

Again, there was silence, but for the clattering of crockery.

"Abel…" the judge began again, "…I will agree to forget about your little attempt to install yourself as judge, jury and executioner in Berylford if you have Lady Vyrrington write to me, informing me she will mention my name to her acquaintances in the House of Lords, as a viable and capable candidate for an elevation in position."

"I will write to her tomorrow."

"Give to me a success in this regard and I will support your candidature as Berylford's mayor."

Abel merely nodded politely, and finished the meal before him, which gone cold in the course of conversation. He knew that, however difficult and full of *quid pro quo*s it was, his relationship with Judge Ezrington was the most profitable one he had forged for some years, and he would be a man worth pleasing.

Chapter LXXI
Lady Vyrrington's Vow

A WEEK PASSED. WHEN 21ST September arrived, at the age of just twenty-six, Jesse Blameford was hanged. The only person present at the gallows besides Blameford himself, the executioner and the priest, was Whitlocke.

Lady Vyrrington had ordered her butler to attend on her behalf, resolved to cloister herself in her study as her late husband had been prone to doing in times of turmoil, in an attempt to shut out the Pandora's Box of pain and anguish from her world.

She was conscious her children needed her – Edward, the baby, cried more and more these days, and her two eldest were not of an age to be caring for their younger siblings in place of their mother. But rendered stiff and numb, as though she were a corpse still cursed with breath, she could not bear to leave her self-imposed prison. The study was to her a sanctuary. Though the books, ledgers, documents and scrolls that adorned the walls and shelves attracted her little, and she attended them as a matter of duty, rather than a matter of interest, she felt the worries and cares of her life could be brought to a halt by getting lost in checking the rents and accounts.

Even that wore thin after a while, however, and when Whitlocke returned (he knew where he would find her), she was writing nothing in particular on a piece of paper – her proper mind in a faraway place. Still, she knew it was him when he entered.

"Is it done?" she asked, putting her pen down but staying exactly where she was seated, not turning at all to meet eyes with her butler. Her voice was bereft of all warmth and emotion.

"It is," he replied in a manner that matched hers.

The Countess shut her eyes slowly, and already the lids were rimmed with tears. By her own election, she had not been to see Blameford in his last weeks, but the notion of *never* seeing him again until after her own death still shook her as though the very Earth were opening beneath her feet.

Though her eyes were still closed, she heard Whitlocke's footsteps, and the soft rattle of a folded piece of paper being placed upon her desk. She opened her eyes again to behold what was before her. A letter of three pages, by the look of things, roughly folded and not sealed. It was accompanied by a second, which was in a sealed envelope, but this she ignored. She was most concerned with the set of folded papers.

"What is this?"

"Mr Blameford made me swear I would give that to you after…" the butler stammered, "…after his death."

Lady Vyrrington nodded a little, her lip curling and her eyes darting side-to-side repeatedly as she contemplated what her feelings were.

"Leave me with this, Whitlocke. I shall ring if I require you further."

After a long pause, the butler replied:

"Very good, milady."

The Countess' gaze remained fixed rigidly on Blameford's letter. Only half of her wanted to read it; the other half wanted to toss it straight into the fire and let its words die with its writer.

'What could be in it that I don't already know?' she thought to herself, 'Will I be opening myself up to further anguish and torment by reading it?'

She could not reconcile herself to it one way or another, but at the same time, she could not have anyone else read it to her. Whitlocke was the only one who knew of their affair, yet she would not be able to bear Blameford's words coming from Whitlocke's mouth.

There was only one thing for it. She would read as far as she could endure, and if it become too distressing to suffer it, she would burn it. Determined, lest she should change her mind again, she unfolded it roughly and quickly, and began to read her lover's parting words.

My dear Countess,
My Lady,
My Oliviera...

She already wanted to throw it away – she never did like him to call her by her Christian name. She did not even enjoy her late husband Lord Wilson calling her 'Oliviera', indeed he usually did it to annoy her.

...I have seen the abyss more than once in this lifetime. I first beheld the starless, nameless sky; the unending black; the torturous darkness, in the days before I knew you. When I was little more than a corpse, scorned and shunned by even the lowest creatures to walk this Earth. You were the angel sent by a God who I believed had long deceived and long deserted me; you were the divine being come of Heaven to absolve me of my sins and allow me to begin my life anew. You, who ransomed me from vice and wickedness and saved this wretch from the unholy pit...

Lady Vyrrington's cheeks were burning, waiting to feel the cold of her tears. Blameford's description was nothing like that which she attributed herself. Such was her belief in her sins that even a God so benevolent or a Saviour so forgiving would condemn her.

...Now once again, I behold the mighty maelstrom of my calumny. My time is running out and I am soon to be engulfed. You may think yourself duty-bound to save me again, but it is I, this time, who must save you.

Seven years ago, when I first beheld your God-sent face, you know that I was accused of the murders of five members of my family – my father, my stepmother and my three siblings. I was set free; as your lawyer said, I was just the victim of ill judgment – the last-remaining member of the family with nothing to lose and everything to gain must undoubtedly be guilty...

The Countess nodded as she read, one hand clasped contemplatively over her mouth. She breathed hard and slowly in and out through her nose. She knew she was at total liberty to stop reading at any time and throw the correspondence to the mercy of the flames, and yet she continued on:

...I have never deceived you, my love...

She screwed her eyes shut, again deploring the affectionate term with which he addressed her. 'We never called each other that. Ever,' she justified in her mind.

...in this regard. I will divulge to you the truth of this matter as I know it to be.

My stepmother died first -- they found her body at the front of the house. She looked to have jumped from her bedroom window, though it was believed that I pushed her.
Then they found my brothers and father in the dining room. My three siblings – all of them younger than I – were shot where they sat, they said. Pistol-shots to the heart and stomach; the carpet around them stained red with their blood.
Our father was at the head of the table with half of his face missing. He looked to have taken the pistol to his throat upon dispatching his sons, though I was believed to have shot them all.

Thus I remained: the sole son of a desperate, twice-widowed sire. My father did not contrive that I should linger here alone, but that I should join them all upon my execution. Little-read into the scriptures was my father. That we should all suffer together in Hell for murder and suicide when my brothers – those lives so young and wastefully taken – should be in Heaven...

Lady Vyrrington had to stand up now, and pace the study, still clutching the letter, even if now the words were not so much eloquent, but desperate and almost delirious. She had never known Blameford to be remotely religious, and yet the words were there before her – he had been a God-fearing young man, at least in mind, if not body and soul.

...But you, Oliviera; you saw to my beginning a second life. How did I repay your kindness? Seducing your pure heart and tempting it into lust. Cuckolding your good husband, by whose will I found myself with a roof over my head. Making free with your affection and using it to my advantage while I succumbed to the spell of the Devil...

Then she read on, his words that she knew to be untrue, of what he told to be his hand in Joshua's disappearance and Mrs Rudgerleigh's death. She made it to the last page, her mind still rent in two as to whether or not to continue. There were but two paragraphs:

...Believe this account or do not, My Lady; it is the truth as I have contrived to tell it. I go hence to my death, to be

reunited with my family. Shame and suffering have governed my life such as it is. And my death, too, they shall attend.

Except from knowing and loving you, Oliviera Vyrrington. Your presence in my life is the closest to God I have felt. I know you feel your sorrows to be His punishment for our affection. In my death, I free you from this. Do not be imprisoned by my memory. Be at liberty to live and love anew.

I take to my grave your heart,
And give to you mine forever

Jesse Blameford

His signature was remarkably elegant, with a series of delicate pen-stroke flourishes underlining it. In all her time knowing him, having him; she had never known him to be so eloquent. The Countess supposed to herself she had never paid much attention to how loquacious he could apparently be. During their encounters there was little call or time for words of elegant conversation. And two people of their starkly differing classes could never be seen in public to enjoy any informal yet intelligent discourse. It was something that the Countess came to regret. Lord Wilson, as a military man, was of few words, though by all accounts when he *did* speak, Lady Vyrrington relished the conversation.

She kept on re-reading Blameford's last few lines to her. '*Do not be imprisoned by my memory. Be at liberty to live and love anew.*' The Countess thought aloud:

"No…" she muttered, screwing the pages up and throwing them in the grate of the study fireplace, before falling slowly to her knees, and leaning against the wall, finally succumbing to her inner pain and weeping.

"…If this agony and despair, and wanton self-destruction is the true consequence of love, then it is not worth the suffering. I am resolved to never love again…"

Her eyes were rushing backward and forward, even in her outer thoughts she felt conflicted as to how she really felt, "…Society will become my only occupation. I abandon my hopes for a better England with a better life for the poor and wretched. My tenants, save for my dearest friends, will be no more than my tenants, and unworthy of my undue attention. And at last I may pay my final penance to the Almighty before I undergo my final journey, for the sin of loving two men."

Then that was her last thought of Jesse Blameford. She left his letter balled up awaiting its own destruction, a funeral pyre that would eradicate all knowledge of him from her memory and soul forever.

28785747R00291

Printed in Poland
by Amazon Fulfillment
Poland Sp. z o.o., Wrocław